Apples
and ICE

THE MICHIGAN MYSTERY

A Novel By

Louise Richie Kunkle

TRAFFORD
PUBLISHING™

Note for Librarians: A cataloguing record for this book is available from Library and Archives Canada at www.collectionscanada.ca/amicus/index-e.html
ISBN 1-4251-0750-8

Printed in Victoria, BC, Canada. Printed on paper with minimum 30% recycled fibre.
Trafford's print shop runs on "green energy" from solar, wind and other environmentally-friendly power sources.

TRAFFORD
PUBLISHING™

Offices in Canada, USA, Ireland and UK

Book sales for North America and international:
Trafford Publishing, 6E–2333 Government St.,
Victoria, BC V8T 4P4 CANADA
phone 250 383 6864 (toll-free 1 888 232 4444)
fax 250 383 6804; email to orders@trafford.com
Book sales in Europe:
Trafford Publishing (UK) Limited, 9 Park End Street, 2nd Floor
Oxford, UK OX1 1HH UNITED KINGDOM
phone +44 (0)1865 722 113 (local rate 0845 230 9601)
facsimile +44 (0)1865 722 868; info.uk@trafford.com
Order online at:
trafford.com/06-2508

10 9 8 7 6 5 4 3

Dedication

For   Judith, Karen, Virginia, Deborah, and David

with love.

Chapter One

Strong slender fingers tapped nervously on the side of the telephone box as the man waited for the response from the local number he had just dialed. As if from force of habit, his eyes scanned the interior of the truck stop. It was the lunch rush hour and the occupants of the restaurant were deeply involved in either preparing, serving or consuming the quickest meal available. Assured no one was interested in his actions, he relaxed his tall frame in the narrow booth. The slightest of smiles crinkled the corners of his mouth and eyes as a soft husky voice came through to his ear.

"Yes, it's me," came the expected answer.

"I just turned off the highway and have eaten lunch. I thought I should check in with you now so I won't have to make another stop. It will take me at least a day to get settled. Since I don't know about the situation there, I'll call you by radio after nine tomorrow night."

"All right. I'll be sure to be at home. How are you doing? Remember, you're going there to rest." She continued anxiously, "it will be a rough time for you a few weeks from now, Whit, darling, and we'll need you desperately then."

"I know, Love. I'm planning to rest and rest. The air here is so much better and I'm feeling the benefit already. Don't worry about me. I'll be in a-one condition in no time." After a quick glance at the clock on the wall above the counter, Whit continued, "I should be on my way again. They're expecting me at two o'clock. I'll just make it."

"All right – but, Whit, you know how much I…"

"Of course I do, Love. Now don't worry. Keep praying for me, and I'll keep in touch, OK?"

"Yes dear, but I'll feel much more at ease when I know you're there and so close to where I am for now."

Then with a softly whispered goodbye and a disconnecting click the conversation ended.

Whit went to the cashier's counter, glanced quickly around the room as he paid his bill and waited for the change. He raised his hand in a friendly gesture in reply to the cashier's automatic comment, "have a good trip."

As the door closed behind him he stretched, breathed deeply of the good air, glanced around the parking area quickly, then walked to the well-packed station wagon he had parked there about an hour before. He drove up to the nearest gas pump, filled the tank and paid the attendant. With a glance into the rearview mirror, he began the last, but shortest lap of the long, tiring journey which had taken him from New York City, to Washington, D.C., through the Pennsylvania mountains, across Ohio and north into Michigan to a small rural community at the edge of a national pine forest near the northern shore of Lake Michigan.

"Tell me his name again, Grandee. Will I have to call him Mister?"

Grandee straightened up from smoothing the corduroy spread on the three-quarter size bed. She gave one corner a final tug, then turned to smile into the pale questioning face of her young grandson who was sitting in a wheelchair near the bedroom door in the small gardener's cottage. As she reached to close the drapes to keep the room cool, light from the late morning sun streamed through the window and set aflame the red in her coiled, gray-streaked hair. As she smiled compassionately on the inquisitive youngster, the same rays painted a bit of copper glow to the fine creases that gathered at the corners of her mouth.

Young brown eyes speckled with golden flecks met the older ones of the same golden hue. The boy continued with more questions before she could answer the first two..."I think he'll like this place, don't you, Grandee? You suppose he'll let me visit him out here, sometime?"

Martha Farnsworth gently ran work-worn fingers through the unruly curls that matched the red in her own hair, brushing them back from the boy's perspiring, slightly freckled forehead.

"Richie, his name is Whitaker Brockman. He will, of course, be Mr. Brockman to you. Perhaps at some time later on he'll give his permission for you to call him something more personal."

She felt the young, still-questioning eyes follow her into the small adjoining bath as she supplied it with fresh linens, soap, and other toiletries. She pulled down the window shade and walked back to the bedroom door. "He will probably drive his own automobile, since he didn't ask to be met at the train or bus station. He isn't a very young man. He's been ill, and working too hard, so he said. His doctor recommended outdoor activities and light physical work for the next three or four months. Since he was the only one who called about the position, your aunt Linda and I feel sure our heavenly Father knows what is best for you right now. Perhaps this is what Mr. Brockman needs also to help him with his life. We trust he will be suitable."

She crossed the comfortably furnished living-dining area to open the front door of the cottage. "He'll be here in an hour to two, so we shall go to the house for lunch. Then you can rest until he arrives."

Carefully, she wheeled the chair down the planks arranged as a make shift ramp from the small low porch to the red brick path that curved toward the back of the main house lawn. "As for visiting in this gardener's cottage, I hope you will wait for a definite invitation, young man."

The sun, now at its highest peak for the day, bathed the countryside in its own particular glow and shimmered on the macadam drive that dissected the expanse of lawn surrounding the large, two-story, white-frame house. Multicolored mums and zinnias extracted extra depth from the sun's rays where they grew in some profusion around the foundation of the cottage and on the borders of the red brick path to the flagstone terrace at the back of the house. Off to the north, rows of marigold blooms formed paths through patches of late vegetables in the old-fashioned kitchen garden. The observer's eye invariably followed on to the thicket of birch trees that lined the stream of clear water twisting through the meadowland, eventually losing itself in the deep green of the young, extensive pine forest beyond. The unmistakable splendor of the Creator.

As they walked along this natural wonder of a path, Richie's thin lightly freckled hand reached and broke the stem of a bright orange mum growing along the path and held it up for his grandmother to take. "Of course, Grandee, I'll wait...here, this is for you."

She accepted his assurance and the floral offering with a quick smile. "That's a pretty one, Richie. I'm sure Agnes will have a vase and a place to put it."

"Grandee, here is a white mum for Aunt Linda. Let me bring it, too. She always smiles when I give her a white flower."

"Yes, Richie, you may give it to her at lunch."

Mrs. Farnsworth maneuvered the chair up a slight incline, across the terrace and through the enclosed patio to the small dining area set apart for quick snacks, lunches, and conversations in the large farm-style kitchen.

When the family dwelling was first built in the early nineteen hundreds, the original homestead was retained as a country kitchen and became the family gathering place. The enormous fieldstone fireplace had been repaired and was kept in working order with a constant supply of pine, apple, and birch logs close at hand in the large log rack. Above the smoke-blackened, hand-hewn mantle hung a great oval mirror, perfect in its reflections and the fine grain of the oaken frame, attesting to its value and its worthiness of this prominent place. Placed at either end of the mirror were two heavy oil-burning pewter lamps that had been brought with the mirror through the St. Lawrence and Great Lakes Seaway with other treasures of Mr. Richard Farnsworth's ancestors.

At one end of the fireplace sat an antique platform rocker. Its walnut frame glowed with the patina of a century of loving use and care. The seat and back were well padded with crewel embroidered, heavy linen. The matching foot stool, now equipped with roller coasters for easy moving, was placed near at hand for comfort. Beside the chair a small table held a silk-shaded reading lamp and a well-used King James Bible.

During an ongoing process of remodeling, the original pine plank flooring was overlaid with fine golden oak. The small windows in the south wall had been replaced with floor to ceiling windows to catch as much of the natural light as possible. Heavy, thermo-lined drapes were hanging, now drawn back to either end of the windows, but available to be pulled closed to retain maximum heat in sub-zero weather. A sectional sofa, with matching chair and ottoman covered in soft leather, formed an oval facing the fireplace. The low, glass-top coffee table and large floor pillows were ready to be arranged in conversational groups or just for relaxing. Tall lamps and a few pieces of antique statuary and pottery sat on low side tables, adding light and color to warm the room and make it comfortable. A large, braided, oval rug fit into the area between the sofa and fireplace, a matching one covered the floor beneath the trestle-type table in the dining area. A hostess chair and four matching side chairs provided seating around the smooth, oak, butcher-block top. A modern cooking area and pass-through window into the dining room filled the wall opposite the window wall. The entrance to the main hall, and the rest of the house, was three steps going up. These were recently equipped with a retractable ramp for the wheelchair.

This was the heart of the house. This was where Richard and Martha Farnsworth had always settled any problems of their early marriage; the place of family prayers and gatherings when their own children were small. Martha Farnsworth was sure that the easing balm for her daughter's present heartaches, and the means of recovery for the boy would be found here. She moved his wheelchair into position so he could wash his hands at the kitchen sink before lunch.

Linda replaced the telephone in the cradle on the desk in the study, noticing the glow of the amber light on the intercom panel. Lunch was ready. Quickly she gathered the papers in front of her. Initialing the top one, she put them all into the folder marked 'W. Brockman,' and slipped it into the top drawer of the desk. She went to join her mother and nephew for the lunch that Agnes, her mother's dear friend and house assistant, had prepared.

On the way, she tucked the tail of her plaid shirt-blouse under the waist band of her blue wrap-around skirt, which was her usual attire for working hours, and tied the belt a little tighter around her much too thin waist. Pausing before the ornate mirror that hung on the wall near the door to the hall, she brushed a few wispy strands of soft auburn hair back into place, cupped both hands around her face and gently massaged above her eyebrows and the throbbing nerves at her temples to relieve the tension that had built up there.

Descending the ramp quickly into the kitchen, she greeted her nephew with a gentle clasp on his thin shoulders and a special wink that was readily given when his searching eyes were fixed on her face in expectation of this special assurance of her love for him, at which he point he reached to the side of his chair for the white mum which his grandmother had wrapped in a wet paper towel and waxed paper. And there was the smile.

As she took her place across the table from her mother, she answered the questioning look in the older woman's eyes with a slight shake of her head. "I haven't been able to uncover anything more about the man, Mother. I have confirmed that he is a lyric writer for some 'off Broadway' musician and that he has been ordered by his physician to live simply, not too vigorously, but out in the open as much as possible for the next few months. This is what we already knew. It seems he had a severe siege of pneumonia and a virus infection, or something that has taken its toll physically. According to him, however, he is completely recovered and only needs to build up his strength. I talked with the lawyer in New York whom he gave as reference, and also checked with the president at the bank on the integrity of the New York lawyer. Everything seems to be in good order. So..." she grasped the small hand resting on the arm of the wheel chair and pressed it gently. "It seems that our heavenly Father has sent us the right person for this very important position here."

"That's exactly what Grandee told me this morning."

Simple conversation continued as they finished the well-prepared lunch, although, Linda noticed again that Richie only pushed his food from one place on his plate to another. Understanding his tension, she permitted him to finish his glass of milk and then go for his rest period. As Mrs. Farnsworth guided the chair up the ramp and through the hall to his room, Linda finished the coffee that remained in her cup, her eyes staring at the orange mum in the slender glass vase in the middle of the table, to which she had added her white mum. Richie had always gathered flowers, bringing them to Linda and his grandmother as he played in the yard. How he must have missed the summer activities.

Surely Doctor Browne could not be wrong. By next summer... this man who was coming... she interrupted her own thoughts with a reminder of the time passing. Agnes was clearing the table.

"Agnes, Mr. Brockman will be dining with us this evening. Regular family fare and service will be fine. Beginning tomorrow he will have his choice about meals, although I will insist that he inform you if he will be dining elsewhere at any time. He just might like to prepare his own at times, since there is a kitchen in the cottage. Seat him next to Richie so they will become acquainted more quickly."

Linda could not distinguish which sound had broken her concentration on the article she had been reading. The grandfather clock in the front hall was just finishing the chimes and had struck the first of two hours, when she heard the sound of the automobile turning into the graveled parking area from the black-topped drive that led from the county road to the house. Appreciating the exact timing of Mr. Brockman's arrival, she put away the magazine, and folding her reading glasses, laid them on the table beside the chair. Linda stood by the window and watched as the driver opened the door of the station wagon and stretched out and up. The sun shining on the window at this time of the day made it impossible for anyone to see in, so she watched with interest and apprehension.

Continuing his languid movements, he stretched his arms over his head and then out to his sides as though it was a great relief to be out of the driver's seat. With a quick hand he gave a light brush to his dark brown slacks and tan short-sleeved knit shirt and a slight check at waist band and pockets. After he had looked around, taking in at one glance the house, drive, and visible expanse of lawn and gardens, he retrieved a light-weight sports jacket from the hanging bar in the back of the wagon. He slipped his arms into it, made the necessary adjustments at collar and cuffs, removed the key from the ignition, then shut and locked the door and dropped the keys into his pocket.

Linda, taking it all in, continued to watch, even though she realized that most people have an inner awareness of being secretly observed. As he came across the drive and up the walk she noted his gaunt frame. Loose fitting clothes and the lack of tan or color in his face upheld the story of a long and recent illness. The quick, almost light-footed measure of his stride, however, spoke of his partial and eventual conquest of the same illness. As he passed the window where she stood and approached the high wooden pillars that framed the leaded glass panels and the huge weather-stained door between them, she caught just a glimpse of silver streaks in nearly black hair that curled slightly around his ears and above his collar, but in severely controlled waves on top and at the sides. Just this swift look at the man was all she was allowed before she heard the door chimes and then the murmur of voices in the hall. She moved from the window to stand beside the desk, rearranged the pens and letter opener laying there, then turned to face the door as her mother tapped, called her name and opened the door.

"Come in." Linda's eyes met the keen look of the man who entered the room behind Mrs. Farnsworth. Pure blue eyes set deep and framed with dark straight brows and heavy lashes held her attention for a fleeting moment. The deep creases at the outer corners could be the result of many past hours in the sun, long intensive hours of study, deep sorrow, intense pain and suffering, or a life of carefree laughter and happiness. Linda felt instinctively sure that those lines were the result of all of these reasons except, perhaps, the last two. High cheek bones, a straight, slender nose and strong faintly cleft chin provided the setting for a full, but firmly drawn mouth with a hint of creases on either side, a companion set to match those etched at the corners of his eyes. His thinness accentuated the six-foot-three height he had written in his application, and belied the two-hundred-ten-pound weight information.

She could see nothing that would discredit the man unless it would be the fact that he had passed his thirty-eighth birthday. How would he cope with a ten-year-old boy, even in a wheelchair? Why would a man of this caliber want this position? Surely there were...

"This is Mr. Brockman, Linda." Her mother interrupted her unspoken questions, and then continued, as Linda stepped forward to meet his out-stretched hand. "My daughter, Mrs. Wilson, is the boy's guardian." Without further comment she turned and left the room, pulling the door closed behind her.

After the usual polite inquiries and answers concerning his trip north, he accepted the offer of a seat in the large, leather chair facing the desk. Linda assumed the unaccustomed position of employer in the swivel chair behind the desk. She rolled the chair closer to the desk, picking up the leather handled letter opener for something to occupy her hands while she conducted the interview. The man across from her appeared completely at ease. Linda put the letter opener down again and, with her hands now loosely folded in the center of the large desk mat in front of her, she began.

"I have never engaged anyone in this type of work before and I'm not at all sure of what I should say to you, Mr. Brockman. You see, we rather wished for a younger man, even a teenage boy, who would take over some the garden work and other odd jobs that will need to be done before winter."

"I assure you, Mrs. Wilson, that in spite of my advanced years," (as his eyes met hers she was sure there was an amused twinkle there as he brushed the sideburns of silver and black with this index fingers) "And," he continued, "my slightly weakened physical condition, I will be able to handle whatever tasks that may arise."

"I am sorry. I'll admit I was considering those two facts, of course, but the last bit of work that needs to be done in an orchard and garden..."

"You think they may be beneath my line of employment?" He arose from the chair and went to stand by the window, looked out through the sheer panels, over the drive and lawn, paused for a moment and then remarked, "I must in all fairness admit to you, Mrs. Wilson, that there were other circumstances that led me to apply for this particular position. There are some very important items on my agenda for while I am here. However, as long as I am in your employ, the first priority will be the care and needs of your nephew."

There was a hesitant knock on the door. Linda called, "Come in." Agnes opened the door and wheeled in a tea cart with a tray of two tall, frosty glasses of iced tea and some small sandwiches.

"Your mother said perhaps you were ready for some refreshments, and – Richie is awake from his nap."

Thank you, Agnes. That looks delicious. We will have it here. Will you ask Mother if she will see to Richie now and we will meet them out on the terrace later."

Later, the shadows of the tall evergreens bordering the spacious lawn and garden to the west were lengthening to reach the area between the house and cottage. As Linda opened the door from the kitchen onto the patio, she caught a breath of hauntingly familiar essence of tweed combined with an elusive aroma of expensive after-shave lotion. Defensively, she clenched and sealed her mind to it as she felt an almost forgotten disturbance in the close presence of this man who followed just a few steps behind her. She deliberately ignored the nearness of the tweed-covered arm as he reached over her shoulder and released the pressure of the weight of the door from her hand pushing it farther open. A familiar tightness at the back of her throat restrained her from responding to his softly suggested, "Let me."

Stepping quickly out into the patio she relaxed as the disturbing aroma was overpowered by the fresh scents of the outdoors. He closed the door softly behind him and followed her through the screen-enclosed patio and out through another doorway to the flagstone terrace.

Linda watched the expression on Mr. Brockman's face as he observed Richie who was turning the wheels of his chair so he could face them. She was pleased as Mr. Brockman met the seriously questioning glance of the golden speckled brown eyes with a flash of assurance from his own. She noticed his observance of the close association between the boy and herself as Richie looked away from the intense blue of the man's eyes into hers and then back to the man's.

Before any formal introduction could be made, Richie wheeled his chair the short distance and held up his hand in greeting. "Hello, Mr. Brockman. I'm sure glad you're here."

Continuing to watch them closely, Linda felt a great sense of relief as the man took the young boy's hand in his own and returned what seemed to be a slight reciprocal squeeze. He answered, "Hello, Richard." Glancing down at the hand he held then back to the eager uplifted face he smiled. I'm glad to be here. I'm sure we are going to be good for each other." Then as he put just a little more pressure on the hand he still held, Linda noted a responding tightening and saw a quick flash of agreement in the golden-flecked eyes of her nephew.

"Since you two have handled the introductions so well, Richie, you and Grandee can show Mr. Brockman the cottage where he will put his belongings and have some privacy while he is here."

The crunch of heavy tires on gravel in the parking area had drawn her attention to the arrival of a pickup truck. "Carl is here and we have a few matters that need to be discussed. If you will excuse me now, I will see you both at dinner."

With a prayer of thanks for her inner good feeling about Richie's care, she met Carl where the walk turned toward the office.

A sense of dread took the place of the good feelings. Linda had to be continually wary of Carl Hickman. He was an excellent manager for the farm and the pine forest and had been part of the original crew when the idea of it all had begun. He was married to one of Linda's childhood friends and they were the parents of a lovely little girl. But.

"Humph. So he has arrived." She watched as Carl's lips formed a cruel, mocking grimace for a smile as his hard eyes swept over the man who was now walking toward the cottage. "He's not much of a man it seems, but then it doesn't take a man to be a nursemaid for a sickly boy, does it?" His contempt for any man who seemed weaker than himself was apparent in his crude laugh.

Quickly she avoided his outstretched hand. As he reached out to put his arm around her shoulder, she hurried through the door into the office. His huge, six-foot-four frame filled the doorway and blocked out the late afternoon sun. She hurried over to the chair behind the desk in front of the window. She needed to keep the width of the desk between them.

"Richie needs help and encouragement, not bullying and sarcasm, and I'm convinced that Mr. Brockman is God's choice and that he will be right for Richie. That's why he's here."

"And what about your needs, Inda? Who will ever supply them, I wonder?" He taunted her as he lowered himself into the great wooden swivel chair near the desk.

"My few needs have been amply supplied here – and don't call me by that name." She glared at him.

"Why not? It was always my name for you until he took it over for his own use. Perhaps I should have used the word 'desire' instead of need,

Inda. Or have you frozen out your desires as you have your friends? Why did you stay here, anyway?" His voice had become coarse with almost a growling protest, seeming to force it at her. "You should have gone away from all the hurtful memories and scenes of tragedy. Why didn't you go? Why hang around here, reminding us all of our loss. Yes, our loss!"

"You know the reason, Carl." Her words needed to be pushed out and around and through the tightness in her throat. "There was no one or no place far enough away for me to run. And then Mother needed me after the..."

"You could have come to me for..."

"NEVER! You know that. I never gave you reason to think otherwise." Her eyes blazing with indignations, burning with a hint of unshed tears met and blocked the intense, most insulting glare of his hard gray eyes. Then in a softer tone she questioned, "Why do you insist on making this transition so difficult? You have Maria and Natalie and a very comfortable home. I appreciate the way you have managed the business for Mother. I don't want to change anything. That is as far as my interest in you, or any other man, goes."

"It can't be possible, Inda! You are still too much of a woman. Just don't shut us out forever. Phil Wilson was my friend, even if he did steal my girl."

"I never was your 'girl' as you claim, Carl – and you know it." Her voice rose stronger in offense at what he was saying. "Besides, you married Maria – and she loves you."

"But I wouldn't have...if he hadn't..."

"That's enough, Carl." she interrupted his angry outburst and deliberately drew his attention to the manila folder he had placed on the desk when he came into the office.

"Is this the harvesting schedule for the Christmas trees?"

He rose from the chair and stood looking down at her hands as she opened the folder and removed the contents. When she refused to raise her glance to meet his eyes, he turned and stood in the open doorway, hesitated a moment, then turned back and sat down again in the chair.

"Yes. Everything is ready except for the mesh bags." There was another brief pause as he rubbed his hand around the back of his neck as though to relieve tension there. "You know," he continued, "that wife of mine should get a medal for that idea." He crossed one heavy cord-clad knee over the other and clasped his hands around it. "It's going to be worth more than their cost in the damage they'll prevent. We'll be able to raise the price on each tree." His voice had lost some of its growl. "She's some girl, that one."

Linda wondered at the softness that had come into his eyes as he spoke about Maria. Surely he must love her in spite of the insinuating remarks he had made to her just a few minutes ago.

"I'm sure she wouldn't expect anything, at least not a medal. What about a pearly necklace, or a small car of her own; something special, just for her," Linda suggested earnestly, as he glanced quizzically at her. "She has been a great help in many ways; and you won't let her help in the office…"

"She doesn't need to work."

"I realize that Carl, but any employee would have received a bonus or reward for suggesting the mesh nets. Take enough out of the profits for her bonus given from the management. We will benefit from this idea for years to come."

She noticed his beginning agitation of embarrassment, and referred again to the papers in front of her. "I see you have planned to cut more trees than last year. Can we do that without taking some of next year's crop?"

"Sure we can. That new crop along the west line has really taken hold. In two years that planting will he ready. The crew is working there these next two weeks, bulldozing the last of the old stumps that are still there and plowing the land for next year's planting. Fifteen years of hard labor and long hours, but it's been worth it, Inda. It has paid the way with a considerable profit for all of us these last five years." His eyes flickered amusedly as he noticed her flinch at his use of that name, but he ignored her silent objection and continued. "Your mother will be pleased that the initial hard work is so nearly finished, then we can relax a little and let things run smoothly, I hope, for the next two or three years."

Carl's remarks hovered in the back of her thinking as she finished the last few bits of work for the day. "Fifteen years of hard work and long hours, but it has been worth it."

"How do you count the worth of a thing?" she questioned aloud. "Who can answer as to what is the benefit and who the beneficiary?"

With the papers on the desk pushed aside and her elbows resting on the desk pad, her clenched hands supported her chin as she stared out the window. The cottage was now engulfed in the shadows of the late afternoon, and beyond it the still heavy laden trees in the apple orchard seemed to blend into the background of innumerable shades of green and brown, shimmering into a blur as though a misty curtain had enclosed it all. The green pine forest gave way to a vivid memory of scraggy, weather-whipped immature trees fighting for existence amid old stumps of the original pine forest. It had been ravaged by men in the early years of the twentieth century and then left to be worn away by the forces of nature. Sand blown from the lake shores and the devastating erosive power of torrential rain and wind storms, melting ice and snow had left the land scarred and almost barren.

Linda recalled the way it had been from as early as memory would allow. She and her brother, Ralph, had spent holidays and occasional odd days of freedom from school, wading or fishing in the stream, romping with pets and friends playing ball and other games on the great lawn in the summer; and the exhilarating fun of snowball battles and sled races on the thick blanket of snow. At that time the outlying property was scrub pasture land used by the neighboring farmers. The house and gardener's cottage plus the vast orchard and garden acreage and the land extending to the east and west of the house along the county road, belonged to her grandparents. Her father and his two sisters had been born here, as were two generations before them.

The lucrative possibilities in the automobile industry, for an ambitious young man had lured her father away from returning to the family farm at the end of World War II. During the first year of his enlistment he had met and married the beautiful girl who worked in the war department, established their home and reared their two children in the ease of substantial suburban living in the Detroit area.

Then had come the late night call. Grandfather had suddenly met death from a massive coronary – Grandmother had passed on years before that night. The farm manager had made the call. The estate needed attention immediately. After weeks of consultations with lawyers, bank presidents and court officials it developed that her father had inherited the home place. He moved his family from Dearborn to the far northern reaches of Michigan.

Her brother, Ralph, had just finished a four-year enlistment in the Army Engineer Corps and had decided to move with them, investing his savings and energy into the family endeavor that resulted. She recalled the energetic, excited teenage girl she had been, working long hours in all types of weather along with her father and brother. Usually

Carl was there, too. He had been one of the boys who had helped on the farm in the summers when she vacationed there. He was the same age as her brother, but always seemed more mature. She had become uneasily aware of him as she grew into her teenage years.

Along with her initial excitement in this new location and way of life, there had also been times when life was not so easy. New clothes, parties, luxuries that before had seemed so essential, had been removed from the expense column of every day living. Her father, her brother Ralph, and Carl had formed a joint contract investing in the reclaiming and developing of the hundreds of acres of the pine forest. After her college years, Linda also invested her time and finances into the business.

Now, after many set-backs and tragedies, the evidence was before her – there in the ledger on the desk. Her father's foresight and her mother's unwavering trust and courage even after the death of her father, had not gone for nothing. And yet, had it all been worth the terrible cost of losing her loved ones and the present situation with Richie? Could God still bring good and healing out of all this misfortune and pain?

Abruptly, she shook her head as though to chase away any doubt, and to forestall any painful memories that would come rushing in if allowed. Slowly she massaged away the tension ache from her temples, praying silently again for the peace of God in her heart. Brushing the loose strands of hair back into place, she cleared the papers from the desk and closed the office for the day.

Linda knew that her mother would be pleased to see the ledger and that, if asked, she would feel sorrow at the price she has paid. She would mourn that the others were not here to enjoy the prosperity. The answer to "Why, oh why?" never came.

The fully packed station wagon was still parked in the gravel turn-around reminding her of the latest addition to the household. Even through Mr. Brockman would be living in the cottage, it would be necessary for him to be included in the family to the extent of Richie's needs. A quick glance showed her that the cottage door was open, but there was no sound of activity or voices coming from within. As she entered her own kitchen through the patio, her mother was placing the service for the evening meal on the trestle table. In answer to her questioning look around the room, Mrs. Farnsworth informed her, "they have taken the tour of the cottage, now Richie is showing Mr. Brockman his room in the house. They are going to wash up together. Would you care for some tea while we wait?"

"Please, Mum." She sat down on the nearest stool and rested her arms along the counter top. "How did the afternoon go? Do you think it will work?"

"The introduction went smoothly, Linda. Richie is very excited, and I detect a depth of compassion in that man's makeup. Not softness and pity, but a strong sense of caring."

Stirring a bit of sugar into the tea put before her, Linda recalled the contrast of expressions on Carl's face and in his voice as he insinuated motives to her and as he mentioned his wife. "Yes," she answered in almost a whisper, "but men have other emotions, some of them not so complimentary, that deny the reality of their so-called finer feelings." She stood up with the cup of tea in her hand. "I'll finish this in my room while I change."

Aware of the deep love and concern this woman, whom she so much resembled, had for her, she placed an arm across the shoulders and gently brushed a kiss on the cheek so near her own. "It will work, Mum. Things are coming along just fine." She emphasized the last two words, daring to believe the answer to her own prayers. She felt the older woman's eyes follow her down the hallway. From an open doorway beyond her room and across the hall, came the sound of two male voices in friendly conversation and the sweet sound of boyish laughter.

Conversation flowed freely between the man and the boy at dinner. Linda discovered that Mr. Brockman had led a very busy life before his illness. She also learned that he had played baseball, soccer, and tennis during his high school years. He had been on the debating team and had played the piano with a song and dance group in college.

"He's been all over the world. Even Russia," exclaimed Richie. "He really prefers a Mercedes or a 'Vett' for his car, Aunt Linda. But he couldn't pack all of his gear into one of those, so he drove the big station wagon." Richie glanced down at the chair in which he was sitting. "Besides, we can put the chair into the back and maybe..." his face and voice combined into one poignant question, "we could go to the club to swim?"

"It could be possible, you know," the man added, "since he did swim before the accident. Of course, the doctor would have to agree and set any restrictions that might be advisable."

"Dr. Browne is coming in the morning for his scheduled call. We will be sure to ask him about it," promised Linda. "We must be sure it's not too soon, Richie."

Chapter Two

There was an unusual sound mixed in with the early morning symphony of bird songs, whispering trees and short wavering wisps of silence. It seemed that a brush beat on a snare drum had been added for this day's performance. It changed the flow of her waking up routine. A few steady, quick strokes of the brush, a pause, three different, one – two – three beats, another pause, then a slight squeak and a thud.

Casting a sleepy-eyed glance at the clock on the stand beside her bed, Linda pushed aside the light quilt and sheet and put her feet into the waiting slippers. She paused a moment on the side of the bed, letting her mind catch up with her body in awakening. Again she heard the strange rhythm, only it was in the reverse order. Squeak, thud, three steps down – someone walking in the parking area, she realized as she noticed the slight pause and then the measured scrunches in the gravel.

She dressed in her soft robe and went to the window. The drapes were open all the way as always, for the night sky was her solace, her sleeping potion – and the morning light a gentle awakener.

She stood for a moment, partially concealed by the drapes, where she could see the man's figure, clad in sweat shirt and gray slacks, removing the last pieces of luggage from the rack on top of the station wagon parked there.

Satisfied, now that she knew the source of the sound, Linda moved from the window and glanced at the clock. It was half an hour earlier than she usually got up. She could take a little longer getting dressed, of course, she thought, selecting the things from her closet and chest of drawers that she would wear, but it wasn't really necessary to spend more time getting dressed. She pushed the button on the alarm to off and turned toward the door to the fully appointed bath and dressing room adjoining her bedroom.

Why she looked out the window as she passed was uncertain, except that she usually did look out the window every morning, just to get a glimpse of the arrival of the new day. She stopped abruptly and stepped back a little so she could not be seen. "What am I doing?" She whispered, "I'm spying on him" But she snubbed her bit of conscience that bothered her. He was now going toward the cottage with a fishing rod and reel in one hand. She was certain that what he carried in the other hand was a case containing a high powered rifle and that thing under his arm was an ammunition clip. No creaking screen door. He remained in the cottage a little longer this time. Hopefully to find a safe place to store that particular piece of luggage. "Why, she murmured, "does he need such a thing as that while he is here?"

Again the spring on the screen door squeaked, and he returned to the rear of the wagon. She continued to watch as he removed a large oblong case which had a hinged top similar to an ordinary foot locker. It was not shiny as though made of metal, the covering appeared more like soft leather or fine dark wood. There were handles on either end by which he lifted it and sat it down on the grass near the wagon. Next he took from the wagon a guitar case and a typewriter case, put them down beside him and closed the back of the wagon.

She continued her clandestine observance as he took the smaller items into the cottage and returned for the chest. She stood with her arms crossed in front of her; her clothes for the day draped over them, forgotten.

Whit stood by the wagon where the chest waited. Slowly he stretched his arms out shoulder high and then up over his head, his chest expanding as though he could not take in enough of the cool, fresh, clear air to satisfy his needs. Lowering his arms he tugged down the waist band ribbing of the sweat shirt, hiding from her eyes the lean narrow expanse of male torso. Then he picked up the handle on one end of the large chest and rolled it behind him up the ramp into the cottage.

She trembled at the vague feeling of emotional awareness that had crept over her; a feeling that had been unfamiliar to her for the past five years. As she went into the bathroom for her shower, her fingers gently rubbed the white marks on her arms where they had gripped so hard just moments ago.

Later that morning Linda found herself on the inside area of that squeaky screen door with the request from Dr. Browne that Mr. Brockman be present for the report of his examination of Richie. In answer to her tap on the door he had invited her to come in while he finished putting away the freshly washed and dried breakfast dishes.

The heavy case that he had wheeled in earlier now stood in a corner of the small living room on legs that had been folded up into the frame. The lid was open, revealing a small electric piano keyboard. The guitar case stood in another corner. The gun case and fishing rod were not to be seen. Of course, she realized, they were belongings that needed to be stored in a safe place. There were other items such as car keys, an expansion-band watch and a neatly folded handkerchief on top of the small table near the door. The faintly noticeable scent of masculinity which she recognized from yesterday's encounter also designated this small cottage as his own private space.

She really hadn't intended to wait for him, but she lingered as he finished in the kitchen. As he turned toward her with, "There, that's finished, shall we go?" Linda only allowed her eyes a brief contact with his and a brushing glance to notice that he had exchanged the gray sweat shirt for a sport shirt made of blue velour with long sleeves, a lay-back collar and neck opening made for lacing shut with a metal tipped cord that he wore loose and untied. That disturbing knowledge followed her as she preceded him out the door and along the walk to the house.

Dr. Browne was very explicit with his instructions for Richie's treatments and the results which he expected within the next six weeks. Time schedules were set, procedures explained and agreed upon. "We need you to be strong, young man, but not exhausted." He declared, "I think a session at the pool in the late afternoons will be a satisfying reward for being persistent in the mornings."

The boy's face beamed with excited determination as his eyes met those of each person seated there with him in the conversation corner of the family room. "We'll do it right, won't we, Mr. Brockman?"

Linda turned her eyes away, not wanting any expression of doubt that might be shown there to take away the confidence showing in his.

Could it all really happen as the doctor set out the schedule?

The well prepared dinner of baked ham glazed with pineapple and brown sugar, tiny white parsley potatoes and freshly cooked vegetables served with cheese and cream sauce was highlighted with the excited comments about the afternoon activities in the garden. As she watched the happy expressions come and go across the lightly sunburned face and noted the way his eyes flitted from her face to the face of the man seated next to him, Linda recalled the scene she had observed from the office window that morning. The reported, 'two bushels of potatoes' brought the remembrance of long lean clad legs; shoulders and back, bared to the waist, that had taken on a dark pink hue from two days of working in the sun, a sinuous network of muscles flowing in unison with the push, lift and turn of the long handled spade.

"...and Mr. Brockman put tallow on my hands so they wouldn't blister..." Richie showed his hands to her as he added to the accounting, "so I could help him."

"Fine, Richie." She sent a quick look of gratitude across the table and then, realizing how her thoughts had drifted she hid the pleasure that might have shown in her eyes, and turned them again toward her nephew. "Did you use sun lotion on your face?"

"Sure. It doesn't burn." He rubbed his hand over the pinkness indicated. "I rubbed some on Mr. Brockman's scar on his back, too. He can't reach it and he said it was still a little tender."

A soft gasp from Mrs. Farnsworth interrupted and Brockman assured her: "It was fine..." then, "I've a request to make. This very formal 'Mr. Brockman' that Richard has been calling me for the last four days is for the more stiff and formal aspects of my life, and if he continues with that, I'm afraid I will have to call him Richard and that would be hard to get used to, wouldn't it?" He teased the boy. "I wonder, could he not be permitted to call me, of course, why not Brock? That's the name most of the fellows I know use." His eyes crinkled at the corners as he caught the glitter in the wide eyes aimed at him. "Except, of course," he continued, "my stern old grandfather, who insists on calling me 'Whitaker' with a definite exclaiming accent to it."

"Oh, he must be old!" Richie's voice and face expressed his reverence to someone who must be even older than his own grandparent.

"Well, yes. He is."

"Will he mind if I call you Brock? Grandee says it's wrong for little kids to call their elders by their first names."

"But you see, dear," his grandmother explained, "Brock is his special name. You wouldn't want to call me Grandmother all of the time, would you? But you should remember to refer to him as Mr. Brockman when you are in adult company, especially those outside the family. We wouldn't want people thinking that you were a brash, impolite youngster."

The conversation drifted back to the activities of the day; the raking away of potato vines, gathering tomatoes, cutting off the tops of carrots and so on, with comments back and forth about the quality and quantity of the garden produce.

Then, over dishes of apple crisp, cups of coffee, and a glass of milk for Richie, Brock broached the question of the upcoming swim sessions. Would he need to make the arrangements? Would he need a personal membership? Where was the club located? As Linda assured him that all of the arrangements had been made and the family membership would, of course, include him under the circumstances, she watched with deep concern as Brock noticed the change in Richie's countenance that had taken place even while they talked.

The happy sparkle in the eyes of the boy seated next to him had changed to sorrow and withdrawal as they raised to meet his own. The small hands were tense on the arms of the wheelchair, his mouth pinched tightly above the barely controlled quivering chin.

"I can show you the way, Brock. That's where Dad and Mom taught me to swim."

Linda turned slowly away from the cupboard where she had just stacked away the rest of the clean dishes from the dishwasher beneath the counter. Agnes had gone to her apartment above the garage for an evening of knitting and her favorite television programs before retiring.

There had been no sound at his coming into the kitchen, but she sensed his presence there. It was that same, but now familiar feeling; not a quiver nor tremble, just an inner knowledge of his nearness.

"Would you like another cup of coffee, or something else to drink?" she asked.

He looked at her, slowly shaking his head in refusal. He slid his hands deep into the side pockets of his slacks and went to stand, feet apart, stiff legged and tense, staring through the open door.

"How stupid of me." His hand came from his pocket and slapped the door frame hard. "I should have thought before I asked about the swim lessons."

"You had no way of knowing..."

"No?" He turned to meet her remark. "I should have realized there was sorrow hiding there. Boys do not have these things happen to them without some resulting emotional pain."

The light for the work area in the kitchen shining down from the ceiling reflected in her eyes, revealing the sadness there, but blinded her vision and concealed the deep self anger evident in his. He stayed by the door, his thoughts hidden by lowered eyelids as he turned again to stare out the doorway. She moved the crystal bowl of fruit from the counter to its usual place in the center of the table. Feeling the withdrawal of his attention from her, she finished the last small tasks of putting the kitchen in order. A deep, uncontrolled sigh escaped her lips as she switched off the light over the counter and pushed back into place the strands that had escaped the soft coil at the nape of her neck.

The sigh caught his attention. As she turned again to face him she became aware of his eyes focusing on hers as the soft glow of the light in the hallway overflowed into the kitchen. The outside brightness was now overcome by definite shadows of the tall pines and great oaks blending with the shadows of the bushes and buildings. The rhythmic scratch and rub of the cricket wings and the mellow deep throated call of the tree frogs accentuated the intense quiet in the room. Even the insisting wings of night insects against the screened walls of the patio became a deterrent to the quiet; gradually increasing the depth of the tension between the two of them.

He pushed open the door and held it there, questioning with his other hand outheld.

"Don't you think you should tell me something of what has happened so that I can avoid hurting the boy...?

She went past him through the doorway and out into the night noises that whispered and chattered and thrumbed around the shadowy enclosure. The air still held some of the heat of the day's sunlight and only the tips of the pines and the slowly drifting clouds gave evidence of the stirring of the night breezes.

"Of course you should know, but there hasn't been the opportunity until now."

She stood with her back to him, wondering how to begin, how much to tell. Finally, determined that he would not learn more than necessary, she began.

"Ralph and June were partners in the family business with Carl, Mother and me. Ralph was my older brother and Richie is their only child. Soon after they were married they purchased a small farm house about three miles north of here on one of the back county roads. The first few years of their life together they spent most of their spare time and money remodeling and making it into a charming, comfortable home. In February of this year they decided to break the monotony of the long winter and have a Valentine's Day party. All of the arrangements had been made, even plans for sleeping here at this house if any guests became storm-trapped. I had spent the entire day before the party at their house, helping with the preparations and everything was going fine." Linda folded her arms across in front of her, her hands gripping her arms tightly through the soft cotton sleeves. Slowly she walked to the end of the patio, clenching and opening her hands as they dropped down to her sides and then each held the other captive as they met behind her back.

"We had finished everything except the hangings around the fireplace and June had decided to wait until morning to do that when Ralph could help. Since it had begun to snow and was getting dark, I left a little earlier than I had planned. According to what Richie could tell us later, he and his father had gone into town before dinner that night to purchase their traditional Valentine gift of candy for June, along with some other party essentials. The clerk in the supermarket told the officers who investigated the accident that they had been in the store and left in a hurry because of the snow. Their purchases were still in the station wagon when they towed it in." "I'm trying to get the picture...they were on their way home when...?"

"They must have heard the sirens. Anyway, Richie said later that they saw the red glow in the sky and his father told him to sit tight because they had to hurry." She leaned closer to the wall, gripping the edge of the shelving that stretched shoulder high along the edge of the patio, where potting soil and empty pots were stored. She had to push hard, it seemed, to get the words through the aching memories that were caught in her throat.

"The car skidded on some snow covered ice and hit a large oak tree. Some of the volunteer firemen found them almost immediately, or Richie would have died, too" She sensed Brock standing close behind her, could feel his breath moving the wisps of hair that curled around the corner of her eye and over her ear.

"But why the hurry? Was Ralph a fireman?"

"He. . . he," she faltered, "Ralph must have realized that it was his own house that was burning." The words could no longer be pushed through the clawing, tightening grip that reached to the very depths of her. NO! She would not allow them to come. Of what use were tears. Her hands gripped the shelf in front of her until the circulation ceased and they were as steel braces holding the shelf in place. She rested her damp forehead on her arms for a moment, swallowing rapidly, forcing back those tears that must not flow. Forcing them down into the depths with all of the other useless, useless, hurting memories. Slowly she lifted her head and focused her eyes as two strong hands loosened each vice-like finger and enveloped them all together in one firm grasp.

He slowly turned her away from the screened wall and with the tips of the fingers on his other hand beneath her chin, brought her eyes up to meet and gain comfort and understanding in the blue strength waiting there so close above her.

She worked her hands free from his, pushed them down over the soft denim of her skirt into the pockets. Shaken, fighting for control, she turned from him and hurried back into the kitchen. The continuing sounds of the night creatures were left outside, shut completely out of her mind. The hum of the heating coils of the stove top burner that she had turned on under the teakettle took its place along with the faint sounds of his footsteps as he joined her in the kitchen. Another unwanted sound alarmed her as she recognized the increase of tempo in her heart beat as he passed close behind her. He reached into the cupboard for mugs, warmed them with hot water from the tap, then took the whistling teakettle from her trembling hands, poured the water over the tea bags as she placed them into the mugs and set the mugs on the table. She felt some of the warm natural color return to her face and hands and a reserve source of calm gained a slight upper hand as she placed the creamer and sugar bowl on the table along with two spoons and a coaster for the used tea bags. The silent sounds of removing teabags, adding sugar and cream ended abruptly with the forceful clink of his spoon on the saucer.

"There's still more, Mrs. Wilson!" The forceful command in his voice and his searching eyes claimed her attention as they faced each other across the table. "I need to hear the rest of it. Now."

A long slow sip and swallow of the almost too hot tea released some of the pressure still in control of her voice. She took another quick swallow and then resting her arms on the table in front of her with the mug between her hands, she agreed. "Yes.

"There's more. It seemed that night would never end. The fireman who discovered the accident called the ambulance on his car radio and in a few minutes Ralph and the boy were in the hospital. But all that we knew at the time of the fire was that Ralph was not at home because the wagon was gone, and Richie was not in the downstairs part of the house."

She felt Brock's searching eyes on her face as her hands began to move the mug they held, turning it around and around. She kept her own eyes fixed on the remaining creamy liquid, concealing from him any idea of who or what she might see in that turning pool. He moved his hands across the table as though he would grasp hers again, but then pulled them back to lift his cup and let her continue.

"The alarm sounded here, and at their house the fire was already out of control. The first men to arrive at the house discovered the family dog barking and whining at the door of the family room that opens to the driveway. They went into the room and found June lying on the tile in front of the fireplace. The ladder she had been standing on was on top of her. No one will ever know why she changed her mind and decided to finish the decorating while Ralph was gone." The mug had stopped turning and was now serving as her ballast, holding her steady as her fingers turned white with the pressure.

"The fire in the fireplace had ignited the streamers she had been hanging. They were strips of old sheets she had dyed a deep red especially for Christmas and Valentine's Day decorations. That's why they..." she paused – a deep shuddering breath filled her lungs and then, "anyway, the fire went up the stairway and the men couldn't get upstairs to look for Richie."

"June wasn't burned, the fire just sucked the living breath right out of her when she fell and didn't know...she was knocked unconscious."

Again Linda battled clawing memories, struggling to force back the persistent tears. She finished the last few drops of tea. Holding the mug with both hands, she slowly put it down on the table.

"They took June and Ralph to the same mortuary – we buried them side-by-side. Richie was unconscious for twenty-four hours. We didn't tell him until after the funeral and then he was in shock for ten days. Now he has no one except his Grandmother and me."

"He also has me, now."

Her eyes, aching and still void of any tears, met his and she permitted a cloud to swiftly form over hers, her lids dropped as shutters and she deliberately turned her head away. He pushed his chair back and put the mugs on the counter. As she pushed her chair back and stood up, he leaned over with his hands spread out on the table across from her and shocked her with...

"There's still more, Mrs. Wilson. What was it that..." Standing there, tense between the table and the chair, she felt the cloud in her eyes spread to a chilling, numbing mask that tightened around her nose, drew her mouth into a grim hard line and stiffened her chin and throat muscles as if to support the weight of the ice block forming there. She moved the sugar and creamer from the table back to their place on the counter, turning her back to him. "Richie is all that need concern you, Mr. Brockman."

"But whatever has hurt you personally, turned you into a..."

"Bitter old maid, Mr. Brockman?" She trembled at his closeness behind her and moved away from his hands before they could grip her shoulders. "You'll never know that. It has no bearing..."

"Never is a long..." They both turned at the simultaneous click of the switch and the lighting of the lamps on the fireplace wall. "Well, he is all tucked in and waiting for you to say good night, Linda." Mrs. Farnsworth stood at the entrance to the kitchen with her hand still on the wall beside the light switch. "He needs some assurance concerning Miss Tucker and what she will expect of him on Tuesday."

"Do you know Miss Tucker, Mr. Brockman?" Linda inquired, noticing a quick flash of interest on his face at the mention of the tutor.

"Isn't she the tutor from the local school?" He evaded. "I believe the name was mentioned in that capacity when the doctor was here."

"Oh, yes, of course." Linda then excused herself to go to Richie.

Later that evening following a brief telephone conversation she joined her mother in the lounging area in front of the fireplace, where Mrs. Farnsworth enjoyed doing needlework or reading a bit before ending the day.

"I've just talked with Carl."

She wrapped her soft robe close around her ankles as she tucked them beneath her in the corner section of the sofa.

"He wanted to know about the weekend plans. I haven't forgotten that it is Labor Day, but I haven't made up my mind yet – should we...?"

"I've been thinking about it too." The older lady removed her glasses and laid them along with the book she had been reading on the small table next to her chair. "There will be memories and some hard moments to face, I'm sure. Although if we cancel it this year it will be harder to pick up again next fall. The question is, do we want to continue with the activities year after year, as we have done?"

"Perhaps we should cancel the Saturday night dance," Linda considered, "just for this year. But, yes, I do think we should continue with the picnic and the fun on Monday." Answering an unspoken question in her mother's eyes, she went on. "Since Richie believes he'll be back to normal by this time next year, I'm sure he will be able to take part in some of the activities, except..."

Mrs. Farnsworth interrupted, exclaiming, "The talent show."

Linda knew her mother was referring to the program which had been Ralph's responsibilities. "We'll need to see about that." She arose from her place on the sofa and walked to the door to the patio, recalling her emotional trauma earlier and noticing the light now burning in the cottage. "Of course, why not?" she continued. "Perhaps there is a person who will accept the talent show assignment."

In the gardener's cottage another two way conversation was in progress. The defused light from the lamp on the small library desk in the corner highlighted the silver in the black hair. It also exaggerated the fatigue lines that still collected at times around the man's eyes and mouth. He was completely relaxed in the large recliner, his slipper clad feet elevated onto the matching ottoman. Beside the chair on the desk surface was a compact disc and cassette player/recorder/AM-FM radio. Concealed in the back of the case was a high powered radio transmitter/receiver. On the front of the radio near the dial was a small unmarked light that was now blinking. The man at ease in the chair talked into the microphone concealed in the hand-held portable fake phone.

Through the tiny speaker in the cassette player came the voice of the same person with whom he had kept in phone contact on his trip north. "I'm glad things are suiting you so well there, Whit. Is there anything more that I should know?" "Your Miss Tucker will be coming here beginning Tuesday morning, to tutor the boy."

"Oh, Whit, no!"

"Yes, I thought you might feel that way. Is she really such a...?"

"I'm afraid so, Dear.. She has her little bid into everything here. She is an excellent teacher, but..."

"Perhaps I should just avoid her. I can always be busy when she is here."

"Of course, only do it naturally. She will insist on meeting you and may become suspicious if you make your absence too noticeable."

"If I were a few years younger perhaps I could just turn on the old charm and get..."

"Oh, you could, even now, but I doubt if that would be the best way to handle her."

"All right," he laughed and assured her, "I'll be able to think of some way to manage the situation, Love. You don't reach my age without learning a little of the art of – something or other."

He glanced at the watch on his wrist and then, "There is one more thing before I let you go. I want you to get a membership for me to the local swim club." He explained about the swim lessons planned for Richie, then said goodnight. Carefully he replaced the fake phone on the clip at the side of the record/tape player.

Immediately the light disappeared.

Saturday morning.

The overnight mist had slowly risen and drifted away, leaving glittering bits and pieces on the bright display of marigolds and zinnias. Linda walked through the patio and stood at the door to the terrace. The bright display of early Autumn colors took hold of her memory. Flashes of happier times rushed through her thoughts, childish romps with her brother on that great lawn, attempts to wash away freckles in the early dew on many first day of May mornings.

The early, every morning sounds of the busy-ness of the tree habitants and bush dwelling mourning doves joined with the human household sounds of bacon and eggs frying. The whir of the blender turning oranges into juice provided ever enjoyable accompaniment for the opening of the day, and brought Linda back to the present. She decided to gather flowers for the breakfast table.

Agnes was busy at the kitchen counter, the table was set for breakfast, and Richie and his grandmother were nearly ready for the meal. She would have a minute or two.

She left her loafers just outside the door and skimmed her feet through the thick growth of well kept grass, luxuriating in the cool, moist refreshment the mist had left behind. Momentarily her arms were filled with some of the garden's brightness, her blouse and skirt slightly stained with the moisture that clung to the colorful petals. For a brief second she stood there as one of nature's own, drawing life for the day from the moisture and soil beneath her feet and the warmth of the sun that now enhanced the gold and copper hues of an autumn sunrise repeated in the soft coils at the nape of her neck.

Her brief reverie ended with the slamming of a car door and the crunch of Carl's heavy shoes as he walked toward Linda through the gravel. She hurried back toward the door unmindful of her bare feet, until he noticed the wet prints they had left as she met him on the walk.

"Well," he sneered. "Don't you think you are a little early for your second childhood?"

She met the scorn that he did not bother to hide with a bit of calm from the inner peace just newly refreshed.

He flipped a hand at the flowers she carried, knocking loose a few petals. "Or are you omitting the 'woman' part of your life entirely?"

Shocked at this renewed attack on her status as a woman, Linda looked first at her feet and then again at him.

"If you have some business matter that needs my attention this morning I would appreciate it if you would wait in the office until I become a 'business woman' for the day."

The day had started so beautifully with her impulsive gathering of flowers, but was soon clouded over, beginning with Carl's inexcusable rudeness. She put on a cheery face for breakfast, but left it there with the flowers as she began the short day's work in her office.

Carl's attitude lately had been rather condescending, even insulting in some cases.

He had always been boisterous and rough when they were younger but he seemed to be losing it in the last few months. He had agreed, however, to manage the contests and the ball games for the men on Labor Day.

She answered the telephone for one call, then flipped the switch that turned off the lights and power to the office equipment. She collected the morning mail that still needed to be opened from her desk, then shut and locked the office door behind her. There should be no need to unlock it again before Tuesday morning. Three of the letters were addressed to her mother so she put them on the table beside the chair in the family room.

Lunch on Saturdays was always a serve yourself arrangement, and according to the evidence in the sink and on the counter she was the last one to lunch. The sound of the vacuum cleaner coming from the apartment over the garage let her know where Agnes was, but the rest of the house was quiet..

Coming from her room later she remembered that her mother had not been in her chair when Linda placed her mail on the table. Seeing her door was closed she fingered a light tap on it and called.

"Mother?" "Oh, Linda." Mrs. Farnsworth turned from the window as Linda pushed open the door.

"Are you all right?"

"Yes, of course, Dear. I was just remembering a little. It will be so refreshing to hear children playing on the lawn again. It's heartening to know that Richie will be able to play in the snow, perhaps even before this winter is over." She picked up the mending from the basket by the window and smiled at her daughter. "So, it will be only one year wasted."

Linda followed her through the hall and to the kitchen. The year had surely taken its toll on her mother. She noticed the silver showing a little more predominantly and a little more sloping in the shoulderline. "I put your mail on your table for you." Linda opened the refrigerator door. "Why don't you read it while I have lunch? Would you like some iced tea or juice with me?"

"No, thank you, Dear, I had lunch with Richie and Brock."

Linda noticed the use of the friendly name, but made no comment. Her light lunch consisted of cottage cheese, lettuce and sliced peaches, with a tall glass of iced tea.

Mrs. Farnsworth glanced up from the letter she had just finished. "Richie and Brock are picking apples this afternoon. They have a contraption rigged up so that Brock can pass the apples down to Richie and he can put them into the crate."

"They seem to get along first rate. It's really too bad we didn't think of it sooner."

"But then perhaps Brock wouldn't have been free to come," reminded her mother, "and then it wouldn't have been the same. God's perfect timing, you know." That with a smile and a slight nod of her head. "Have you finished with your lunch?" Her mother changed the subject abruptly.

"I'll put the dish into the sink, have a little more tea. Can I get you something?"

"No, but bring your tea over here. There's a letter I think you should read," she continued as Linda sat on one of the footstools near her chair. "Do you remember the note we received in the spring from that friend of your brother Ralph's in Australia?" As Linda nodded Mrs. Farnsworth offered her the last of the three letters she had opened.

"Well, this is from him." Linda took the letter as her mother glanced at the post mark and said, "It's from Montreal, not Australia." "Oh?" Linda questioned, and then read quickly through the first part of the typed page to herself, and then as if to make what she was reading seem more clear she read aloud...

"...I had written to Ralph questioning about the working and living conditions in your area. My wife's family are in Canada and we are in the process of moving from Australia.

"I received a letter from your son last November extending an invitation to visit, expressing the fact that we would be welcome at any time. I know that he is no longer there and I deeply regret not being able to come sooner.

"We have severed all of our connections in Australia and are now with her family in Montreal. I will be in Saulte Ste. Marie on Saturday and Sunday and then I must go on to Detroit for an early appointment on Wednesday morning.

"Since I am going to be passing so near, I will take the time to come to you. Since it is a holiday I realize that you may have other plans, but would like to share a few moments with you, if at all possible..."

and the letter was signed, Sincerely, HAROLD VAN FLEET

Linda folded the letter and handed it back to her mother. "I remember Ralph talking about him. They were in the service together for a while and then Harold left for special training or something and Ralph came home. He told me about writing the letter, about Harold wanting to move back to this country." She slowly turned the now empty tea glass between her hands, concentrating on the motion. "He doesn't say if he only wants employment or if he wants to invest in something, and become a part of it." Linda glanced at her mother, and continued. "Why don't you and I talk with him as a friend when he comes Monday, and then decide." She took her glass to the kitchen and rinsed it at the sink. "Carl hinted that he needed a few more men helping with the Christmas trees this year. It would be a good way for Mr. Van Fleet to learn what our farm is all about."

The sound of the door opening from the apartment above the garage interrupted the conversation. Agnes stepped heavily into the room and Mrs. Farnsworth began discussing the arrangements needed for Labor Day weekend. Agnes had been a friend and helper for many years. Her build, slightly shorter than Mrs. Farnsworth, with similar rounding shoulders. Her hair still shone black with more than a few silver streaks. Her demeanor as quick as her snappy, brown eyes.

Leaving the two elderly ladies to a friendly chat and their after lunch duties, Linda walked to the apple orchard for a quick glimpse of the activities there. "It's coming along fine," she remarked as she noticed two full crates of apples on the gound near the cottage. She picked one out as she walked by, polished it to a deep burgundy red on the sleeve of her blouse. She went on, rustling her feet through the assortment of leaves scattered around her. She stopped at the low fence that marked the beginning of the orchard. The sense of faint and undiscernable feelings stirred within her again as she observed the scene under the trees. The man, again with no covering on his back or arms, and with his back toward her, was sitting in the bed of the large coaster wagon, his feet set firmly on the ground on either side, a half eaten apple in his hand. The sun shining through the trees added a soft sheen to the golden tan that outlined in stark relief the pale scar that followed the line of his lower ribs on his right side. She recalled the mention that Richie had made of it, and Brock's remark that it was nothing. She stood for a moment unobserved, and watched as the boy in the wheelchair and the man astradle the boy's wagon shared a quiet time of food and fellowship. Not wanting to interfere with this new found companionship for her nephew, she returned to the house, munching the apple that she held unaware of its flavor or texture; only thinking of the boy and the man together in the orchard.

Later, at the evening meal, the question of 'Why' came to her mind again. Seated across the table from her was a well educated, refined person who could successfully hold a high position in many different types of business organizations or associations. Surely being a musician, a writer of lyrics, was just a sideline. She watched as the strong, tanned hand, lightly covered with dark hair, unadorned by jewelry, held the delicate handle of the teacup as unconcerned as if it were not a fragile thing. The urging pull of some magnetic force commanded her eyes to follow the cup as it was raised to his lips. From there it was just a quick lift of her lashes and she met the source of that power.

She could not be sure of what he was thinking. There was no mockery in his eyes.

None of the sneering insinuations that had been in Carl's eyes were evident here. Yet, there was something vaguely familiar.

"I was down at the orchard after lunch. You two were so engrossed in sampling the crop and a bit of conversation that I didn't bother you." She reached for the sugar in front of her to add a little to her already too sweet coffee. The moment had to be passed over and stirring coffee was a good excuse for turning her eyes away.

"We didn't see her, did we, Brock?"

"No, we didn't." He lifted a questioning eyebrow toward Linda. "Was there something you needed?"

"No." She covered her blushing by finishing that last drop of coffee in her cup. "Just a bit of exercise after a tiring morning."

Chapter Three

Linda and Richie were making quick work of spreading the table cloth and laying the place settings for Sunday dinner. Most of the preparation of the main meal on Sundays was always done early in the day. Today was no exception. The crock pot steamed full of New England pot roast and the salad sat chilling in the refrigerator. This preparation gave opportunity for Mrs. Farnsworth and Agnes to attend church with the neighboring couple, James and Louise Roberts, who would call for them and bring them home after the service.

Linda gave the cut fall flowers and fern that made up the low centerpiece a twist and a pull here and there, then, satified with the arrangement, put it on the crystal circle in the center of the table. As she folded the matching napkins for Richie to put at each place, they heard the sharp rap of knuckles on the kitchen door.

"Come on in, Brock. We're in the dining room."

"Richie!" Linda admonished. "You are to go to the door, not just call out like that!"

She despised the embarrassed flush that tinted her cheeks. "Good morning Mr. Brockman." She greeted him.

"Aw, Aunt Linda. Can't you call him Brock like Grandee and I do? After all, he's your friend, too."

"I certainly am," laughed the man now standing in the doorway.

She watched as the laughter wrinkles deepened at the corners of his eyes and a thought slipped invitingly through her mind. Brock was becoming more than just an employee and perhaps even more than a friend. "Perhaps you would rather call me 'Whit' as my sister – and my mother did?" "I think, if you don't mind, it will be Brock." Again there was that strange something in the intense blue eyes that caused her to turn from them. "Good." He took in at a glance the stage of preparation for sitting down to the meal. "Since I have nothing to do right at this moment could I fill water glasses, set the chairs around? And," stepping close to her he took command of her eyes again,

"may I call you Linda – for want of the right to call you..."

"Of course, Brock," Richie was not reprimanded for this bit of rudeness. "That's what her friends call her!"

Turning sharply toward the kitchen, she informed him, "Richie is in charge of the dining room on Sundays, so perhaps you can do it together." She found it hard to speak his name. "Brock will be dining with us, so – places will be the same as in the kitchen, Richie." Why did she falter around like this. Anger at herself for some unknown reason brought a glow to her cheeks, as she hurried away into the kitchen.

Linda's mother lingered longer than usual at the table after dinner. Linda and her mother usually enjoyed the clean up task together, but at this meal Agnes was clearing the table. Linda waited until Agnes had gone back to the kitchen and then spoke, "Mum, are you feeling all right?"

"Of course I am, dear." There was just a little too much emphasis on the first two words, Linda was aware, as her mother put her folded napkin on the table and then, "I was just recalling something of the sermon..."

As Agnes returned from the kitchen for the remaining dishes, Linda wondered at the stern set of the housekeeper's mouth. It was a definite sign that she was upset, or worried about something. Evidently something was said that upset them both, Linda decided. The ladies of the Aide Society were always bickering about things.

Linda followed as her mother went into the kitchen and stopped close beside her as she paused at the bottom of the steps. Just briefly she put her arm across her shoulders in a quick hug, a little endearment she had copied from her father. She allowed her arm to linger there, inwardly alarmed at how thin her mother had become, and vowing to take more notice of her mother's health.

Later that day, since Brock had agreed to direct the talent show for the picnic, Linda and Brock were working on the program together at the umbrella table that had been moved onto the lawn near the drive. The rattle and scrunch of tires stopping in the gravel and the following sound of a car door slamming took their attention from the papers on the table between them. No other person in the area drives like that, she realized, as she turned to see Carl striding across the lawn toward them. She felt the uneasiness and that certain anger begin to mount within her as she noticed the antagonism that Carl deliberately showed as he ignored Brock, greeting only her.

"Hi, Inda," using that name for her with an insulting intimacy. "Maria is out in the car. Natalie is with her, so she won't get out, but..."

"Surely she can come and sit for a minute or two?" Linda put it as a question.

"No, it's not necessary." He picked up a lawn chair nearby, put it down between her and Brock and sat there with his back to the other man. "The gang is having the dance at the lodge tomorrow night, seeing that you didn't want to do it this year. Since you don't have a guy to take you, why don't you come with Maria and me." He reached for her hand that gripped the arm of the chair in which she sat. "I'll personally see that you have a real good time."

She stared at the hand covering hers and then glared at him, meeting his sensuous, insulting leer, holding his eyes with hers until he slowly took away his hand. "I really don't think I can accept that invitation, Carl. In fact, I shall even forget that it was offered, for Maria's sake."

"Well LA-DE-DAH," he sneered as he stood up, slamming his chair back to its original place. "Don't worry. I'll make sure that they all know that you were invited, but you..."

"She has a right to choose not to accept your invitation." The chill of cold steel in the curt spoken words impelled Carl to finally face the man now standing behind Linda's chair, carelessly relaxed with his thumbs hooked through the belt loops of his low-riding jeans.

"What do you have to say about anything around here, Brockman?" Carl threw at him, clenching both fists at his side. Fiery green eyes locked with those so like the ice blue steel in the cool voice. Linda, not wanting any physical clashes to take place, stood up between the two men.

"Carl, I cannot accept the invitation. Maria will understand." She took the papers from the table and turned to Brock as Carl stomped back through the grass and gravel to the car where his wife and daughter waited. Linda stood for a moment, collecting her composure as she had collected the papers she was now reading. Brock pushed the chairs closer to the table and adjusted the umbrella, then nodded toward the papers.

"Are there any more names that should be added?"

"Not that I know. If someone else does want to take part I'm sure you can handle it."

The sun was quickly dropping behind the pines as she and Brock walked toward the house. She felt the chill of Autumn in the breeze that flicked her hair in soft wisps around her ears and throat. Gently it moved around her, playing with the soft material of blouse and skirt. Linda was, all the while, unaware of the appreciation in the blue eyes which were squinted to avoid the low rays of the sun. Not realizing that the persistent breeze was piquing his interest, she offered..."Won't you come in for coffee, or tea, or something?"

He stepped closer beside her as she handed him the papers she had carried.

"Thank you, but no. I need to get this organized and plan a little patter to go with it." He turned toward the cottage – then turned back again.

"Linda?"

Something caught her breath and held it for a moment as she heard him speak her name, then released it as she waited for him to continue. "If you would like to attend the dance Monday night, I could, as Carl hinted, be your 'Guy'."

"It's kind of you to offer, Brock, but..."

"Won't a lot of your friends be there?"

"Not really. It's mostly the rowdy crowd from the logging camps and the forestry crew who attend the dances that Carl and his friends organize. I'm sure we both would be out of place there."

The night sounds filling the air drifted into the room as she turned off the light on the beside table and opened the window part way to welcome the stirring, refreshing coolness. The soft cotton gown brushed just below he knees as she sat on the edge of the bed. Slowly she removed the pins that held the coiled braids in place, letting her hair fall down her back. As if it were a type of sleeping potion, her fingers worked from the end of each braid, deftly parting and combing through each strand, reaching the back of her neck, combing and massaging away the tensions of the day. This was a ritual that Phil Wilson had anticipated for their intimate times after their wedding day.

"Oh, Dear God," she breathed, "Don't let me think of those things, now that they will never be." She gave the soft auburn flow a few strokes with her brush and fastened her hair in a loose braid that was comfortable for the night, then slipped between the fresh cool sheets.

She blocked out of her mind the hurtful memories of the past and considered the events of the day just ending. Would Harold Van Fleet want to stay in Michigan. She tried to recall if she had ever seen the man and decided that she had not. There were four bedrooms, two baths and plenty of storage space upstairs. They would fit in there, she was certain. It would be great if it worked out that her mother could have some extra help for awhile.

Her mind wandered from the Van Fleet family to Carl and then to Brock. What had he thought of Carl's actions that afternoon. Why did Carl persist in unwanted attentions. And Maria, did she think that Linda encouraged him. She turned on her side, shrugged her shoulder into the softness of the pillow and cuddled the soft comforter under her chin. The breeze coming through the window caressed her cheek as she turned off all thoughts of recent disappointment and ideas of joys that could never be, closed her eyes and waited for sleep to come. In her last moments she caught the faint, plaintive sound of music. A medley of familiar tunes from the past decade accompanied the chorus of crickets and tree frogs.

"How strange." She concentrated on the direction of the sound, then recognizing the sound of an electric keyboard she identified the location and the attractive yet disturbing source.

By early afternoon on Labor Day, the area in front of the house near the road marked with logs for parking was filled with mini-vans, an ancient mini-bus, family sedans in all available parking spots. Three pickup trucks and a couple of four wheelers were parked on the gravel strip along the driveway and near the blacktop of the parking area. The loggers and Christmas tree crew were in the seventh inning of the play-off game of two out of three series for the annual championship. The teams had taken a burger and soda break between the second and third games, and were now back playing baseball "as hard against each other as they had worked together," Linda noted to the elderly neighbor waiting next to her for her turn at croquet on the front lawn. Some teens and their younger siblings were skating on the blacktop and front walks. A few mothers were playing with their toddlers in a portable wading pool beneath a huge oak tree. "We had thought about a swimming pool for that area," Linda mentioned, "but the cost and problems were too extensive for the time it could be used."

Everything had worked out perfectly. The trucks had arrived early with the barbeque pit. The tables, chairs, and benches were all set in their places. Jonesey and his crew were busy with the food preparation and would be ready to serve at five o'clock.

Right on schedule.

She filled her lungs with a clean fresh breath of autumn air and released it slowly, drawing invigorating strength. Linda walked with Brock around the house to the back lawn. Near the cottage where chairs sat in semi-circle rows facing the small porch where microphones and speakers had been put for the talent show.

"I'll play a tape of carnival music as soon as the ball game is over." Brock straightened a few wires on the porch, then continued, "The show should run perhaps an hour."

"There will be cold drinks and popcorn for the audience," Linda informed him.

They stopped at the side of the cottage where Richie and a group of boys his age were in the middle of a lawn darts contest. She reveled in the sight as she noticed that no allowance was made for Richie when it was his turn. Her eyes followed Brock's to the scoreboard taped to the side of the cottage, and beamed in answer to the pleased look on his face. "He does hold his own, does he not. I was afraid he would be reluctant to take part."

"We talked about that in the orchard on Saturday," Brock informed her, as they turned back toward the house. "He's a very sensible boy. Not a trace of self pity there.

Do you know he has challenged me to a snowball battle some time before I leave in January?"

"He and his father always built forts on the lawn..."

They stopped suddenly as they reached the screened patio when the sound of raised women's voices came from within.

"Martha, you mean you didn't say anything to Linda?"

"No , I did not. She has too much to worry about as it is"

The third voice cut in. "I'm that upset about the whole thing, Louise. I found her leaning against the table just a few minutes ago..." Linda swung the door open with Brock following close behind her. Mrs. Martha Farnsworth, Agnes, and Louise Roberts all turned to face them.

"Mother. What is this that you haven't told me?" She pleaded with the other women. "Agnes, Louise, – what?" Brock opened the door to the kitchen and urged them into the family room. "Why don't you ladies come in here, sit down and explain to Linda. The ball game is over and it might be a little rowdy outside for a while. I'll send someone in with cool drinks."

Linda nodded her appreciation of his offer as he turned to leave, then..."You've been ill all this weekend haven't you, Mum." She accused. She couldn't keep her tone any lighter. "Is this the reason for Agnes being so stern with you yesterday? Were you ill in church? That is what you didn't tell me?" Her voice trembled now belying her growing concern. "Oh, my dearest Mother." She exclaimed. "Didn't you realize it would be best for me to know, so that I can see that you do something about it?"

"It was just a little twinge in my side," her mother protested, as Agnes helped her to her chair. Her protestations were denied as Linda observed the concerned look from Louise who was standing behind her mother's chair slowly shaking her head.

An hour later, after cool drinks brought in by Maria, Linda had heard the details from the ladies, the talent show had ended, and Mrs. Farnsworth, much rested, was back in her chair on the lawn chatting with her friends.

In the study, however, Linda, by telephone to Dr. Browne's answering service, made arrangements for him to see her mother the next afternoon. She wrote down a number to call if an emergency developed, and a notation of the time and address. Then rested her head in her hands. All of the pleasure of a smooth running day, dampened by the frightening thought that her mother could be seriously ill. Not understanding how she could not have noticed, she sent up a prayer to her heavenly Father, got out of the chair and went to the window. The ladies were taking up the wickets and stakes of the croquet game and the babies and small children from the pool were resting in strollers or on blankets. The skaters had abandoned the walk and drive and the record player had been put away.

It had been a good day, surely. Now all that was left was the meal at the long tables and her mother's little speech that everyone expected. Linda promised herself to see that the speech was extra short and to the point. Looking forward to better times ahead. *No looking back, for only sad things are there to recall.*

Her attention was drawn to the sun reflected on the windshield of the VW Rabbit just making the turn from the road into the driveway. She recognized the Canadian plate on the front of the car and hurried out the front door to the bottom step as the bright red mini car was being parked in the small space left vacant by the removal of the record player and speakers. Linda stood at the bottom of the steps, waiting.

She had wanted to meet this man before anyone else knew that he had arrived.

The first glimpse she had of him was a crop of bright yellow curls gleaming in the sun, over the top of the VW. She blinked her eyes in disbelief. "Oh, my" she gasped.

"That is one of those 'Bushy-Bushy' hair do's." Then she caught the full effect of the sun on his face as he came from the back of the car. A golden brush of neatly trimmed beard, side-burns and mustache joined with slightly shaggy eyebrows to form a complete circle around a huge pair of dark sun glasses. He was not much taller than she and very slim.

His pale green knit shirt was open at the throat and his arms were covered with long sleeves. His skinny legs were clad in tight buff-colored levis and bottomed off with sand colored Dockers. He strode up the walk to meet her, his hand outstretched and his white teeth dazzling in a broad smile.

She noticed the golden hairs on his suntanned hand and wrist as he gripped the hand she extended in greeting.

"G'day and Hey. I know you are Linda." His greeting a mixture from the many places he had lived. "And you are Harold, of course. I remember Ralph telling about the blonde curls and some of your attempts at getting rid of them." She was relieved that he laughed as she did. "I was never so glad of anything in my life as I was when all of this came into style. He laughed again as he brushed his hand over the golden mass. "My skin burns so badly in the sun, so I'm grateful that I can wear a natural sunscreen."

They went through the front hall and into the study where he removed the glasses revealing eyes of deepest emerald green glittering out at her from ovals of golden eyelashes very masculine in spite of their length and thickness.

"Won't you please make yourself comfortable here for a minute or two. Would you care for a soda, iced tea, or fresh lemonade? You are just in time for our Labor Day dinner."

"How about a tall frosty glass of lemonade, since I have a choice." He went to the window. "I'll just wait here."

Linda hurried to the back lawn, let Agnes know of her needs, and then stopped by her mother's chair. "Mr. Van Fleet has arrived. I'll bring him out in time for dinner. We can talk with him together after our meal. Should I have Agnes make up the small room upstairs?"

"I believe she has, already."

"Good. Are you all right?"

"Yes. Don't worry so! I'm going to be fine." Then, as she saw Agnes go into the house with the frosty glasses on a tray, Mrs. Farnsworth urged, "You had better go or Agnes will be there before you." Linda hurried ahead to open doors and to inquire about the room upstairs, then took the tray from Agnes and went into the study. They enjoyed the refreshing drinks and exchanged brief get acquainted questions and answers. Then Linda directed him to the first room on the left at the head of the stairs. "There's a small bath connected to the room if you want to freshen up a little. I'll be in the study when you come down. The festivities have been going strong most of the day." *I can use a few minutes to recuperate.* Before he went up the stairs she added, "You'll have about thirty minutes, so if you want to get something from your car, you'll have time."

The clear emerald eyes that met hers glittered with a hint of a smile. "I think I'll just stretch out for those twenty or so minutes." He turned and went up the stairs.

She folded her arms in front of her on the desk and lowered her head to rest. It was impossible to stop the names as they whirled around in her mind. Carl and his insolence, Brock and the mystery that was building in her mind concerning him, her mother and her sudden illness, Dr. Browne and Richie's operation: Carl. Brock. Mother. Richie. And now the Van Fleet family.

He's surely personable. Linda figured he must be at least forty years old because he was older than Ralph, and that he must be a responsible worker and family man otherwise her brother Ralph wouldn't have invited him to come to the tree farm.

The soft swish of shoes on carpeted stairs and the gentle tap on the door frame aroused her from her troubling thoughts.

"It's not been quite twenty minutes yet, but..."

"Oh, Harold – I'm sorry, perhaps I should have said Mr. Van..."

"Not at all." He assured her, that smile flickering again in the emerald eyes. "We reached the Linda and Harold stage as I came up the front walk and saw the welcome look on your face, even though it wasn't a smile."

"Very well, then – Harold – we'll go out the back door where Mum is waiting."

Most of the crowd had moved closer to the tables when Linda and the newcomer reached the back lawn, but James and Louise Roberts, the neighbors from down the road were sitting in the shade with Mrs. Farnsworth. Linda introduced Harold to them, excused herself and walked on toward the head table. Brock's microphone, bench and electric keyboard were at the end of the table for Brock's convenience. Richie and a small dark haired girl were examining the keyboard, running their fingers back and forth over the keys. Linda stopped a few paces away to watch and listen.

A gruff voice sounded behind them. "Hey, Richie, you going to learn to play that thing? It sure won't take the place of a good game of ball, will it!" Linda gasped and moved closer. Carl's back was toward her and he had not seen her standing there. "But I guess you can play darts, or doodle on a piano or toodle a horn, even from a wheelchair." The taunting voice continued.

"Lots of men play piano – and darts, Mr. Carl." Richie answered politely.

"Yeah, but not real tough 'He' men." Carl jibed. Linda took an angry step toward them but a firm grip on her arm stopped her and she felt Brock beside her.

"Let me handle..." he began, but the boy handled it his way.

"My DAD played piano and he wasn't a sissy – and my Uncle Phil played guitar and sang, and I saw him beat the TAR out of you – Mr. Carl."

The grip on her arm slowly relaxed and she looked from Brock to Carl and then to her nephew in the wheelchair. The boy's chin was firm, even a little belligerent, while his lips quivered and his eyes glistened with a hint of unshed tears. Carl mumbled something about a lucky punch and where was Richie when all of that was happening. Seeing the reminder of the occasion evident in the scorn in Linda's eyes, he turned and walked away.

"Aunt Linda, I'm sorry but he's always saying..."

"I know, Richie, and we know about things like that, don't we."

Brock wheeled the chair to one side and grinned at the boy in it and the frightened little girl still close beside them. "It's not much of a man who will bully a couple of kids, is it, Richie?" Brock pulled the bench up closer to the keyboard and began to play. First some soft classic pieces then some lively popular tunes and finally the familiar notes of the 'Mess Call' which caught the attention of the assembled crowd. The last few notes interrupted conversations, brought smiles to faces, young and old, as families gathered with friends and fellow workers, along with their employers around the table.

How could I have even considered not having this company Labor Day picnic today? Linda chided herself as she watched them gather and noticed the pleasure on her mother's face as she walked through the crowd, her hand held firmly in the bend of Harold's elbow.

Because of the informal nature of the dinner there were no opening speeches. Mrs. Farnsworth simply welcomed them all and introduced the pastor of the local interdenominational church who prayed for God's blessing on the people gathered there, their fellowship together, and of course, the food that was so bountifully supplied.

Linda slowly became aware of a feeling of tension at her table. It seemed to hover, pushing down. As she tried to locate the source, she realized that no one sitting with her at that table was involved in even polite conversation. Glancing down at her side she noticed the slight trembling hands on the wheelchair. Slowly, Richie's eyes met hers, then flashed toward the jeering face of the man sitting beside his grandmother.

Surely Carl can't still be angry with the boy. The dull ache in her throat increased at the thought. She felt other eyes questioning her, demanding to be noticed.

Hesitantly, she glanced to the far end of the table as the firmly drawn lips surrounded by that golden beard were a sure evidence of the anger inside the man seated there. Her attention shifted to Brock who was seated at the other end of the table nearer to her and Richie.

She wondered if Harold's anger could be toward Brock. She gasped and almost cringed at the idea. Observing the coldness of Brock's eyes as he glared, not at Harold, but at Carl seated beside her mother. Then she realized their anger was at Carl not each other.

Dear God, she thought. *How will these three men ever work together calmly?*

Where will it all lead? She searched her mind frantically for a way to break the deadly silence and was relieved when her mother pushed her own chair back from the table and stood up.

After a slight bit of moving plates and cups around on the table in front of her, Mrs. Farnsworth asked Brock to switch the microphone to on. Then she called the attention of the people gathered there. She invited Brock and Harold to come and stand beside her. She introduced Brock and explained his purpose and position there, and recognized Harold as a dear friend of her son Ralph whom they all remembered and explained that he was her special guest for the day.

Her mother had really kept her speech short; thanking them for their support and looking forward to a good year ahead. Families were already packing chairs and blankets, into their cars as Linda positioned Richie's chair near the corner of the parking area. It would be a good place for him to wish his friends goodbye. Most of them he would not see again until after his recuperation from the operation and he was back in school.

In a much shorter period of time than it had taken to set them up, the tables were cleared, folded and loaded onto the trucks to be returned to the lodge. As the guests made their way in family groups or last minute gossip clusters to their vans and cars, the chairs they had occupied were swiftly folded and stacked on the trucks with the tables. Before the sun had set all evidence of the day's celebration had been cleared away, except the barbeque pit, which was too hot to be moved. Linda experienced a bit of embarrassment when Maria came to her and quietly apologized for Carl's insistence on inviting her to the dance, explaining that Maria had asked Carl not to ask her. Linda assured her that she understood and that Maria was not to let it bother her. She wished her a good time at the dance then bid her goodnight, as she noticed Carl striding across the lawn with their little daughter, her legs wrapped around his neck, holding on with her hands gripped tightly under his chin, riding on his shoulders.

The sun had disappeared behind the pines, casting their long shadows over the lawn. But the darkness that had moved in was more than shadows. The sky above and beyond the trees, the place where the sun had last been visible was now filled with a dull gray; and a chill had taken the place of the sun's warmth.

Her mother and Harold were just going through the patio to the kitchen, and Brock was waiting on the walk beside Richie's chair. There was again that strange but somewhat familiar something in his look as their eyes met above the boy's head. Linda murmured a quick thank you as he offered to see to the task of getting Richie settled for the night.

Chapter Four

He was not sure if it was the rattling of the barbeque pits in the truck bed as they were being hauled away, or the pelting of the rain against the window beside his bed that disturbed his sleep, but Brock woke with a start. He sat up immediately. It was still a shock to his nervous system to be awakened from a sound sleep by sudden or unusual noises. *Will it ever be back to normal?* What was normal, anyway. Ten years of secret places; mysterious lonely journeys; exciting, nerve wracking, extremely dangerous situations. That had been typical, but definitely not normal. He glanced at the clock on the bedside table. Seven-thirty and it was still dark outside.

Standing up by the bed, he pushed his feet into the slippers waiting there and covered his lean nakedness with the short velour robe that was draped across the chair.

Suddenly he felt the air blowing the curtains in at the kitchen window. It was cold and damp and he realized it was still dark because of the rain.

During the process of shower, shave, and getting dressed, he stopped suddenly, taking a more observant look into the mirror. Good! The eggs, pancakes and sausages he persistently prepared for himself each morning, along with the meals he ate with the family were already doing what the doctor had assured him they would do. The energizing warmth of the sun along with his careful regimen of exercises and activities had definitely helped. The old physique was coming back in good shape. Soon the only outward evidence of the last episode would be the scar. "It's about time," he remarked to the image in the mirror. "It's hard to tell what will occur during the next few weeks."

After breakfast and the simple housekeeping chores of the morning, he pushed his arms into the sleeves of the brushed denim jacket that matched the thigh hugging gray slacks and closed the door behind him. The sharp, cold, pre-autumn air penetrated deeply into his lungs as he stood for a moment on the steps taking in deep breaths. He walked through the small rivulets racing over the surface of the walk. Enjoying the cool rain on his face reminded him again of his distinct privilege of being alive. The Volkswagen Rabbit just turning from the drive onto the main road recalled to his mind his meeting of the overnight guest and a feeling he had barely noticed at the time. An awareness of recognition between them!

He glanced at his watch. Not quite nine yet. By the time he drove to the small town, Brombke would be in the Washington office. He knocked on the screen door and then went through the patio into the kitchen.

Agnes answered his knock with a 'good morning'. "Good morning to you, Agnes." He greeted her then remarked about the refreshing pleasantness of the cool air.

"Yes..." she agreed, "it's a sure sign that winter is rushing to catch us." She noticed he was dressed for town. "Miss Linda and Richie are in the study with that Miss Tucker who is going to teach the boy, and Mrs. Farnsworth is upstairs. Is there something you need?"

"Yes, as a matter of fact, there is. But I need to go into town for it. Is there a department store or sporting goods store there? I need to purchase swim trunks."

"Oh, yes, there's Penney's and Sears." She gave him names and locations of those and two other places that should sell the supplies he needed.

"Thank you. I won't be here for lunch, but I will be back in time to take Richie to the pool."

"But don't you want to meet Miss..." "Oh, I think there will be many opportunities for that." Brock excused himself out the door and hurried through the now heavy rain to his station wagon, knowing that there was one appointment he had to keep before any shopping trip. Twenty minutes later the station wagon was parked in the driveway of a small house in the residential area of town, and he was waiting on the step of the house for an answer to the doorbell. Feeling a strong sense of being observed, he was ready when the door swung inward and a soft voice greeted him.

"Whit, dear. Come in."

With one continuous movement he closed the door behind him and gathered the slender woman into his embrace. He lifted her off the floor as she wrapped her arms around him and planted a profusion of light kisses at random on his cheeks and chin and finished with a resounding 'smack' of a kiss on his tenderly smiling mouth. "Hey! Someone would think you were glad to see me." He held her close for a moment longer before putting her back with her feet on the floor. Then holding her at arms length away from him he demanded. "Let me look at you, Love." The dark hair, slightly streaked with silver, would have covered her head in a riot of tight curls if it were not skillfully arranged into tidy waves and brushed into place. Although she was seven years his junior, the lines of care and heartache evident in her gentle, delicate features made her seem much older. *Surely, some of those lines around her mouth and eyes could be from laughter during the happier years, not merely the indication of the uncertainty of their plans for the near future.* The lashes surrounding eyes that appeared as deep pools of amber glowing in soft brown velvet, were long, thick, and softly curled upward. In her soft one-piece shift style dress which she wore belted at the waist, she appeared trim and fit.

Grateful for how much he had benefited from the abundance of food and working in the fresh air the last week, Brock hope that their reunion would be beneficial to her.

He shoved his hands deep into the pockets of his slacks. The tension, a mixture of apprehension and hope, increased in his facial muscles. He prayed a silent prayer. *God, don't let anything go wrong now. Please let our plan work.*

"I have made coffee, Whit." He followed her into the kitchen. "It's so good to see that you have finished this part of the plan and that you are here. You do look healthier already. But, I'm wondering – has something changed?"

"No, no." He took the serving part of the coffee maker from her and filled the two cups she had placed on the table. "I need to call Washington and this is the most private place I could think of, besides, I needed to see you."

"But if Miss Tucker should see you here..."

"There's no danger of that, Love. She's at the Farnsworth's tutoring the boy this morning, so I wasn't needed." Brock sat at the table across from her and helped himself to sugar.

Since she seemed unable to take her gaze from his face, he attempted to reassure her. "There is nothing wrong, Love. I just need to call for some information."

He turned his attention to the living room, centering his concern on the front door.

"How did you know I was at the door? There's no evidence of a spy hole. Yet I did feel as though someone was watching me."

She grinned slightly at him, then called his attention to a small square section of clear glass in the ornamental mirrors on each side of the doorway. "Those are opaque decorations at the bottom of the coach lamps on the outside. They are tilted up just enough so I can see the face of whoever is there without opening the door. There is one at the back door also."

He watched as she clasped her hands on the table in front of her. It's only a few more months, Love, and he'll be here again."

"Will he, Whit? Oh, I pray it is so."

At the anguish so evident in her face he drew her hands across the table into his and gently began to massage them. "You aren't worried about Rosella, are you?" He felt the tension gradually leave her hands.

"Oh, no, but I miss her so."

"Of course, but it would be harder to see her, be with her for a few days, and then have to leave her again. Nan is a good nurse and Rosella loves her. They will be fine. We must concentrate on making it possible for all of us to be together again."

Releasing her hands from his grip he pushed his chair back from the table.

"I do need to make that call. You can listen in so I won't have to explain it all to you."

After some delay the call was put through and Brock identified himself. "I need some detail on a Harold Van fleet; Australia last four years; recently returned to Canada. His face is now covered with a heavy blond beard, but his eyes and voice seem to ring a faint bell, not necessarily an alarm...probably Army...maybe Intelligence." He paused. "Could you call me at this number before one o'clock this afternoon? " He gave Love's telephone number and hung up the receiver.

"I'm glad he is calling back later. Now you can tell me about the boy and the job you are doing. Did I tell you that you look so much better than you did two months ago? Wasn't it an answer to prayer, this job opening up right at this time?"

He took her hand in his again and they sat together on the sofa in the small, simply furnished living room. Each desiring to shut out the past almost three years they had endured being in separate places and having different assignments.

He told her what little he knew of the Farnsworth family situation, including the activities at the company picnic, described the cottage, assured her that he was quite comfortable there. Then he asked for any information she could provide that might help concerning Richie. "I haven't heard much about the family, Whit. Except the barest details concerning the accident and the fire. Richard is an 'A' student, so I didn't have any contact with him at school, since I work with those who have reading problems."

"You will have to meet him soon. He is the epitome of child faith and courage. Of course, we cannot let him know of our relationship until after the first of the year." The ringing of the telephone broke into their conversation.

She quickly mentioned that she would fix lunch while he talked.

Later, he relaxed in the living room in one of the two large arm chairs near the window, the pad from the telephone table in his hand. Love, curled up in the other chair, listened as he explained Harold's arrival at the picnic and his friendship with Richie's father. "He may be returning to the family for a prolonged visit, or even employment, so I needed to know some facts about him."

"It took Brombke a little longer to find him because I didn't have much information. But he did come up with what I need."

She pulled a low, wheeled ottoman close to his chair and sat beside him, deep brown eyes met steel blue ones in an exchange of deep affection. From the pad he held in his hand he read. "Harold Roland Van Fleet, age thirty-nine, born Vancouver, Washington, USA. Served twenty years in the U.S. Army in construction and transportation, and the last four of those years served in intelligence. He took special training to serve in the Antarctic at..." he named the military training station, "before he was assigned to his post in New Zealand."

"Whit, that was the year after you were there as instructor."

"Yes. That is why he seemed familiar. He began his special training about six weeks before I left. He received numerous citations and Brombke gave him an excellent report. Evidently he plans to settle somewhere in the area since his wife is Canadian."

He took the top four sheets from the pad and slipped them into his shirt pocket.

"So, now you also know about Harold Van Fleet." Glancing at his watch he stretched himself up out of the chair. "I'll need to rush now. I have to buy some swim trunks and a beach towel on the way back.

By the way, did you get your membership as well as mine for the local swimming pool?"

She assured him that she had. "About Mr. Van Fleet. Were you thinking of including him in our plans?" "No, not right now. But if he remains in this area at least I know that he is not someone I need to worry about."

"Do you think there may be someone? It pays to be wary of strangers, you know."

They walked to the front door together. A quick 'good-bye' and he was gone.

The rain continued off and on for a few more days. Brock spent the time after Richie's therapy catching up with correspondence and working on the lyrics for the musical. *If the show ever makes it off the ground, it would still only be a fly-by-night.*

But then, it did make his story of being a musician legitimate.

During therapy time on Thursday morning, Richie seemed very concerned about something. It was evident in the tightness of his back muscles. "Hey, fella, you'd better relax or this won't do you any good. What's on your mind? Maybe we should talk about it while we're alone like this, huh?"

"It's a lot of things, Brock. First of all Doc says Grandee has to take things easy for a while. Aunt Linda found out from Agnes that Grandee had a 'spell' with her heart in church last Sunday. Doc gave her some medicine to take every morning. Then – that Mr. Van Fleet that was here Monday – well, he and his wife and little girl are going to move into the rooms upstairs. Aunt Linda said Mr. Van Fleet wants to buy into the business and his wife is supposed to help Grandee with her part of the work."

"Isn't there plenty of room upstairs for them?" Brock turned the boy over onto his back and began to slowly bend first one knee and then the other. "Oh, sure, there are three rooms and a bath they are going to use. The other room with the small bath will be kept for guests."

"Then what is the problem? You want your grandmother to be able to do what the doctor recommends, don't you? She does an abundant lot of work around here."

"I know that, Brock. But it's Carl. He put up a big fuss. He doesn't want anyone else here!"

"But don't your aunt and grandmother own the business?"

"Well, Carl does own part, but the lawyers had the last say, and they said yes. But Carl still doesn't like the idea."

"Perhaps we should just let the ones concerned about it worry about the business, and you and I will concentrate on getting you ready for that very important repair job that is going to be done, O.K.?" He pulled soft cotton exercise pants onto the legs he had been massaging, helped the boy finish dressing, then lifted him into the waiting wheel chair. "Didn't I hear you say the Van Fleet's have a little girl?"

"Yes, she's three years old." Richie sounded skeptical at best.

"Someone to laugh and giggle with, someone to hold and hug. Did you ever hug a sugary, dimpled, curly haired little girl, Richie? Or hear one laugh and try to sing?" "No, there aren't any around here, except Carl's little girl and he never brings her here." Brock folded the table he had been using, pushed it next to the wall out of the way, and then, wheeling the chair out of the room and through the hall to the study, he reminisced aloud.

"I don't know if the one who is coming is curly haired with dimples, but in a house on the Hudson lives a perfect little charmer, a soft cuddly little armful, just waiting for her mother and father to get their lives together again. She's almost four now and things are finally going to work for her." Under his breath he pleaded, *Please, God, let it be so.*

"I didn't know you had a little girl, Brock." Richie's next comment shocked Brock out of his remembering.

"Oh. She isn't mine!"

"Does she live with her grandfather?"

"Yes." Brock maneuvered the chair around to the portable desk where the boy did his lessons. "She is there now with her nurse and the rest of the household."

"Gee! It must be bigger than this house even." Richie's eyes were wide with wonder. "I'll tell you more about it another time. Now it is time for lessons with Miss Tucker." He noticed the grimace flicker over the boy's face but only commented, "I'll see you at lunch today, O.K.?" Since the rain had ended in the early morning hours and the sun was now appearing above clouds drifting away into the eastern horizon, the time was right for last minute outdoor tasks. Already the chill of autumn was gaining in the battle for supremacy over the sun's warmth, and as Agnes had told him, 'Winter was hurrying in.' Brock found window cleaner, sponges, and a ladder with other necessary implements in the tool shed. By lunch time the windows were clean and storm sashes fitted securely in place; garden tools were treated with rust preventative and stored properly. Brock showered and dressed in a clean knit sport shirt and brushed denims.

Realizing there would still be a few mild days, he raised the storm window over his bed and lowered the screen. He could always sleep better in a cool room and this one could be shut off from the heat. He wondered about the arrangement for the new arrivals and when they were expected. Richie hadn't told him and he didn't like to seem curious. That part of the arrangement did not concern him. But nothing – not anything – must interfere with his personal reason for being here. Everything would work out in timing as far as the boy was concerned, he was sure. Richie would be on his feet by then. He could not let anything interfere, not now, nor later. The last bit of fussing with the window screen had made him a few minutes late for lunch so he just rapped lightly, opened the screen door to the patio and went to the kitchen. Everyone was in their usual place and someone else besides. *The Tutor*, he thought to himself and quickly blanked his expression so no one would get a false idea of his reaction. He purposely concentrated on unfolding his napkin and placing it on his knee. Then turning to Mrs. Farnsworth he smiled. "Excuse me for being late. I remembered something at the last minute, and it took three minutes to do instead of one.

She smiled back at him. "Of course, Brock. We have only just now sat down."

She waited for Agnes to fill his cup with coffee, then continued. "I do not believe you have met Richie's tutor yet." She turned her eyes toward the person seated across the table from him. As she made the introduction he quickly scanned Miss Tucker from the top most sculptured curl in definite shades of bottled blond, down over tinted blue eyelids and cherry colored lips which parted sumptuously over glittering white teeth as she murmured, "Howja do, Mr. Brockman!"

He allowed a pause in his scanning to meet her glance briefly with a very articulate, "How do you do, Miss Tucker?" She made an inane comment about something and he continued with his summary. Down the rather thin, corded neck, following the line of the deep V in the jersey knit blouse. He shifted his glance to the flashy turquoise and silver rings on fingers tipped with pearly pink elongated nails.

He turned his attention to a soft, now familiar voice, Linda's. "Miss Tucker needed a little time with Richie for giving him his week-end study assignments. This is the only time it will be allowed, though; it makes lunch too hurried for swimming at two."

"I heartily agree." Brock glanced again at the face across the table. Richie needs time to relax before lunch."

"Then perhaps I could explain his weekend assignments to you, Mr. Brockman."

Miss Tucker stared directly at him, batting the fringe glued to her eyelids. Brock's voice dripped sarcasm as he answered. "No, Miss Tucker, that won't be necessary, I'm here for his physical revivification, only." He quirked his lips slightly as she showed her confusion at the word he used. "You can explain to his aunt or grandmother if necessary."

"Of course, Brock." Mrs. Farnsworth assured him. "I'm sure I shall be able to handle any assignments without difficulty."

He hurriedly swallowed the remaining few drops of coffee in his cup and rose from the table as he noticed Richie lay his napkin on the table and push his chair away. He excused them both politely but emphatically and followed the boy as he wheeled his chair up the ramp and through the hall. They entered Richie's room and Brock closed the door behind them with a definite slam – then turned a quizzical grin toward Richie.

"Is she **really** a teacher?"

"Oh, yes." Richie grinned impishly at him and blinked his eyes rapidly. "She has been waiting all week to meet you, *Mr. Brockman.*"

That evening Brock questioned Mrs. Farnsworth on the arrival time of the Van Fleet family. He offered to help with whatever needed doing when he discovered they would be arriving in time for dinner the following Monday.

The weekend was spent doing much the same things he had done each spring as a teenage boy in his parent's home on the Hudson River. Only now he worked with Agnes, who was a more lenient task mistress than his mother had been. Rooms that had not been aired or changed since February were cleaned thoroughly.

Fresh linens were put on each bed, drawers and closets emptied, dusted, sprayed with a faintly scented air freshener. Windows were opened to allow cool fresh air to circulate through. Heat vents and air ducts cleaned and storm windows were put into place ready for the cold of the winter.

During this time he became more acquainted with Agnes and learned little things about the history of the Farnsworth family . She obviously, perhaps deliberately, avoided any reference to Linda's marital situation, making him even more aware of the unknown something that haunted Linda. Why was she referred to as Mrs. Linda Wilson? Where was her husband? What had happened to him? He could not be in the Armed Forces or surely he would be mentioned. Was he in prison for some reason? Was he the Uncle Phil to whom Richie had referred so proudly at the picnic? It was almost as though the man were a myth; had never existed at all.

He recalled the tremor in Linda's voice as she had defied him that night in the kitchen with 'You will never know that. It has no bearing on Richie's case.'

Sunday afternoon Brock stood unobserved at the study door and listened as Linda and Richie finished the assigned lessons for Monday. *It could be her own son – or daughter there with her, why not?* he wondered, as he leaned against the door jamb. The patience and understanding, the love enveloping this, her brother's son, could one day be surrounding her own child, also.

Hey, man, is that what you see in front of you? He reprimanded himself and turned quickly away. Forgetting why he had come down from upstairs, he went through the kitchen and out the back door to the cottage. There could not be any complications in his life now. There were three precious lives that were depending on him for their future happiness But still...

It had been a long time since he sat on a porch, knees drawn up to his chest leaning against a post like this. The last time, he recalled, was when he had decided on his career. The place was the boat house on the Hudson. Then, his daydreams had drifted into scenes of danger, adventure – far away places. Now, they included the face and form of one so newly met, but so deeply impressed on his mind. Linda – in the house on the Hudson. But what of her secret? He vowed that he would know that, too, before the end of January.

It seemed that the heat of the afternoon had followed the sun behind the row of trees. He felt a sudden chill. How long had he been sitting here. He could see the lights from the kitchen showing through the screen enclosed patio. His daydreams had gone out with the sun. What was it that Agnes had wanted – oh, yes, some of the plants from the patio for the lounge upstairs. He went to the patio for the dark green pots containing fern and geranium.

Monday dinner was practically on the table as he entered the kitchen. He found Mrs. Farnsworth and Agnes relaxing in the corner by the fireplace.

"This is great. Walking into a pleasant situation such as this seeing two of the nicest ladies I know relaxing, enjoying a bit of leisure."

"Why, Mr. Brock! I didn't realize you were given to a bit of flattery."

The sounding of the front door chimes pre-empted an answer.

"They're here," Richie called as he wheeled his chair from the living room into the hall. He waited as his grandmother went to greet the new arrivals. Richie looked at Brock with a questioning brow.

"I watched from the front window when they got out of their car. She's not curly and dimpled," he whispered, "more like – pixie blond"

"Sounds delightful," came the answering whisper.

The next two mornings Brock and Harold finished getting the house ready for the winter. Storm windows were put in place around the lower floor of the house, the patio and the office. Bins were moved from the floor of the garage to overhead racks making room for the additional car. He was surprised to discover the small Mercedes that occupied the first space. It was not a late model, probably seven years old, in perfect condition as far as he could see. Whose, he wondered. He had not seen anyone drive it.

As they worked together, Harold revealed that he had recognized Brock from the time and incident that Brock had mentioned to Love. Each man casually exposed bits and pieces of their personalities to the other as they worked.

"Linda has accepted my credentials and is presenting them, along with my offer, to the lawyers and the bank officials tomorrow," Harold confided relaxing over coffee in the cottage kitchen, late Wednesday evening. "I wish we could have come sooner, when Ralph was here, but it just wasn't possible."

"I believe that now is the right time for it to happen." Brock encouraged. "Especially since it is going to be a permanent arrangement with your family. I will be leaving in January. Richie will be back to normal by then."

"Is the doctor sure of that?"

"As sure as he can be. It's a matter of repairing some damaged nerves, but he has done it many times before with success. Richie was just run down because of his extended recovery period and they needed someone to help get him back into condition."

"From what I understand you needed some shaping up, too," Harold commented. Brock pushed his chair back and took his cup to the sink, delaying his answer, not wanting to open up to the man just yet. "Yes," he turned to Harold. "I had a little bout with some adversaries about six months ago."

"Can you talk about it?" came the normal question.

"Well, I could, officially, but I don't really think I should. And as far as anyone here knows, I am a 'has been' of some kind, who now writes lyrics for off-Broadway musicals. I am recovering from a bout with pneumonia after an accident. It has to stand like that for a few more months, but since you know some of the truth I can tell you a little more." He relaxed, resting his lean hips against the edge of the counter behind him. He continuted. "One of these adversaries slipped a knife between two ribs in my back while I was officially occupied in subduing two of his buddies. But they were all taken out of circulation, and I'm here, so..."

"Enough said," Harold grinned. "I understand how you feel about rehashing those terible incidents. Many of life's miseries are better forgotten, even if the good guy wins."

Harold took his empty cup to the sink, rinsed it and checked his watch. Noting the lateness of the hour, with a sincere 'thanks for this' he motioned toward the coffee cups and looked around the room. Walking together through the living room to the front door, Brock realized Harold had meant more than just the coffee. Brock turned to Harold agreeing to the strong expression in the other man's face for a demand of trustworthiness between them.

Chapter Five

Early Thursday morning Linda parked the Mercedes coupe in the parking lot adjacent to the bank. It was just ten o'clock but evidently Carl was already there since the company pick-up truck, mud-caked, dust covered, and with huge logging chains, wenches and other equipment piled in the truck bed, was parked in front of the bank.

As she opened the door on the passenger side of the small car and helped her mother out she wondered if Carl had actually expected them to accept his offer to bring them to the meeting in that. Not that she hadn't ridden in it many times when Ralph had offered to take her places or bring her home. But the Mercedes was more comfortable, more proper for her mother. Besides, it had been a gift to her mother from her father just a few months before he had suffered his fatal heart attack. Linda drove it because Mrs. Farnsworth no longer drove and she insisted that it be used.

Linda opened the bank door, and they went directly to the office where the meeting was to be held. Mr. Reams and John Arnold, the bank representative who was handling the transaction, had the papers spread out on the table when the two women walked in.

The men had evidently been discussing the transaction for some time, even before the bank opened. Mr. Reams had a nearly finished cigar which he quickly extinguished.

The smoke and aroma lingered for a minute or two until the air conditioner whisked it away. John Arnold was rapping his finger tips nervously on the table top.

Carl, red of face, turned quickly from the window. "I've no objections to the man. We just don't need him – or his money," he said with force to match his red face.

Carl's outburst was countered by a greeting from Mr. Reams. "Good morning Mrs. Farnsworth, Mrs. Wilson." He rose to his feet and extended his hand to them. "We have taken care of a few preliminaries, as you can see." He turned his hand toward the table and then nodded his head toward the man beside the window. "And Carl is expressing his opinion, as you can hear."

John Arnold moved a chair nearer to the desk for Mrs. Farnsworth. Mr. Reams began, "Now since you are both here we can continue in a more formal manner."

After running his hand through his already rumpled hair, mumbling, Carl sat down at his place at the table. Linda had realized he would act belligerently, and now that he had made his opinion known, she was just as sure he would settle down and become the shrewd, knowledgeable businessman she knew him to be.

Realizing that a certain fact needed to be clear to him before the meeting could go ahead she carefully explained. "You know, Carl, Ralph's share of the business will go to Richie, so that money is financially secure. My share and yours is the same. We have that investment to work with. But mother's is different. When she retires her share comes out of the working capital and goes into a retirement and trust fund."

"But she is still working. She works as hard and as long hours as you and I..." He stopped suddenly, his face swiftly becoming flushed with embarrassment.

"Yes, Carl, she does. That's part of what this meeting is about. Doctor Browne has ordered her to slow down. He would like for her to quit, but he knows that would be asking the impossible."

Carl apologized with an unspoken quest for forgiveness as his eyes met those of the elderly lady seated across the table.

Mr. Reams, clearly impatient to get the meeting underway, indicated the credentials that Harold had supplied for him. "There can be no question about Mr. Van Fleet's character or ability..." The meeting concluded later to Linda's satisfaction.

Linda turned to Carl and held out her hand. "Thank you, Carl." She flinched a little at the extra pressure he put into that hand clasp. She shifted her attention to her wrist watch as she withdrew her hand. "It's lunch time already, Mum. Should we treat ourselves and Carl to lunch at Chiffero's?"

"Oh, hey," Carl interrupted, "let me do the treating." Refusing to listen to their objections he ushered them through the bank and out into the cool brisk September air.

Although the sun's rays were still warm, the chill in the air and the force of the breeze required fast walking and buttoned or zipped up jackets. Linda noticed with some alarm that her mother did not walk as briskly as usual. She wondered at the gentleness Carl unconsciously displayed holding the older woman's arm and walking a little ahead of her, shielding her from the force of the wind they walked against.

Linda worked through the afternoon and a short while after dinner in the study with her mother and Marci Van Fleet, getting acquainted with this new friend and introducing her to the work she would be doing in the company.

Later Mrs. Farnsworth left the study to say goodnight to Richie, and Marci went upstairs with her daughter. Linda had not had time to talk with Harold until now, and he was waiting for her in the family room. There were many responsibilities he would be required to handle. But first there was the Christmas tree marketing. Carl surely needed more help, especially in handling the shipping crew. Well, she would put it to him.

Certainly Harold was the right person to fill the spot.

"I'm sorry to keep you waiting, Harold."

He put down the logging magazine he had been reading and stood up as she came toward him.

"Marci and my mother are close friends already." They sat in the chairs facing each other by the windows. Harold agreed with her and commented on the compatibility of all those in the family.

"Even Richie and Angela hit it off right away."

"She will be very good for him."

"And he with her." Harold smiled.

Fully intending to keep the conversation on a business level, Linda deliberately turned the direction away from the personal path. "I must tell you tonight so you will have time to prepare for the weekend ahead. You will be working with Carl for a while, handling the crew that packages and ships the Christmas trees."

"That sounds like an interesting place to start." "The actual shipping preparations do not start for some weeks yet, but you will need the time to get acquainted with the entire operation so you will understand more about what is happening."

At a questioning look in his eyes she told him he would need to be ready to leave for the lodge early Monday morning. "You will be interested to know," she continued, "that everything went well this morning. Mr. Reams will call you when the papers are ready for you to sign. He will call you at the lodge and you can plan to spend a few days here with your family at that time.

"I must admit that Carl was a little reluctant. Not that he objected to you personally, but he didn't see the need for more money or people in the business.

However, when I explained mother's situation he was completely in accord with the plans.

"You see, he was a teenager, two years older than Ralph, when Ralph and I used to come here for vacations. The farm belonged to my grandparents and Carl worked for my grandfather. He loved my grandmother. I suppose it was because she treated him as she had her own sons, and thought of him as a young man and not a rowdy boy. And he was *rowdy*. His mother died when he was just a child and his father was an angry man.

When my grandfather died, the farm manager asked Carl to move into the gardener's cottage and take care of the house until we came from Detroit. That was twelve years ago.

He continued to live in the cottage until after he and Maria were married and their house was ready for them to move into."

Linda hadn't intended to tell all of this and she could not go on in that direction, but since she had opened up the subject she continued on in a slightly different vein.

"Carl had met my mother during the times we were visiting here on holidays and when we came to live here he just seemed to transfer the love he'd had for Gram to her. He doesn't show it as much as he did when Ralph and he were younger – but it came out today."

Talking to Harold of Carl, she realized the truth in what she was saying. Carl was indeed a hard man, but in spite of his rough, sometimes crude ways, the destructive anger that was in his father's nature was missing in Carl.

"Whatever else he is, Harold," she assured the man seated across from her, "he is a fair man to work with."

"I'm sure we will have our differences. Hopefully we will be able to solve them like sober men – instead of *rowdies*." Harold grinned at her, his green eyes and white teeth highlighting the golden beard." After all, he is a lot bigger than I am."

"I have seen Carl fight, but always it was with someone bigger than he."

"Was Phil?" he questioned.

"No." The answer was barely a whisper as she rose from the chair. "How did you know?" She turned to look through the window.

Harold now stood close behind her. She could feel his nearness.

"Richie's voice travels pretty far in the open air. A lot of people heard him the other day."

"He was just a little boy when that happened."

"But very observant, I'm sure."

"I'm sorry, Harold, but I cannot talk of that."

"O.K. But you will have to talk about it sometime. Just remember, I make a very good listener."

She stood staring through the windows into the darkness outside. How could she let any of that come out – the deep injury, the aching sorrow of a passionate love...that was never to be fulfilled. Phil, forever gone. All of that needed to stay buried beneath all the tears that never flowed after the initial flood had passed. *Oh, why?*

Linda turned to face Harold. "But I'm not going to talk about it. It does not concern anyone but me..."

He turned from her to greet Marci as she came into the kitchen.

The conversation had not gone as Linda had planned. Why was everyone bringing up these painful memories. First Brock, then Carl who had often managed to bring them up, and now Harold. How could she ever talk about it to another man. And now here were Marci and Harold waiting for her to – but how could she possibly tell – and then it was not necessary because...

"There's a little girl waiting upstairs for her daddy..." Marci reminded Harold.

"But don't be long, darling. There'll be a big girl waiting down here..." Linda could not help but see as Harold cupped his wife's chin in his hand and gently brushed a light kiss across the tip of her nose, then hurried away, up the stairs.

These were familiar scenes of past years, only the actors had changed. She had not been reminded in the past seven months of how much they could hurt.

"If you and Harold would like tea or coffee, or anything, Marci, feel free to help yourself. The sofa in front of the fire is a cozy place..." She caught her breath sharply as yet another painful memory came through. The sofa had been a special place.

"I'll say goodnight. Mother has already gone to her room so will you see to the lights?" She could not meet the concerned questions that she might see in the gentle eyes of this new friend so she turned her face to the hall. "The night light will come on when these are turned off."

She went to the hallway, then turned to face Marci. "I'm glad you and your family are here, Marci. Please feel that this is your home."

After receiving Marci's quiet thank you, Linda turned and hurried through the hall to the lonely room that had become her hiding place, her refuge for the last five years.

Even though it was Saturday Linda was up early. The sun was just pushing its warming rays through the open spaces between the pine trees that marked the eastern edge of the fallow field that had been the scene of the ball game a few days ago. The light moisture that would show as frost in another few days now glistened and glittered as the sun's rays caressed and the breeze stirred the blades of grass it clung to. All of this she saw and enjoyed in a quick glance through the drapes at her bedroom window, before her brief morning shower. Breakfast would be ready, and she had planned a short meeting with Carl.

Mrs. Farnsworth and Agnes had breakfasted early with the children. Linda joined Harold and Marci as they finished their sausage, pancakes, and eggs, along with toast, juice, and coffee. As they lingered over their last cups of coffee, Brock and Richie came from Richie's room and stopped on their way out through the patio.

"We're going to get some wood for the fireplaces today, Aunt Linda." Richie informed her. "Brock said there are some apple tree branches down and some other limbs along the creek that we can cut and bring in."

"You be careful with the saw and axes," she warned, glancing quickly from the boy to the man behind his chair. "Richie is going to help with the transporting from where we cut to the wagon," he assured her. "Harold is going to help later on – unless you need him."

"I won't need him. His official duties will not start until Monday."

"Great." Harold grinned. "Today I can refresh my memories of being a teenager in Vancouver." He promised Richie he'd join them. " I'll finish my coffee and see you out there in a few minutes."

"Be sure to get some heavy gloves from the tool shed before you come." Richie advised as he wheeled his chair out the door.

Linda's morning session with Carl went easily and fast. They made decisions about numerous accounts and confirmed orders and shipping dates. By eleven-thirty she was putting stacks of papers in their respective folders, and Carl was relaxing in the large leather chair by the window.

With a trace of gruffness in his voice he remarked, "I didn't realize the amount of work your mother was handling, or that she had been ill, Inda." He quickly rushed over her irritation at his use of that name.

"It's a good deal – having Van Fleet here. He's got the head for the job." She recognized his sincerity, since Carl never praised anyone freely. She picked up the folders, pushed back her chair and stood up to file them.

"At least he has his wife and daughter with him. I won't have to worry. . . "

"Carl." She turned to face him as he rose from his chair. "You have no cause..."

"No, not as far as he is concerned." He came closer to her, turning his back to the door, "but why did you have to hire some grown man for Richie? Why not some young girl?" He leaned his hands on the top of the desk, glaring at her. "Gad, Indie, I know some of what you've missed during these last five years. Remember, I was there. I was in at the beginning. Remember, I was even one of the losers."

"Carl. Stop. You have no reason to bring all that up"

"Someone has got to make you face up!" He reached out to take her by the shoulders as he moved around the desk. She evaded his grasp and moved to the filing cabinets where the drawers were pulled open.

"Not you, Carl. There is nothing that you can say or do that will..."

"Inda. Whatever you think of me – I'm in love with my wife. I'd not be the one to waken you. Only Lord knows I would have, years ago. But when Phil came, everyone knew right away..."

"Carl, please don't." She pleaded now. "Please don't."

He scowled. "Do you think it's easy for the people who know you and care about you to see you throwing your life away? It wasn't your fault that he died. He did it himself – Indie! He knew he could never..."

"CARL!"

The file cabinet rocked with force as she shoved the drawer shut and turned her angry face to him. "You don't know that."

"I do know. I knew from the time of the accident. I was at the hospital when they took him in."

"Then there is nothing more to say, is there?" Suddenly all of her angry strength was gone. Exhausted, she pulled out the swivel chair at the desk and sat down with her elbows resting on the desk blotter – her forehead pressed into the palms of her hands.

Again his tone changed and a note of tenderness crept in. "Yes, Inda, there's this." She flinched at the endearment, but he continued. "I realize now that the love I felt for you was more as a brother, like Ralph. But how was I to know that then since I didn't have a sister of my own?" He sat on the corner of the desk, his huge hands wrapped around his knee that was hooked over the edge.

She could not grasp the change in him. Could he be sincere. Carl, who was so hard, so rough? He continued in still a different tone. "You know, I think you should spend a month or two at the Lodge, working with Maria, where you could meet some of the guys. They're men. However much I hated him at first for taking you away from me, at least Phil was a *man*."

She raised her eyes in astonishment at the sudden change she now noticed in his tone. His last words had almost snarled at her. And then she noticed through the window the man striding over the grass, coming toward the office.

"You've collected yourself a couple of men," he sneered. "One of them is married and the other one is a gardener, a handyman – a boy's nurse maid."

She shoved back the chair as she jumped to her feet. "Carl."

"How do *you* judge a man?" Once again the hard steel of Brock's voice cut at the offense in Carl's attitude. His eyes were as cold and hard as his voice. "I would say it takes a *man* to do anything that needs doing at the time it is required of him. I wonder how you will measure up, if that time ever comes your way?"

"Why you..." Carl lunged toward the man now standing in the middle of the office, his fists were clenched, the cords in his neck straining.

"Some other time." Brock offered him, then turned to Linda. "Don't be upset, but Richie has had a slight mishap. Marci is taking care of him in the kitchen."

"So, you can't even do that simple job right. How could..." Brock ignored this last slur from Carl as he followed Linda from the office. "It's only a skinned elbow and a little fright," he assured her. "His chair rolled back and he scraped his arm against a tree. He braced himself with his leg against the side of the chair so he would not fall out. Is he supposed to be able to do that?"

"I don't think so, but if..."

"If he did it unconsciously, that surely is a good sign."

"Yes, she whispered, "but let's not tell anyone except Doctor Browne. She put her hand over his as he reached for the handle of the screen door. "You saw it, for sure?"

"For sure." He pressed his other hand over hers. "I think he noticed it, too. But I won't mention it unless he does."

"Thank you." She couldn't keep from smiling. As they went into the house she was aware of the scrunch and scattering of gravel in the driveway and noted that once again Carl had left the office very angry and upset – with her, or with himself?

Sunday passed as quietly as possible with additional people in the house. The Van Fleets attended the morning church services with Mrs. Farnsworth and Agnes. Linda and Richie prepared the dinner, with Brock again assisting with the table setting. Linda found herself constantly watching the boy. Had the incident yesterday injured him – or benefited? Doctor Browne had seemed interested, but not concerned. He promised to come to the house early Monday morning to do some simple tests.

An easy, comfortable silence prevailed between the three as they worked together in the dining room and kitchen. *How simple, how comfortable*, Linda thought. She remembered the strange, vaguely familiar feelings that whispered when she reached over the table to arrange the centerpiece and he stepped behind her, the tremor that coursed through her arm yesterday when their hands touched on the handle of the screen door. *Did he notice that?* She wondered. And the tenderness that showed around his eyes when he watched, or talked with or about, Richie. Once it had appeared momentarily, when she had met his glance briefly, but it shaded over before she turned her eyes away. Dinner was pleasant, the time shared around the table and through the rest of the day was spent in casual conversations. This extended family becoming acquainted.

Monday, after an early breakfast with the family and a few goodbye tears from Angela, who wasn't sure she wanted her dad to go away – even after he explained about his equipment: heavy shoes, gloves, mackinaw and a well-packed duffle bag plus a very explicit map. Harold drove down the drive in the VW Rabbit just as Doctor Browne was arriving.

After a quick examination, the doctor explained to Linda. "The reflexing in the back muscles is a good sign. He is shaping up just as I wanted him to do and the possibility of a complete recovery is more sure than ever." He gripped Richie by the knee in a friendly gesture. "They'll soon be able to take you wherever you want them to, son."

Richie grinned his thanks as the doctor left the room.

The week moved on in the set pattern of activity. Since Harold had gone the upstairs lounge was closed and Marci and her daughter became intimate parts of the family circle. The rain that had varied from downpour to drizzle, with brisk winds to gentle breezes, finally ended early Thursday morning. The front lawn and drive were covered with patches of gold and brown mixed with deep shades of red. Spots of green grass and shiny black driveway glistened through the fallen leaves. In the early afternoon the sun added an extra brightness to the color, but Linda was not deceived. There would be little warmth in its rays through the months ahead. Already there had been snow flurries along the lake shores. She turned from the desk where she had been working with Marci until a few minutes ago, and went to the window, looking out on the great expanse of lawn. She dreaded to see winter come – it would only bring painful memories.

She sensed Marci coming into the room from upstairs.

"Well, Angela is down for her nap. I do enjoy these few minutes with her. She always seems to need and give more loving at these times. Sometimes I feel she is frightened to spend even naptime away from me. We've always been so close since Harold has had to be away so much."

"I'm sorry, Marci. Perhaps we should have..." Linda turned away from the view outside.

"Oh, no. I'm sure he needs to be away right now. He's so excited about this new venture. He needs to get right into it, with both feet – so to speak."

"Everything should be finished with the Christmas trees by the middle of December, so he will be home for the Christmas holidays." A crunching sound brought her attention back to the window and the driveway area. "I wonder who?" she began before she recognized the woman getting out of the unfamiliar green station wagon.

"Oh, it's Maria." Linda turned back to face Marci. "Good, now you can meet a dear friend." She hurried across the study. "It's Carl's wife. I wonder why she's here."

Linda excused herself and opened the front door, waiting to greet Maria as she came up the steps.

She made the simple introductions then invited them into the family room where quick cups of tea were prepared and served with thin slices of freshly baked coffee cake.

"Is something wrong, Maria?" Linda asked, noticing that her guest was unusually quiet and a little pale.

"No, not now. I guess you didn't hear – of course you didn't, or you would have called me right away!"

"What was I supposed to have heard? Is someone ill? Not Natalie?"

"Oh, no, she wasn't with me."

The three women were seated around the coffee table in front of the fireplace.

Linda on the sofa and Marci and Maria on the low floor cushions.

"You saw the new wagon I drove today? Well, the brakes went out on the old Chevy on my way home Saturday. I had to stop it by running into the side of the bridge on Turner Hill."

"Turner Hill, Maria, how..."

"You know the dip there where it levels off first and then goes down and the road turns at the school yard? I tried the brakes at the top of the hill – I guess because I knew they were weak, but they didn't work at all. I knew that if I didn't do something I would not be able to turn at the school yard, and it..."

"Oh no. It was game time and there is always a crowd of young people there by the fence."

"I knew that." Maria swallowed all of the remaining still hot tea, then, holding the cup tightly in her hands she continued. "By that time I was about thirty feet away from the bridge over the conduit there, so I steered for that so the passenger side of the front would scrape and stop the car – I hoped!"

"Were you hurt?" Marci asked.

"No, only shook up a little, but the car was badly damaged. Two boys on their way to the game stopped. One of them stayed with me while the other one went to call the highway patrol, and Carl."

"Why didn't you call here, Maria? Surely there was something I could have done."

"I didn't want to worry you, and Carl was there. He was so upset – he called himself all kinds of hard, ugly names. Linda, I've never seen him in such a state. Even when Phil had his..."

"He loves you very much." Linda assured her, recalling her conversation with Carl on Saturday. The day the accident had happened.

"If ever I doubted it, I don't any more. We went to the emergency room at the hospital where Doctor Browne checked me over, then sent me home, ordering Carl to not let me do anything until Monday. Carl and Natalie gave me dinner on Saturday night and breakfast in bed on Sunday. They treated me like an invalid until Monday morning." She paused to stop her lips from trembling with the fingers of her right hand. "All I could think of was how glad I was that Natalie was not with me." She continued, "Carl couldn't leave for the lodge on Monday because of it. So we went into town, filed the insurance claim and picked out my new Chevelle wagon. He was so apologetic, cursing himself for not getting the brakes fixed sooner, endangering my life.

Oh, Linda, I had a terrible time trying to convince him that I wasn't angry with him. But such a wonderful time afterward, loving and being loved." She reached into her bag that was on the floor by the cushion and, bringing out a long jeweler's box she placed it on the table and continued, her eyes sparkling with unshed tears. "You know how much I love Carl, and that I don't have any family or close friends except you – so please don't think I'm bragging or trying to show off, but I just had to tell you. She picked up the box, still not opening it, and continued.

"Carl left the house about seven-thirty Tuesday morning, supposedly to go to the lodge, but he was back before lunch. Natalie was at kindergarten and I was there in my old blue jeans and sweat shirt, sorting the laundry when he came in. I thought perhaps he had forgotten something. But then I realized he wasn't angry as he would've been if that were the case.

"Anyway, he came into the laundry room, kissed me on the cheek, then turned me around with my back to him, facing the mirror that hangs on the wall over the folding table. He winked at me and told me to close my eyes." She released the catch on the box but still did not open it. "Linda, I was so thrilled. This was Carl, the way he was when we first began to date, when I fell so much in love that I couldn't stand it. Well, after he kissed me behind the ear and fastened something around my neck the first things I saw in the mirror were his wonderful loving eyes and smile, then I looked at these..."

She carefully opened the case to display a double strand of perfectly matched pearls resting on a bed of blue velvet. "I didn't know what to say, so I just threw myself into his arms and sobbed like a baby." She giggled a little as she recalled the tenderness of the episode.

"He whirled me around in his arms then carried me into the living room and sat down in the big rocker there – said if I was going to cry like a baby he would treat me like one. He tucked my head into the hollow of his shoulder, cuddled me close and rocked. I just wrapped my arms tightly around him and enjoyed every minute of it."

She handed the jeweler's box to Linda so she could see the gift closer and Linda passed it to Marci.

"Later," Maria explained, "he told me that he had ordered them on Wednesday of last week."

Linda recalled her suggestion of a reward, but a double strand of matched pearls was love and not just a reward.

Maria's face gleamed with the excitement and the pleasure of her gift but she relaxed a bit as she continued. "He made a special trip back into town this morning to get them. Aren't they gorgeous?" She giggled again. "I will certainly have to wear something nicer than an old gray sweat shirt as a background for these, won't I?"

By this time the fire had burned low and Linda got up to add another log.

Maria glanced at her watch. "Oh, my, it is late. I'm sorry I took so much of your time, but I just got the car today, and I did want to share with you."

"I'm glad you came, Maria. I'm so happy for you. Now," Linda and Marci had walked with her to the front door, "let us see your new car and then we will let you go."

Chapter Six

By four p.m. on Friday the clouds from the northwest had moved nearer, obscuring the sun. Slow moving, hanging low, they were familiar to Linda as she watched them approach. The first snow of the season would blanket the ground by morning. The farm and the house had been prepared for the winter weather. The transfer of positions in the business was coming along nicely. Yet there was still something needed. Something lacking. She felt suddenly so alone. Business and home running smoothly. Even Richie seemed not to need her. She realized that was good for him.

What would happen when Brock went away in January? Would life go back to normal?

What was normal, really? Surely not the way summer had worked out this year.

She turned from the office window, the storm still coming on, and slid her arms into the sleeves of the wool plaid jacket that had been draped over the back of the chair. She let her glance go quickly around the room, then, satisfied that her work schedule was up to date, she flipped the switch that shut off the electricity, closed and locked the door, and stepped out into the invigorating air, hesitating a bit as she slowly filled her lungs with its refreshing goodness. Then she hurried into the house.

During dinner that evening she sensed a quietness in Richie's attitude, caught a strange glance between the boy and Brock and a denying shake of the man's head. Maybe they had a difference over something. Perhaps they were trying to keep a secret from her?

She questioned Richie later as she bid him goodnight. "How was swimming today?"

"All right."

"Just all right? Did something go wrong?"

"No. Why?" Richie raised his shoulders so he could brace himself on his elbow, sitting part way up in his bed. "What could go wrong?"

"I don't know, I'm sure. But you seemed a little quieter than usual at dinner. I noticed the little signal that flashed between you and Brock."

"Oh, that." He sighed. "After we came out of the locker room and were having our milkshakes in the snack room, guess who came slinking over to our table, batting that fringy stuff she has glued to her eyelids?"

"From your vivid description, I'm sure it was Miss Tucker."

"You guessed it." He looked at Linda, blinking his eyes rapidly and mimicking Miss Tucker's sultry voice. "OOOoooh, Mr. Brockman! How fortunate that I'm here on time." Richie took on his own boyish tone of aggravation. "She said she had an additional reading assignment for me so she brought it to the club. She wiggled and fluttered around getting it out of her bag. I could see that Brock was embarrassed.

"There wasn't an extra chair at our table so she didn't sit down, but she leaned across the table in front of Brock to hand it to me. Then she made a big thing out of Mrs. Johnson being there."

"Mrs. Johnson?"

"You know, the reading teacher."

"No, Richie, I've never met her."

"Oh, well. She brings three girls from her class to the pool on Wednesday and Friday to teach them to swim. She's cool. Brock and I talked with her once while we were waiting for our refreshments. But, anyway, Miss Tucker kinda stared at her then looked at Brock and back at Mrs. Johnson, and said, with her lips kinda twisted up into that funny smile 'Aren't you lucky that there were some girls who wanted to learn to swim, Mrs. Johnson. Be sure that swimming is all they learn while they are here with you.' Then she turned back to us and batted her fringe at Brock again, but said to me, 'I'll see you on Monday, Richieeee', and then she kinda bounced out the door."

"Oh, Richie!"

"Mrs. Johnson just turned her back to her and helped the girls with their jackets."

"What did Brock do? He must have..."

"He went over and talked with Mrs. Johnson for a few minutes. She just smiled at him and asked him not to worry about it, but he sure was upset about it all the way home."

"Do you have the reading assignment?"

He nodded his head toward the closet. "Yeah, it's in my jacket pocket."

"Very good. We'll make sure that all of your assignments, including that one, are up to date when Miss Tucker arrives on Monday."

"Oh, do I have to?"

She assured him that it was very necessary. After he was again settled in his bed with blanket and sheet tucked in around him she drew the window drapes as far open as they would go so he could watch the clouds and stars before going to sleep.

"I think that all you will see tonight will be clouds," she teased, dropping a kiss on his forehead, "but there will be snow in the morning, I imagine." Linda turned out the light and left the door open as she exited the room.

Music from a favorite cassette coming softly from speakers concealed in the hearth ledge accompanied the snap and crackle of the apple wood logs burning in the fireplace.

Linda poured a glass of milk from the carton in the refrigerator and, taking it with her, sat down in the chair opposite the older woman at ease in lounging robe and slippers, relaxing in her favorite chair beside the window. Mrs. Farnsworth, sensing that her daughter wanted to talk, put aside the ever-present therapeutic needlework and looked questioningly at her as Linda sipped from the glass of milk.

"I'm afraid we need to make some changes in Richie's schedule, Mum." She began. Then at her mother's inquisitive 'Oh?' she repeated the story Richie had just told her.

The first heavy snowfall of the approaching winter season had dropped a two-inch blanket of the soft, downy, white substance over fields and highways, frosting the shrubs and trees, flattening the few remaining blooms of the fall flowers in the garden area. The return of sunshine and the surface heat of the ground and roadways quickly turned the snow to slush which became rivulets, seeking the ditches and streams. By the time another day had come and gone, so had the snow.

Harold returned to the farm on Sunday evening so he could be at the meeting that had been arranged for early Monday morning, to sign the documents making his partnership in the business official. Mr. Reames had the documents ready for all the signatures. The transfer of Harold's investment had been completed, so there was no delay. Harold then hurried back to the farm to spend a few hours with his family, and Carl returned to the lodge to get on with the work he had planned.

Linda took her mother with her for a quick visit to the elementary school for a special conference with the man who would be Richie's teacher when he returned after the mid-term break. Thoroughly pleased with the results of the meeting with the school principal and the teacher, they hurried from the school with folders, work and text books, and a satisfactory arrangement with the teacher. They returned home for lunch with some apprehension about the unpleasant task that needed attention. However, the only cars in the parking area when Linda drove the Mercedes into the garage were the VW Rabbit and Brock's station wagon. Miss Tucker had already gone. Linda wondered if anyone had given her problems. She hoped not. It was a situation she thought she should handle.

The sounds of congenial voices and children's laughter greeted her as she opened the door from the garage into the kitchen. Agnes and Marci were putting the finishing touches to a chef salad and a relish plate while Harold cut generous slices from a large roast of beef. Brock was preparing refreshing drinks for the simple celebration. Richie and Angie were laughing over a board game they were playing at the coffee table.

Greeting everyone with a general 'hi' and 'we're home,' she and her mother went into their rooms to shed coats and put away gloves and purses. Linda sighed in relief as she realized that the unpleasant task of dismissing Miss Tucker had been delayed for another day. It was good not to have to bring in a disrupting incident to spoil the next few hours for Marci and Harold.

When she returned to the dining area of the kitchen, the table was spread for the occasion. There was a small low centerpiece with fresh mums and marigolds, which had been cut from a sheltered place in the frost ravaged garden, arranged around a large glowing candle which filled the air with the pungent aroma of ginger and cloves.

That particular scent from the candle and the array of fall flowers along with the crackle of the fire in the fireplace impressed again on her mind the quick passing of time.

September was over.

Three weeks remained before the scheduled operation. She glanced lingeringly at her nephew now seated across from her. How well he looked. The sparkle had returned to his eyes, his face had lost that pale, sunken appearance. She knew that beneath the long sleeves of the knit shirt his arms had filled out with muscle and his shoulders were straight and strong. What toll the stay at the hospital would demand could now easily be met. As her glance shifted from Richie to the face of the man seated next to him, they met the intense blue beams that had, she was sure, been watching her for some time. She glanced again at the boy and then back to the man. It seemed that everyone else was talking to each other and her quiet 'thank you' was heard only by Brock. His 'you're wel- come' and his nod toward Richie was unnoticed by the others at the table. Only Richie seemed to sense something as he flashed a quick grin at Brock and a smile and his customary wink across the table to his aunt.

Tuesday morning Linda was waiting at the desk in the study when Miss Tucker arrived. All of the textbooks and teaching supplies the tutor had been using were gathered together in a neat pile on one corner of the desk. Richie, Angela, and Brock were in the family room watching a children's TV show. Mrs. Farnsworth, Agnes and Marci had gone to town shopping immediately after Agnes had opened the door for the tutor.

Miss Tucker hesitated a moment before she entered the study, her eyes searching hurriedly around the room. "Oh! Is Richie ill this morning? You should have called me, saved me a trip..."

"No, he isn't ill, Miss Tucker. Please come in and have a chair." Linda rose from the chair behind the desk and motioned to a straight chair near the window. "I need to talk to you a bit. Please sit down," she invited again as Miss Tucker hesitated.

At Linda's insistence, the other woman sat down on the very edge of the chair. Linda picked up a prepared envelope that was laying on the desk, holding it carefully in her hand, as she heard...

"I'm sorry, Mrs. Wilson, but if Richard does not have his lessons up to date and is not ready for today's session, then I do not have time to stay." She picked up her purse from the floor where she had put it, preparing to leave.

"Miss Tucker." Linda stepped quickly in front of her. "I'm only requiring a few more minutes of your time today and then you will not be needed any more."

The wide fringed eyes and the glistening red-orange mouth flew open equally as wide and as fast as she gasped "WHAT." The force of her exclamation pushed her back into the chair.

"Yes, Miss Tucker." Linda offered her the envelope she held in her hand.

The tutor automatically accepted it, shifting her stare from Linda's face to what she had given her.

"I don't understand!"

"The check in that envelope is enough to cover the rest of this month and two weeks more, in lieu of notice. We have decided that Richie does not need your services any longer."

"Oh," she sneered, "isn't he going to be able to go to school as soon as you thought, after all? If he is he won't be ready without my..."

"That is no longer your concern." Linda informed her. "We have talked with the officials at the Board of Education and they are aware of the circumstances..."

"You mean you had the nerve to go there and tell them..." She got quickly from the chair and took a few hesitant steps toward the middle of the room, looking frantically around for something to grasp hold of, finding only the envelope in her hand which she clutched so that it wrinkled between her clenched fingers. "Surely," she raged, "just because I gave the boy a little extra work to do isn't a reason..."

"No, Miss Tucker, and please do not raise your voice. It was not because you gave it to him, but the manner and the place in which you chose to do so. My nephew has enough difficulties in his life to cope with without being part of a scene such as you created on Friday."

"What scene? I just met him at the pool...That Mrs. Johnson. Did she call you and tell you a pack of lies? Honestly, you'd think she'd have a little more disgr dis – "

"Discretion, Miss Tucker? You apparantly have no concept of the meaning of the word." Linda gathered the things that were stacked on the corner of the desk and placed them in a large canvas book bag. "Richie told me of the embarrassment you caused Mrs. Johnson and Mr. Brockman that day."

She offered the book bag which Miss Tucker almost jerked from her hands.

"What embarrassment? If you want to protect your nephew from talk then you should keep him away from those two. Maybe you should cancel his swimming, too, Mrs. Wilson, then you won't have to worry about what he sees and hears."

"*Miss Tucker.*" "Maybe then you could be sure to keep Brockman away from her and have him all for yourself." As Miss Tucker turned away from the astonishment that flooded Linda's face the door flew open and Brock filled the open space.

"That's enough!" Brock'svoice slashed through the sudden quiet that filled the room. "Your accusations are sounding through this house so loudly that they are frightening two small children, Miss Tucker. Let me remind you that slander, character maligning and moral abuse of other teachers or pupils are some reasons for losing a teaching certificate."

She had never seen him so angry before, Linda realized, staring at the angry, tightly drawn mouth. Never would she want to face that.

Brock had gone back to the door, his hand now grasping the knob. Some of the anger had gone from his voice as he continued. "I suggest that you quit this conversation and leave immediately and quietly, while you still can." He stepped aside for her to pass through the doorway as he held the door open.

Still defiant, she swung her heavy hips, with her shoulder bag bouncing against them and the canvas book bag draped over her arm, through the hall and out the front door which he had opened for her, then down the walk to her car. The sound of the slammed car door and the racing motor as she drove away was shut out by the quiet closing of the front door.

Brock stood for a moment, his back to Linda who had followed them from the study. His hand slowly released the door handle and he turned to face her. I'm sorry you had to hear that." He began to apologize as she watched the storm of anger fade from his eyes. She returned to the study, feeling his nearness as he followed behind her, closing the door. She turned to face him, expecting a continued apology, but he began...

"Regardless of what that woman said, you must believe that there is no truth in her accusations of Mrs. Johnson." His eyes demanded her attention, as would the center of a blue flame draw and hold, challenging the observer.

Linda, deeply aware of the demand they held for understanding, and aware of the strange uneasiness she felt at his nearness, answered in a stiff cold tone.

"The same as there is no truth in her accusations to my motive for dismissing her."

As she faced him, her mouth and chin lifted, tense defiant and proud as she watched his eyes. The blue fire diminished as though hastily smothered. An icy glare took over, harsh, full of scorn, mocking her at her helpless bitterness.

Standing tall, her head erect, she turned away from him folding her arms across in front of her, gripping her upper arms tightly in her long slender fingers. This time she was not quick enough to escape as his hands reached and grasped her shoulders, turning her around to face him. She did not immediately jerk away. The force with which he had turned her drew her against him. He loosened his hold and remarked with a hesitant gruffness in his voice, "I have not seen an indication in your behavior that such an idea has occurred to you, Mrs. Wilson. But I am an impatient, enduring kind of a man. His blue eyes flashed down from beneath the dark brows. "I do wonder, could ever a man break through that ice chest surrounding your kind heart."

He held her away from him. "Think about it, Mrs. Wilson, when you lie awake tonight, staring at the stars through your window."

"How do you know that?" She turned away asking her question in unsteady voice.

"Richie told me that is what he does at night. And that you told him that you do it also when you can't go to sleep. His eyes sparkled just a tease as she turned to look at his face.

"No, he wouldn't." *I will have to talk to Richie – soon.* All she could think of right now, was how she felt just now being so close to Brock and seeing the look in his eyes. No one had caused these sensations before. Not even Phil.

"Perhaps not. It is time to forget the past, if you can, at least the hurt of it. There's a lot of future stretched out ahead of you, Linda. You should be preparing to meet it."

She had thrust her hands deep into the pockets of the wrap-around skirt to hide their trembling which she could not control even by clenching them. She would not let him think that she had been affected. But her eyes could not resist the insistent pull of his as he hesitated by the door. She forced the cloud of coldness to conceal any other emotion that her eyes might reveal.

She shifted her concentration to the hand, and did not look up as he turned the knob, then closed the door behind him with a firm pull and the sound of the latch clicking.

Shadows and shapes moving over the leaf strewn lawn attracted Linda's mind from the reports on her desk, a short while before lunch. Her mother, Agnes and Marci had returned from their shopping but no one had interfered with her work. It had taken a few minutes to settle her nerves and thoughts before she finally could concentrate on the work before her, then she had worked steadily for an hour and a half.

Now she pushed the papers back from the edge of her desk and rolled back the chair. She heard noices coming from the front lawn, walked to the window and pulled the drapes farther apart, separating the sheers a small space where they met in the middle so she could see out. The sun and the wind had driven away the gray mist that had lingered over the area earlier, and now they were working together scattering and drifting the remaining leaves from the trees, arranging them on the ground that had so recently been blanketed with snow. Richie in his wheel chair and Angela with a diminshed sized rake were assisting rather noisily with one last raking of the leaves. Unbidden, her eyes filled with tears. The thought that she and Phil could possibly have had a child the same age of the little girl running and jumping into piles of leaves, brought a faint image of Phil's fine features. "Oh, Phil, how could I ever forget." She looked around hoping no one had heard her speaking aloud to herself. When she glanced out the window again she discovered that Brock, the foreman of the raking chore, was watching her and had brought her to the attention of the children. She briefly returned their wave and let the sheers fall back into place, returning to her desk. A few minutes later the sound of voices coming through the back hall and Marci going with Angela up the stairs let her know that the raking session was over. She lingered over the work in front of her, determined not to leave the study until lunch was ready. Her apprehension about facing Brock over the lunch table was unnecessary, however. Richie enlightened her as she glanced over the table that was set for only six. "Brock had some letters to write, so he's going to have a sandwich in the cottage while he does that."

Richie wheeled his chair into place at the table. "It sure was fun rakin' and playin' in the leaves this morning. It was the first time Angie ever did." He grinned down at the little girl seated beside him. "You had fun, too, didn't you?"

The little head bobbed in agreement and she sighed. "Yes. Now, am I ever tired."

Marci laughed as she set a plate of food in front of her daughter. "O.K. little Miss, you finish this and then off to bed with you while Richie is swimming."

The remainder of the day passed quietly. At dinner that night the family was informed of the dismissal of the tutor with a simple explanation that Richie needed the outdoor activities and the man who would be his teacher when the new term started would take care of any needed tutoring at that time. She received a cheer of agreement from Richie, looks of approval from her mother and Marci, and a probing look of understanding from Brock as their eyes met briefly across the dinner table. "I really hadn't intended for you to spend all of your time as a child attendant." She felt her cheeks flush as she offered the apology. "No? Well, that is basically why I'm here, isn't it? To see that Richie is as strong as possible for what is ahead of him?" Just a hint of a smile flickered in her direction as he continued. "I need the benefits from it, too, so don't apologize."

She had forgotten that his deteriorated physical condition had been part of the reason that he applied for and accepted this position six weeks ago. Surely his shirts and sweaters, jeans and slacks did not hang so loosely on his tall frame as they had then. She allowed her eyes to briefly scan his strong tanned face. She turned to examine Richie's browned face and sun bleached hair. "It is plainly evident that you both have fared well in that respect."

Immediately after the meal Brock excused himself and returned to the cottage.

She wondered what he did there, noticing the light still burning in the cottage when she turned off her own light that night. *Oh, yes, he's writing lyrics for an off Broadway musical. What kind of show, a revised classic, a comedy, a mystery?*

Chapter Seven

Linda let her fingers sink into the rich softness of the fine woolen fabric of the coat that she was trying on in the clothing store in town. The urge to remove it from the rack gained precedence over her reluctance, and she held the soft, beautifully simple creation cuddled in her arms, brushing her face against its luxury.

Uuummm, it reminds me of warm, creamy, vanilla pudding, she thought. Just the pleasure of trying it on would be enough. She shrugged out of her serviceable London Fog and into the lovely garment. A soft quilted satin lining extended into the sleeves and the fleece lining hung to a half way place between her hips and knees providing a warm cozy feeling. Pulling back the front of the coat she discovered that the lining was the zip-in, zip-out type and the body of the coat was lined with shimmering satin that matched the quilted lining in the sleeves. Her hands lingered over the cream colored wool as she buttoned the six buttons down the front and pulled the detachable hood over her head to fasten it snug around her face. The rich cream color highlighted the perfection of her gently tanned complexion and deepened the color of auburn in the wisps of curl that had not been tucked inside. Tags hung from the sleeve giving dry cleaning instructions, manufacturer's and merchant's information – but no price.

She hadn't intended to purchase a new coat this year, although she did need one. Where was the salesperson? Walking around a display of hats and purses she came face to face with a young woman wrapped in an identical coat. It really was a good looking coat. It enhanced the appearance of the girl facing her - she looked so familiar.

"That is a beautiful garment. Don't you think it should bring a warm smile to the face of the one who is wrapped so snuggly inside it?"

Her eyes flew to meet the deep blue gleam in the eyes of the man standing behind the girl facing her. She turned away from the full length mirror, her hands swiftly undoing the fastenings at the neck for the hood. "I didn't realize it was so late." She avoided Brock's eyes and question as she looked at the clock above the cashier's station. "It isn't late." He stepped behind her and the touch of his hands on her shoulders prevented her from removing the coat At the slight pressure of his hands Linda stood quite still, her heart racing. His hands moved from her shoulders to her neck, his fingers gently brushing against her face as they followed up the front of the hood, lifted it, folding it into place, to hang down at the back. "It is a lovely coat." He assured her as his hands slid down its soft surface to grip her arms through it. "It suits you." His breath stirring the hair around the back of her neck and ears, the nearness of him, and the racing of her otherwise sensible heart alarmed her.

"We have time! Finish your shopping." His blue eyes were cool again, but that unknown yet vaguely familiar something was hovering in their depths. He, helped her out of the coat and nodded his head toward a counter of sweaters. "There is a saleslady over there. I'm sure she will be glad to help you." He glanced at his wrist. "I have an appointment at eleven. How about lunch at Shapiro's – say at twelve thirty?" He picked up the package that he had placed on the nearby chair and waited for her answer.

Her heart slowed for a beat or two. *What is the big problem? I've had lunch with him at the house almost every day for weeks, why hesitate now?* She let her eyes follow the slim line of dark green corduroy which began at the brown, suede loafers, upward, taking in the snug fit at the knees and on up past the well-tailored jacket, open, displaying a beige, knit sport shirt. She mocked her questioning heart. Her eyes continued their upward journey.

"Well?" The slightly bemused mouth asked, "Is it yes – or no?"

Still not smiling she felt her mouth form the words, "Yes, thank you."

Her eyes ended their journey with a quick upward flicker of copper tipped lashes.

"Good, I'll see you there." He turned away hurrying his tall frame through the aisle of the department store to the street exit.

Minutes later she found herself on Main Street, her dark blue London Fog buttoned securely against the cold of the rising wind. Her mind dismissed the thought of the lovely garment she had returned to its place on the rack. She needed to buy some things for Richie warm pajamas, a new robe, **bedroom slippers**. A warm feeling flowed through her and the lump crowded her throat. Bedroom slippers. *Oh, God! Please make them needed* – the plea rang through her mind. Everything else will be bearable if that can be so. She hurried on to the young men's shop, made her careful selections and returned to the street.

It was still forty-five minutes until time to meet Brock. She would use the time for shopping for Thanksgiving and Christmas linens and accessories. The town's only linen and specialty shop was just a few steps away. She could have her purchases delivered later, if necessary. She had come with Brock in his station wagon – had his offer been thoughtful, or had he just been amused? He had started to drive away just as she opened the garage door that morning. Before she could back the Mercedes out into the driveway he had driven the wagon behind it, blocking her way. Rolling down the window he inquired, "Are you going to..."

"Yes," if you will move out of the way." She was hardly civil to him, she realized.

Why was she acting that way? There was no reason.

"Are you planning to be there long?" He seemed not to notice her cutting attitude.

"I'm going in for a few hours, why not share the ride?" He had opened the passenger door for her. "It seems rather silly to follow each other down the road and back."

She had realized he was only being sensible and friendly and she did need to apologize for being so snippy. "Yes, it would seem strange, wouldn't it." Closing the garage door, she went out. "Thank you, Brock," she offered as an apology, fitting herself into the passenger's side of the front seat.

The drive into town had been pleasant. Simple conversation flowed between them of Richie's progress, her mother's benefiting from Marci Van Fleet being there, even the pleasure of having their daughter Angela in the house. There had been something puzzling about part of the conversation. She had remarked about how well Richie and the little girl got along together and Brock's hands had gripped the steering wheel as though he were suddenly angry. The muscles in his face around his mouth and chin had tightened and he stared almost defiantly at the road in front of him. His voice, however, had become husky with emotion other than anger – but what? "Yes, there is something special about the presence of a curly haired energetic bundle of femininity. The laughter, squeals, giggles, even a few tantrums and tears..."

"I didn't realize that you noticed her so much." Linda interrupted.

"Oh. Aren't all little girls like that? Natalie, Angela..."

"Yes, of course." She had agreed, neither meeting his eyes as he glanced at her, nor answering his suddenly amused smile. She only questioned if there were any little girls he had been thinking of to add to that list – and Angela's hair was straight. Linda returned her thoughts quickly to the interior of the linens and gift shop as she closed the shop door behind her. In a few short minutes she purchased scented and tapered candles for the Thanksgiving table, ordered new table linens and candles for Christmas, and placed her mother's order for Christmas greeting cards. She still had fifteen minutes to spare, she would window shop the three blocks to Shapiro's until twelve-thirty.

As she approached the intersection her attention was caught by three men in front of the meat supply house near the corner to the left on the cross street. They were gesturing forcefully with their arms as though they were arguing. One man she recognized as the cook from her farm lodge. The other two wore lumberman's clothing, one in bright red plaid with a knit cap and scarf – the other wore dark blue. Both men were heavily bearded, one gray, the other one dark, she could not tell whether black or brown from that distance. The argument ended suddenly as the cook motioned with his hand toward something across the street from where they were standing and then turned and entered the supply store. The other two men turned their heads in the direction the cook had indicated and then swiftly walked away, going in different directions.

The cause of their sudden flight seemed to be the man and woman who were lingering in the doorway of the jewelry establishment located there. She missed a second chance to cross the street with the green light as she watched the familiar form clad in dark green corduroy put a small package into the hands of the woman standing close beside him.

Suddenly the wind whipping around her legs seemed bitingly cold. The sun had lost any of the warmth she had felt earlier. Crossing the street with the next green light, she noticed the woman draw his face down to hers and kiss his cheek before he drew her arm through his and they turned the other way toward the station wagon that was parked along the curb.

"SO!" She stormed inwardly at her slightly aching heart, "*Did you think, perhaps...? What is it to you that his eleven o'clock appointment was with a woman at a jeweler's shop. He's only your employee, working with your nephew.* Obviously he is interested in Mrs. Johnson – for it must be she, what other woman has he met while he has been here. He must be more interested in her than he wants anyone to know. Her steps faltered as she drew closer to the next corner. How could she meet him now. *This is really foolish. He might be going with her and has forgotten about lunch. Oh, no. What if she comes with him.*

There was a drugstore on the corner before she reached Shapiro's. She would go in there. She didn't want to be waiting at the restaurant if he should bring Mrs. Johnson.

Besides, she did need some hand cream and some special greeting cards. The store was crowded, so she lingered over the display of cards. With her selections in her hand, she turned toward the counter where the hand cream was displayed. Then the door opened and Brock came striding to the counter.. He was not angry, merely amused, sounding a little sarcastic as he glanced at his watch and then at her. "Shapiro's at twelve- thirty? Couldn't these have waited until after lunch?" Taking her cards in one hand and her elbow in his other hand, Brock guided her to the cashier, paid for the cards with some change from his pocket and ushered her out the door.

"It's twelve forty-five, didn't you intend to have lunch today?" He stopped at the curb beside the station wagon that was now parked near the restaurant. "You can leave your packages in the back," he offered, and taking them from her, deposited them on the middle seat. "I saw you go into the drugstore just as I parked. Were you going to stand me up? You didn't have to accept my invitation, you know."

She was quietly fuming at her own actions. Why couldn't she have just gone on to the restaurant and waited. It would have been less embarrassing even if he had brought her with him.

"I'm sorry," she offered as they followed the waitress to a table beside a lighted fountain. "I didn't realize that I was taking so long with the cards."

He helped her off with her coat and hung it on the nearby rack, then held her chair for her. After the waitress had taken their order he relaxed and looked at her quizzically. "Relax, Linda. Forget everything else and enjoy this time off, the place, and – perhaps the company?"

She felt a fleeting softness around her mouth and eyes; restful, relaxing. Of course, there was no sun glare and the lights were soft and rose-hued. She let herself relax a little more and met Brock's glance again, this time steady and sure across the table. .

"That's much better." He commented, noting the slight change in her facial expression. Her simple lunch of French onion soup and chef salad was followed with a deep dish apple pie ala mode. Brock enjoyed a burger and chips with pie and no ice cream.

"That is a hefty meal" Brock remarked as she relished the last little bit, "for someone who seems not to gain an ounce." His glance took in the thinness of her sweater-draped shoulders and arms, lingered at the point of the V that was formed by the slight fullness of the lift of her breasts. She felt the heat of a girlish blush flood her neck and face.

"You have your meals at the house, Brock, so you know that this is not my usual fare." She pushed the empty plate aside and lifted the cup of lukewarm coffee to her lips, consciously diverting his focal point. "With Richie confined to his chair and mother's heart condition this type of food is not included in their diets."

"So, everyone diets and you indulge once in a while." His eyes teased and she knew that he had noticed the color rise to her face.

The waitress interrupted their conversation with her friendly, "Is everything all right here?" and the usual offer to refill coffee cups. At their refusal she presented the bill.

Brock helped Linda with her coat, a quizzical expression in his glance. By the time they returned outside the sky had filled with dark rolling clouds hurrying in from the northwest. "Those clouds mean that we should head homeward as soon as possible," Linda warned. "It will be snowing before very long."

Without any time wasted they were out of the town, approaching the top of Turners Hill. Linda broke the silence that had invaded the wagon as Brock drove into the wind that accompanied the approaching storm. She found it a little easier to relax as she told him about Maria's recent accident with her car and the related incidents, including Carl's reaction and the presentation of the pearls. The telling of it filled the time until they arrived at the driveway from the road to the house. By then the snow was falling fast.

The lawn and paved surfaces were already covered with a light sprinkling of its softness. Brock stopped the car just before turning into the drive. "I'm glad that you told me about Carl. It eases my mind somewhat."

"Oh, how do you mean?" She felt cautious. Surely he didn't think that she and Carl...

"Not what you obviously seem to think." He laughed at her. "I'm just relieved to know that you still believe in that special deep feeling that can exist between a man and a woman."

"Oh, I know it exists. I've had too many good examples lived before me not to believe."

"But for everyone else, not for you?" he asked.

"I was not so fortunate – it ended before..."

"How did it end, Linda?" His hands remained on the wheel in front of him.

She could feel his eyes staring at her, pleading that she look at him, give him an answer. "Please, Brock. Let's just go on up to the house. I'm not going to talk about that. Not ever!" Her eyes dropped to stare at her hands as she clenched them together in her lap. They would not stop their trembling, no matter how hard she tried.

He removed his right hand from the wheel as if he would reach for her hands, but she tucked them under her arms out of his sight, and shivered slightly. "Not ever is a very long time, *Mrs. Linda Wilson.* You could freeze solid long before then." He shifted the car into drive and marred the white carpet in front of the house. His impatience with her was near to anger. It showed in the whir of the station wagon tires as they tried to make contact with the driveway under the snow.

She pressed the button on the garage door control that she carried with her in her shoulder bag, and the door was open when he parked as near to the garage as possible. As he helped her with her packages he asked, "What did you decide about the coat?" He noticed that none of the packages was big enough to contain such a bundle.

"It was much too impractical. I think I would never go any place to wear it." "But there is no reason why you should not go to those kinds of places, and never is a very long time." He reminded her again. Irony, sarcasm, a little bitterness, and yet another something in his voice taunted her as he opened the door from the garage into the family room. "Thank you, Brock." She murmured as he dropped her packages onto the sofa. "I did enjoy lunch, and..."

"You don't need to thank me." He hesitated a moment then hurried out the door through the patio, saying, "Tell Agnes that I'll not be here for dinner, and if the storm gets too bad, don't worry if I don't make it back. I'll just bunk overnight at the inn."

She caught a swift draft of the cold air before he closed the door behind him.

That can't be the telephone or the intercom, Brock reasoned, throwing back the sheet and blanket, to sit, still hardly awake, on the edge of the bed. The furnace had switched on during the night, he could hear the hum of the blower. But what...? It was chilly. Then he remembered that the thermostat was set low, allowing just enough heat to keep the temperature at fifty through the night. As he shivered he decided it was foolish to encourage a cold at this time and pulled on a pair of cotton drill trews left over from army days, rubbed his hand through his hair, over his chin and around the back of his neck and suddenly realized it was the radio. That was the sound that had awakened him.

Now he discerned the flashing on-off signal. He pulled a plaid shirt from the closet, shoved his arms into the sleeves as he hurried into the living room and flipped the receiving switch to on as he sat down in the chair beside the radio/recorder.

Immediately the voice came through.

"Brockman – sorry if I disturbed you, Old Man, but I need to talk, so switch to two way. O. K?" Brock recognized the voice of the young radioman from Brombke's office and the Old Man tag he had attached to him – he switched to two way and answered. "If it's so important that I need to hear it at five thirty on a Monday morning, quit wasting time."

"O.K." The young voice coming through the speaker laughed. "Put this in your tape player and listen to it."

"How do you know?" Brock frowned as he picked the fake phone off the tape recorder.

"You forget so soon, Old Man. I designed it and put it all together, remember?"

"Oh, yes. A very ingenious idea, wasn't it. I trust it is still the only one of its kind."

"Of course. Each to his own, you know. I think the last special one was for a dog trainer. That one failed. His bite was worse than his bark.."

"All right, all right!" Brock laughed. "Now give me the information."

"First here is the message identification. You know what to do with it, of course."

He read a line of jumbled numbers and letters which Brock carefully wrote down on the pad near the night stand.

"Got it?" The voice questioned.

Brock read them back to him.

"Right. Now, the merchandise has finally come through. However, the outer wrappings were damaged so they had to be replaced. The merchandise was badly scratched, but nothing was broken. It will need to be in the repair shop for a while since it did receive some rough handling at one of the shipping points. Got that?"

"So far." His hand clenched the pen until the knuckles turned white. Concern deepened his voice as he asked. "What about the shipping point?"

"Don't worry, Old Man, we closed it down without any problem. We'll not go that way again."

"Do you have a new shipping date, so I can inform my buyer?"

"It will be on schedule as planned, arriving at..." he gave Brock some more letters and numbers to write down. After checking to be sure they were right, the radioman continued. "Remember that if there is no one there to receive the merchandise it cannot be marked 'Return to sender' and put back on board."

"That's definitely understood. And thank you for your part in this."

"Was glad for the privilege, you know that." There was a pause from the other end and then... "Old Man?"

"I'm still here"

"Your customer doesn't need to know about the damage ahead of time. None of it will show when it is finally unwrapped."

"Good. Time enough for that when the merchandise arrives."

"Right." The radio voice agreed. "Have a good day."

Brock hung up and the little red light went out. He sat back in the chair, his head thrown back against the padded rest. It had been a long, hard time. Two years ago they had found what they had been searching so hard and long for, in a small village just over the border of Austria into East Germany. Two people had lost their lives in the recovery operation, and the secretive movements of many others had caused much hardship and delay. But it was worth the results. He had nearly given up hope when he had been set aside for six months because of his injury and the illness that followed. Even now, there was still danger. They could not relax and become careless at this, the last part of the desperate action which had been undertaken, and which still needed a few weeks for its completion.

He reached for the desk calendar near the chair and marked the day's date with a circle. October the fifteenth. Was it that late already. No wonder it was cold outside.

And not so warm inside either, he noticed, rubbing his hands together to warm them. He lifted the three top sheets on the calendar, yes – there was the sheet for January on it.

Turning back to the sheet for December he marked a red line through the dates twenty-one through twenty-eight then marked January third with a green "X" and the seventh with a question mark. No one would understand the reason for the markings, nevertheless he opened the drawer and put the calendar beneath the typing paper and envelopes that were kept there.

An hour later he had showered shaved, dressed, and eaten breakfast. He wondered if he should make some explanation to the people in the house. But what could he say? Surely not that he had spent the weekend with Mrs. Johnson. How would Linda react to that? Perhaps he should just say that very thing. Would it shake her out of her icy casing? That shell was not as thick as he had imagined and something like that might just add another layer to it.

He hadn't had any plan to kiss her that day. But she...*Oh, man,* he scoffed at himself. *You are acting like a fuzzy-faced love sick youth. You know what's happening, but cool it. You have a promise to keep – a commitment to Love and Grandfather – plus that little curly haired girl who has no idea of what is happening.* His thoughts came to a sudden halt as he realized the cup in front of him had given up the last drops of its already cold contents. He allowed himself one more mental recall of the lovely face and person as he saw her wrapped in the luxury of that coat and he was certain that underneath all of the chilly sadness there had to be a warm loving woman. He was also certain he could reach that woman if he could just find the right way to crack the ice.

He shook his head, pushed the chair back and filled his cup with the coffee still in the pot. He took three swallows of it, poured the remains down the drain and rinsed the cup and pot. There was snow to shovel. Richie needed his exercise.

And why should I need to explain my weekend to anyone!

Brock had finished shoveling a path from the cottage to the house through the three inch layer of snow that had fallen overnight and was working his way to the door of the office when the storm door of the patio opened and Richie wheeled his chair out into the cleared space.

Richie squinted through the reflected glare and smiled as Brock called to him.

"Good morning, Richie. How do you like this snow?" "Isn't it great? So smooth and white – of course you get kind of tired of it after it gets dirty and all marked up."

Brock rested his arm on the handle of the shovel he had thrust into the pile of snow at his feet. "But you don't have to wait long do you, before more snow comes down and covers up the dirt and tracks." He reached down and gathered a handful of snow and quickly formed it into a ball. To the boy in the wheel chair he said "Here, catch." He threw the snow ball. Richie caught it and thus began his physical therapy for the day.

Brock realized his own mental, physical, and, yes, emotional balance had been set back into the right perspective. This day and the days ahead even with the difficulties still unknown would pass as fast as the last few days had gone, and then...*There is a lot of future ahead...* he reminded himself of the words he had flung at Linda a few days ago in the study.

Chapter Eight

Doctor Browne informed the family, as he finished his scheduled check-up at the house, that Richie should cancel the swimming sessions. The danger of catching a cold from the early onset of cold weather was more of a risk than the swimming would be a further benefit.

"As of right now he's in top shape for what is ahead of him," Dr. Browne assured as he tousled the curly hair and met the questioning eyes that were lifted to meet his. "It really is a simple adjustment that needs to be made, Richie. Nothing to worry your young head about." The doctor pushed himself up from the chair beside the boy's bed, patted the still useless legs that were stretched out beneath the covers. "By Thanksgiving you will be using these instead of that chair."

Mrs. Farnsworth remained in the room to finish Richie's preparations for the night. Angela, dressed in warm footed pajamas and quilted robe, slipped into the room as Linda, Brock and the doctor left. At Dr. Browne's raised eyebrow, Linda explained, "Angela and Richie share story time. Sometimes Mother reads and other times Marci has that privilege."

Later, in the family room Dr. Browne talked with Linda about her mother's condition and reminded her of an up-coming appointment, and then..."Are you taking the vitamins that I recommended? You are going to need some reinforcements for those ten days, too, you know."

Brock had remained silent through the examination and now as he stood by the fireplace sipping some of the hot coffee that Agnes had left ready for them, he deliberately let himself become involved. His eyes followed the lovely slender hands as they slowly brushed back the forever escaping strands of hair, drawing his, and he was sure the Doctor's, attention to the hollows in her cheeks and the pale pink tremble of her mouth.

She doesn't even realize that she is beautiful. He mused. He didn't think it would it matter to her, even if she was aware of her own beauty.

Doctor Browne took one of her hands in his, examined the texture of the skin, the color of the nails. "It won't do, Linda. You have to keep yourself well."

She pulled her hand from his and turned to the coffee pot, filling one of the cups waiting on the counter, asked the doctor if he cared for some coffee, then met Brock's eyes with an offering glance. He looked down at his empty cup and shook his head. "No, thank you." The vague wish speeding through his mind for that look to be offering something more precious than a cup of coffee. He shook his head again and took his cup to the counter. "I will join you over a sandwich of left-over roast beef. I'll even make it." He dared her with his eyes to refuse, since he had noticed her playing and nibbling at her food during dinner. "I'm sure that will atone for your neglecting to take your vitamins today." He smiled at Dr. Browne who stood, replied negative to the offer of coffee, excused himself and walked to the door. Linda followed him to make a proper farewell and promise to keep up her health.

Brock took the roast from the refrigerator and was cutting thin slices ready for the prepared bread waiting, along with two dessert dishes filled with bread pudding, when Linda returned.

"Really, Brock, this is too much. It's too soon before bedtime to eat all of this."

She paused at the counter to put down her coffee cup.

Completely ignoring her objections, he piled more slices of beef onto the bread.

Although his mind was filled with apprehension recalling what he needed to know about her, wondering what would come of this evening's conversation, he smiled slightly at her as he placed the open-faced sandwiches on two small steak platters along with slices of cheese and tomato wedges. After he had deftly arranged the snack on the table he pulled out the chair for her. When she began again to object he interrupted her. "I'm sure you must have dined on more sumptuous fare than this and at a much later hour than eight-thirty, in your courting days, Mrs. Wilson." He smiled at her, letting a bit of amusement sparkle in his eyes. Some way he had to break through that reserve.

He waited for her to sit, letting his hand brush lightly across her shoulder before moving her chair in. He did not expect her to answer his jibe, but, taking his place across the table from her, he did notice a stiffening of her shoulders and a tremor in her throat as if she were desperately trying to swallow something difficult. He respected her silence as she concentrated on putting the top slice of bread on her sandwich.

He held a moment of silence himself. *Lord, I don't know her story, but whatever happened, let me help her to talk about it.*

Gradually, as they began to enjoy their snack together, her shoulders relaxed a little and the tightness eased around her mouth. She had managed to consume half of the sandwich.

"We need to do some talking. That might make your bedtime maybe a bit later tonight."

Her gaze lifted from the plate in front of her and shot a questioning glance at him before she picked up the napkin by her plate and thrust it in a tight clinch into her lap.

"What do we need to talk about?"

"Richie will need activities to occupy his time and we need to discuss what happens during and after his hospital stay."

"The operation is scheduled for October twenty-fifth, which is only ten days away.

He should be there for ten days after, receiving special therapy. Hopefully he will be ready to use crutches when he comes home."

When Linda brought the crushed napkin to the table top and he could see how she twisted it in her wavering emotions, Brock longed to place her long, slender, almost transparent fingers into his own two strong hands.

"Then it will be over. The long hard period you've all been through."

"Yes, if Doctor Browne is right there will be 'Thanksgiving' in this house again."

She managed a wistful smile.

He shifted his concentration from her face to her clenched fingers and then to the unfinished sandwich on her plate. "Let me get you another napkin and a fresh cup of coffee while you continue that delicious, nourishing sandwich, if I do say so myself." He took the hardly recognizable napkin from her. Realizing that she would not eat if they continued talking, he picked up his empty plate and went to the counter with it, then said, "I'll replenish the fire while you finish, then we'll talk again." With that he set down a napkin and a hot cup of coffee.

He moved the nearly consumed log around on the grate sending crackling sparks and flames up the broad chimney, giving her a few extra moments. As he finished arranging the split log of apple wood on the remaining coals, she finished her sandwich.

He watched her sure movements as she gathered up the coffee cups and took them to the sink, rinsed them, ready for the dishwasher.

"Would you like some hot chocolate to go with the bread pudding?" She asked.

"Chocolate is fine, Linda." *Isn't it amazing what finishing a nourishing sandwich will accomplish in mood adjustments.* Brock watched as she reached for the chocolate, spooned it into empty heated cups and stirred hot milk into the cups. As he observed, his mind changed the background of this kitchen to the efficient stainless steel and brick kitchen in the house on the Hudson. The setting he saw would suit her perfectly. *Will she ever be there?* he wondered. He cleared the picture from his mind. *Not now*, he reasoned.

He took ceramic coasters from the rack on the counter and placed them near the dishes of pudding on the table, then moved near to the counter to stand by her side. "That smells delicious." He realized that the aroma of the chocolate mingled with a more delicate, fascinating perfume. He lifted the mugs of chocolate from the counter and placed them in the coasters on the table.

"Now," he motioned for her to sit down again, "it's time to talk, eat bread pudding, and hold cups in our hands." He smiled, seriously with his eyes, but faintly with his mouth as he sat not across from her but at the end of the table near her chair at the side.

"What do you need to know?" She leaned back in her chair, then answered his questions about Richie's needs for the next ten days.

"He will just need to be kept busy so the time will not seem so long. He enjoyed throwing snowballs in the snow this morning. I realize that playing in the snow in a wheel chair is not much exercise."

"Don't worry about it. He mentioned a snowmobile. Is there one?"

"Yes, it's at the lodge. Can you handle one?"

"I have driven one, a few times."

"Then I'll have Harold bring it down in the truck tomorrow. He needs to pick up some supplies for the lodge anyway. We only used it for emergencies and when the men went hunting."

"There are two more things I need to know. Richie said something about a fishing shack. I will need to keep busy while he is in the hospital and you might as well benefit from my activities. If I could set the shack up, on the lake..."

"Carl and Richie know where they are."

"Where would I get a permit for hunting and fishing?"

"Those licences are provided by our company so you are entitled to them. There are deer along the lake front but hunting is not permitted until after the Christmas trees are shipped out, which is two weeks before Christmas. There are probably still some geese and ducks around. The fishing shacks are at the edge of the lake near the lodge, but they can't be set up until the first of December." She hesitated for a moment, taking a spoonful of pudding and a swallow of chocolate. "But you don't know the area, Brock, and it isn't the best idea to go alone."

"I'm a careful person. Besides, Harold mentioned that his young brother-in-law would like very much to come and work with him for a while."

At her quick glance he stopped, got to his feet and walked over to the window.

"Evidently Harold hasn't mentioned it to you as yet, but the young man has finished four years of military duty and needs to take some time to decide where to go now. Harold thinks that this would be a good place for him to work while making that decision. There is room for him at the lodge and Carl has agreed to take him on a trial basis as a member of the crew until the first of the year."

He noticed that she did not show much interest in this idea as she answered simply. "Well, if Carl agrees to it."

"He won't be a permanent employee until the first of the year, Linda." Brock came back to the table and sat in a chair across from her. Surely she was not objecting.

"The fellow needs this chance." His voice had taken on a little more force than he had intended, it seemed,for she raised her eyes to meet his with a slight bit of anger in them.

"I'm not objecting. But shouldn't he be here in the house with Marci and Angela?"

"Yes, when Harold comes back from the lodge then Steve will come, too"

"The house will be full again. Mother will enjoy that."

"And how about you, Linda?" He allowed his exasperation at her seeming upset come through in his tone of voice. "Will you find pleasure in that?" He watched as again the color faded from her hands as they clung to the now empty, cold mug.

"What makes you think that nothing pleases me? I'm not unappreciative of kindness and beauty, or good happenings." She took her empty mug and pudding dish to the counter. "Must I jump for joy, clap my hands, and shout 'Oh goody' as Angela does?"

"No," he breathed, and in a few steps was standing again beside her. His arms ached to draw her close as he gently turned her around to face him. Those tears that he knew were being pushed back and down so desperately, would they break through if he did? The sorrow he felt at the hurt that had made her this way flowed through his hands and his grip tightened somewhat. He would have drawn her closer."But isn't there even a smile near the top somewhere? Or are even they all buried or drowned in all of those years of pushed down sorrow, tears and self pity that has accumulated?" In his own frustration he would have held her in his arms, allowing the tears to flow, but...

"I thought I smelled chocolate," Mrs. Farnsworth announced, as she came into the room.

Brock released Linda, watching as a faint color returned to her face. As he turned to gather up his mug and pudding dish from the table, he thought, *maybe she's not so cold, for only inner warmth would cause the color to return, and maybe she's not really bitter, for she does care for other people. What will it take?*

Questioning, his eyes caught a look of warmth in the older woman's eyes. Linda offered hot chocolate to her mother. "Would you like some, Mum?"

"Oh, no, just a glass of milk will do for me. I didn't mean to interrupt you, but Richie is a little restless and I thought a cup of milk might be just the right persuasion."

"Of course, Mum, I'll take it right away."

The older lady poured the glass of milk and with the same grace of movement as her daughter, she sat down in the chair that Linda had occupied a few minutes before. Brock, still standing by the counter, his lean hips pressed against the ceramic tile that formed the edge, watched as Linda left the room. The interruption had been deliberate, he was sure, but why? He felt that he would now receive some of the answer, but would it suffice?

"The tears, sorrow, disappointment, yes, even self-pity are very deeply buried, Brock." Her voice reached him, although the words came in a softness as though she were only breathing them. "They cover a devastating tragedy. Five years it has been, with a few more tragedies piled on top." She lifted her head and he saw the deep aching sorrow in her eyes, sorrow that stemmed from the tragedy that had struck her family. She cleared her throat, speaking with a little more force.. "It will take more than mere picking to clear away the covering."

Is that what she thinks am doing, picking at Linda? The thought of that word used in that way, when he only wanted to challenge her. "I am sorry if that is the impression that you got from our conversation. Surely there must be some of it that you can tell."

"It is not my story to tell, Brock. But I feel that you should know."

He moved to the chair facing her, this was her mother, surely she could tell him some of it. He ran his hand through his hair, down the back of his neck, trying to relax his impatience.

"Mrs. Farnsworth, there are other activities which claim my time while I am here, duties that I need to carry through, concerning people whom I dearly love, – but Linda, how do I get through to her?" He could not confide any information to her about Love and Grandfather. His mind again filled with Linda as he clasped his hands together and rested them on the table in front of him. The warm compassion and understanding of the woman across the table flowed through her strong, work-worn hands as they reached out and wrapped around his. "Brock, one tragedy is about to be answered. That could be the beginning of the clearing away. Perhaps if you act carefully and be patient for just a while longer, you may reap many answers."

"Thank you, Mrs. Farnsworth." Brock watched as the amazed and puzzled look vanished quickly when she realized that Linda was coming from the hallway into the kitchen. "It's good to know where the reliable merchants are located in a strange town. McFaddens sounds like a good place to do all of the Christmas shopping I'll need to do."

He smiled at Linda as she came into the room. "I have to send some things early," he explained.

"Of course, I'm sure they will have everything that you need."

Brock doubted that Linda believed they were discussing shopping places, but sincerely hoped she didn't discover the real topic of their conversation. *That,* he thought as he said goodnight to them, *would surely tamp down the covering a little tighter and freeze the ice even more solidly.* He closed the door silently behind him to walk through the night air scarcely feeling the coldness of the rising wind. After all, he had just been exposed to the effects of a solid ice wall, the cold of which was more penetrating than that of the north wind. He hurried the last few steps and shivered in his flannel shirt sleeves as he entered the comfort of the gardener's cottage.

He stripped off the heavy plaid shirt and jeans, reached into the closet for the velour robe hanging on the inside of the door, hesitated, and then drew the obnoxious pajamas from the dresser drawer. He hated the things with a passion, but it sure got cold during the night. Stripping off the remaining bit of clothing, he drew the pajama pants up over his strong, once again healthy, muscular legs and snapped the gripper at the waist. Might as well be warm he decided and pushed his arms into the sleeves and fastened the grippers down the front of the jacket. Suddenly remembering the change in the schedule for Richie, he wrapped the robe around him and went into the living room.

Minutes later the phone was glowing, the red light gleamed and he was in earnest conversation with Love. "I remembered that you should know about the change so it gave me an excuse to call."

As he talked with her he could not avoid comparing the two women. What if events had made a different path for Love three years ago when her life had been turned upside down. If the end were definite. If she had not had some measure of hope to cling to, what would she have done? But he could not deal in 'what ifs'. Life was coming together for Love. Perhaps after all his duties were accomplished, and they were back together, there would be time. Yes, he would be sure there was time and opportunity.

That ice wall would have to be crushed, perhaps melted.

He finished the conversation with Love. "So, I'll be shopping on Friday. Can you make it for lunch, and is there a place other than Shapiros?"

"Yes, meet me at the school at eleven and I'll direct you to a small place out of town a little way."

"Meet at the school? Won't Miss Tucker be there?"

"She shouldn't be. She doesn't have classes there."

Harold arrived with the snowmobile, and a new employee, soon after breakfast on Wednesday. Opening the cottage door, Brock was surprised to see Richie on the terrace wrapped in mackinaw, muffler, and hat with ear tabs, plus a heavy blanket around his legs, watching as the men from the lodge unloaded it from the truck.

Excitement beamed from his eyes as they met Brock's. "Can you drive it, Brock? It's simple once you learn how."

"Oh, I've driven a few of them, here and there." He hunched down beside the chair. "Do you know how to make the thing go?"

"I sure do. Dad used to let..." He faltered a bit, swallowed, and then continued. "He used to let me drive it over the fields when we went for firewood. "

"Good." Brock gripped the mittened hand that was wrapped tightly around the armrest of the wheelchair. "You can show me how it goes."

Brock understood the battle the young boy just waged as he stood up by the chair watching Richie quickly brush an escaped tear from his cheek. *I imagine all his tears have been shed and dried away, except for a few leftovers now and then.* Soon, he was sure, Richie would be ready to face that long future that was ahead of him. Brock shook his head slowly as the recurrent thought crowded in – the boy's aunt had a greater problem.

Brock talked with Harold and the man from the lodge for a few minutes while they were loading supplies to take back with them. The man, named Sam, had just been hired as a part time employee, along with two other men. Something about Sam bothered Brock. He was sure he had seen that bright red mackinaw in combination with the grey beard before, but he could not recall where. Well, no matter, if it became important to him it would come to mind.

"Is your brother-in-law, Steve, coming?" He inquired of Harold just as they were getting into the truck to leave.

"Oh, I've not said anything to Linda about it yet." Harold replied.

"She knows. I inadvertently let it slip, yesterday. She seems agreeable."

"Good. I'm looking forward to some hunting and fishing later on." Harold climbed into the driver's seat of the truck. Brock hesitated a minute not moving out of the way so Harold could drive off. *Now, why did I do that?* He wondered. The man named Sam had stopped abruptly, one foot in the vehicle and one still on the ground, his eyes staring at Brock. Why would the man jerk and pause like that at the mention of fishing? Brock held the man's attention in the stare until Sam blinked his watery eyes and looked away.

Well, he needed to probe a little more. "There is a shack at the lake that Linda said we could use."

"There are three or four up there. You can have a choice."

"We'll really need two, in case it gets a little crowded." Brock kept his eyes trained on the grey-bearded man who was now climbing into the passenger seat of the truck. "We'll take a look later in the week." He lifted his hand in farewell and Harold drove away.

The question of Sam's identity lingered in Brock's mind all through the day.

During the morning Richie put him through the routine of driving the snowmobile, explaining how to fill the tank, where the fuel was kept, and guiding him around the area, pointing out the low places in the ground where roots pushed up.

"The snow isn't really packed solid enough yet," Richie informed him, "but it will be before long."

Before long, Brock mused later. *Ten days in the hospital, two weeks recuperating.* He should be completely well by Christmas. That would be great. Then, if everything went without a problem – It had to. *Oh, Dear God, let it be so.* He had his own future to get on with, now that he was sure where he wanted it to go and who he wanted to share in it with him. "How would you feel about spending New Year's Day all cozied up in a snow bound cottage with a certain person?" Brock smiled compassionately as his question took by surprise the woman facing him across the table in the little out of the way restaurant on Friday noon.

"Oh, Whit. What a place to ask me such a question. You did it purposely because you knew I would cry all over the place if you waited until you take me home." Her fingers went from her throat to her lips, stilling the trembling he noticed there. "Are you sure? Why so long? Can't it be before Christmas?" The excited questions tumbled over one another.

"No, Love. A few days after Christmas." He reached for her hands as she brought them down in front of her to rest on the table top, and held them gently in his own. "It is still risky, remember."

His eyes searched her lovely face, so drawn and faintly lined with the strain of the last three years. It was not hardness that fought against the havoc that tragedy could reek in the life of a person. And surely it was not weakness that allowed its effects to develop, he assured himself. The inner strength of this woman, and the apparent strength in Linda's makeup, were proof of that.

He continued holding her hands in his, deliberately caressing each wrist with his thumbs, soothing, quieting the throbbing there. "You have so much in common with her. If only..."

"With whom, Whit? Linda?"

He met the question in her eyes. "With Linda," he answered. "You'll meet her at the hospital I'm sure, while Richie is there."

He released her hands "I couldn't risk telling you over the radio. I received the news early Monday morning. But you need to know. He's in Norway now, at a hunting lodge. He was very weak and rundown so they are letting him work as a busboy. Clearing tables, picking up empty cups and soiled napkins in the lounge, that sort of thing, not too strenuous."

"Busboy. Oh, Whit, what a..."

"I know, but it is a good cover, and he will be building up his strength. That's all I can tell you for now. He set his coffee cup at the edge of the table hoping that the waitress would refill the coffee cups, then checked the watch on his wrist. "Do you need to be back at any special time?"

"No, but I do need to go back to the school. My car is parked there, and I shouldn't leave it overnight."

"I'll drop you off and see you at the house later. Will that do? I need to check some things at the post office and do my Christmas shopping at McFaddens." He glanced down at the front of his shirt, drawing her attention to the strain and pull at the button holes. " I think I need to buy myself some new shirts, too. These last few weeks have been good for me. I've gained back all the weight I lost, my arm and back muscles are fit. The scar is still a little tender but that will take a bit longer."

The road from the old farmhouse where they had lunch took them through the rough, rundown part of the small town's business section. The lunch hour traffic was heavy, mostly due to the typical one-lane, two-way traffic pattern, with parking allowed on both sides of the street. As he slowed the car to a stop at the traffic light, Brock's eyes picked out the flash of a bright red mackinaw.

"Quick, Love. See the two men on the steps of that building, there on the right?"

"Yes, I see them." "I'm going to turn the corner, you get a good picture of them in your mind." The light had turned to green and he turned the car around the corner, but the two men had turned their backs and were walking in the opposite direction.

"*Damn.*"

"Whit!"

"I'm sorry, he quickly apologized, "but I need to see – here' s an alley. It should take me back a block. If they go all the way to the corner – just maybe..."

"What's so important about those men?"

Brock drove the length of the alley and turned right at the cross street. There was an empty parking place at the corner where he immediately parked at the right angle.

"One of them was with Harold at the house on Wednesday. I've seen those two someplace, but I can't remember where." He slouched down in the seat so he could see directly into their faces as the men came toward the car.

"You mean those two? I don't know if you saw them, Whit, but they were standing across the street from the jeweler's the day we picked up..."

"Right. That's where I saw them. The man who was with them that day was familiar, too." He turned to watch as the two men crossed the intersection. "Of course. The one in red is Sam. The other one must be from the lodge also. They work at the lodge with Carl and Harold." He explained. "But one of them, Sam, doesn't look much like a lumberman. His face is too weak, his eyes too watery and blurry. That's all I could see through the grey tangle of brush on his face."

He backed the car out of the parking space. "I have to see where they are going."

"Why is that so important, Whit?"

"Just a feeling. Sam acted very iterested the other morning when Harold and I were talking." He rounded the corner and followed the men along the street. They crossed in front of him and got into the back seat of a blue sedan waiting there. "New York license." He read the number aloud. "Remember it, Love, and put it down on something for me. The man driving the car. Grey hair, clipped moustache, wire rimmed glasses. Are you writing all this, please. Fifty to sixty years old." He drove on down the street.

"What do you think it means, Whit?" She asked as her pen rested. She was alarmed at his intensity.

"I have to suspiscion what I don't know, or actions that set me wondering, Love. It's in my training. At least now I remember that the man with them the other day was the cook from the lodge. That visit to town was legitimate as far as their job is concerned. Why they should be making another trip to town when they should be working is another question."

He relaxed slightly behind the wheel, accepting the slip of paper she handed to him. He patted her hand for a moment. She sighed. "Sorry to put you through this."

Brock glanced down at her as he continued on to the street on which the school was located.

"Are you all right?"

"Yes, I'm fine." She smiled at him. As he turned into the parking area on the school grounds, she requested, "Let me out at the side door. I need to get some papers and then I'll go right home. I'm so happy about the news, Whit, I'll probably get home, have a bit of a cry, and then wash away the evidence before you arrive."

She gathered up her purse and gloves that were on the seat between them, opened the car door and stepped out quickly when he stopped at the walkway leading to the side door of the building. He drove slowly through the crowded, icy streets, back and forth, looking down the allies, in crowded parking areas, following streets to the end, searching for the blue sedan with the New York license plates. Finally convinced that it was not in the vicinity, he parked in the downtown area, made his purchases and piled them in the back of the station wagon.

He paused before getting into the car as a pleasant picture flashed through his memory. A gentle face surrounded by wisps of auburn curls framed in the soft hood. She had walked out of the store without it. The clerk in the fashion department of McFaddens was very pleased with his selection and appreciative of the fact that he had come to her to make the purchase. But doubts of the appropriateness of the purchase began to form in his mind even as he placed the large bag containing the gift-wrapped package in the back with the rest of his purchases.

"Well," he spoke to himself aloud as if to be more convincing, "if I can't use it as a Christmas gift there will be a time, later." He determinedly pushed down the lock button and closed the door.

Two hours had passed and he still needed to go to the post office. He hurried there, mailed to a New York City address the bulky package containing the words and music for the first act of a musical which would never make it to Broadway. He also sent a smaller package to the Pentagon in Washington, DC.

Another brief stop at the florist shop and then he was offering yellow roses to his hostess as Mrs. Johnson opened the door to his brief ring of the bell.

"Oh, Whit, dear. You do know how to cheer a person after a very foolishly weepy afternoon."

The sincere warmth of her greeting cheered him as she lifted her face, freshly washed and faintly made up to conceal the stress he knew was there. She smiled at him. "Make yourself at home while I put these in water. Dinner will be ready in just a few minutes."

Chapter Nine

Another Monday morning. The early morning sun stretched out shadows of the house and pine trees across the snow that covered the back lawn and garden. In the distance beyond the shadows, the glittering white bounced blinding reflections into the crisp, cold air. Linda hugged the softness of her robe close around her. The temperature must have dropped to below zero during the night. She turned the thermostat in her room up a few degrees. From the room across the hall she heard her mother getting Richie ready for the day. He was going to be disappointed if the temperature didn't rise a little. The air would be too cold and dry for him to be out.

By the time she had finished with her shower and brushed her hair into its usual tidy bun her room was warm. Last year's corduroy shirtwaist dress that she had started to button down the front, hung at her shoulders like a heavy sack. With a self reproaching sigh she put the dress back into the closet, and took down a pair of brushed denim slacks and pulled them on. They were just as loose as the dress was but the matching top was belted, so she simply tied it a bit tight to hold up the pants and folded the excess carefully into pleats. There, it didn't look so bad now. Doctor Browne and her mother would really fuss if they knew specifically how much weight she had lost.

The smell of fresh coffee, perked to perfection greeted her as she went through the hall into the kitchen. Everyone was seated at the table where Agnes was serving sausages, eggs, and pancakes. Breakfast smelled and looked delicious; it was just a problem getting food down. Perhaps after next week.

"Good morning Aunt Linda. Will you eat some breakfast with me? Grandee said you had to start eating or you would be in the hospital before me."

"Richie." Mrs. Farnsworth objected. "Well you did and I don't want her to be sick."

Linda took her place next to him. "All right Richie. I'll eat as many sausages and half as many eggs and pancakes as you do." She held up her plate for Agnes to fill. "Is that fair enough?" The increased amount of food that she forced upon herself at breakfast and again at noon had settled heavily, making an uneasy weight in the pit of her stomach. She sat staring out the window of the study from behind her desk. Food just didn't seem to be what she needed. Perhaps milk in her coffee, more butter on her toast. Surely when Richie was well life would be easier. But then soon he would be a teen-age boy, a young man, by then 'Mum' would need her more than ever. *Dear Lord, What am I doing? Pushing my life so far ahead – what happens when there is no one who needs or wants me around?*

Brock had really jolted her when he had accused her of being cold, full of self pity. *Perhaps when Richie is well and into high school I can sell my share of the business to Harold, or maybe his brother-in-law will decide to buy it. Mother and Agnes will always have a home here. Richie could go on to college.* The thoughts continued, building a world of maybe's. Maybe she would go away. Leave all of the sadness and heartache behind. There were many places where she could go – but wherever she went the unfulfilled ache would always be there. Why couldn't she shake off this hurt? It had been five years. All personal thoughts; feelings, desires had gone when that four week period of shock had ended. Carl had nagged, fought, taunted, even tried to humiliate her. She realized now that Carl had suffered much, also, at that time because Phil had been his friend. Her hands trembled upward to massage where the throb repeated at her temples. This won't do. She almost screamed at herself. She picked up her glasses from the top of the desk where she had unknowingly laid them and put them on, trying to focus her thoughts back to the work in front of her. *I'll be so glad when this is over and Richie is well. Mum and I can relax a little and Whitaker Brockman can repack his station wagon and go back to wherever he is from, really. I have never been so uneasy around anyone before. He just seems to bring out the worst in me.*

The sun suddenly reflected off of something in the front of the house, distracting her as a bright beam of light streaked across the ceiling of the study. Marci had been to town for the afternoon. The western sun, overly large through the barren apple trees, flashed its last rays of the day against the windshield of the VW as she drove into the garage.

Where had the day gone? The manila folder holding the day's correspondence still lay open on the desk in front of her. This would never do. Glancing at the clock on the corner of the desk she realized there would still be time. She picked up the folder and swiftly checked through the remaining work, finishing it before the amber light beckoned her to the evening meal.

Marci had purchased bright gourds and Indian corn at the market to be used for Halloween decorations.

"Angela enjoys them in her window and around her room. There's plenty if Richie would like some also."

At dinner, Linda took and finished a good portion of her meal and finished it off with a glass of milk. She questioned Marci about her trip into town.

"Oh, I found everything I needed, thank you. We have a tradition carried over from Harold's childhood and I hope you don't mind, but I found some beautiful large orange pumpkins for our early celebration of Halloween."

"Oh! Goody! Jack-o-lanterns!" Angela clapped her hands and smiled at Richie. He returned her smile.

Linda caught her breath at Angela's expression. Her eyes instinctively sought Brock's eyes across the table. Should she answer his searching, mocking grin with a truly spontaneous smile? Of course. She was glad for the happiness of these two youngsters.

How little it took to bring shouts of joy from them.

Richie's eyes sparkled with anticipation. Halloween would have come and gone during his stay in the hospital.

"The pumpkins are rather large. The man at the market put them into the car for me. They are still in there."

"I'll get them for you," Brock offered.

"Perhaps they should be left there until after breakfast, tomorrow," Mrs. Farnsworth suggested. "You see, our children always liked to draw the faces onto paper first and then do the carving. That way changes can be made without so much trouble."

"That's great. Angela usually needs a bit of instruction about putting one eye on each side of the nose which should be in the middle," Marci laughed.

Agnes finished clearing the table. Brock was stirring the fire. Linda quietly escaped. *Would he offer to clean the pumpkins. That had been Ralph's job.* Even the smallest memories seemed to hurt so much. Linda went to get the drawing supplies for the next morning. The large mats of paper used for such projects were kept in the library. Excited laughter and bustling sounds followed Linda through the study. The cupboard was just inside the library door. There would be no need to turn on the

... "How can you see without a light?" Brock had followed her. "What are you trying to find?"

"The supplies are right here where we've always kept them." She pulled out the wide shallow drawer between two shelves and withdrew a large pad of foolscap. "This is what they can draw on, and here these are what they use for drawing."

As she held out a large box of crayons for him to take, he saw tears streaming down her cheeks. Instead of taking the crayons he clasped her wrist lightly in one of his hands and cupped her chin with the other, causing her to meet his stare.

"Even in this happy project for the children, you find sorrow. Are you so sad that you cannot find pleasure in their joy?"

She stared back at him, pulling on her wrist that he still held. She tried again to free herself and dropped the crayon box. Brock loosened his grip. "Leave them. I'll get them."

But, already she had pulled away from him and was gathering the crayons from the floor.

"Oh, yes. Pleasure! Perhaps you can watch that small boy tomorrow. Perhaps you..." She could not collect her composure as quickly as she had the crayons. He took the crayons from her as soon as she stood up and put them on the nearby shelf. Then he lifted her hands again in a smooth movement.

"I hope that Marci does not see that what she has done has upset you like this. She has done it in kindness..."

"Oh, I'm not upset with her." She moved her head from side to side, fighting the tears that were trying to come. " I was thinking of Richie and his father. This is one of the many things that Ralph and Richie shared – the fun they had together as father and son." "And you think the boy cannot handle it? Already I have wiped away spilled out, left over tears from his soft cheeks, Linda. Already I have held his head close to my shoulder when his lower lip refused to quit trembling. Yes, perhaps his tears will spill tomorrow. I understand that you can cry for Richie. Yet, you seem too bitter to cry for yourself."

"I do not care to speak about it, Mr. Brockman." She clenched her teeth at the pain this was causing her.

"Is this all they will need?"

"Yes."

"I will see you in the morning, Mrs. Wilson."

Tuesday morning, as she had planned, Linda finished her work in the office before turning that part of the business over to Marci. The files were straightened, all old unnecessary papers, communications, and pamphlets discarded. Agnes had knocked at the door with a tray and pot of coffee at lunch time, reporting that the jack-o-lantern project had over-run the kitchen so they had decided to have lunch on trays.

"It's a mad house in there, Miss Linda. He put the pumpkins on the floor and they're sitting around on pillows cleaning out pumpkins. Even Richie is..."

"Who put them on the floor?"

"Why, Mr. Brock. He said they couldn't fall and burst then. He spread out the vinyl cover for the picnic table so nothing would get on the carpet, then rolled his sleeves up past his elbows and just dug in." She hesitated a moment. "I've never heard that boy laugh so natural for a long time." She shivered slightly and then her expression changed to one of concern.

"It's a little cool in here, Miss Linda. The coffee is fresh and hot. Why don't you eat your lunch while it's warm and – turn up the heat a bit."

"I have my sweater, Agnes. Thank you for the lunch."

"Be sure to put the sweater on then, we can't have you getting sick." She opened the door to leave and then returned to the other subject of the conversation. "Wait until you see. Marci bought six pumpkins and they're carving them all."

Wednesday, the early afternoon sun brought with it a warming trend and then swiftly disappeared as grey, rain-filled clouds blew in from the northwest. The fireplace crackled and blazed, burning with apple tree logs. The aroma filled the room, leaving an elusive trail as it drifted through the rest of the house, mixing with the acrid scent of burning candles in grinning pumpkins on the mantle in the family room and at the large window in the dining room.

Even in the laundry room where Linda was busy preparing summer clothing to be stored away and winter washables for immediate use, the scent mingled with the usual laundry room odors of water, detergent and fabric softeners. The washer and dryer had both finished their final cycle. Last year's flannel shirts, both hers and Richie's would probably be too large this winter, but it would not take him long to fill his out again, and hers, well what did it matter. Anyway, it was better to be thin than...

Suddenly the sound of voices had taken the place of the laundry room noises. Brock, Richie, and her mother were engrossed in a game of Scrabble around the coffee table in front of the fireplace. Apparently Angela had abandoned her coloring book to observe the game for it was her voice that attracted Linda's attention.

"That's 'M' and that's 'A,' she exclaimed excitedly. "I know a word that starts like that. They're the natives of New Zealand. Maori. They make beautiful things and sing and dance and have lots of fun – of course, they work hard, too."

There was a slight pause and then. "It rains hard there, too, and gets real hot."

"Does it snow in Australia?" Richie inquired.

"Sometimes, but not much, where we live." Then the informative changed to the inquisitive. "Does it snow where you live, Mr. Brock?" A giggle followed the question.

"Of course it does," she answered her own question, "cause you live here." The Scrabble game seemed to be forgotten as the conversation continued after a slight outburst of laughter.

It was pleasant to hear them like this, Linda realized as she carried kitchen linens to be put away in the cupboard drawers and on the shelves.

"Yes, I live here for now, and yes, many of the places where I have lived in the past ten years have had lots of snow." Brock answered them.

"How about rain?" Richie seemed interested in everything Brock had to tell.

"Yes," Brock said, "It rained all the time when I was in Southern California, and drizzled most of the time I spent in England. When I was in Spain and in Washington D.C., the sun shone most of the time."

"Was that where you were when you got that scar, in Washington?"

Linda was surprised at the hint of mystery and intrigue that was so evident in the boy's voice, as though the U.S. Capital was indeed a dangerous and mysterious place. She was going to object to his questions but realized from Brock's glance and shaking of his head that he did not object so she continued her work in the kitchen without interfering with the conversation.

"No, Richie," he answered slowly, "it happened on a chilly, clear night in one of the most dangerous, evil parts of the most fascinating city I know."

"In Moscow – or Hong Kong?" Richie breathed the names of the cities.

"No, in our own *New York City.*"

"Oh, Brock, that's not a fascinating place."

"Don't you believe that. It's a wonderful place. At least most of it."

"Did you live there then?"

"Well, I lived on Long Island, which is part of it. The headquarters for the agency I was a part of was in The Bronx, which is..."

"Yeah, I know." Richie" interrupted. "We studied about that last year. It's one of those 'burroughs' they have there. Did it happen there? How did you. . . "

"Richie. Please remember your manners."

"But, gee, Grandee. It *is* exciting."

Linda closed the kitchen cupboard doors and went back to the laundry room. Brock's voice carried very well. She wanted to hear, but not be observed as she listened. She could see his reflection in the mirror over the work counter in the laundry room and she watched as he walked to the sink, filled the teakettle with water and placed it on the burner to heat. He put out four mugs, continued with the telling as he put heaping spoonfuls of chocolate drink mix into each mug.

"It happened about three miles from my agency, in an old tenement area. A partner and I were looking for a young man who was in some bad trouble who needed our help. He lived in this neighborhood and we had to go there to look for him. We finally found him and a friend of his who we thought might be with him, hiding in an empty poolroom. They were glad to see us and go with me to my apartment. While my partner and I were going with them to my car, someone jumped out from another store room. There were two of them. One shot my partner and the other one pushed his blade between my ribs while I was hurrying the young people into the car. The young man laid heavy on the horn and they ran. There was no one else around. Though the young man and his friend were very frightened they helped my partner into the back seat of the car and went with us while I drove to the nearest hospital."

"Didn't they know you were hurt?"

"Yes, but not how badly. My partner was losing a lot of blood and someone had to drive. I called the police on the car radio and they met us at the hospital."

"Did your partner die?"

"No, she's recuperating in Washington, DC, now."

"She." Richie gasped. "A girl?"

"Well, no.

"She was a mature woman, a well-trained police captain with the New York City Bureau of Narcotics."

"But why a woman?" Mrs. Farnsworth wondered.

"One of the youngsters we were looking for was a young girl."

"What happened to them? Did they catch the ones who hurt you?" Angela needed to know. "The boy and girl are being helped through a very difficult time, and so is the man who stabbed me, which is good because he thought we were members of a gang and he was trying to help the two get away from us. But the one who shot the police officer was later killed in a gang street fight."

By this time Brock had poured the water over the chocolate. Linda stopped to help pass the cups around the table and to share the cookies that had been put out for them. She watched the excitement increase in Richie's expression as he fired more questions.

"Are you an F.B.I. agent?"

"No."

"A C.I.A. agent?"

"I couldn't tell you that, now, could I?" Brock teased him. "But, no, not one of those either."

"Are you a private eye?" The questions continued.

Brock shook his head. "No."

"I know! You're Army Intelligence?"

"Well, I was for a while, but not now."

Linda listened intently while finishing her tasks in the laundry room. Why she was interested in this question-answer bit, she could not have explained, but the man continued to be an enigma to her. On his application for the position he had written...His voice reached her more distinctly and she realized he was watching her in the mirror, and was directing his remarks to her.

"There isn't that much excitement in what I do, Richie. I'm a partner in a law firm in New York. I am retired from the Army, and..." his eyes laughed as they caught Linda's swift glance into the mirror, "I do write lyrics for my friend who is an Off Broadway little theater producer."

Linda stepped back so they could not see each other through the mirror, but continued to listen as she sorted and folded the remaining clothes from the dryer.

"I also work with a private agency that has its national headquarters in Washington. Primarily we help people who find themselves in great personal difficulty and danger."

"Is that why you were in New York?" Some of the excitement had faded from the boy's voice, but there was still a sense of intrigue coming through. "Yes, the father of the young man in this case was a member of the C.I.A. and he could not get involved in it, so he called on us."

"And you said it wasn't exciting!"

"Well, to hear about it, I suppose it is, but to live it – I would say it is more terrifying than anything else."

"What will you do after I am better and you won't need to help me any more?"

"Oh, I'll just keep on doing whatever comes my way that needs to be done."

Linda realized that he deliberately ended the questions there, getting up from the table, collecting the empty mugs and taking them to the counter.

"You know," he said, including Linda in the conversation as she went from the laundry room into the kitchen, his eyes shifting to meet hers. "This is one of the most rewarding and relaxing jobs I've had."

He tousled the boy's hair in a friendly gesture as his eyes looked away briefly from Linda to Richie.

"I'm certainly glad it came my way."

Linda caught her quivering lower lip between her teeth and began putting away remaining cookies and dishes from the table. The sincere interest he had taken in Richie was evident in everything he did. What would come after – would he just go on out of their lives with the satisfaction of a job completed, as he had before? How many more dangers would he...

Feeling again the demanding pull of the look he directed at her, she turned away, going to rearrange the floor pillows around the coffee table.

His voice seemed to be directed only at her as he continued. "Perhaps it was fate. He seemed to be thinking. After a brief pause, he said, does anyone still believe in that, I wonder? Anyway, thank you for needing someone to help."

The rain had washed away the snow, the sun and wind together had dried the land, and by Saturday morning the air was clear and cold.

On Thursday, at dinner Marci had informed them that according to a call from Harold, her brother Steven had arrived at the lodge and would be spending the weekend at the house, if it was agreeable with Linda. "Of course, it is all right," was her ready reply. Brock studied the young man who arrived with Harold and the clear and cold air early Saturday. He was perhaps two years younger than Marci – a tall, masculine, near duplicate of his sister. The exuberance of youth still flowed from him as he greeted his sister with an exaggerated hug and a noisy kiss. He then swung his vivacious niece high into his arms, planting a teasing kiss on the top of her head.

For all of these boisterous greetings there was a deft smoothness in his movements - the evidence of complete physical control. His eyes sparked with the same exuberance plus intelligent, interesting questions as he offered his hand to Brock. It was a firm straightforward greeting, not just a young man trying to impress.

The women had made plans to make the transition from fall to winter throughout the house and had made it plain that the men were not needed. Therefore, by ten-thirty Richie was bundled into appropriate wrappings and with his wheel chair, was in the back of the Land Rover with Harold. Steven had the motor warmed and ready to go as Brock climbed into the front passenger seat.

Brock had explained to Richie what he was interested in and was amazed at the boy's knowledge as they followed the east bank of the river, going north and west toward the lake shore. It was an old logging trail, Richie had explained, but only used now for hunting and fishing trips. The road veered off to the right as the river took a sudden drop into rapids and turned away. "This is the area where the deer are, but it's too close to where the Christmas trees grow," Richie explained. "There's a high electric fence so the deer cannot get to the trees. Grandad had it put up so the deer could stay here and still not bother the trees." He paused, then added, "The current isn't powerful enough to kill them. It just shocks them so they'll stay away. Since there is snow on the ground you can probably see..."

His sentence was cut off as Steve slammed the brakes down, bringing the vehicle to a sudden stop.

Out of the trees ahead of them came a doe and her nearly grown fawn, stepping delicately, cropping the tall, dry, hay-like grass growing in the wide space between the stand of trees and the edge of the trail. Even as they watched from the Land Rover, the deer sensed their presence and possible danger; they bounded from their grazing stance in great leaps. Mother and offspring crossed the road in front of the truck, into the safety of the dense growth of trees beyond the road, nearer the lake shore.

"Aren't they beautiful." The thrill of the sight was in his voice as Richie continued. "Dad said it was a shame to shoot them, but if we didn't there would be so many they would get sick, even starve to death."

"Do you allow hunting parties?" Harold asked.

"No, but my dad and Carl used to hunt them and dress out the meat for the Indian families and the children's home. Other places, too, I guess. Last year they took twelve bucks that were good for meat. I think Grandee still has some of that in the freezer. They had to shoot two does. One was trapped in the ice flow in the river and one had broken a leg. That meat they sold to some company in Canada that packages meat for sled dogs.

The matter-of-fact way in which the boy was giving them this information brought wonder to Brock's thinking. *What a heritage for a boy to have. This background, knowledge and way of looking at life brought fiber in his character. Not only his, but also in his aunt Linda and the other women in his family. They gritted their teeth, clenched their hands around something firm - like coffee cups. They swallowed their tears, and went on. Only those very few closest to them would know of their deepest sorrows and disappointments.*

"But there has to be a weak spot someplace," he said aloud. "And, with God's help, I''ll find it."

The trail they were now following was no more than a wide path. Scattered throughout the forest were scrubby pines still standing from the old forest growth. Harold who had now taken over the narration of the trip, explained that the pines had been part of land devastated over a century ago when the pioneers had used it with no thought of conservation or of replanting. The wood had been there, they had used it.

"The forest is productive again." Harold pointed out fine white birch and pine which would be used for furniture and fine interiors; and, of course, the evergrowing firs for the yearly crop of Christmas trees.

The path, as they approached the edge of the forest, turned to connect with a heavily gravelled road. They followed it to a wide gravelled area surrounding a long, low – roofed, log building. Along the front ran a porch, enclosed with thermo window sections.

Steps led up either end of the porch into a sheltered doorway. Smoke curled from two wide chimneys rising above the roof at each end of the center peak. Brock turned to the boy behind him. "Is this the first time you've been here for a while, Richie?" he asked.

"Since last Christmas. Dad and I came here to cut our own Christmas tree. It hasn't changed any, only the parking lot is bigger."

Harold laughed. "That's a sign the business is growing. The bigger the business, the more machinery you need and the bigger the place you need to park it."

"Someday I'll be a part of the business, won't I, Harold."

"You surely will. I think you have a big part of it right now." "Yes, I know, but I want to work in it like my dad and my Uncle Phil."

"Was your uncle part of the business, Richie?" *Surely,* Brock thought, *that isn't a prying question. What if it is. I need as much information as I can get. Richie seems to be the only one who is willing to talk about the recent history of his young life.* Information which Brock felt he desperately needed. "He worked in the office most of the time until Aunt Linda came home from college, then he moved to the lodge, He wasn't really my uncle until later, but he said I could call him that anyway." Richie told him. "Then he really was my uncle for a few weeks after the accident."

"Accident?"

"Yes, you see, he..."

Richie's answer was cut off there. Steve had parked the Land Rover near the closest entrance to the lodge and called out 'lunch break' and immediately swung his door open and dropped to the ground.

There were still unasked questions whirling around in Brock's mind. What accident? Where did it happen? Who was involved? *Dear Lord. Had Linda been in the accident? Did she cause it somehow?* That could surely be the answer to her unwillingness to speak of it. The answers could not all come from Richie. He had been just a five year old at the time. Brock vowed that he would continue the search in the very near future. But first must come the successful finish of the mission of rescuing someone from great personal danger. For that he needed to know about the condition and mobility of the fishing shacks.

After lunch, a short five mile trip north of the lodge took them to a cleared space beside the road that was enclosed with chain link fencing.

"They put up the fence to keep the animals away from the shack." Richie explained.

Steve and Richie stayed in the Land Rover while Harold accompanied Brock. The wind had increased considerably and blew in cold from the lake.

Harold turned his collar up closer around his neck. "Man, this is going to take some getting used to." He strode along beside Brock, matching his steps to those of the taller man.

They entered the nearest of the five shacks. "Are you really planning to spend time sitting in one of these six by six cubicles with a string dangling down through that hole?" Harold joked.

Brock hesitated before answering. *Not as much time as I want people to think.*

"Yes, I am." He examined the benches constructed along opposite walls and the small wood-burning stove with the flue connected to it. "Are they all like this one? It seemed to me as we drove in that there was a larger one farther back on the lot."

"Oh, you think you might have company?" Again Harold tried to joke with him, but became serious as Brock met the question in his green eyes with a serious nod. "I'm going to need company on a few occasions. That's why I brought you along." Brock eyed his friend closely to see what effect his statement might have.

"Then this isn't just a fishing project?"

"No." Brock motioned for the other man to sit down on one of the benches.. "I don't have time to explain everything, but I can take about five minutes now. " He took his wallet from his pocket and opened it to display a card holder. "This will make things a little clearer to you. We are expecting a package from overseas about Christmas time, just before the channel closes. It will be dropped from a freighter headed for Chicago, after it passes through the Mackinac Channel."

"You're expecting what?" Harold got to his feet.

"Yes. It's all hush-hush, but definitely legal as far as this country is concerned."

"You know, Brock, I have the idea that I've been thoroughly investigated during this last month, clear back to where I was born."

"Oh, even further back than that, my friend." Brock assured him. "You were a God-send. One of the best assurances that this whole thing is going to continue without a hitch." He put his wallet back into his pocket. "Our five minutes is up. I can assure you that this is a desperate effort to right a terrible wrong, Harold. And I do need your help. But first I need your agreement to do it before I can tell you any more."

"The only package I can think of that would be so important to your associates will need a very thick wet suit and a much larger opening in the floor through the ice than a twelve inch circle."

Brock grasped the gloved hand held out to him as Harold said, "I'll check out the larger shack and see to making those holes bigger when the time comes." With that they returned to the Land Rover.

Harold helped get Richie resettled for the ride back and adjusted his wraps and cushions. Brock deliberately guided the conversation around Harold, Marci and Angela, who Richie knew and Harold's brother-in-law, Steve, the driver. They discovered that Steve had spent two years in law school after graduating high school, then four years in Army Intelligence. Brock could see from Harold's reactions that he was pleased with the young man. Still, Brock knew he'd have to call Brombke in Washington concerning Steve's credentials.

The first hard freeze of winter moved in from Canada, bringing with it a blanket of snow that covered the frozen ground. Although the snow had accumulated to only a few inches, Brock could feel the permanence that was evident in the way it scrunched and packed beneath his boots. The storm had moved on to the east by noon on Monday, and by three o'clock he had cleared the snow from the walks, driveway and paved parking area in front of the garage.

The tension that had prevailed inside the house through the morning had diminished somewhat by the children's excitement at the first big snow storm.

Running beneath that excitement was the apprehension in the women's conversations as they prepared for the trip to the hospital and the surgery scheduled for early Tuesday morning. It had become so noticeable during lunch that Brock had called Linda into the study.

"What can possibly be so important at this time?" She demanded. "There is still so much to do. We need to be ready to leave by four o'clock!"

He hesitated a moment, watching as her hands nervously twisted the belt of her wrap-around skirt. *She's so thin.* Her cheeks already had paled from loss of her summer tan. Hollow places in her cheeks only emphasized the fatigue lines at the corners of her eyes and mouth.

"It won' t do, Linda." He had taken her cold hands in his protective clasp. "You'll be in the room above his with a bad case of nerves, if you don't settle down."

"Nonsense, I'm fine." She tried to pull away.

"You are not fine. You are worked up and not calm. Of course you are worried."

"Sit, Linda. Let's talk." He moved behind her and began massaging her shoulders. At first she objected but as the muscles began to lose tension, so did she.

"Relax," he whispered. The muscles that held her mouth in such a tight grip released just a little as his fingers moved along her jaw line. "I know it's hard. Even if there is not a smile available, how about some tenderness, hmmm? Richie needs to see you calm and hopeful. And how about a little faith?"

The hint of warm softness that had come into her face matched the tone of her voice as she stood up. "I didn't realize. I wasn't thinking. Thank you."

A slight change had come into her face. He brought her toward him. Pulled her close into a brief embrace. Not so brief, however, that he could not feel the racing of her heart and a quickly drawn breath before he let her push away. He went back to the task of snow removal.

Inwardly, Linda's fears and doubts were not yet transformed into faith and confidence. Anything could still go wrong. But, Brock had given her a sincere challenge.

Chapter Ten

Brock pushed back the cuff of his jacket. "Three-forty-five. Good timing," he assured himself. The snow removal equipment was put away. He had showered and changed into a brown corduroy suit with turtleneck sweater. He took his great coat from the closet and, with it over his arm, was in the garage waiting at the door to the family room as Linda opened it to wheel Richie to the Mercedes.

"Hey there, Richie. It looks to me like you're all set for the great event." Brock gripped the boy by the shoulders as Linda stepped back from the chair. "Want to ride in the wagon with me?"

Richie looked for consent from Linda. She nodded. He grinned at Brock. "That will be neat."

Tuesday Morning. Linda knew, of course, that it was still too soon. Only a little over an hour had passed since Richie had been taken into the surgery. She and her mother had had two cups of coffee and two or three banana nut and raisin bran muffins in the cafeteria. *Why does it take so long for time to pass?* She must remain outwardly calm because of her mother who was waiting in the lounge for Linda to return from the cafeteria.

She returned to the lounge to find one of the volunteers speaking with Mrs. Farnsworth. Linda recognized the woman as a friend of her mother's. Glad for the distraction from 'waiting' for her mother's sake, Linda turned and walked the opposite direction to where the hallway crossed the central corridor. A familiar figure had just come away from the information counter and was walking toward her. She waited.

"Good morning." Brock greeted her as she turned to walk beside him back toward the lounge. "I tried to get here sooner, but didn't expect a traffic jam in this small town."

He stopped her just before they reached the lounge and asked, "How is she?" He glanced toward the two ladies in conversation.

"She's better now. Her friend has come along."

"And how about you? How were your accommodations at the inn? And have you had breakfast?" He smiled. "Answer in any order."

"Apprehensive. Fine. And yes, thank you."

She guessed she answered all of those questions satisfactorily, because he continued. "The attendant at the desk couldn't tell me anything. But, it's still too soon. Did you sleep last night?"

"Not very well."

"It shows." He frowned. More than just a friendly concern in his expressive eyes.

Linda turned from him and went to the window at the far side of the room. In the early morning sun, the snow glistened on the lawn. The thought of the cold caused her to tremble and rub her hands up and down where the sleeves of her blouse covered her arms.

She sensed the movement behind her. Felt his hands drop a coat around her shoulders.

His voice was close to her ear.

"Your mother is doing great. Her friend is talking volunteer opportunities to her, so the time will hurry by." He took the coat from her shoulders and held it out to her.

"Put it on. A walk in the crisp fresh air will add some needed color to your cheeks and occupy your mind for awhile."

She hesitated. *He isn't serious. How can I leave Richie?*

"The doctor can report to your mother," he reasoned. "The doctor will give last minute instructions to the nurse, so he won't be out immediately after the surgery, anyway. You need some fresh air and then a good nutritious meal."

"Just never mind objecting," he insisted. "Richie doesn't know a thing about what's going on. He won't miss you." He turned her around and buttoned her coat. Pulled the hood over her head and around her face. "Where are your gloves?" he asked as he took her arm and walked her through the corridor to the lobby.

"I left them at the inn." She could feel the tingling freshness of the air as he opened the outer door. The breeze was gentle enough so small wisps of snow whirled along the walk in front of them. If she allowed them, many heartbreaking memories could overwhelm her in this place, but surely this time it would be different.

"Don't worry so much, Linda." It seemed he had read her mind. She allowed him to take her hand in his gloved hand for warmth. "Relax and enjoy the snow." He smiled down into her eyes as she lifted her face to look at him. "There, that's better."

Quickly she turned her head away and looked out over the snow-covered hospital grounds. She was surprised at the calm she felt walking with him hand in hand. She relaxed the muscles in her arms and legs, wondering at the effect this man was having on her. *Could he be all things a man should be to a woman?* Her thoughts could not take that direction.

It really wasn't all that cold, she decided trying to change the course her thoughts had been taking, and she breathed deeply of the fresh air. They had walked halfway around the city block that was the hospital grounds and the sun felt warm as its rays touched her face. She drew her other hand from her coat pocket, pushed her hood back from her head and folded it down across her shoulders. She lifted her face into the breeze. It caught some loose wisps of hair, worked them into their natural curl, then tossed them around her cheeks and tangled with her eyelashes as they reflected the sun. She felt his reaction to this slight change in her. With his hand still holding hers he managed to draw her closer to him, sometimes touching as they walked, no faster, no slower around the next corner of the square, into the walk leading to the front door. She could feel his eyes touching her hair, lingering there. She could not possibly look at him now. She could not explain even to herself this feeling, nor could she reveal it, not to anyone.

Slowly he released her hand and opened the door. Unpredictable, this lack of need for conversation between them. The walk had relaxed and refreshed her for a while. Of course, the fresh cold air had a lot to do with that. But, back inside the hospital she could feel the tension returning.

They stopped in the corridor and, turning her toward him, he unbuttoned the top button of her coat as she released the two bottom ones. Their hands met on the second one from the top and he caught hers in both of his, cupping them together.

There was that strange something in his eyes again. Her eyes met his over their clasped hands. She lowered her glance as he drew her hands close to his mouth. She had never had a man kiss her hands before. *Even Phil had never.* He held them, gently. "They seem so fragile they could shatter in the strong winds of these northern winters." He spoke huskily as though the cold had affected his voice. His breath was warm as he breathed into her cupped palms and then gently released them together. A little flustered at the stirrings his actions sent through her, and at a loss for some reply, she simply shrugged out of her coat as he held it.

While Brock hung their coats on a nearby rack, Linda paused at a small mirror above a table and tucked in the stray wisps of hair which the wind had disarranged. Her cheeks, chin and tip of her nose were pink from the effects of the cold. She pressed her hands to each side of her face enjoying the fresh cool feel. *They are rather thin,* she admitted to herself. "As soon as this operation is over you have to begin taking care of her, you know." Brock had come to stand behind her. "If Richie should think that you are ill, he won't recover as quickly as he could.

She could not answer as they turned along the corridor to join her mother in the lounge. The leather sofa was now empty and Mrs. Farnsworth was seated in an armchair near a low coffee table. There was no one else there. Linda sat quickly on the end of the sofa near her.

"Has the doctor been out yet?"

"No, dear. You've only been gone twenty minutes." She smiled at Brock as he came nearer. "I see you did get her to go out for some air. She insisted on driving the three blocks from the inn."

"It was icy, Mum. I didn't want you to fall."

"We had a very pleasant walk, Mrs. Farnsworth. What time did you arrive here this morning.?"

He's getting her talking, that's good.

"We were here at seven o'clock to see him before they took him in at ten minutes to eight."

"But," Brock glanced at his watch, "it's only ten thirty now. Time for a coffee break."

Mrs. Farnsworth got up from her chair. " Good. I cannot just sit here any longer."

"Come, Linda. Neither must you. If you insist on being nervous about it, at least do it with a cup of coffee to hold onto." He smiled.

She threw a questioning glance at him and then, recalling the number of times she had done just that in his presence, she followed him as he walked with her mother down to the cafeteria.

Brock guided them the long way around and down the stairs to the cafeteria. He seated them in an ell section where the clock could not be seen.

Linda hoped that the operation could not last more than two or three hours.

Slowly she drained the last few drops of her coffee and took another look at her watch. They had been in the cafeteria for over an hour. She met his cautioning look across the rim, telling her not to panic. He held her gaze as he pushed away and turned to her mother with tenderness and a hopeful expression in his voice. Again they took the long way, waiting for the elevator in the busy rush of the morning. As the elevator doors opened at the surgical floor the questions came again. *Why the delay?* Brock took her mother's arm and accompanied them back to the lounge. Then Brock went to the desk where a nurse and receptionist were busy. He asked a question. The nurse shook her head. Then checking her chart she gave him another answer.

Linda left her chair and met him as he turned away from the desk.

"I need to know right away, Linda. Did your mother take her medicine this morning?"

"Why?"

"Just yes or no. And does she have extra for an emergency?" His voice was low but urgent.

"The answer is yes to both." She gripped his arm. "But why, Brock. What is it?"

"You need to get a tight grip on something more than a coffee cup, now. The nurse said there was an emergency and the operation was delayed." He placed his hand over the one holding so tightly to his arm. "She didn't know what the emergency was but she did say everything was going all right now. Come," he turned her around, "we can't stay here any longer. Your mother already senses that something is wrong."

She kept her voice low as she suggested, "Couldn't we let her believe it was someone else who was involved in the emergency?" She took a deep, faltering breath as she felt the pressure on her hand increase and heard the understanding in his voice.

"Of course – perhaps..."

After Brock made a brief explanation of the delay to Mrs. Farnsworth, Linda and her mother walked the length of the corridor to a window alcove at the end. Even the halls in the small community hospital were busy at that time of the morning as nurses and aides hurried about their various tasks. A few ambulatory patients made their slow progress depending on the wall rail for support. An orderly pushed a wheelchair with an elderly patient dressed in coat and scarf to the elevator to join the companion who had come to take him home.

Linda called her mother's attention away from the cares of those patients. They stood beside the fernery near the windows and watched as the coming and going traffic made tracks in the new snow that tried to dust a fresh layer on the drive and walks. There had indeed been an emergency, Brock explained as he came for them a few minutes later. It hadn't been Richie. "A little girl was rushed in from the children's ward for an emergency tracheotomy, and the only surgeon available at the time was Doctor Browne," he reported.

"After he finished her case he had to scrub and change before doing Richie's surgery. What a morning." Brock exclaimed. "But everything has gone well with Richie."

At Linda's searching look he continued. "He is in the recovery room now. Doctor Browne said you could see him after lunch."

"But, Brock."

"After lunch. *He said. Not me.*" Brock asserted. "Richie is still under the effects of the anesthetic and won't be awake until then anyway."

He stepped between the two women and walked with them to the coat rack. "We have time before lunch. Why not go back to the inn and rest, take a nap, relax for this time."

Linda caught the shift in his gaze as his eyes shifted his attention momentarily to her mother who was already gathering her gloves and scarf from the nearby table where they had been since their early arrival that morning. "Rest an hour or so," he stressed.

"See that your mother takes her medicine." For a moment, as he helped with her coat, he brushed back a rebellious curl of her hair, held it in place and then turned away to assist her mother.

She was still in the spell of his tenderness as he accompanied them in the elevator and out to where the Mercedes was parked. Helping Mrs. Farnsworth into the passenger seat, he explained. "Dr. Browne wanted me to assure you that things went well with Richie. He was sorry he couldn't talk with you now. Because of his emergency, he was behind schedule. He'll talk to us when we go in after lunch. "I'll meet you at the inn for lunch."

By Wednesday afternoon she was convinced that Richie was going to be well. Doctor Browne assured her that everything was going as he expected. The therapist was to begin his preliminary work on Thursday morning. Richie should be ready to leave the hospital on the following Monday afternoon. Her mother would be staying at the inn until Saturday. Her volunteer friend had asked her to help in the program for the elderly patients. Linda was going to object until the friend assured her that she would see to Mrs. Farnsworth's transportation and that she took her medication. After talking with Richie over an early dinner with him, and since his grandmother would be still at the hospital, Linda decided that she would return to the farm that evening. The lighted windows in the upper rooms reflected a bright glow on the banked snow along the drive as she turned off the main road. It was her first time since February to arrive home after dark and see them glowing. Marci was there along with Angela, Steve and, of course, Agnes. It was encouraging to feel this warmth for others, again. Of course she had always loved Agnes almost as much as she did Mum. Richie was very precious to her. But, the closeness that had developed between herself and Marci was like having a sister. *And what about him?* She could not avoid the question that invaded her thoughts as the lights from the gardener's cottage crossed her view. How could she abide that hauntingly familiar feeling? She could not allow it to linger, increase, become identifiable. He would be gone.

She parked the Mercedes in the garage and hurried into the warmth of the kitchen. *His care for Richie seems to be genuine. Even his concern for Mum seems real. But does he truly have feelings for me? What does he wish me to do – weep all over the place, walk the floor, wring my hands? I could have done enough of that for two life times. It wouldn't have changed anything. It would not have brought back my only brother and his wife. They are gone. Phil is gone.* "Agnes," she called. "I'm home. Marci? Where is everyone?"

She heard voices then, coming from Richie's room. Agnes called back.

"We're in here."

Still wearing her coat she opened the door to Richie's room. "What are you doing?"

The book shelves were empty, dresser drawers open, the curtains were from the window and the bed stripped.

"We thought it would be a good time to get his room ready," Agnes replied.

"It looks as though you have worked all day."

"Oh, no, just since lunch;" Marci answered. "We finished all of the office work so we thought we should get started in here." "Let me hang this up." Linda slipped her coat off her shoulders and went into her room. Her thoughts, however, remained in the room across the hall. *This is where my contentment in life will be found. Richie is going to be well again. He will be the center of my life. I can be sure of his affection. His happiness and welfare, his goals and attainments are to be all that is important to me now.*

Reality returned as she joined the other women in his room and in making plans. The paper on the walls had been put there four years ago, the furniture was all still nursery white. "Agnes, now that everything is down and stripped," she motioned to the bare windows and shelves and bed, "why don't we make some major changes? Do you remember the furniture in Ralph's room before he went into the Army?

"Of course. The bookcase bed and the corner desk and shelves."

By the time the evening was over, the plans for altering the room were complete. the furniture from Ralph's room had been located in the attic, and the new colors had been decided.

A warm glow of inner peace came to Linda as she stood at the window in the darkness of her room. The feathery clouds were moving into the east on this moonlit autumn night. She could sense a bit of melancholy coming on. Could it be the softness of the velour robe as she wrapped herself in it. The warmth of the collar against her chin.

She involuntarily recalled the closeness that she had felt to Brock earlier in the day.

His hands were gentle, and lingered. Why? She glanced at the still lighted cottage windows. *I wonder what he did while I stayed in town? What will he do while Richie remains in the hospital? What will be his next move?* "Stop it," she scolded herself in a whisper. *He's temporary, he will be leaving in a few weeks. To him you're just a cold-blooded, sour, old maid.* "Am I?" she heard herself ask aloud. "Nonsense!" *There aren't such women any more. So what if I don't want those feelings again?* But the warmth that seemed to flow from his touch came over her again.

More clouds began to drift in from the west, hiding the warm glitter of the far distant stars. She wondered if Richie could see them from the window in his hospital room, as she drew the drapes together before the clouds hid the stars completely from view.

The clouds that had passed over during the night had added another inch to the snow cover. Brock had cleared the walkway around the house, and the driveway. The county plows and salt trucks had gone through the area, and someone had driven an automobile through the new fallen snow from the house and back again. Linda did not linger on the thought of who it might have been. She was only thankful for the act. After all, it could just as well have been Steve. It made the trip into town easier and safer. Marci went with Linda and checked off the items on the shopping and 'to do' list as accomplished. First they visited Richie in the hospital and took Mrs. Farnsworth for coffee in the cafeteria. Linda was pleased at Marci's excitement when Mrs. Farnsworth suggested that the white furnishings from Richie's room be moved to Angela's room, and that some 'girl-type' paper and drapes be purchased to go along with these changes. They went shopping and checked off the remaining items on the list.

By noon on Saturday the two rooms had been painted and papered, and furniture transferred. Both rooms were completely transformed to better suit their occupants.

Linda was planning to leave directly after lunch to visit Richie and bring her mother home. Everything was going smoothly now. Perhaps it was a good sign.

She had showered and changed into a soft wool plaid skirt, cotton, long-sleeved blouse and crewneck pullover. Like most of her clothing, it fit loose and clumsy on her. As she brushed her hair back into its soft roll to allow it to fall into soft waves over her ears and around her face. Perhaps that would distract form the hollows and shadows around her cheeks and eyes. She applied just a slight touch of lip gloss to protect against the icy winds that had begun to blow outside. She disliked the taste of lipstick, and so had Phil. Her hand still held the stick of gloss to her lower lip recalling the kiss she had received that day in the study. Determinedly she put the tube back on the dressing table and went to join the others for lunch.

When Linda arrived at the hospital and got to Richie's room it was crowded. It seemed that everyone had decided to visit him this day. Dr. Browne was firm in his demand. "No more visitors today young man. You need your rest now, if you want to go home on Monday."

After everyone else had gone, Linda had a few minutes with Richie. He delighted in showing her the gifts and cards he had received. Especially important to him was a new edition of a series of mystery stories for young boys. He seemed to treasure it because Mrs. Johnson had given it to him earlier in the day having been one of the many visitors. Richie told her, "You just missed Mrs. Johnson by a few minutes, Aunt Linda."

Then she tucked him in, kissed him quickly on the forehead and admonished him to get his sleep. "We are taking Grandee home with us this afternoon, so don't expect her tomorrow. Steve and Marci are coming tomorrow, and then you'll be home the next day." That assurance had seemed to satisfy him and he had relaxed. He opened one of the new books and began his mystery adventure.

She pulled the door softly shut behind her as she left the room. She wondered about Mrs. Johnson. *Who is this woman? Why does she take such a special interest in Richie? Is it because of Brock?*

She was to meet her mother and Brock in the lounge downstairs near the cafeteria. She hurried along the corridor and down the stairs. There was no sign of either her mother or Brock as she neared the bottom of the stairs. Then she heard his voice coming from an area near the stairs, secluded among some rubber tree plants and other potted greenery. She hurried around the newel post and then paused. It was not her mother he was talking to.

"The boy should be on his own by the middle of December, Love, and then we can..."

"Oh, Whit. It's been so long. I don't know if I can stand any more delays."

Linda stopped and turned her back to the pair standing there. She could not walk away without being seen, yet she really did not want to hear. She was startled to see that they were reflected in the mirror on the wall which she was now facing. but their backs were turned to the mirror. She watched as Brock placed his arm around the woman's shoulders and kissed the top of her head. He said something more to her but Linda could not hear.

She moved to the foot of the stairs and stood in plain view because Brock had turned his head and caught sight of her.

"Oh, Linda." He kept his arm around the woman's shoulders for a moment and then took her hand in his and brought her forward with him to meet Linda. "Have you been waiting long?"

"No." He had not known she had been standing there. "I expected mother to be with you." She glanced at the woman beside him. Her face seemed familiar, the dark silken hair and something about her mouth reminded her of someone, but the tinted glasses she was wearing were a detriment to recalling her face.

Brock was speaking now as the woman looked up at him. "Mrs. Wilson, this is Mrs. Johnson. I'm sure you have heard Richie speak of our meeting at the pool. She is also a teacher at the elementary school.

"It's nice to meet you at last, Mrs. Wilson." The woman smiled and offered her hand.

"Thank you, Mrs. Johnson. Richie has told me much about you. Her friendliness seemed sincere as she held her hand firmly a few seconds. More questions went whirling in Linda's mind. Then she heard,

"I really must be going. I'm happy to hear that your nephew is making good progress." She turned then to Brock. "You have much on your agenda, so I'll just..."

"That's all right. We need to wait for Mrs. Farnsworth, so I'll walk you to your car. Linda will excuse us, I'm sure." He reached for the coat draped over the arm of the nearby chair and held it for Mrs. Johnson.

"Love." Linda thought, and turned away, walking swiftly through the lounge to the cafeteria. *Where is my mother and why am I so tense?*

"Linda, dear, where have you been? I thought we were to meet in the cafeteria."

"Oh, Mum. I'm sorry. I thought we had agreed to meet in the lounge."

"No, dear, at least that isn't what I understood. You seem upset about something. Get a cup of coffee and sit down for a minute." She motioned to the chair across from her where she sat at a near-by table. "Brock should be here soon." As always, the trips into town were used for shopping for needed items. Today was no exception. This morning's purchases were now packed in the back of Brock's station wagon along with Mrs. Farnsworth's overnight case.

Linda had insisted that her mother ride in the front because it was warmer. As she had hoped, the three way conversation had led to a general exchange of comments. Mrs. Farnsworth began telling about the volunteer work she had enjoyed so much these few days. Linda relaxed, half listening, with her head resting against the window, her eyes barely open, watching through the thickness of her lashes.

In the darkness and at that angle she could not see the lines around Brock's eyes and mouth, nor the silver streaks above and in front of his ears. Only the strong set of his chin and jaw, and the line of his throat were plain against the background of the blowing snow. The strength was there even though he was relaxed as he carefully handled the wheel, driving through the storm that was blowing great gusts of snow in front of and around the wagon, almost cutting off his vision as it whirled against the windshield..

He must have felt her eyes upon him.

"There's a pillow back there somewhere, Linda. Why don't you fit it behind your head, then you can sleep if you want."

Realizing she had been caught staring at him, she reached for the mentioned pillow, murmured a thank you but it's only a few more miles. She bunched the pillow between her shoulder and the window and stared out into the night, trying to keep her mind a blank.

The end of another trying, uneasy period. The weekend was over, the time of waiting past. Richie was coming home. Today. Now everything should be going uphill. Of course, he would need to be careful, and it could be ten days or more before he would be able to walk. "He will be home in just a few minutes," Linda said aloud. She felt like shouting it. It was so childish to get so excited. Everything must be just right. Brock and Mum would be back with him soon. They were to be there for dinner.

Agnes and Marci and even Angela had helped prepare everything. The long trestle table was covered with the bright orange and brown cloth, the harvest gold dinnerware and amber glasses made the table festive. Agnes had prepared a special roast of venison with wild rice and Richie's favorite vegetables. Fresh apple dumplings were even now baking in the oven. *The kitchen seems unusually warm.* Linda thought. She turned on the exhaust fan over the counter, then prepared the coffee maker and set the timer. With all those sounds in the kitchen she did not hear the humming sound of the garage door opener. As she turned from the counter towards the door leading to the garage, the space where the door should have been was filled with a boy in a wheel chair and a man standing behind it. Before she could say a word of greeting the boy grinned at her, flung away the lap robe that covered his knees, lifted his feet and exclaimed, "Look! Aunt Linda. They work." "Oh Richie, I'mmmm..." Suddenly the boy with the wheel chair, and the man behind it began to tip. The fireplace along the wall seemed to rise to meet the ceiling and everything in sight joined them to become a crazily spinning pinwheel. Linda clasped both hands over her ears to stop the persistent whir. She was trying to answer whoever had shouted her name. But the pinwheel whirred louder and whirled faster as her knees refused to hold her. The whir developed itself finally into one fierce scream. The wheel whirled off into blackness.

The spinning had stopped. The blackness had gone away. But it was still dim and shadowy. *Where am I? Who is calling me?* "Not Phil?" Was that her own voice? *Of course it wasn't Phil, but who else would call me Darling? Who would hold my hand, caress my wrist with his thumb? His thumb?*

"No, Linda. Not Phil." He took his hand away and placed a cool, damp cloth on her head.

"Where am I? What happened?" That voice seemed weakly hers, but far away.

"You fainted away when you saw Richie move his legs."

"I never faint." She raised her head and shoulders from the sofa. But everything began to spin and the blackness moved in again. Through the dark grayness another voice came from somewhere.

"He said to keep her warm, get her into bed. He'll be right out."

Who are they talking about? Who is coming? Suddenly she felt strong arms lifting her effortlessly, holding her steadily. *Am I the one who needs to be warm? Is this the way they're doing it?* She did feel warmer already. Could she get closer? She felt the arms do her bidding, it seemed. They drew her closer, held her there, and then she seemed to float through space.

What's going on? It's getting dark again.

Chapter Eleven

"I know. The doctor told me that you might sweat it out during the night, and that if it didn't happen you would be taken to the hospital about seven this morning. So, no trip to the hospital. That's good."

He kept her hand in his, sending tingling alarms up her arm from where his thumb again caressed the pulse in her wrist. It was becoming a disturbance she didn't want to cope with. She withdrew her hand back into the warmth of the covers.

"What time is it, anyway?" She turned her head away from his searching eyes to locate the clock, but she could not see it in the dark.

"A little after three." He put the covers in place again under her chin, letting his fingers brush over the pulse that throbbed evenly there, and around her cheek, brushing back the ever straying strand of hair. "You should sleep without any problems now. I'll leave the drapes open for you and take your damp things into the laundry room."

He stood up, then leaned over her, brushing his lips ouickly across her forehead. "Um, very nice and cool as it should be now. Goodnight, Linda."

Even then she was almost asleep. From somewhere a voice answered him, but the clouds were hurrying by and she might miss the stars if she didn't watch. She didn't hear the door close behind him, nor did she see the snow blowing against the window as it rode in with the great bank of clouds that now filled the sky.

The next two days were little more than a blur to her. A mixture of frantic efforts to again lower the elevated temperature, insistence from everyone that she remain in bed, almost forced feedings of the monotonous chicken broth and herb tea, a faintly remembered time when Brock had wheeled Richie in to see her.

Again the night moved in. The clouds seemed to swirl into her room. They were cold and damp whirling around her as she seemed to be standing in an open doorway.

The wind caught at her hair, blew her sheer night gown into angry tangles around her bare feet. Off in the snow-filled clouds she seemed to see them. Phil, Ralph, Father. What were they doing there? Calling to her? She must catch up with them. It looked so warm and peaceful there, but they were moving away leaving her behind in the cold.

"Wait. Phil." She called but could not make him hear. "Phil, it's so cold here!"

"Aunt Linda." From behind her another voice called. She turned her head and saw someone standing in a square of bright light.

"Aunt Linda." Again the voice. "You should stay covered."

The clouds had disappeared, the figures vanished, only the cold remained. The figure in the bright square of light moved closer in halting, jerking stages. The light was blocked out as though a door had been shut and only the pale light of the storm-filled night was there. Now the form was leaning over her, gentle hands drew the covers close around her, warm, caring hands. Something to hold onto. But she became aware that it was cold in the room. Insistently she folded the covers back, gently pulled the warm young body in beside her, wrapped the covers close around both of them and forgot the cold and the storm.

It couldn't be snow from the storm in her dream. It was too warm. The satin edge of her comforter assured her that she was in her own bed, in her own room. But what? Then she realized that Richie had come into her room during the night. It was his soft, tumbled, auburn curls against her throat and chin. Richie. It had been years since he had sought early morning comfort in her bed, now, here he was. He had come to her in the night. But where was his chair, how had he gotten here? She found the answer as her eyes rested on the polished wooden crutches that were leaning against the bedside chair. At least that part of the dream had been real. She could feel the warmth of his young body as it was curved to fit with the bend of her knees and hips as she cuddled him close in front of her. He must have heard her call out in the night. She could not see his face, but she sensed he was waking.

"Aunt Linda?"

"Yes, Richie."

"Are you all right now?"

"I'm sure I'm going to be now." She met his eyes with a reassuring look as he turned to face her. "I didn't mean to frighten you last night. It was only a dream."

"But you called out twice, and I didn't want to waken Grandee, so I..."

"Oh, Richie, I love you so." She drew him close to her again, rubbing her face in his curls. "I'm so thankful that things are going to be right for you again."

The gray of the winter morning gave way to arriving sunlight as the two in the warmth of their cozy wrappings kept their voices low and talked of the happenings of the past five days.

"You were really sick, Aunt Linda. Brock slept on the family room sofa, even on the nights when it wasn't his turn to stay with you. Doc has been here every day."

"I'm sorry I frightened everyone so, but everything just seemed to give way when I saw you move your legs. Now you are moving about on crutches." She tightened her hold on him. "I'm so glad you came in last night."

"So this is why we haven't heard you moving about in your room." The door had quietly opened. "You should have let someone know that you were coming in here. Your grandmother was worried." Brock stared at the smaller of the two snuggled in the bed. "Or have you been here all night? Really, Richie."

"Aunt Linda cried out..."

"I had a nightmare and Richie heard me. He was concerned and we just reversed roles for a change." She watched as realization lighted Brock's face when he saw the crutches near the chair. His concern for the boy, the pleasure of his progress was in his voice as he came to stand by the bed. "You did it. You came from your room to here. That's great." He reached down and caught the boy's hands, pulled him to a sitting position on the edge of the bed and then slowly onto his feet. "I'll hold you and you move one foot to the side so your feet will be about eight inches apart. That's right."

Linda propped herself up with her head resting in her hand, her elbow bent against the pillow. Her eyes moved in wonder from the face of the man to the straight back of the boy now standing without any support there in her room.

"Now," Brock continued, "I want you to sit down on the edge of the bed." He moved back a few steps to give the boy assurance that he expected him to be able to do what he asked.

"Do it slowly and only use your hands for balancing. You can brace yourself if you...*good*."

She felt the bed sag a little at the slight drop of his weight onto the edge, but he had done it. She lifted her glance to meet the blue eyes that watched her. Met the compassion she saw there with a brief plea of her own for understanding, then turned her attention back to the boy. How could she express the pleasure of this moment? No smile would come, not that it would suffice, tears were of no avail. Yet, as she met again the blue searching gaze she felt he could understand from what he discovered in her face. "Well, it looks as though the sick room has been turned into an early morning meeting room." Harold quipped as he and Marci came through the open door. He grinned at Linda. "I'm glad to see you're awake and back among the living."

"Harold. She was very ill, but not dead." Marci went to stand by the bed.

"Harold has to go back to the lodge this morning, but he didn't want to leave until he knew you were better."

"Thank you both. It seems I have been a nuisance and an inconvenience for everyone."

"Yes. It has been a very upsetting week." Brock's voice was strangely hoarse as he lifted Richie's crutches and handed them to him. "Meeting's adjourned. Time to get ready for the day." He followed Richie through the door.

"I'll see you, probably on Thursday, Harold. By then this house should be back to normal."

Linda frowned as she watched him cross the hall to Richie's room. "What did he mean, Harold? Surely my illness has not interfered with your schedule."

"It was a little touch and go with you there for a few days. Now we are glad to have you back." Harold turned toward the window.

"We are going to get the fishing huts ready to be moved. Fish a little; do some hunting. The Christmas trees are ready, waiting to be loaded on the customers' trucks when they arrive, so we thought now..." he hesitated, did not finish the sentence but turned to Marci. "We need to get going." He leaned over and kissed Linda lightly behind her ear and left the room.

Marci, with tears in her eyes, said, "We were all so worried about you. Especially Brock." She gave her hand a light squeeze and followed her husband.

The next four days were definitely convalescing days. Linda was not allowed out of bed except for bathroom needs and an hour in her chair beside the window. The latest issues of her favorite women's magazines were read from cover to cover. Richie spent some time with her, making good progress in getting around the house with the crutches. Her meals were brought to her on a tray that fit across her lap in bed, with instructions to eat every bit of every meal delivered.

Now it was Thursday, only one week before Thanksgiving Day. She trembled at the thought of all the work involved in preparing for that favorite holiday. But this year it would be full of reminders of sadness. *Would it be worth the effort?* But there was the rest of the household, Harold, Marci, Angela, Brock and now Steve – none of them had made plans to go away!

"Well, I'll leave it to Mum and Agnes." She finally decided, as she stood by her bedroom window.

It seemed she had been completely removed from all that was taking place in the house. Business was running smoothly. Marci was in full charge of the work her mother had done. Steve was picking up his responsibilities without any problems. Richie was well on the way to complete recovery. A series of shudders followed the deep gasp of breath she took suddenly.

"Oh, Linda. What brought that on?"

She turned from the window, still in her flannel gown and velour robe.

"Oh, Marci, I was just wishing."

"For what?" Marci asked, coming into the room and joining her friend by the window.

"That I was fifteen again and could be out in the middle of that." She indicated the scene beyond the window. "Making snow forts, having snowball battles with Ralph from behind them." She shrugged her shoulders and walked away from the window. "Or perhaps that I could now be standing here watching Richie and Angela, perhaps Carl's little girl and one of my own..." She drew her robe closer around her and sat down in the chair near the bed.

"I'm sorry, Marci. That's maudlin. I really was wondering about Thanksgiving, and when I am going to be allowed to get into some clothes." "Doctor Browne is here checking Richie's progress now and he will be in soon to give you the answer to your last question." Marci sat down on the edge of the bed and continued. "About Thanksgiving, Steve and Brock have gone hunting for the weekend. Carl said that any geese in the area would either freeze or starve to death anyway, so a roast goose would be very tasty."

By the time the week end passed, Linda was back in the busy-ness of the household. She was weak and tired easily. The constant dosages of vitamins and minerals insisted upon by the doctor and enforced by Agnes seemed to no avail. Her clothing was still too large and an ache persisted as if she were missing something. She wondered if she should mention it to Doctor Browne.

The brittle glare of the Thanksgiving morning sun danced and glittered on the wide expanse of snow as Brock hurried from the cottage to the patio door. Entering the kitchen, he was assailed with pleasurable aromas as Agnes and Mrs. Farnsworth were busy at the counter and stove. He greeted them with a smile and a quick good morning, then glanced briefly at the fireplace area where Harold and Steve were engrossed in the previous day's newspaper. Angela was absorbing the antics of the characters in the Thanksgiving Day parade, cavorting in review across the TV screen. He avoided the dining room as he heard the voices of Linda and Marci working together there, and hurried through the hall to tap lightly on the door to Richie's room.

"It's me, Richie," he announced as he pushed open the door. The boy standing at the window slowly turned to greet him. In the corner facing the wall was the abandoned wheel chair with the crutches resting against the wall.

Brock grinned at him. "Agnes has arranged to serve coffee and punch along with other goodies in the living room in about half an hour. I'll try to have everyone there. That way it won't be such a shock to her. We surely don't want her to go through any more trouble."

"She'll be okay, Brock. Doctor Browne said she was better. Although I can't see much difference." Brock agreed with him that there was no evidence of any improvement and quietly left the room.

A few minutes after twelve-thirty, all but Richie and Steve were gathered in the living room for the family tradition of coffee hour on Thanksgiving Day. Linda's wing-back chair near the fireplace had been turned a fraction so she would be facing the passage from the hall into the room. A serving table was near her chair at her left, waiting for the refreshments to be placed there.

Brock went swiftly to stand behind her as he recognized the faint sound of a door opening and closing. Now he caught the familiar fragrance that was exclusively hers, saw the few silver hairs she did not attempt to hide and the pallor of the thin, yet shapely, hands in her lap as she failed to relax even now. Simultaneous with his placing his hands on her shoulders and pressing them back against the velvet covering, Richie appeared in the room. He stood tall and slim, clad in a corduroy blazer with matching pants and knit shirt. Brock added pressure with reassurance to the hold he kept on her shoulders as Linda whispered, "Richie." Brock felt one of her hands seek and clasp his as she watched her nephew walk the few steps that brought him into the room and to the chair where she was seated.

"Good morning, Aunt Linda." He leaned forward bracing himself with his hands resting on the arms of the chair, and kissed her on the cheek.

"Forgive me for being a bit slow."

Brock tightened the grip on her hand for just a moment, then relaxed the restraint he had kept on her shoulders.

"Richie." She turned her head for just a quick glance at Brock and then back to the boy standing in front of her.

"OH! How wonderful! Just let me look at you!"

Brock moved from behind her chair to stand by Richie, his arm resting lightly across the boy's shoulders. "We thought this might be the proper day to let you know."

He shifted his glance around the room to see smiles on every face, and then back to the young boy's face to meet the grin he saw there with a smile of approval.

"How long?" Mrs. Farnsworth had come from her chair to stand close to her grandson.

"Tuesday morning was the first time without the crutches." Richie put his arm around his grandmother's waist and hugged her. "You almost caught me when you came in to make my bed." He laughed.

"Why the secret?" Harold wanted to know.

"We wanted to be sure, and not raise any false hopes." Brock met the question in Linda's eyes. "Of course he'll not be able to run any foot races for a while, at least not until Doctor Browne gives permission."

Steve interrupted any more questions and answers as he wheeled in the serving cart with coffee and punch, and Agnes placed the plates of sweets and tiny sandwiches on the table next to Linda. Richie pulled the wheeled ottoman that matched the winged chair nearer and sat beside her. Brock watched the expression of happiness on his face turn to concern as the boy noticed the tremble in her hands and the tension around her mouth. The dining room was arranged for semi-buffet service. The table was covered with a beautifully aged linen cloth and set with the matching napkins, heirloom silver, crystal, and fine china. Autumn colors of brown, orange and deep burgundy accented a low centerpiece of preserved flowers and leaves, with highly polished acorn and shelled hickory nuts arranged on and around an antique pewter tray and matching candle holders.

Brock allowed his attention to roam around the table, noting the grace with which Mrs. Farnsworth presided as head of the house. He was sure she was not a product of society's influence nor an exclusive girls' school, yet he felt certain that his grandfather, Love, Oscar, and those nearest him would fit into a setting such as this. They would have entered into the friendly conversations and spontaneous laughter as they shared the good food and fellowship.

Richie and Linda frequently looked at each other, his eyes offering assurance, smiling. But there was never an answering smile from her. She looked somewhat troubled. *Dear God, what will it take?* Brock searched silently for an answer. *I know she is pleased.* He caught her glance as she shifted her gaze from Richie's and by force of command he held her attention. Almost, he could see the color deepen, a glow come into them, perhaps an inner show of happiness, or was it pain? *Was she desperately ill and didn't know – or was that the truth and she did know and was trying to hide it?* Slowly she hid her eyes from his searching, dropping her long golden-tipped lashes to rest in the faint dark circles there. Her mouth tightened a firmness developed in her throat and along her chin line. The gentle pulse just above the soft chiffon scarf she had folded into the neckline of her dress throbbed rapidly. She was excited or upset about something. *I wonder,* he mused, *could my attention be what is getting to her?*

After Marci and Steve had removed the soiled plates and silver and while dessert was being served, Mrs. Farnsworth reviewed the items that were relevant to the family in the year that was soon ending. The success of the business, the tragic events of the fire and accident, the arrival of Brock and his assistance, the inclusion of Harold and his family into the household.

She hesitated a moment before concluding with an invitation to all assembled to lift a heartfelt prayer of thanksgiving to 'Our Heavenly Father' for bringing us through this year and for the wonderful recovery of Richie's ability to walk.

"Now," she gave them a radiant grandmotherly, smile and announced, "we will have coffee, tea or hot apple cider, whatever you desire, in the living room."

In no time at all Brock and Steve had the dining room back in order, Steve had gone to the study to finish reading an article in a magazine and the clock in the foyer chimed the hour of ten as Brock left the room.

The fireplace in the living room had been banked for the night. Harold and Marci were in the love seat now pulled up in front of the fire and Angela was curled into the warmth of their closeness. The house was strangely quiet after such a busy day. He hurried through the hall, stepped into the softly lighted room where his eyes immediately found Richie propped up in bed reading one of his newest mystery books.

He had been waiting for Brock to come.

"I did it, didn't I?" He grinned, closing the book.

"You certainly did. How do you feel?"

"A little tired, but really great."

Brock sat on the edge of the bed rubbing his hands gently over the young legs and knees.

"Do they ache – or shake?"

"No. Aunt Linda rubbed some lotion on and worked them a bit." His face suddenly puckered into a frown. "Why doesn't she smile, or cry, or something, Brock? I know she's glad about my being able to walk again."

"How long has it been since you saw her smile?"

"Last Christmas she seemed to be a little happy, and…" He paused a moment, "and just before the party she laughed at something Dad had said, but then Carl began teasing her about stuff again."

"What kind of stuff, Richie?"

"Oh, I don't know. He used to call her a frigid old maid. Stuff like that. But she did love Uncle Phil, and they always had lots of fun together." His attention suddenly shifted to the door to his room. "Hi, Grandee. Brock has come to say goodnight."

"It sounded as though you were saying a bit more than goodnight."

Brock quickly noted the reprimand in her tone and apologized, adding, "It wasn't intended to be idle gossip, Mrs. Farnsworth. I'm sure you realize..."

"I understand more than you think, Brock, but Richie has been asked not to discuss certain things with outside..."

"Again I apologize. I sometimes find it difficult to remember my status here."

"Brock. Now it is I who need to apologize. Please, there will be a time for you to know, I'm sure."

"My time is running out, Mrs. Farnsworth. Richie is well, or almost, and..."

"She'll never tell anyone, you know that, Grandee." "Nevertheless it is her story to tell." With that she pulled his covers up around him, kissed him goodnight, and opened the window drapes to the night sky. Brock had already left the room when she went out.

The living room lights were out, the loveseat was empty, and the light in the study revealed Steve at the desk engrossed in the magazine as Brock went through to the family room where the fire had died down considerably and only the lights at the work counter were on. Linda was sitting near the fireplace. He stopped for a moment, observing her before she could realize his presence. The glow of the waning fire flickered over her hair and face accentuating the pallor that still lingered there. *Will she object,* he wondered, *if I just sit?*

"Oh. Brock." She straightened up in the chair. "Come and sit for a minute." She motioned to the chair opposite her. "There's some coffee if you would like it."

"No thank you. I've had sufficient coffee." He moved quickly to where she was and sat down on the ottoman near her. "I've had enough of all of the things I don't really need, or want. I've had enough..." He broke off the remark, shocked at the bright glare of her eyes reflecting the fire. Had they suddenly filled with tears? But, no, she kept them fixed on his for a brief glimpse and then hid them from him as she lowered her head to stare into the fire. She said, "I don't understand why you should be so upset. I only meant to try to thank you in some way for what you have done for Richie."

"Don't bother about it. I do not need your thanks, it's what you hired me to do. It's your attitude that needs explaining. You know he lost so much more than you that night of the accident and fire and yet you are a continual reminder to everyone of your tragic loss."

Brock was nearly beside himself with frustration at this point. He intensely searched her face as she continued to stare into the smoldering embers, her jaw line firm as she clenched her teeth. He raised his voice deliberately to break through her resistance.

"Linda!" Then dropped to almost a whisper as he saw her shoulders tighten and her hands twist around each other. "Can you not show a little happiness, a bit of emotion over his recovery? Your attitude is taking more out of the boy than he can spare. Are you so hard, so cold that you..." She pushed back her chair, almost upsetting it as she jumped to her feet. "What do you know about me, MR. BROCKMAN? What can you possibly know about my feelings, or my loss?"

He caught her hands and held them in his hard grip as he got to his feet facing her.

He was aware that she was distraught, upset because he had angered her. She would have turned and run out of the room had he not blocked her way.

"Not nearly as much as I intend to know." He answered her question and would have pulled her close to him, wrapped his arms tightly around her and made her cry from pure anger at him, but she managed to slip her hands free one at a time as his attention was distracted by a movement at the door.

"Oh, I'm sorry." Steve paused at the bottom of the steps leading from the living area. "I didn't mean to interrupt. I was going to turn out lights and..."

"Don't worry about it, Steve." Brock moved the ottoman back in place regaining some composure. "We were just discussing Richie's recovery and the progress he is making." His eyes lingered on the woman in front of him as she, too, struggled with her reactions. The soft velour dress she wore clung to her slight form emphasizing her thinness, almost hiding her soft shape in its many folds.

"There are still a number of problems we need to clear away, iron out, but we will pick it up again – very soon." He emphasized the last part of his statement as she lifted astonished eyes to meet his. Just as quickly the shrouds of sadness swept over them, and Brock turned away to go to the cottage.

"Good night, Steve. We must let the ladies get a good night's rest."

Glimpsing Mrs. Farnsworth in the hall he added, "They have earned it this day."

Chapter Twelve

The next evening the house seemed strangely empty, as though everyone had found things to do in the far corners, or behind closed doors. The ring of the telephone stopped Brock as he passed the door to the study. His intentions were to go to Richie's room for a quick visit before the boy went to sleep, but no one seemed to be about so he stepped into the room and answered the ring.

"The Farnsworth residence." He smiled as he recognized the voice coming through. His voice filled with special tenderness as he explained it was just chance that he had picked up the receiver to take the call. He listened for a moment and then replied.

"Every thing went fine. He made his entrance in good form and everyone was very pleased."

He listened again as Love expressed her pleasure over Richie's recovery and then to her more personal concerns.

"There's no need for you to worry, Love, things are going smoothly and everything will be perfect in a few weeks." He listened to her reply.

"I know, Love..." he spoke softly into the mouthpiece. He heard a gasp of indrawn breath behind him. He turned to see Linda behind him in the room. He walked toward her, carrying the phone and speaking into it as he went.

"Listen, Love. I'll be able to tell you more later, but I need to hang up now. I'll call you tomorrow." He put the receiver down on the cradle, carrying both pieces in his left hand.

Linda turned to leave the room. She rushed into a small table near the door, upsetting a tall pewter vase and scooting a book onto the floor. In her confusion she hesitated there, setting the vase upright. Brock stopped her from picking up the book, his hand gripping her arm.

As she met his glance briefly, he caught a fleeting look of, what...? It was there and then gone! Surely not fear! *Why is she afraid of me?* The question flashed through his mind as he kept her from leaving the room.

"You don't need to run off, Linda. It wasn't that private a conversation."

"No? Then you didn't really need to cut it short, did you?" She motioned to the instrument he still held in his hand, the long cord of which stretched to the connection near the desk. He put the telephone on the stand where the book had been, then taking her firmly by the shoulders, turned her to face him. The indirect lighting from above the study windows cast a soft glow over the lovely face turned up to his, highlighting the golden flecks in her amber eyes. Again he noticed a fleeting something there. He released the grip on her shoulders, allowing his hands to move slowly down her arms, caressing through the soft velour of the shirt that had replaced the checkered or plaid ginghams that she usually wore with her denim skirts.

"Brock, I came to..."

He ignored her remark, still watching the light and shadows of her face, his hands now enclosing hers. They were cold. Gripping them tighter, he felt a slight tremor go through them.

"Your hands are freezing." He scowled at her. "Have you been outside?"

"No." She pulled her hands away and pushed them into the pockets of her skirt. "I came to tell you that Richie is waiting to tell you goodnight."

"I'll go to him in a minute." He took her gently by the arm and turned with her to walk through the hall to Richie's room.

"But there is something else on my mind at this moment."

"Oh?" It was just a whispered question as she looked up at him.

"Yes. Something very serious has been happening in the lives of people who are very dear to me. I will be deeply involved in the conclusion and perhaps the results. I will be able to handle it from here so I won't need to leave..."

"But Richie is better." She reminded him. "You don't need to..."

"He'll still need me for a week or two, and by then..."

"Well, of course," she reminded him, "the agreement was until the first of January."

"Thank you. Now I need a promise from you concerning the rest of my stay here."

"A promise? I don't understand."

"I can't explain it yet, but..." his voice dropped to a murmur as they approached Richie's door. "I want you to promise that you won't discuss anything you might hear Harold or me talking about either between us or on the telephone, or question about where we go or what we do. Not even with Richie or your mother. I cannot let you in on this. Only Harold knows, and then only because I need his help."

"But, Brock."

"No buts." He lifted her chin with his free hand so he could impress on her the importance of his demand. "Lives are involved, Linda. I need to know I can depend on you. He saw the answer in the expression on her face. "If you have any doubts or questions they will have to wait, I'm afraid. But I can assure you this, it is not criminal."

"I realize that." She turned her head away, forcing him to release his clasp of her chin. "If there is anything I can do..."

"No. We just need your understanding and discretion." He held her arm for just a moment longer and when he noticed the slight nod of her head in agreement he released her, lightly caressing the place where he had gripped. Then he turned the knob and opened the bedroom door.

The cottage became a place of seclusion for Brock. Richie was moving around freely now without crutches or any other assistance. He needed only a short period of simple therapy in the mornings to relieve stiffness and tension. Brock used the remaining part of each day to tie up loose ends.

Late Wednesday afternoon he mailed the lyrics for the final score to his off-Broadway friend and had a relaxing dinner with Love. *Relaxing?* He scoffed at the thought. *How can Love relax? The time is getting short. Once the ship has passed the drop off point and the crew is dismissed for shore leave, then she can relax.* "Until then, nothing must go wrong," he emphasized to Harold while they discussed plans the next evening. The image of Love's face as he had assured her the evening before blotted out what he was going to say to Harold. Harold's obvious throat clearing brought Brock's thoughts back to the conversation.

Harold continued. "Carl has agreed that Steve will be an asset to the company, especially in the forestry division. So all Steve needs to do is decide what he wants."

"According to Brombke he is still in the service of the government, working on something in this area. Highly confidential, as is what we are doing, but you know the system. One hand cannot know what the other is doing, even though they might work more efficiently together."

Brock walked to the small kitchen, poured two cups half full with the freshly made hot coffee and filled them the rest of the way from the liquid chocolate sitting on the table. He took one to Harold and went back to his chair with the other one. "Whatever it is, he's keeping it to himself."

"Aren't we all?" Harold laughed.

"He seems to be interested in the shipping channel, the shipping schedules and..."

"Do you suppose we'll be working next door to him?"

"You mean in the fishing shacks?" Brock held his cup between his hands with his elbows resting on his knees. "He seems to be extremely interested in the one farthest north, doesn't he."

"But those men are really fishing for the lodge."

"Perhaps we should, too. Not for the lodge, of course, but couldn't you stand some good, wide-mouth bass and lake perch on the dinner menu for the next week or so?"

"We wouldn't have to be such good fishermen, just be able to act the part."

"Right. We do still have some work to do there." Brock glanced at his watch as he continued. "I should be getting a call from Brombke about now and I want you to listen in on the conversation."

Right on schedule the red light signaled on-off-on-off. In a matter of seconds the little red light was glowing and the conversation began.

"Brockman here."

"Right. Is Van Fleet with you?"

"Yes, he is here."

"Welcome to the crew, Harold." Brombke finished his greeting and then, "I need to know the exact location of the fishing huts so we can calculate the exact time and place for the package to leave the ship. The substitute package will be put on board the ship at Detroit, make the substitution at the time of the drop, and go with the ship on to Chicago remaining there to be returned to Detroit another way."

"Won't that be risky?"

"No. It won't be missed until shore leave is over and the crew reports back to the ship."

Brock passed on the information that was needed and then Brombke assured him, "you have permission to use Steve if he will accommodate you in any way. But only you and Steve are to know the full story, and

Harold is only to know that Steve is in when the package arrives. Is that understood?" "Right." Brock threw a questioning glance at Harold and then replied, "Except if it becomes absolutely necessary..."

"Why should that be?"

"I told you about the two men."

"Are they still there?"

"Right. And they are fishing in a hut about a quarter of a mile north of the two we are using,"

"Give Steve the job of watching."

"He already is."

"Well I'll dig a little deeper on that. We can't have anything go wrong at this point."

"It would help to know."

"I would say we have to know." Brombke's voice was silent for a moment. "You take a little more precaution than usual, this time, you hear?"

"Yes, Sir, I hear you." Brock chuckled.

"All right, see that you do. All of you "

Brombke softened his tone of voice to finish. "I'll be in touch with you as soon as I get the facts on Steve's assignment." The red light flickered – then went off as Brock replaced the phone on the track.

Harold parked the Land Rover loaded with fishing gear, snowshoes, emergency medical supplies, canned and packaged food, and other odds and ends of needed equipment between the two fishing shacks.

The wind rushed at them as he and Brock dropped from the high vehicle to the snow packed ground. It continued its assault as Brock struggled to open the door of the larger shack. The loose snow swirled and twisted in great streamers above and around the shack and off across the great expanse of frozen land and water. To the north and west the great white plain was broken only by a line of huge, piled up boulders of ice stretching as far as could be seen to the shipping channel, the waterway was still open for ocean going vessels. The sun glared its shimmering brightness, forming rainbows in the ice crystals that flew before the wind.

Once the door was open it took much of Brock's strength to keep it from slamming shut while Harold hurried the supplies inside where they would be stored. Later they would take what was needed to the other hut. The wind whistled around the door continually, finally gaining the victory as Harold carried the last armful of supplies through and Brock followed him in, allowing the door to slam shut behind him.

Brock's eyes immediately focused on the obviously new lumber that formed the two and a half foot square trap door that had been recently put in the middle of the floor.

"There's an opening in the ice the same size." Harold explained. "That was a tough one to do. Do you realize there is six to eight inches of insulation between this floor and the sub flooring underneath? There's a sliding door in the sub flooring. I haven't figured yet how we are going to keep that from freezing."

"You'll find a way, Harold " Brock assured him.

Harold did not seem so sure of that as he went about laying a bed of kindling and arranging firewood in the small wood burning heater. Although light through the one window that faced south was sufficient for the days when the sun shone, for those times the sunlight was not enough, Brock fitted an oil filled lamp in the bracket above the table.

Then he lit it to be sure it hung level. The two men worked quickly and efficiently in spite of the small space. By the time the stove was providing heat the bunks in the corners had each acquired a rubber pad with air mattress and blankets – even pillows. The food and other equipment was neatly stored away except for what would be moved to the other shack. Water and coffee had been set to perk on the two burner cooking unit. "Well, all the comforts of a sheep herder's camp in the south of New Zealand." Harold picked up his hooded parka from the chair where he had dropped it and hung it on a spike driven into the window frame for that purpose.

"Oh, sure..." Brock agreed, a wry grin widening his mouth, "or a line shack in the Wyoming mountains." He laughed as his mackinaw took its place on the other spike.

"This is really set up for just two men, isn't it? Two places at the table, two chairs, two bunks, and two spikes. The other is the same only smaller and only one bunk. We can make people believe there have been four people here most of the time, if we need to do that. So there won't be any questions about it later."

Harold made no answer to that comment. Brock wondered if he had said too much.

"Why the two huts?" Harold asked instead of answering Brock's comment.

"For camouflage, mostly. The smaller one is closer to the channel. That will be where we conceal the package until we can move it safely."

"How do you propose to get the 'package' from there," Harold motioned from the direction of the channel to the shack, "to here?"

Brock deliberated his answer as he filled the two mugs on the table with coffee from the steaming pot. He slid one of them across the table and, motioning for Harold to sit across from him, sat.

"That's what we need to work out between us in the next two days."

Brock watched his friend, noted the changes of expression around his eyes, the slight quiver of the red beard as his mouth and jaw relaxed ready to accept any explanation. How much more should he tell this man? It would be so easy to confide everything, even his feelings for Linda, but...He grasped the mug in front of him feeling the warmth from the coffee penetrate his fingers. The coffee was still almost too hot to drink, but he took a slow sip, letting his mouth become accustomed to the heat and cool the liquid so he could swallow it.

"You'll know all of it before the event actually takes place."

"Fair enough." Harold relaxed on the chair, grinned across the table and finished his coffee.

By the time the fire had burned down, the work was finished. Coffee mugs rinsed and turned upside down on the small utility table. The oil lantern put out. They let the wind slam the door behind them before they locked it, and drove down the narrow snow packed trail in the emptied Land Rover.

"It's too rough under there, man. You'll never be able to guide anyone through that. The chunks that you see standing on end go deeper underneath." Harold sat on the bunk nearest the stove, removing the wet suit as he talked. "It would take too long to get a man through."

Brock looked from his kneeling position as he closed the sliding door that covered the hole in the subfloor of the hut. "So, you've decided that the package we're expecting is a man."

"I guessed that almost at the start." Harold grinned at him and became serious again as he finished changing into his heavy clothing. "And I'm warning you, you're going to need a different plan." Brock noted the sincerity in the other man's voice as he finished closing the opening in the floor.

Harold continued. "I was under there how long? Five minutes? And I only passed the halfway marker. I'm sorry Brock but I think it will be too risky." He laid the wet suit on the padding on the floor to dry, poured two cups of coffee and joined Brock at the table.

"If we could just get closer to the channel," Brock expressed his thoughts. "There has to be a way. Things are happening like clockwork with the rest of the plans, and now this."

"I don't think it would help to move closer. It will have to be over the top instead of underneath. In that narrow channel he could be drawn right under the ship."

"Could we do it with ropes?"

"How would we get a rope to him?"

"Maybe we wouldn't need to supply the rope. There are always ropes on freighters."

"Sure, but how?"

"How strong is your casting arm?" Brock inquired.

"But wouldn't he be spotted? I mean, a man leaving a ship in that fashion."

"The ship is scheduled through here at two a.m. Only the night watch will be on duty and two of them will know what is happening. Perhaps some knock-out drops for the others," Brock suggested.

"Or a little commotion on the other side of the ship." Harold flashed his ready grin as though he had some ideas in the back of his mind concerning distractions. "How close to the channel can we drive the Land Rover?"

"I don't know. The ice is thick enough, but it's pretty rough out there." Brock studied the bit of coffee lingering in the bottom of the mug in front of him. A thought flashed through his mind. *How many answers do I think can be found in the bottom of one of these?* He mocked himself as he recalled fleetingly the expressions he had seen come and go in Linda's face as she had seemed to seek answers from this same source.

No time for even those thoughts now. The eminent problem was this one and the expedient solution was essential.

He took the coffee mugs to the dry sink, rinsed them in the small amount of water remaining in a bottle, and turned them upside down to dry. He could sense the questions rising in the other man's eyes – not about the problem they had been discussing, but a private wondering, as though Harold had an inclination to the thoughts that had flitted so faintly through Brock's mind. He was going to have to keep his mind on the problem in which Harold was involved. He could not share his feelings in that other direction.

"We'll have to see tomorrow about another plan, so we can report the changes that will have to be made to Brombke." He nodded toward the string of bass hanging from a hook over the dry sink. "Do you think we have enough evidence to prove we really have been fishing?"

"I think so. Richie will be proud of us, I'm sure."

Harold accepted the answer that was not an answer but only a postponement of an important decision. "Then we had better go."

"So it seems we'll have to do some practice casting along the channel." Brock pushed himself up from the chair where he had just finished talking with Brombke, went across the room to the closet and continued talking with Harold as he changed his light sweater for the heavier jacket that matched the corduroy jeans he was wearing. "Do you have a rod and reel here?"

"No, but I could get one."

"That won't be necessary. I brought one with me."

"You did?" Harold seemed surprised.

"I had it in New York so I just brought it along with some other bits and pieces of camouflage."

"Just something you happened to have handy."

"It's a good strong one with an extra long line. We'll go up there tomorrow and try some fishing in the channel."

"Hey. Do you have another receiver hidden somewhere?" Harold laughed as he asked the question, but Brock noted the seriousness in his eyes as he nodded toward the amber light blinking on and off in the light switch panel near the door.

"Oh, no, that's the signal from the house. Dinner is almost ready." He handed Harold the jacket that was dropped over the sofa when the two men entered the cottage a little over an hour before.

"Isn't there one in your room upstairs?"

"Now that you mention it, there is." Harold shrugged into his coat. "I've seen the lights blinking here and there, but," his eyes twinkled up at the taller man, "I seem to have a sixth sense when it comes time to eat."

Brock pulled the door firmly shut behind them following Harold along the snow-banked walk toward the house.

Already the early darkness of the long winter nights had moved in. The glare from the security light in the parking area threw the outlying area into deeper shadows. He noticed at once the light shining through the office window onto the snow-covered lawn. She usually tried to be finished in there by this time of day. The head bowed to the desk top showed definitely auburn in the glow of the desk lamp shining down upon it.

Brock glanced at Harold, who had paused to look questioningly toward the office.

Brock motioned him on into the house. Then he hurried along the short walk to the office and through the door.

The effects of her recent illness were still noticeable in the thinness of her arms and shoulders as they were stretched out amidst the papers on the top of the desk. The bones down the middle of her back and the edges of her shoulder blades showed clearly beneath the tightly drawn sweater.

"Linda!" He hurried to her chair and then stopped abruptly as he noticed her gentle breathing. Her right arm was turned so her left cheek rested on the back of her right hand. It rested on her other arm which was stretched out in front of her on the desk. *What ever can I do about you?* His mind questioned as he let the back of his fingers brush the soft palor of her cheek and then down her neck to the pulse that kept steady time in the hollow of her shoulder.

"Linda?" He cupped her chin in his other hand, raising her head a little, trying not to startle her. Soon, he noticed her eyes were open. The blur of sleep was still there as she blinked at him. His glance lingered on that softness and watched as they opened wide and she raised her head. With the waking, the softness hurried away and, although the flush of sleep still lingered, he felt the cool reserve return. She pulled away from his touch and straightened to sit up in the chair.

"Why are you here, Brock?" She glanced out the window and then shifted her gaze back to him. "What time is it?"

"You're cold!" He ignored her question. "Why are you still in the office? The heat shuts down in here at four o'clock. You know that." He didn't want to yell at her.

He yanked open the closet door and pulled out her jacket. When he turned back to her she was busy tidying the papers on the desk. "Leave it, Linda. If there's not another day to do that it won't need doing. How long have you been sleeping?"

"How do I know? I didn't look at the clock and then just decide to take a nap."

She picked up the folder lying on the desk, pushed back her chair and started toward the filing cabinet.

"I said leave it." He took the folder from her hand and slammed it down on the desk."Put this on." He forced the jacket into her hands, switched the button on the electric typewriter to off and turned to face her. She had not put the jacket on, only draped it across and around her shoulders as she turned to go.

He stopped her with a quick hand on her arm. As she turned the motion caused the jacket to fall to the floor, and the unexpected twist of his hand threw her off balance.

With one quick move he held her, wrapped his arms tightly around her. He felt the firm thrust of her body as she braced herself against his hold. But he held her there, one hand pressing against her shoulder and the other just at the top of the gentle curving below her waist. Her struggle against him sent exciting thrills of desire coursing through him. He smoothly moved his hand from her shoulder around to catch her chin between his thumb and fingers, tipping her head back.

"Look at you. Even now, this close..." and he tightened his arm around her. "You are cold, unfeeling. Well..." He lowered his head to capture her tightly closed lips within his own. She did not respond except her heart beat against his chest just a bit stronger, quicker, because of or in spite of her resistance, he could not determine. *Brock*, he thought. *This won't work. You'll never reach her by force.*

Just as quickly as it had begun, it ended. He turned from her and picked up the jacket from the floor. "Here. Put this on. Although I'm sure it can't be much colder out there than it has been in here the last few minutes." He held the jacket for her, then turned her again forcing her by sheer demand in his voice to look at him. *There is so much hurt there*, he noted.

"It doesn't mean a thing to you, does it, that your self pity causes so much pain and unhappiness to those around you? At first you give the impression of an unawakened school girl overgrown and unloved." At that remark she tried to turn away from him but he caught her by both arms drawing her close again. "But you're more like a frost-bitten embittered premature old maid."

He glared at her, wanting to shake her, anything to break through to her, at the same time hating himself for this outburst, but not being able to bring an end to it. "It would take more time than I can afford to use right now to cut through this iceberg." He let go of her, feeling guilty for the pain he knew he had caused with his words. He turned toward the door.

"But someway it has to be done."

She followed behind him and waited for him to open the door answering him softly.

"There isn't anyone around that could, or that really should, be concerned about it."

He hesitated about opening the door and stormed back at her. "Then leave this place to Carl and Harold. Take your mother and nephew with you to some sunny place. Surround yourself with sunshine and warmth. Make yourself available for God's sake. Somewhere there is a lovely, warm person under all that ice. Share it with someone soon or it will completely disappear."

He felt the cold in her voice, watched as it gripped her face and filled her eyes as she answered. "Don't concern yourself, Mr. Brockman. You'll be gone in a few weeks and it should not matter to you."

"No, it shouldn't, should it?" He wrenched open the door for her to go through and slammed it shut behind them.

Fishing for three days in a row. *This will have to be the last one for a while, or people will get suspicious.* Brock watched as Harold approached the smaller hut farther north of where he stood. It was necessary to see inside that hut as soon as possible. He was still very uneasy about those men and what they really were doing there. Good. Harold was signalling with the kerosene can. No one was there. Leaving the door to the hut unlocked he hurried across the snow-covered ice.

Other than what they had added, the interior of this hut was identical to the smaller one that Harold and Brock were using. The bunk was empty except for a sleeping bag and blanket. A small radio was on the shelf, a tackle box on the small table and some pasteboard packing boxes on the floor. A careful and thorough search of the pasteboard boxes disclosed packets of food that could be dissolved in hot water, a jar of instant coffee,a jar of sugar and small packages of instant coffee creamer. In the small, box-like cupboard nailed to the wall near the window Harold discovered two mugs, some plastic spoons, two badly scarred melamine plates, a jar of instant coffee, a bowl with sugar in it, and more packets of coffee creamer.

On top of the two-burner cooking plate was a beat up aluminum tea kettle and a sauce pan. Harold stood in the center of the floor looking around, his hand customarily running through his beard. "Well, whatever it is they are hiding, they surely know their business."

"We aren't sure they're hiding anything, but I still can't deny my suspicions. Why would they follow me, or us? Why are they here? You and I know they aren't fishermen."

Brock flung his upturned hand in distaste toward the cheap, porno-filled magazines.

He replaced the fishing equipment in the expensive tackle box open on the bunk. "Maybe they are lovers hiding an illicit love affair." Harold scowled at the thought and watched as the idea brought an expression of disgust to Brock's face.

Harold rubbed his hand around his head and down the back of his neck, tangling his fingers there as he sat cautiously on the one chair. "Although I can't see those two in a situationlike that. But, then, you never know."

"No, I can't see that sort of thing here; but there is something. I can't take a chance on believing that it's just coincidence." He stopped in his slow pacing around the small area, his back to the door. Training over the past fifteen years alerted him to slowly turn and face the opening door. "By the looks on your faces I think you haven't found it, but if you have I hope you didn't..." "Steve!" Harold pushed himself up from the rickety chair, his eyes suddenly filled with questions.

"What's your interest in this tent?" Steve flashed directly at Brock as he closed the door and stood in front of it. "And how did you get in?"

Harold displayed the set of master keys he had 'borrowed' from the lodge. "No one will know we've been here," he assured Steve.

The decision had been made for him, Brock realized. This man would have to know some of the facts anyway. He withdrew his wallet from his hip pocket and displayed it to Steve, showing him the identifications he carried.

"So, what has that to do with this hut?"

"Perhaps we should trade tales of woe or something," Brock suggested.

"We know, Brock, that Steve is here officially, so we..." Harold started.

"You know what?" Steve asked.

"Only that you are here in some official capacity for the government." Harold assured his brother-in-law.

"How did you discover that? I don't appreciate it, no matter how you learned what you think you know." Steve had entered the room and was sitting with one leg draped over the corner of the small table.

Brock was now leaning against the window frame, his arm resting along a shelf that was almost shoulder high and reached from the edge of the window to the corner. He had listened to the conversation between the two men, as he decided how much more he should tell. If he was going to need this man's help he would have to let him know some of the details. He felt the pull of flashing green eyes. Harold was trying to assure him of Steven's fidelity, he was sure, but other brothers had betrayed brothers many times before. He kept his gaze fixed on the toe of his shoe, feeling the draw of Harold's eyes. Then he looked directly at him – then at the younger man and gradually felt the tension of the situation dissolve and that inner assurance that had never failed him before was there. It only took a minute to make the decision.

Harold grinned at him, relaxed, and sat down straddling the chair he had left, his arms resting across the back of it, facing Brock.

Steve glanced from one to the other and then asked, "Well, who is going to talk?"

Brock changed his position near the window so that his other arm rested along the shelf and he could watch the expression on Steven's face. "We were very curious about your being here right at this time, so for security reasons headquarters in D.C. checked you out. Only what was ok'd for us to know. We haven't put any pressure on our source yet, if you know what I mean." "No deep dark secrets revealed yet." Harold assured him, then continued. "Carl has the two guys from this tent running errands in town, but I don't know how long they'll be gone. Let's not waste any more time."

"I still don't know why you two are here." "We think these two men are hiding something and we want to know what." Brock let his glance search around the hut again, his eyes checking for some place they might have overlooked. "This is the first time in three days that both of them have been away."

"Did we check the radio?" Harold motioned toward the small box-like object on the shelf near Brock's elbow.

"A RADIO." Brock jerked his arm away and looked at what appeared to be an inexpensive digital lock which was not running. Have they been listening?" He reached to pick it up, but kept his arm extended in mid-air as Steve commanded him not to touch it. It's it a..."

"What is there has nothing to do with you, I hope. But what's there has to stay right where it is." Steve surveyed the hut. "I hope you put everything back as you found it."

Harold closed the lid of the tackle box, leaving it on the bunk. "Now, everything is as it was." Later, after Steve had sped away on the snowmobile that had been parked between the two shacks, Brock waited in the Land Rover while Harold checked inside making sure the fire was out and everything was in order.

He watched, fascinated, as the wind whipped and whirled the light dusting of snowy powder erasing the evidence of their visit to the other hut, now only faintly visible through the whirling whiteness.

Was it just coincidence? The two ships going through the channel on the same night? Steve had assured them it was. This was the only channel and it was quickly becoming impassable. These two would probably be the last ones to come and go until the thaw in the spring and this was where they always passed. That was the only connection between the two happenings. He hoped Steve was sure of his men.

There couldn't be a leak now, not when Love's waiting was so nearly over. Yet, as Harold had suggested, perhaps since the two events were happening so close together both in time and place, the one could be played up to distract attention from the other.

Everyone was more concerned about the harm caused to thousands of people through the drug traffic than they would be about the safe return of one man.

He revved up the engine as Harold locked the door of the shack, flung the string of now frozen fish into the back of the Land Rover and climbed into the seat beside him. "Agnes will have enough fish to last until spring," Harold surmised as Brock turned the Land Rover toward the trail that Steve had taken a few minutes earlier.

Chapter Thirteen

"I wish Brock could have come with us today."

"Oh, why?" Linda glanced down at the boy walking so straight and tall beside her.

Richie replied, "He would have been surprised."

Linda looked closer at the rosy cheeked face turned up to meet her questioning glance. "Why should your recovery surprise him?" They hurried along the snow-cleared walk leading from the hospital. As they talked, the cold air caught their breath turning it into clouds of frozen vapor that drifted back over their shoulders.

"I didn't mean that." He turned his head away, watching for traffic before they crossed the street. The act of crossing over icy patches and through snow piled at curbs and the middle of the street between the two-way traffic lanes delayed further conversation until they were on the opposite corner. Turning toward the department store, they braced themselves against the rising wind.

With the idea of Brock being surprised at something, the good news of the morning became mixed and tangled with other thoughts racing through Linda's mind. Doctor Browne had just pronounced Richie completely recovered. When the two of them had come out of that examining room, so sure, so confident, Richie smiling so full of life, it felt as though her heart would burst with the joy that flooded through it. Richie had wrapped his arms around her and hugged her close.

"It's great, Aunt Linda." He had pushed back from her, searching her face.

"Aren't you glad?" She had watched as his gold flecked eyes brimmed with glistening moisture. She felt hidden strings being pulled, tense muscles relaxed and she smiled down into that beautiful, happy, little-boy face before she pulled him into her arms again. Surely this was a good sign that her life was coming to right again.

They pushed through the busy entrance to the department store into the comfort of a warmer place. She glanced at him again as he pushed back the hood of his parka and shoved his mittens into the slash pockets.

"Are we doing Christmas shopping?" he inquired as he watched her undo her coat and lay the hood back across her shoulders. "I didn't bring any money."

"Well," she felt the slightest bit of a smile pull at her wind-chilled lips. "I think there's an account open here for that purpose." As she put her gloves into her shoulder bag before going into the shopping area of the store, she heard Richie exclaim, "There, that's what I mean. That's the second time you've done it, and Brock sure would have…"

"Did what, Richie? I didn't do…"

"I know you didn't do it on purpose, that's what makes it so great."

She walked quickly away from him toward the area around the jewelry counters where the crowd was thinner, then stopped and turned to face him.

"Now, Richie, what have I done that seems to be so shocking?"

"You still don't know, do you? When Doc and I came out of the examining room and you realized I was okay and I hugged you, you smiled at me – even with your eyes.

Just a minute ago you did it again."

Of course. Richie would notice that. Strange, it had felt so natural. It was such a good feeling to have something to smile about; and, yes, Brock would have been sarcastically surprised, she supposed. She took the boy's hand in hers gave it a hard squeeze and felt the pressure returned.

"There haven't been many things to smile about it seems, Richie." *As for Brock being surprised, that wouldn't count for much, would it?*

She smiled deliberately this time, ruffled and then quickly smoothed his hair back in place. "Come on. We have some shopping to do."

Friends and acquaintances they met in the crowded aisles greeted them, some cheerily commenting on his quick recovery while others recalled painfully the accounts of the accident. Soon the fleeting smiles she felt come and go began to be achingly superficial. How could people force to mind the memory of the tragedy. Soon that pressure in her throat returned, harbinger of tears to come. She forced them back. Even Richie began to be irritable and sad faced.

Finally, after he selected slippers for Grandee, boxes of powder for Agnes and Marci, they made their way to the toy department to find some hand puppets for Angie.

While they were trying to make a decision on which puppets to purchase, Richie suddenly lost interest in the selection. He concentrated his attention on an area farther along the aisle. Two boys stood together there, watching Richie and Linda. Immediately she recognized them and her heart thrilled with a sudden warmth as, when they decided for sure who he was, the boys grinned and hurried through the shoppers toward Richie.

"Hey, Rich. Look at you. Man, this is great." The bigger boy grabbed him by the shoulders and swung him around, then gasped. "Wow, it's okay isn't it? I mean – I didn't want to hurt…"

Richie laughed with them, bent his knees, turned around. "Everything's fine, well almost. I can't play football or hockey for a while, but, I'll be back to school after the first of the year."

The younger of the two brothers, who was Richie's age, turned to Linda. "Mrs. Wilson, our mom is going to pick us up here in about an hour, can Richie stay with us until then?" We've got a lot of talking to do."

Linda checked her watch. I still have some shopping to do." Richie did need some time with his friends. "All right."

After arranging to meet him at the entrance where they had come in, she finished the purchase of the puppets and took them along with the other purchases to the gift wrapping center to be wrapped and picked up later.

Suddenly purchasing gifts for others lost its appeal. She really should buy something new to wear for the holidays. Everything she owned was too old and too large.

She wandered through the dress department, hesitating, waiting for others to make their selections, being pushed or crowded out of the way. Was it so important? Nothing seemed to matter as far as she was concerned. Her hands instinctively brushed the sleeve of a dress, checked the length of a skirt or examined the neckline of a blouse. Then, she saw it. A soft, eggshell-white, dinner dress. It was almost extreme in its simplicity.

Long straight sleeves, fastened the wrist with tiny crystal buttons. A slight fullness had been worked into the shoulder seams, a perfect disguise for the amount of weight she had lost. The back of the neck

was trimmed with soft, matching braided cord that followed the vee neckline in the front as it crossed on its way to the waistline.

"It's very attractive," the salesgirl assured her. "It's the only one of the style in the store, and it will go beautifully with your coloring. Would you care to try it on?"

"No, thank you. I wouldn't have occasion to wear such a dress."

"Oh, but Christmas, the holidays, even at home..."

"No. But, I think I am interested in a coat you have."

"Oh, well, the coats are..."

"Yes, I know. Thank you." Now why had she mentioned that coat. Of course she did need a new one. She glanced at her watch. There was still time. She turned in the direction the sales girl had indicated. Yes, there was the style on the model but it was red.

There was no salesperson in the area so she searched the displays, hoping. It was a beautiful coat, it had fit perfectly, comfortably snug and just as she liked. Or was she just imagining that because, but, no. She had liked it even before he had stopped behind her, before their eyes had met in the mirror. Was she letting his opinion determine even what she wore? No, of course not. She did like the coat and would...Yes, here it is.

"May I help you with a coat?" The salesperson seemed to come from nowhere.

"Well, perhaps, but this one is much too large. Do you have it in a smaller size?"

"No, I'm sorry. That's the last one in that color in that style."

"Oh, I see."

"We do have it in red..." The salesgirl indicated the one on the model, "and we have the color you like in another style." She removed the coat from a nearby display.

"No thank you. I was interested in that one coat only." As Linda turned away the salesgirl offered to try to order what she wanted. Linda politely refused, turning slowly toward the entrance.

She still felt the need to buy something new for herself, but...she stopped to examine some scarves on display, softly shimmering in their attractive arrangement.

Some were of brightly colored silk, others softly shaded pastels in wispy chiffon, one, a softly shaded green with a shadowy print of pine tress outlined with a faint line of gold would have been just the thing to wear with the coat, but...oh, well.

It was almost time to meet Richie. Quickly she made her way back to the dress department, the same salesgirl was there. In a few minutes the white dress, exactly the right size and length, was among the order of things to be collected after lunch and she was on her way to meet Richie. She could see him waiting, not too patiently , for her at the main entrance.

He was full of excitement and chattered about what his friends had been doing and the unexpected chance of getting to see and talk with them. They turned the corner on their way to where the Mercedes was parked when he stopped suddenly.

"You did say that I could buy a present for Brock while we were in town today."

"Oh, yes, and this is the Games Shop. All right, I will help you find something.." Then the thought came pushing through – should she purchase something? Richie would expect her to have a gift under the tree for Brock. But what? She noticed that the shop was more than just a store with games. There were bar supplies, chess sets, desk sets, barometers, etchings in crystal made into paperweights. There were bookends, pen holders, and ornaments set into wooden bases. One of them especially caught her eye. Yes. And if he was not at the farm for Christmas, or if in some way it was not proper to give it to him she could always give it to Harold or Steve, or keep it as a remembrance. She would buy it just in case. The six inch crystal oval with the delicate carving of pine trees on a snow covered hillside, on a sturdy base of polished wood took its place on the counter along with the already gift-wrapped game of Richie's choosing.

The clerk produced its duplicate from the stock room and it, too, was quickly packaged in an attractive gift box.

The Mercedes was parked in a parking lot between the game store and the coffee shop where they were planning to have lunch so the packages were put into the trunk of the car as they passed.

As usual it was a busy place but the hostess led them to a table set for two near a window. It was Richie's first time in the restaurant since the accident and, as there was a favorite sandwich on the menu, he wasted no time in telling her what he wanted. Then he began exploring the surrounding tables with his eager eyes. Linda watched his expression change, his smile come and go as he would catch someone's glance or wave at a friend, and then...

"There's Brock and Mrs. Johnson."

She glanced quickly to where he indicated.

"Can we..."

"No, Richie, we don't..." She reminded him of his manners. "It might be intruding on their privacy."

They are truly acting as though they were the only ones in the restaurant, she thought. Evidently they had not yet been served for they were holding hands across the table, deeply engrossed in each other's words.

Meanwhile, the young waitress was prompt with the service, and because Richie was hungry they were soon finished. Richie had concentrated his attention on the other table and had at last attracted Brock's attention.

"Can't I go and say hello to Mrs. Johnson, at least?"

She could do nothing else. It would seem rude indeed not to let him say hello.

Quickly he was back with an invitation from Mrs. Johnson to join them for coffee and as Richie added his plea to it, she agreed. It would be just as rude to refuse.

Apparently their meal had also been a simple one for the waitress had cleared away the dishes and was there with the extra cup for coffee and a glass of milk for Richie as he and Linda were seated. Whatever else Linda could feel about the woman seated between herself and Richie, she knew without a doubt that she was beautiful, quietly, simply beautiful in every way. How could she have imagined anything else – even her voice now as she inquired, "How was the doctor's report, Mrs. Wilson? Whit told me that today was the day."

That achy feeling was there again. This softly speaking woman with her gentle use of that special name for the man seated at the table, had the power to do this. There were no tears to force back, but she needed to make her reply around that uncomfortable grip. She tried to smile, but it didn't come.

"Everything is fine. He will still be a little stiff if he neglects the exercises, or weak if he doesn't eat properly, but there's no danger of either of those things happening."

"That is wonderful, I'm glad for you, Richie." Mrs. Johnson's eyes glowed with her sincerity. "You will be going back to your classes after the first of the year?"

"Yes, Ma'am. I never thought I would be this glad to go back to school." He grinned as he answered her.

Brock laughed at his comment and then... "Aren't you happy about this, Linda?" There was a strange, almost angry deriding look in his eyes and his mouth was drawn into a grim hard line.

"Of course she's happy, Brock. We're celebrating with a shopping trip and lunch here. She even..."

Linda quickly interrupted his exuberant reply. "Thank you for your part in it, Brock. I am very pleased about it." Her thanks to Brock had begun with a warm feeling in her heart, but by the time it had been pushed up around the lump it came out cold and hard. She must leave. She could not finish the coffee she had not even taken a sip of, had not wanted.

"It was very nice meeting you again, Mrs. Johnson, and thank you for your kindness to my nephew." She pushed the cup of coffee back from in front of her.

It was certain that the coffee was the only thing she could object to, other than the upsetting feelings going rampant inside her.

"We really must go, Richie." She slid her chair back and continued. "Thank you for the coffee, Brock." Barely raising her eyes fleetingly to meet the hardness in his as he stood while she left the table.

She could feel those eyes following her as she stopped at the cashier counter to pay her check, even as she slipped her arms into her coat and buttoned it. Buttoned it!

She had almost turned to look back at him while her fingers worked up the front of her coat, lingering, remembering, as she buttoned the top button and pulled the hood up to cover her head, leaving the ever present wisps of hair blowing loose.

They went out into the biting cold of the rising wind. The drive home was more bothersome than she had anticipated. By the time she stopped to collect their purchases and negotiated the traffic through the main street the wind was blowing extremely hard.

She needed to hurry on the straight roads so she would reach the curved, winding road before the drifts made it impassable. If only Richie weren't along, or if he could possibly go to sleep.

But he sat stiffly erect in the passenger seat, watching as the wind whirled and piled the snow like a white froth of whipped cream being pushed and peaked with the broad blade of a baker's spatula. Twice he turned his face toward her, seeking assurance.

"It will be all right, Richie." She smiled at him, offering what he so desperately needed.

"I won't have to hurry now. We can make it home before the roads get icy or the drifts get too deep. Relax if you can."

How can I offer him any comfort, she mocked at her own trembling nerves. It was even difficult for her to keep from recalling that other winter night and the pain of it. What could she do for him? One more curve in the road and the turn into the drive. At least it was still daylight and she could see where the road turned and went on between the two parallel fences. Finally, she turned the car into the driveway and heard Richie release his tense body with one long shuddering sigh.

"We're here." He relaxed, leaning his head back against the plush covered seat.

"I'm glad I made this first trip through a snow storm with you, Aunt Linda." He pushed the handle down that opened the door next to him as soon as she stopped the car inside the garage. "It won't be so bad next time."

There was no need for more words between them.

She put her arm across his shoulders and drew him close to her as he waited for her to open the trunk and remove the packages.

All the necessary work in the office was finalized. Everything finished or put away until the new year. The New Year! What would it bring? With her part of the business concluded she had time to wonder about the other reason for Brock's coming to the farm. Surely an end to the secrecy, the tension she noticed in the movements of Brock and Harold. Could it concern their frequent fishing trips. There had been no suspicious telephone calls or people coming and going as Brock had inferred. *Who is Mrs. Johnson or the grandfather he had mentioned.. he had said it involved people who were very dear to him and obviously Mrs. Johnson was that. He had called her 'Love' and 'Dear'.* There had been no evidence of violence but, she did sense the building up of tension around the two – no, three men. She was certain Steve had become involved in whatever was happening. Whatever it was, she felt it would in some way affect her life and Richie's. She prayed fervently there would be no more tragedy. There had been heartaches enough to last both of their life spans and some left over. Whatever was imminent she had vowed, it could not hurt anymore. She just would not permit it. She would in some way keep from becoming involved. After all, Brock had warned her, cautioned her about it. But he had not said what was going to happen. They seemed to be very casual about the trips they made. But why should it bother her? They must be fishing as they would have everyone believe – there were all those pounds of fish in the freezer.

Marci did seem a little concerned about Harold being out so late – and what would Agnes do with any more fish? But, after dinner they had gone in the station wagon and they were surely not dressed for fishing.

The house was exceptionally quiet. Marci and Angela were already asleep, or at least upstairs. Mum and Agnes had finished a few chores in the kitchen and then retired. Richie had eagerly accepted an invitation from the parents of the boys he had met in the department store and was spending the night and all day Saturday at their home.

The deep cover of snow across the front lawn glistened in the moonlight. The tall bare birch trees stood stark like guardian sentinels along its boundary. The clock in the foyer had already chimed eleven. Linda stood by the study window where she had stood many times during the happier years of her life, watching for automobile lights to come around the bend in the road, trying to judge which car would turn into the drive. *Dear Lord. Is that what I am doing? Am I waiting for him? How can I do this? Where is my pride, my common sense? He can never mean anything to me.* She berated herself as she pulled the soft collar of her velour robe closer around her neck and chin. Her throat ached, her hands trembled. This was preposterous. She remembered that there had been something special in the way he had touched her. The feelings he had caused to stir deep inside her would no longer be denied. There were times when she was sure he could have seen the iceberg was slowly melting – from the inside at least.

But then, she remembered, *He has Mrs. Johnson. For some reason they are only waiting and she will be so right for him. There's warmth and tenderness there as she looks at him. She didn't even try to conceal her love for him as it glowed in her eyes that day in the lunch room. The gentleness of his hands as they held hers across the table.*

Then the memory of her own hands being held in his caused her to clench them even more tightly as they held her robe in place. Her shoulders quivered slightly – a flood of jealous envy for what she could never have swept through her. Letting herself love him would be too painful, too dangerous to her peace of mind.

This would never do. If she could just bear it through the next few days. These feelings needed to be curbed. *I shouldn't be standing at the window.*

Oh, too late. Lights from the road had turned into the driveway. Already the station wagon had parked in the snow-cleared area.

The fire was still burning in the living room fireplace as she hurried from the study thinking to get to her room before Harold came through to go upstairs. But as she reached the area leading into the living room she heard their voices in muted conversation as they entered the family room through the door from the patio. The living room sofa was turned to face the fireplace, its back toward the kitchen area. Quickly she slipped into the room and stretched full length on the sofa, fixing her eyes to stare into the flames. Surely if they saw her they would think her asleep. The men's voices mingled, the words indiscernible at first, as they lingered in the family room. Their conversation became clearly distinct as they approached the living room area.

She tucked her chin further down into the softness of her robe hiding as much of her face as she could to seem, indeed, to be asleep. She closed her eyes. Oh, why had she not been more alert and hurried to her room before they came in. She really did not want to eavesdrop on this conversation. People always heard things they should not know in these situations.

"Well, she is packed, ready to leave the house, Harold. Cartons with her personal things are ready for the movers when they arrive next week."

There was a pause and then the soft click of the switch accompanied the gleam of light illuminating the stairs and upper hallway. Their voices became clearer as they passed behind the sofa.

"Every thing of mine is out of the cottage except the radio and record player, of course, the things I will need for the next few days." Her eyelids quivered and her lashes fluttered until she had to force them to lay still against her cheeks while her eyes adjusted to the light filtering through them. Surely they would see her soon and quit talking. *I can't fake a waking-up scene now.*

They did not see her and Brock continued. "These next two nights are going to be rough. I'm glad you and Steve are here." Another short pause. "I hated not to be able to tell Linda but, well, when all of this is settled we can all get on with plans for the rest of our lives."

She dared not open her eyes. This was not something she should be hearing but how could she leave now. The quiet creaking of the first step up let her know that Harold was on his way upstairs and Brock would be coming back through the...

"Three years is a long time to be separated from someone you love so desperately, Brock." Harold paused to remark.

"Yes. Thank the Lord it will soon be..."

The sound of Brock's voice dropped abruptly. Linda knew she had been discovered.

"Linda?" The surprised questioning in his voice halted Harold on the second or third step.

"Where?" He hesitated, waiting for an answer.

"She has fallen asleep on the sofa. Go on up. I'll just leave."

Linda had to continue feigning sleep. The soft sound of shoes brushing through the deep pile of the carpet told her he was coming toward the sofa. She quickly snuggled her chin a little lower, hiding more of her face in the folds of her robe. She felt the extra warmth over and around her as he covered her with the knitted afghan that had been folded over the back of the sofa. She ignored the tremor that passed through her as his fingers brushed cool against her cheek and, again, when he folded the other end of the soft woolen cover around and under her nylon clad feet. He paused for a moment leaning over that end of the sofa and she realized she had left her slippers there on the floor. She sensed him standing there at the side of the sofa. She could not open her eyes now. Then she heard two deeply drawn breaths – drawn, then slowly released. What was he going to do? She heard him move away.

The fireplace. She could hear the sound of the log being turned, the embers stirred. Then the density of the light changed. Harold must have turned the upstairs light off. A gentle glow along with a crackling sound now filled the silence. Mingled with that sound she heard the soft swish of his shoes again through the carpet. He passed behind the sofa, paused just a step there before going on. With closed eyes she followed him, hurrying now, out through the door to the patio and the walk to the cottage. The click of the patio door latch signaled to her that she could now 'wake up'.

The glow from the log now blazing in the fireplace filled the room with renewed warmth. She could see that Brock had turned the log and brushed back the embers making it safe to burn a little longer.

Linda remained there as he had left her, snuggled warmly under the afghan. She recalled the gentleness of his hands, the nearness of him as he leaned over tucking her in. What would have been his reaction if she had pulled him down close, winding her arms around his shoulders. What would it be like to kiss him as she would like, not a hard angry.... He had Mrs. Johnson, "love" as he so tenderly called her. They were planning to go away together. Hadn't he just said "Three years was a long time." But what about five years?

What about five years? Strangely, revealingly, Phil's death seemed a long ago unanswered incident, a feeling forgotten, or replaced by something more forceful, more urgent. The only familiar haunting sensation was the stinging moistness at the back of her eyes, the throbbing ache of loneliness at the base of her throat. She flung the afghan away from her, pushed herself up from the sofa, and hurried to her room. A quick splash of warm, then cold water to her face, a glass of water to wash down the capsules Dr. Browne still insisted she take and then her robe was folded and placed on the nearby chair, and she slipped into bed between the cool sheets. Not even the open sky visible through the pulled back drapes made a difference this night.

Richie arrived home late Saturday evening filled with excitement from the day he had spent with friends. "They insisted that I have hot chocolate and cookies and a sandwich before I came home, Grandee, so I really can't eat much dinner." The pot of rich vegetable-beef stew simmering on the stove filled the room with its own special aroma. On the counter adjoining the stove top was an assorted supply of crackers and cheese spreads and a large crystal bowl containing a freshly tossed salad and a selection of the family's favorite salad dressings. At Linda's insistence Richie did agree to a large glass of milk and some of his favorites from the crackers and cheese selection. He took his regular place at the table while the others served themselves from the stew crock and salad bowl then joined him.

"Where are Brock and Harold?" He looked at Marci. "And Steve isn't here either."

"They went away – fishin' again." Little Angela informed him, very adult in her exasperation. "We don't need any more fish." Linda, working in the study and library with family accounts and correspondence most of the afternoon, had not especially noticed the absence of the three men. She tried to soften the little girl's agitation.

"Oh, it's rather dark to fish..." she hesitated, noticing Marci's uneasy silence. "Is something wrong, Marci?"

"No – no. Only they seemed very tense about something and Steve doesn't usually go along." She shook her head slightly at Linda as though she didn't want to say any more where Angela could hear. They sent the children to bed and enjoyed the warmth of the fireplace with after dinner tea.

The clock in the entryway had struck the eleventh hour and then chimed the quarter hour, with the two young women still waiting. Marci spoke. "Well. They are three grown men. I'm sure they can do for themselves whatever they need when they come in. I need to be up early with Angela in the morning, so I'm going to bed."

In the dim light from the dying fire the signs of strain and concern on her friend's face seemed to soften but Linda knew they were there. She wondered if Harold had not told his wife even as much as Brock had revealed to her. She could not betray Brock's confidence, but she did try to comfort Marci. "I agree with you, and I'm off to bed too."

The effect of the tiny pill Doctor Browne had recommended to solve her inability to go to sleep was just that, tiny. She needed only one to relax her tensed nerves, allowing her to drop into a shallow unconsciousness and to sleep without drugging her senses. Only occasionally did she feel the need, and so, even though she had gone immediately to sleep after taking this one, the light flashing through the open drapes at the window and reflecting off the dressing table mirror awakened her.

Her first thought was that something had gone wrong and then she realized what it was. "He's back. Nothing went wrong. That's the Land Rover."

She pushed back the comforter and hurried to the place near the window where she could see and knew she could not be seen. Yes, it was the Land Rover – but only two men – Harold and Steve. *Where is Brock?*

He was not with them.

Why, oh, why?

She continued to watch – perhaps he was in the back. But no, no one else was there. Her eyes flashed to the clock on the dresser – four a.m. *Four a.m.?*

The next half of that early morning hour was spent in deriding herself for permitting her emotions to become involved. The tears came unbidden burning her cheeks with a deep longing that had never been completely smothered. She had loved

Phil, surely, but not with such urgency. She was admitting she loved this man. Desired him. Wanted his arms around her to share her love. The tantalizing memory of those few brief incidents only made her want more – to be completely possessed by him – to share...

There was no escape for her. He belonged to Mrs. Johnson. Three years they had been separated and there was no way she would try to come between them.

Faintly she heard the two men enter the house and make their way up stairs. She stopped her pacing at the bathroom door. If ever she needed to lose herself in sleep it was now. Determinedly she washed down two of the tiny pills with very warm water from the tap and then stretched herself, face down on the rumpled bed. Haphazardly pulling the soft sheet and comforter over her back and shoulders she rested her cheek on her folded hands and waited for sleep to return.

Neither of the two men put in an appearance for breakfast. Marci assured Linda they were both all right, just sleeping. "Do you know what is happening?" Her eyes held anxious questions that she seemed not to want to put into words as they met Linda's across the table while preparing breakfast. "Harold seemed so tense and it was evident they had been out in the cold for a very long time. I've learned not to question him, only he is not in the service any more..."

Linda tried to give her a comforting answer, but how, when she so desperately needed to know herself. "All I know is that Brock is involved in something that concerns someone he loves very much. Harold is helping him and their plan is to be completed before he leaves here."

"But what?" Marci's frustration was evident.

Linda only shook her head.

Words refused to be pushed through the mounting pressure in her heart and throat.

Linda turned from the table to reach the coffee cups on the counter and to hide the fear that was flooding through her. "We will just have to wait and see." She managed the familiar platitude in an almost normal voice, and set the cups carefully on the table.

"They can sleep while we are at church, and get their own breakfast when they want it."

She moved a chair out from the table as her mother and Richie came into the kitchen. "You have time for breakfast, Mum. Agnes has gone for the early church service."

"The men are not in for breakfast?"

How could she tell what she didn't know. *Perhaps it has already happened. Brock didn't return with them.* Suddenly, part of the conversation which she had overheard flashed through her memory: "She is ready to go," and "all of my personal things are out of the cottage."

Her mother looked at her with a questioning glance as Linda repeated, barely audibly: "We will just have to wait and see."

Chapter Fourteen

Once again Richie had accepted an invitation to spend the afternoon with friends eager to renew relationships with classmates with whom he shared both school and church backgrounds. Linda could not, nor would she deny him these pleasures. His recovery was the only thing she would recognize as the source of peace that had in some measure returned into her life. Perhaps there would be a few uneasy times yet ahead for him, but they would... Deliberately she changed the direction she knew these thoughts would take her. She must not let them wander back.

Carefully she guided the Mercedes through the garage doors and turned off the engine as she stopped at the foot of the steps leading into the family room. She pocketed the keys, got out of the car and opened the door into the house for Marci, who held a sleeping Angela against her shoulder. She continued to hold the door open for her.

Agnes was in the kitchen. Lunch was nearly ready.

The fragrance that filled the house, however, was not from what was being served for the meal. Men's voices came from the living area, so apparently did the fragrance. Marci followed Mrs. Farnsworth through the hall, accepting her suggestion of putting the little girl on Richie's bed to finish her nap before lunch. Although Linda intended to follow them through to her own room, the scent and the sound of the male voices deterred her progress. She stopped at the entrance to the living room.

Harold's voice came from the far corner beyond the fireplace. "You're going to have to move it out about another foot. The branches are too tight against the wall."

Linda gasped in surprise. The "it" the men were trying to position in the corner was the "it" that was emitting the wondrous spicy aroma that filled the house. The beauty of the silvery blue spruce filled the corner beyond the fireplace, touched the ceiling and spread its branches out into the room as though eager to receive the adorning that was to come.

"When did you bring it?" Her question was little more than a whisper, but Harold grinned at her and replied, making his way out from among the enveloping branches.

"We thought you would like a surprise." His glance caught and held hers. "Brock and I cut it the other day and we, nodding his head toward Steve, thought today would be a good day to bring it in." "Agnes said it should go here this year," Steve added with some force in his voice as he tightened the screws that held the tree firmly in the stand.

"Yes. It's beautiful there."

The blue lights, a family tradition since Linda's earliest memories of her childhood, reflected throughout the areas adjoining the living room wherever there was a polished surface or glass or metal. They especially highlighted the delicate crystal and silver ornaments that were in open boxes on the floor and chairs around the tree, ready to be carefully placed in prominent places or snuggled away among the branches.

Later, the significance of the tree's presence in the house seemed, like a cloak of finest wool, to wrap her heart in a protective garment, enclosing her in peace.

Marci had much to do with creating that feeling, Linda was certain. The first moments of seeing the tree brought apprehension. Brief memories of other years, the tragic years, flashed through her mind. Marci, sensing what was happening, insisted that they couldn't just stand there. "Let's have lunch first and then get at the trimming of this new Christmas tree."

Together they brought to the living room lengths of garlands, more strings of lights, delicate ornaments and many family keepsakes and treasures of past years were carefully placed in their special places on that stately tree. Linda took the empty cartons back to the attic for storage again in their proper places until after the Twelfth Night celebration.

The amber light in the wall switch had just begun to glow when Linda finished her task and went down for the evening snack that was ready in the kitchen. The tree, the fireplace, the warmth of the seasonal amenities glowed in the living room as she passed through – yet a chill surrounded her. Her hands were cold. Any physical warmth had quickly fled in the chilled air of the unheated attic and the chill clung to her arms and shoulders even now. Although there was some semblance of peace returning to her life, it all seemed to come from those in the house with her at that particular time. That inner glow was just not there.

Glaring lights of the returning Land Rover flashed through the windows of the patio and shined briefly into the kitchen and family room as the vehicle turned on the snow packed lawn between the house and cottage then turned to flood the lawn with light as it stopped there.

"What on earth." Mrs. Farnsworth caught her breath in a sharp gasp and hurried to look through the door.

"Harold said they would be bringing back the fishing equipment;" Marci offered in explanation.

"But that goes into the storage shed," Mrs. Farnsworth reasoned.

"Brock was using some of his own. Perhaps they are returning his."

Linda was busy at the counter sorting candles, folding linens, choosing what to use during the coming holidays and what should be stored away for another time. The sound of doors slamming after the lights were extinguished carried into the house, but the sound of the voices of those who had arrived, if indeed there was any conversation, could not be heard. The light inside the cottage flashed on casting a large rectangular reflection through the open door onto the snow. There should have been three men, Linda pondered, but as she watched through the window she could not be sure. Some of them made two or three trips from the Land Rover into the cottage. As she continued to watch she noticed that two of them seemed to remain in the vehicle as the other two – two? (But there should be three.) Now one came from the cottage and seemed to be assisting someone out of the Land Rover. But who, and why? Was one of them injured? Evidently not, for the two went into the cottage and the other one drove the Land Rover away.

It all happened so smoothly and quickly!

Mrs. Farnsworth turned away from the door. Marci glanced up from the floor in front of the fireplace where she was sitting wrapping gifts. "There, at least that is finished. Harold despises gift wrapping, and I've finished just in time."

Linda felt her questioning glance reach out to her and caught the concern in her friend's eyes. "What is happening?" Marci's voice came in a mere whisper.

"They surely will want some coffee." Mrs. Farnsworth murmured and set about making a fresh supply. Still the question remained in Marci's expression as her eyes pleaded with Linda. "Can there have been some trouble?" She quivered, hastily packing the brightly wrapped packages into a large department store type shopping bag. Then Marci moved closer to the table where Linda had just finished her task. "It's not like Harold to be so secretive about things. Do you think..."

How could she explain to Marci, Linda cried inwardly, when she did not have an answer for her own fears and doubts. She gathered her sortings, put the storage-bound into boxes and the decoration-bound on the far end of the counter to be put in their proper places later. She tried to answer Marci. "You know Harold will tell you about whatever it is, Marci, when he is free to do so. It does seem that the three of them are involved, so whatever..."

The opening door interrupted their conversation.

"UMmmmm that coffee smells great." Steve hurried into the room, removing knitted gloves and cap.

Harold followed, going directly to embrace Marci and plant the usual noisy hello kiss on the eager, upturned, trembling lips awaiting him. "Hi, Darling. I'm sorry to be so late but a few difficulties developed." He glanced at his watch as he removed his gloves.

"But we aren't very late, are we? It seemed like it took so much longer than we expected."

He included Linda and her mother in his glance as he apologized and grinned at them.

"Anyway, the fishing is a thing of the past. I hope you have enough fish to see you through the winter," he joked and then turned to Marci.

"Honey, that coffee will hit the spot. We'll go up and change," he paused a moment as Steve excused himself and went toward the stairs, "then we'll be right down. Brock will be in later."

"Harold, is anything wrong?" The anxious words came through before she could stop them.

"Why no, Linda." The soft, understanding, green eyes held the same assurance as was evident in his voice. "What could be wrong? We're all just a bit cold and tired."

"I'm sorry. Don't let me detain you. Go and get comfortable." Linda turned to the cupboard for the mugs and sugar for coffee. Of course, she reminded herself, Brock would change in the cottage. Why should she be so uneasy about his not coming in with the other two men. He was a grown man, could do for himself. Besides she had not the right to...*But who had driven away in the Land Rover?* The question would not quit going through her mind.

A slight commotion at the front door interrupted Linda's musings as Richie returned from visiting his friend. Linda hurried through the hall from her room into the kitchen to greet the father of Richie's friend, talking there with Mrs. Farnsworth who had offered him a cup of coffee. "No, thank you. I must get back to the family. Richie was no trouble, We all enjoyed his visit and are pleased at his recovery. Good night."

"How was your visit, Richie?"

"I had a great time, Aunt Linda." Richie removed his hooded parka, mittens, and snow boots, put them into the laundry room, then slipped his feet into the warm slippers waiting there for him.

Where is Brock? Does he know that Richie has come back from his visit? she wondered as she closed the patio door just as the man was leaving. And there was Brock coming quickly down the steps and walk to the patio door. He came in and went to the kitchen just behind Linda. The scent was familiar. Just the faint aroma of after shave lotion entered the realm of her senses as it always did, causing an unwelcome awareness of him to stream over and around her. The increased depth of the lines around his eyes and his tightly drawn mouth denied Harold's assertion that nothing was wrong. When she asked, he avoided answering her question. Instead, he reached for her hand, held it firmly in his for a brief pressure, then turned to greet Richie as the boy closed the laundry room door behind him.

Her eyes met Brock's for just a moment. In them she saw understanding of her concern for her nephew. She hoped desperately he would believe what he saw in her eyes was only that.

"What smells so good?" Richie exclaimed. "It smells just like..."

The young eyes searched the adult faces for confirmation of his own answer to his question. He smiled, "You have a fire in the living room. And a Christmas tree!" He turned from them and hurried in, only to stop suddenly in the middle of the living room.

Immediately, Linda was behind him, her hands resting firmly on his tensed shoulders.

She felt the shudder build up inside him and heard the deep sob come from him as he flung his arm up across his forehead to hide his face. Suddenly, he turned to rush staggeringly to his room, the sobs becoming louder and more forceful.

Marci and Harold sat silently observing as Brock took Linda into his grasp when she turned to follow Richie.

"Let me go." She gasped, trying to remove the restraining hand. "He needs..."

The hard steel shining in his eyes caught the angry fire blazing in hers as she tried harder to free her arm from his grip. The fire only added a glow to the shine as he held her gaze. Lowering his hand to grasp hers. He lessened the grip on her arm. "He knows only one way to handle his grief, Linda, but spare him the humiliation of doing it in your presence. Let him cry, while he is still tender enough to indulge."

The incredulity of his seemingly harsh remark flooded her face with the strength of her anger. Slowly she lowered her attention to the hand holding hers. She shook her head slowly in denial of his reasoning and slipped her hand from his. She stepped aside to pass Brock and go into the boy's room, only to be stopped by the concerned plea in her mother's voice.

"He's right, my dear. This is a difficult thing for Richie to face. But he must face it in his own self. Let him cry. Find his release from the tragedy that is still fresh in his mind and at the same time he will find and recognize his own inner strength."

In the sincere concern evident in those words, Linda recognized the strength and wisdom that had always been the guiding factor in her mother's life. She looked from that dearly loved face into the eyes of the man standing so near. She let her eyes travel to the strong tense mouth, down the length of him and back to the broad shoulders and strong arms where she longed to find... It was either fling herself into those arms seeking comfort for her own heartaches or... She clenched her hands stiffly at her sides, turned her back to the others and went past the still closed door of her nephew's room and entered her own. She closed the door and pushed the button on the lock to insure her privacy.

There were no lights lit in the room. Only a dim grayness showing through the closed drapes guided her to the windows. Quickly the cord was pulled and the drapes parted, displaying for her the ever present source of her only comfort. There were the trees, resplendent in their lacy covering of white. Hushed and silent, just the tops of the tallest ones gently swaying in the whispering breeze.

The cold which had been held captive between the thermo drapes and the window glass reached into the room, surrounded her, gently cooling the heat of the anger that engulfed her. It was still necessary, even after five years, to keep the tears from coming and endure the burning behind her eyes. The desperate groan of loss which she would not allow to come forth from the back of her throat was again forced down. As she watched the trees, the clouds, the stars, she tried in vain to lose her sorrow in the ever expanding nothingness beyond the view from her window.

Am I mourning Phil forever? This seems too recent, too new. That memory had diminished. These new yearnings were no longer connected with the tragedy of five years ago. The events of the present time, the happenings of the past few weeks – other than Richie's recovery – seemed to at once bring new hope and dash all expectations. In this moment of accepting the new realization, Linda willed the very personal loneliness, the heartache of the present and despair for her future into that great expanse of nothingness.

And sent a prayer along with it: *God, if You can bring something good out of it into my life, it would be a miracle.*

Suddenly, feeling the cold, she changed from the corduroy, wrap-around skirt and plaid shirt into a soft, fleecy gown and wrapped herself in the warmth of her velour robe.

Then she curled up in the chair by the window. Slowly the sense of pain turned to numbness and she drifted into sleep. By noon the next day she finished her Christmas correspondence and decided, with her mother and Marci, on the menu and special treats for Christmas day and the weekend that followed. She had taken special time for a satisfying conversation with Richie while they shared some milk and cookies. She assured him there was no reason for him to be embarrassed by his crying. "It's not a sign of weakness," she told him. "I'm sure you'll gain control over it as you grow older, but don't be ashamed of your feelings." She tried to comfort him and by the end of their talk he seemed back to normal.

Richie was cheerful and receptive to Harold's and Steve's banter as they talked with him at lunch. They were making tentative plans for a sledding party after Christmas. "Do you think you will be up to it?" They teased.

The coming and going of the two men whipped through the back of Linda's mind all day. There was the faint recall of the snowmobile returning while she slept in her chair the night before, and Carl had gone away in it again just before lunch. Brock had not come in for breakfast, but had driven away in his station wagon in the middle of the morning. Harold and Steve had been in and out with arms full of firewood, baskets of apples and vegetables from the storehouse that would be needed for the holidays. Being very helpful – it seemed to be a special effort. Soon after lunch they both went away in the Land Rover and returned near dinner time, one driving the Land Rover, the other on the snowmobile. Brock had not returned. Harold tried to explain his absence from the dinner table. "He needed to go into town on some personal business." His eyes met Marci's warning glance. Then he turned to fix a questioning look at Linda, which he held until she felt an embarrassed flush creep up from the open neck of her shirt to blend with the soft shading of her hair. *What is Harold thinking? Does he know of my internal feelings? Does he expect me to voice my concern of Brock's comings and goings? Surely he has no idea.*

The work of the day had kept her hands and mind occupied. The fellowship of the other three women eased the inner tension. The two children were now in their beds.

Steve claimed that he had a chore to finish and left soon after dinner in the snowmobile.

Harold finished stacking the wood by the fireplaces and hung some mistletoe here and there. He and Marci seemed very much at home in the house. After her mother and Agnes retired, she quietly slipped away to her room, leaving her friends time to enjoy the fire and the tree in the living room and to share some precious time alone together.

Sleep eluded her. She lay in the dark of her room watching the darkness of the winter sky with clouds drifting across the expansive display of stars, only allowing a few now and then to be seen. She could have taken one of the little pills, she knew, but it was as though she must wait for – there, she saw the lights of the station wagon as it was parked in the drive near the cottage. When the lights were turned off and she heard the car door shut softly, she turned onto her side to go to sleep, now that she knew he was safely back.

Much later, in the early morning hours, she had no awareness of the sound of the Land Rover leaving and the return of the snowmobile later, nor of Steve's quiet entry into the house and upstairs to his room.

The study and the library were always the last rooms to receive small bits of Christmas decorations. There was a special candle arrangement for the window in the study, just above the wooden creche arrangement, and a small ceramic tree with a miniature pine forest scene for the table in the library. Linda had just finished testing the lights in the small tree, the final bit to be done, when the telephone rang.

By the time it rang three times she realized she was the nearest to it so she hurried into the study to answer.

"Linda Wilson speaking, may I..."

The raspy voice coming through the receiver to her ear was obviously an attempt to conceal the identity of the caller. "Well, I see you finally sent him packing. Or did he run out on you?"

"Who is this?"

"You forget my voice so soon, Mrs. Wilson," the voice continued. "What is the matter? Did you finally learn about his little affair with Mrs. Johnson, or did he decide she was a little warmer, had a sweeter disposition..."

"Who are you?"

"Well, if you don't recognize my voice that's fine. I just wanted to tell you that your high and mighty airs have lost you your boyfriend. He has moved in with Mrs. Johnson – didn't you know? Where did you think he would go when he left your place?"

So dazed at this onslaught from some unidentifiable person, Linda did not replace the phone in its cradle but asked, "When, who left where?"

"Dear Mr. Brockman, or *Whit*, as she calls him. You didn't even know he had moved out, did you? Or are you just trying to hide the fact that he's gone?"

"Do you realize this call is malicious slander?"

"Oh, no, Mrs. Wilson. Truth is not slander. His station wagon was parked at her house two nights in a row last week, and I saw him carrying boxes in and luggage out. Could be they are going away together? Too bad, Mrs. Wilson." Then the silent sound of a wire gone dead rang through her ears as Linda slowly replaced the receiver.

Miss Tucker. Why did she...but Brock had not left. Surely he would say something. Harold would have mentioned...but Harold had been very quiet and secretive about something. Brock would be leaving the first of January. But why to Mrs. Johnson's house? But there would be nothing of interest to keep him here would there? She mocked herself. She had definitely seen to that. *No man would want to take time to chisel away an iceberg. But hadn't that started to melt inside?* The tenderness he showed toward her during her illness, his concern for Richie had given her some hope. If only... there were still too many if only's running through her mind. The rest of the day was like a heavy pall hanging over her. That woman thought she could hurt her by that telephone call. Did the entire community think there was some truth in what Miss Tucker had suggested? Oh no, surely it was just spite on the caller's part because she had been dismissed from tutoring Richie. There also had been reports of trouble caused by her indelicate suggestions concerning other people in the community that had caused the school board to release her as tutor from their teaching roster.

"Oh, I'll be so glad when things are truly back to normal." She found her voice at last. Linda glanced around the study, taking time to get her thoughts away from the unpleasant experience, making sure that everything was finished in those two rooms before she left.

After lunch Harold and Steve bundled Angela and Richie into heavy clothing and took them to the stream bordering the edge of the garden to test the ice covering for skating.

She spent the afternoon with her mother, Agnes and Marci in the kitchen making surprise treats to stash away from small hands until Christmas Eve finally arrived, beginning their celebration of the holidays. Linda could not hide the moody, upset feeling that persisted because of the telephone call but, although there were some anxious questioning glances sent her way as she worked silently, none were put into words. She was glad of that, for she would not – indeed could not – tell of the call. She could not abide the humiliation it would bring. The well of tears even now were becoming harder to control. The dam must not break from embarrassment over a petty telephone call. Shortly after dinner Linda noticed the Land Rover leave again, following the tracks of its previous journeys through the trees toward the fishing huts. "I thought you had finished with the fishing, Harold? Is there still more work to be done at the lodge?" It seemed rather odd to her that they should need to go so often.

"Oh, Carl has some last minute things to take care of, and he has asked for some extra help." His green eyes met hers directly, offering gentle assurance. "Everything will be finished by Christmas, don't worry."

She accepted his explanation, noticing that he had included Marci in his answer, wrapping his arm cozily around her waist, hugging her close to his side. "As I told you before, it's just taking a bit longer than we expected."

Later they gathered in front of the fireplace in the family room and shared the greetings in brightly decorated cards that had come that day. Those addressed to Brock and Steve were put aside. The rest were displayed in various card holder arrangements placed around the room.

The single light of the snowmobile reflecting on the snow near the cottage proclaimed Brock's arrival, so Linda was aware of his coming before he opened the door from the patio into the kitchen. He had removed his heavy outer garments and hung them on the rack provided near the outside door. From where she sat, facing the door, she caught the glance that passed between the two men. An alarming question in Harold's eyes as he stood to face Brock was answered with just a brief nod, and "It's beginning to blow out there, but things are all falling into place."

A soft sigh escaped from Marci and, since the brief answer seemed to satisfy Harold, Linda refrained from her anxious inquiries. It did not seem to concern her in any way and she certainly did not want to pry. Richie told Brock about the fun he'd had skating and mentioned the fact that there would be skating activities at school. "Are you all set to return to your classes?" Brock's voice had a hint of teasing in it.

"Yeah! It's going to be great – going back!" He talked a bit more about it. All of his friends would still be in his class since he was not behind in any of his subjects.

A warm thrill stirred within Linda as she listened to their conversation. Brock had done so much toward Richie's recovery. She must be sure to mention it to him.

"Did you know that Mrs. Johnson is not going to teach the second term?" Richie asked.

Linda tensed, waiting for the answer.

"Yes, I know. She is..."

Linda deliberately blanked out the rest of the answer. She got up from the chair and went to the sink to rinse coffee cups to be placed in the dishwasher, turning the water full on to hide the sound of the answering voice. Brock and Harold pulled out the chairs at the table and were enjoying this short time of relaxing.

"Now's your chance, Brock!" The boy's voice rang with merriment and Linda turned her head quickly, a question gleaming in her eyes as she met Richie's, just before he raised his gaze to indicate the cluster of mistletoe hanging directly above her head.

"Would you like to see that, Richie?" Brock teased back at him, rising from his chair as if he meant to take the boyish suggestion. It was all meant in fun, Linda was sure, but she felt the trembling begin in her middle and travel quickly to her knees as she moved back from the sink, and reached for the tea towel to dry her fingers. How could she hide any more hurt, from where would the strength come? She pressed the damp towel to her tightly closed lips and turned her face away from those teasing eyes hurrying as swiftly as her traitorous trembling knees would allow toward her room. Richie's "Aw, Aunt Linda!" completely ignored. Trying desperately not to lose control she stiffened her back and arms, demanded her knees to stop their trembling until she reached for the knob to the door of her room.

Brock grasped her shoulders from behind and smoothly turned her around. The soft glow from the light beside her door cast a shadow, deepening the lines and hollows of his face showing to her the deep anger – *it must be anger* she surmised, that made his eyes burn like fire. "What is there in me, that utterly repulses you, Linda? Or are you so embittered that any man who is free to think you desirable, is your enemy?"

She pulled frantically away from him, hurting her arms as she wrenched them from his hold. "What does it matter to you," she challenged him, "since you are not free?"

He pulled her back into his arms and held her there, his eyes blazing down into hers. "And would it change things between us if I were? Could you forget that bitter resentment of fate that took away the man of your dreams? Could you do away with your pet pain and be the warm, tender woman I'm searching for – if I were free?"

He wrapped his arms even tighter, his urgency increased, bringing her closer to him as he hoped the warmth of his arms would further melt the ice barrier.

Unaware of the tears now streaming down her face she clenched her teeth and stared into his gaze. "But you are not free, are you, so what does it matter?" She desperately needed to fight him and the feeling of weakness flooding through her. "I'm not your problem, why don't you just go!" She struggled to be released, trying to work her arms between them to push away. "Your job here is finished." She tried hopelessly to put an angry force into her words. Amazed at the sudden gentleness in his voice as he answered, "I am going away, very soon." She relaxed in her struggle but felt the trembling return to her knees and the tears continuing to flow.

"In the meantime..." His voice came as a deep growl from within his chest. His arm tight around her waist, he pulled her close against him. He moved so swiftly she could not pull away nor prevent it as his fingers caressed their way up her back to the nape of her neck. All at once it seemed to be happening! She could hardly swallow.

There was no longer any strength to oppose his demands of her. She turned her head into his shoulder to prevent his seeing the effect he was having on her and trembled as he brushed the back of her neck and deftly removed the pins holding her hair in its soft roll, letting them fall heedlessly to the floor. Pain coursed through her as those fingers became strong and insistent and twined themselves into the soft strands. Forcing her to lift her head from its hiding, he finished his sentence, "think about this." He held her there answering the uncertain defiance that still lingered in her tear-filled eyes with something unreadable, growing and glowing in his. A soft moan emitted from his throat but she scarcely heard it as he drew her face to his, closing both of her eyes with a gentle kiss on each lid, brushing the tears from her lashes, collecting them on his searching, eager lips, his mouth leaving feather light kisses over her cheeks. Finally, as she allowed her arms to creep up over his shoulders and around his neck, he took full possession of her unresisting, trembling mouth. Her ice wall weakened. Her trembling came from desire and not anger. A deep sigh forced the sob that had hung in her throat. Her mouth answered his in its seeking, her fingers buried in the crisp curls at his collar line, gripped and held his head there. She was fully aware of the tension building in him.

Suddenly his mouth was gone. The sweet taste of him was lifted away causing her to release her hold on him. His arm and hand no longer held her so closely. The gentleness had returned. She did not want that, she surprised herself with this realization.

It made her weep. Deftly his hand cupped the back of her head pushing it into the hollow of his shoulder. *What a weakling I am.* How could she respond to this man in this way?

He was involved with another...She began to push away, forcing strength back into her weakened arms and knees. He tightened his hold. She felt the pressure of his kiss against the top of her head and his face as he brushed his cheek against her hair and down across her ear. His warm breath stirred the stray strands that always curled there.

"There!" The word was a mere whisper coming from the depths of his desire. "I think *that* fire will melt the ice and burn forever, once the smoke has cleared away." Completely stunned by his onslaught and her shocking response, she clung to his arms for just a moment before he reached behind her, turned the knob of the door, and gently backed her into her room. Haltingly, she only watched as he pressed her trembling lips faintly with his fingers and backed out into the hallway. He pulled the door firmly shut hiding from her the unreadable expression she had caught in his eyes.

Outside Linda's window the morning sun shot off glittering sparks from the new ice crystals that had formed where the strong night wind and the lowering temperature had altered the slopes and crests of the drifted snow covering the ground. In some places the tracks left by the Land Rover and snowmobile were obliterated. Someone was still out there. She had no idea of what was occupying their time. Surely the work was finished, but they had said that Carl needed some extra help with something.

She shrugged her slender shoulders and pulled the drapes closed again to trap the cold between windows and drapes. Her mirror told her she looked the same. Her hair was again neatly wound at the back of her neck, her mouth, a little more red without the aid of any make up, but who would notice. In spite of the change inside and the fact that she could not meet the eyes that searched her face in the dressing table mirror she vowed to herself: *last night was just a happening, nothing had altered, the barrier had not crumbled.* She could not let it happen.

Deliberately, she planned the order of chores that needed to be done through the day. Thankful that she had not given way to the onrush of tears that had started to come as soon as she was alone in her bed room. Almost in a daze she had prepared for bed, taken two of the recommended little pills with the glass of hot water, and slept easily.

So the day hurried away almost as quickly as she had planned, beginning, of course, with breakfast. Then she finished last minute gift selecting and wrapping, and lunched. She helped Richie neatly wrap and tag his gifts to be placed around the tree.

Oh, yes, and dinner came and went. There was no time or need to permit what had happened at her door the night before to make a change in anything. *It had just been a highly emotional incident and not worthy of recalling. What would be the good of it?*

How many times during the day have I had that same thought? She wondered.

Besides – he was gone.

There were lights showing from the cottage now. Steve had gone into the cottage two or three times during the day, but the station wagon had been gone since early morning. "You would have thought," she taunted herself, "that he would have said goodbye to Richie." But then she recalled he was going to leave in a few days. "So he is probably in town with Mrs..."

She finished wrapping the last piece of nut bread, put it with the other sweets she had prepared, turned off the kitchen lights and went quietly through the hall. The next day was Christmas Eve day and her mother would deliver the brightly wrapped little packages they had prepared to her friends and shut-in neighbors.

There were no thin lines of light showing on the hall carpet beneath either Richie's or her mother's bedroom door as she passed them. She felt sure they were both sleeping. The two people who meant everything in her life. How could she ever feel the need for a more personal involvement, someone to share...but the ache was still there. Tonight she would pray for a quick ascent into sleep. She hated to depend upon those pills.

Tomorrow...

Chapter Fifteen

Brock paused for a moment after pulling Linda's door quietly shut behind him, then hurried back to the kitchen. He answered Richie's alarmed, questioning eyes with a wry grin and a tousle of the boy's hair while passing through to the patio where his coat was hanging. "She'll be fine, Richie, but perhaps we should not have teased her, hmmm?" He lifted his hand from the boy's head into a slight farewell sign toward the others in the room, then hurried into his coat and out the door.

The air was still and cold, turning his breath into clouds of frosty vapor as his long strides carried him over the short distance to the cottage. In a few short minutes he pulled a handy ski mask over his head, tucked the attached shawl-like collar into the neck of his mackinaw, checked to be sure everything was zipped and snapped securely, went out to the waiting vehicle, and drove away. The tracks stretching out ahead of him were so familiar now he could almost follow them automatically. At least the sun was down so there was no glare from the snow which had taken on the appearance of a warm fleecy blanket. *How many more trips*, he wondered. *We had so many unscheduled trips.*

Everything should have been settled by now but how could they have imagined the unforeseen events.

Again he went over the unexpected happenings of the previous Saturday night.

What an occurrence that was. It was fortunate for them that Carl had offered to help. The growing tension and suspense when the two men from the other hut lingered around the fire they had built so near the channel had kept Brock's nerves on edge while Harold and Steve stood in the larger fishing hut in darkness, waiting with him for – they knew not what. Except, come to find out, Steve had known all along. He had slipped out of the door after showing his credentials to them and warning them to stay where they were – the lights from the outgoing tanker coming into view around a slight bend in the channel.

As a ship passed the area, Brock thought, *too soon, too soon*. Search lights beamed from a stand of trees near the edge of the frozen lake, flooding the area with their light. Several men hurried from the same place. Steve answered signals that were coming from aboard the ship with the light in his hand. After the shadowy action-filled drama had ended and the floodlights were extinguished; after Carl had smothered the fire near the channel that he had come to investigate, Steve explained to Brock, Carl and Harold that he had just completed a drug bust. "Remember the radio on the shelf in their hut? Well, that's where it was hidden. Just a small case of cocaine shipping – payoff money wrapped in water-proof packages."

Those two fishermen were quickly on their way with the narcotics agents Steve had working with him. Their two accomplices on the oil tanker would be taken into custody when the ship passed through the locks at Saulte St. Marie. Half an hour up the channel, two ships would pass in the night and in another half hour the Norwegian freighter would pass the fishing huts on its way to Chicago. The adrenalin flowed harder and knots formed in his stomach muscles when the freighter came into view. How could they know if it would work? Then there was the signal from the ship, the hum from the deck as a small harpoon was fired and the 'zing' and slithering sound it made sliding over the ice. Within a minute the heavy cable from the pick up truck was fastened to the line attached to the harpoon and was pulled back to the deck of the ship. It was strange that no one on the ship had seen the action and interfered, but the agent that was to replace the "package" for the remaining part of the passage to Chicago was a reliable and clever man. Carl had been commandeered to drive the truck and had parked it at an exact angle with the ship and set it to hold the cable taut. It had been a breath-holding situation from the start. Then to see a man begin his descent over churning icy waters to the rough frozen surface using just a pulley with hand grips and his own legs wrapped around the cable to control his speed, made Brock wonder at his own audacity. Surely, there could have been a safer...Then something cracked like a pistol shot – the end of the cable sprang from the ship and came ringing through the air, dropping the man with the pulley still in his hands and dragging him over the sharp ice as part of the hook, still attached to the cable, fell dangerously near the truck. Harold had been the first to reach the man on the ice. Brock remained for a moment where he was watching the ship; almost immediately a man appeared at the ship's rail, held aloft the remaining part of the hook so Brock would recognize it, then heaved it as hard as he could so it would land on the ice. He gave a signal which Brock recognized as the 'all clear' and disappeared into the shadows of the deck – the ship continued on its way. Steve brought blankets from the bunks to carry the injured man to the warmth of the larger hut. Harold contacted Doctor Browne by radio from the truck while Carl rewound the cable and stored it in the bed of the truck. An hour later the long gash made in the man's thigh by the jagged ice had been cleaned and stitched together, the deep abrasions on his back were cleaned and medicated before Doctor Browne wrapped his chest and back to protect the three fractured ribs. By three o'clock Sunday morning calm prevailed. Carl had gone with the truck. Harold and Steve – with a warning reminder of the secrecy of the night's events – had gone back to the farm in the Land Rover. Brock had spent the remainder of the night and into the morning, closely watching the man on the bunk in the large hut. He was precious cargo. The man's life, a woman's happiness and a small girl's future, depended on the success of this endeavor. The fire had continued to burn, the lantern flickered and then glowed again when he had turned up the wick – then he waited. Doctor Browne had administered antibiotics and sleeping pills finally the man on the bunk slept. In the morning, the return of the Land Rover with Harold and Steve had awakened both of the men in the hut. They removed the fishing equipment from the hut. They moved the blankets, food, lanterns and fuel plus any remaining firewood from the smaller huts into the larger one. Carl came with the truck, showed Brock the piece of the hook that had been fastened to the cable. Carl offered to stay at the hut while Brock, Steve and Harold returned the no longer-needed equipment and closed the other two huts against the weather. Brock kept reviewing the week. There was the incident with Richie and Linda Sunday evening. It seemed as though he was involved in the upsetting experiences of her life in the past few weeks If he could only take her into his confidence, then he could take her into his arms and comfort...*Oh, dear Lord I desire more than simply to comfort her.* There was some deep remorse in her. He was certain now that it had something to do with the death of her husband. She must have been about twenty-one or two, not just a love-sick teenager. But why the bitterness. No, it wasn't exactly bitterness – more like an unfathomable sorrow. Just the short time he had been in the house it had been evident. Of course, that had been more concerning the loss of her brother and Richie's parents, but even that should have been softened by now.

He had hated to leave her then, but there had been nothing he could do and Carl had been at the hut for a long time. There had been some response tonight when he had held her in his arms there at her door – perhaps he had gone a little too far – but he had waited so long, and she was…she had some antagonism against love. *Could it be jealousy? She really doesn't know who Mrs. Johnson is.* Yet, he could not tell her. After Doctor Browne's early morning visit to the hut, he had declared the patient was doing as well as could be expected but still needed someone there to keep the fire going. Steve offered to stay. Brock had accepted his offer. He had to get to Love with this bit of good news/not so good news. Later in the afternoon they stopped at the cottage. Brock told Harold, "I know I don't have to remind you of the secrecy we still need to keep. You know how important that is." He paused before going into the cottage. "Make my excuses to the family, will you? I have something to do in town as quickly as possible." In a short time he had loaded the station wagon with his luggage, the portable keyboard; this he favored with a grimace as he realized he probably would never use it again, perhaps Rosella would, some day. For now it fit in with the other things that had served as camouflage for his purpose here. He hesitated about leaving the cottage and farm in this manner, but the events of Saturday night had made it necessary.

The drive over the snow-packed country roads and the cleared streets through the town had only taken a small part of an hour. He was glad for the early darkness of the winter evening when he parked the station wagon in the drive leading into Mrs. Johnson's garage. He blinked the lights on and off twice. Almost immediately the garage doors opened. There was not room for the wagon inside the garage, but he unloaded his things and stored them in the readied space. Then he locked the doors to the wagon, leaving it parked in the drive. Love met him at the door leading from the garage into the house, her lovely but tired eyes raised to look anxiously and inquiringly into his.

"Tell me, Whit! Is he all right? How did it go? I've been so worried…"

"I'm sorry that I took so long to get here, Love." He began his explanation as he removed his gloves and heavy coat. Then he took her hand, which seemed even colder than his own, guiding her into the living room to the sofa.

"He's safe, Love! We had a little problem." He explained briefly the occurrence on the ice, assuring her that everything was going to be fine.

"He has some fractured ribs and we cannot move him until Christmas Day."

"Oh, Whit"

"We still have to be cautious, Love. There may still be someone..."

"But the two men are gone!"

"True, but until Brombke clears it through Chicago..."

"Oh," she interrupted him, "he called here about an hour ago. You are to call him back. I'll put dinner on the table while you do that." .

After the call and the quiet dinner for two. They went outside as he packed Love's already filled luggage into the back of the wagon.

"You be sure to call Grandfather. Let him know some of the news but do not alarm him. It will not be necessary to tell Rosella anything just yet. You should be able to let him know without any risk..." He lifted his hand to warn her as she seemed about to protest. "Even private telephone lines, sometimes are not private, Love." Then as she stood beside him in the cold night air, he drew her close in the warmth of his mackinaw covered arms. He lifted her face to his and kissed her gently on the forehead. "You need to go inside. The three years of waiting are over, Love. Just a few more days."

The drive back to the farm had been just as quick and made with the same ease, although he suddenly felt the strain of the last few days. But in his mind the phrase "just a few more days" echoed along with the memory of another pair of sad eyes, and thoughts of Linda flooded his entire being as he had parked the wagon near the cottage on Monday night. All of this recalling had hurried through Brock's mind as he drove the snowmobile back to the hut. He did not realize he had followed the tracks as though the wheels of the snowmobile were on tracks in the grooves. Now it seemed strange to see just one light burning in one hut there on the broad expanse of ice and snow. He parked the snowmobile near the door to the hut, forced the door open against the wind, and closed it firmly behind him. The glow from the hanging lantern made the shadows waver as it swung in the draft of air from the opened door. The fire in the grate provided heat and added light to the small hut. The trap door they had enlarged in the middle of the floor had been securely sealed and was now covered with a thick piece of carpet.

Brock removed the thermal mittens and ski mask and dropped them into a corner along with his mackinaw.

"Doctor Browne left about an hour and a half ago." Carl informed him, sitting up straight in the chair near the bunk. He stretched his arms above his head and indicated to Brock to have a cup of coffee. "It's fresh, or was, when Doc was here." After he filled a mug from the pot of a now very strong brew, he turned to face the man by the bunk. "What did Doc have to say? Is he. . ."

Another voice interrupted from within the bunk. "I'm going to make it, brother mine. Don't fret so." The man on the bunk raised his head, groaning as he tried to move into a more comfortable position.

"Hey. Take it easy. I hadn't any doubts about you making it. Just wanted to know how soon we could move you out of here?"

"How rough is the road?"

"Not too bad in the Land Rover. We've worn the path fairly smooth in the last weeks," Brock assured him with a smile on his face.

The man in the bunk eased himself into a more comfortable position and made his voice a little stronger. "Your esteemed doctor says not before Sunday unless it's absolutely necessary, and then it would have to be by ambulance or helicopter."

"Oh, no, a helicopter. That kind of attention we do not need." Brock glanced at Carl. "Did he say why?"

"He's afraid that long of a ride would..."

"We cannot take him into town. Not yet...I need to get..."

"Then where?" interrupted the injured man.

"I was thinking of the cottage." Brock stopped his pacing and stood by the bunk. "How painful are the ribs, Oscar? Could you stand fifteen minutes in the back of a well sprung and padded station wagon?"

"By when?"

"Friday evening."

"That's Christmas Day."

"Yes, I know, but it can't be arranged any sooner." Brock shrugged his shoulders,

"The ship should have reached Chicago by now."

"Yes, and the call should come through by Thursday – but we can not take any chances."

"Who will know this far away?" Oscar glanced from Carl to Brock and then his eyes returned to study the face of the man who had been with him through the day.

"You surely are trusting a great number of..."

"I know, Oscar. We had a bit of a fracas here just before you arrived. Some narcotics officials made a slight haul from the ship that passed yours in the channel. One of the undercover men lives at the farm. Carl is responsible for the property around here.

It's a good thing he was here. You might not have been as lucky as you were." He motioned his hand toward Carl. "You should know a bit about this 'package' that you helped retrieve from that passing ship, Carl, but all I can tell you now is that he is my brother-in-law, Oscar, and has just arrived from that illusive place referred to as 'somewhere behind the Iron Curtain'."

As Oscar reached out to grasp the hand Carl offered to him, Brock continued.

"This is a friend and business partner of the people I work for, and also a friend of mine."

The eyes of the two men met and held over their gripped hands and Oscar added to Brock's comments. "Mine is a story that will never make the headlines, friend. Too many other lives would be endangered if it were made public. Perhaps sometime later Brock can..."

"Don't let that worry you. There have been others farther out in the seaway, dropping off in the Maine woods and near Montreal. They all seem to make it to safety from there." Carl tried to assure him.

Not all. For some had not made it. Brock did not voice his thoughts. "Their bid for freedom had been desperate, and desperate men take desperate measures when they are offered." Carl gathered his coat and gloves from the bench near the door, remarked that he had a wife and daughter at home who might be anxious.

"We appreciate your taking this time, Carl."

"Hey, don't mention it, and don't worry. "I'll think of a simple tale to tell," he assured them, with a nod toward Oscar. "I'll see you again, I'm sure."

According to Oscar, Doctor Browne had been there earlier, changed the bandages on the thigh, rewrapped his broken ribs and left more pills for the pain and to fight any infection. "But that's not what I need. Where are they, Brock? Are you sure they are..."

"Lovellyn is fine, Oscar. She's in the small town up the road. She knows that you are here and that you have a few cuts and bruises."

"And Rosella?"

"She'll be coming with Grandfather late Thursday afternoon. We'll all spend Christmas Eve together and most of Christmas Day. After the evening meal I will bring Love to the cottage – but we can't make a move into town until..."

"Yes, I know. Until Brombke calls. How will he contact?"

"There 's a radio in both places so I'll call as soon as he knows for sure."

"Man, I hate to seem so impatient, but three years..."

"I know. It's a long time." Brock reached for the packet of capsules. Shook out one of each kind into the palm of his hand and offered the medicine to Oscar along with a mug of water. "Now why not take your medicine and sleep away the next eight or ten hours."

"Yes, the good doctor said I would not need a night nurse beside my bed any more, so you can get some sleep, too. Tomorrow I can sit up if I'm able to prop my game leg up on something."

"We'll surely see to that," Brock assured him, as he set the empty mug on the counter and turned down the wick in the lantern.

Both men slept soundly until just before the sun appeared over the snow covered cliffs that bordered the river bank toward the east. The fire had burned down with just a few embers remaining.

Brock's breath wrapped around his face in a mist as he hurriedly stirred the ashes down through the grate, providing air passage so the few remaining embers would ignite kindling and logs he carefully placed on top. There. It would burn now.

He felt Oscar's eyes following him and turned to meet their still questioning darkness with assurance in his own, and an affectionate grin. "You stay wrapped up, you hear? I'll have coffee going in a minute."

An hour later he was back on the snowmobile nearing the cottage. There was no reason for him to go into the house so he hurried into the cottage and was quickly back out and into the station wagon, hurrying it out the drive toward the town. It was Wednesday already and still much to do. He spent the day with Love, handling the arrangements for the moving company to empty the little house and transport the furnishings back to the rental agency and her personal belongings to that special house on the west bank of the Hudson. The little snatches of song on her lips and the happiness shining in her beautiful eyes made all of the efforts and secrecy worthwhile. That alone would have been compensation enough, but to have found what he had been searching for, finally. Now perhaps, some way, there would be a future for him in the larger house on the west bank of that famous river, too.

The day passed in a hurry and again he was back at the cottage, late at night. The house was dark as he parked in the drive. The night had turned extremely cold. The wind whipped in his face and the snow scrunched under his feet. It nearly took the storm door from his hand before he could close it behind him.

Soon the glow from the fireplace was casting a flickering light around the small comfortable den as the logs snapped and burned, sending blue flames and fragrant curls of smoke to scent the air before they drifted with the draught up through the chimney. The aroma from the quickly brewed coffee in the steam rising from the cup in his hand mingled with the output of the fire, bringing an almost overwhelming sense of aloneness to him. He began again to sort out the events of the last few days.

He almost wished he could have gone into the house when he had returned a few minutes ago, for a late cup of coffee with her, to continue the ice melting and barrier destroying. To explain to Linda. But that could not be, not yet.

Everything needed to be accomplished with Oscar and Love first, and then he could take her into his confidence, into his arms, his life, his home, his...He had hated to leave her, especially after last night. He was sure there had been a response, even if she was not aware of it. But the next time he wanted to be able to come closer to feeling some warmth of melting ice.

Determinedly he closed the door of his mind on those prospects, and relaxed for a few more minutes in the lounge chair by the fire. He switched his thought track to Monday at Love's.

Where did she get the strength, the patience to hold on, he wondered. *But then, she has always been sure Oscar would return. Everything is finally falling into line. Her temporary household is ready for the movers, her personal needs for the weekend are even now in the closet and dresser drawers here in the cottage.* Brombke had been informed of all that had happened. Most of Brock's stuff had been shipped to his Grandfather's house to the other bank of the Hudson. Only the radio equipment and one case of his personal items remained.

Thursday morning Brock drove the station wagon over the well-packed trail to the fishing hut, satisfying himself that it could be used to move Oscar on Friday, if it didn't snow again before then. Everything had to be finished today and, like a well maintained machine, his mind accurately scheduled the hours ahead. He arrived at the hut just as the sun was beginning to scatter its daily supply of glitter across the wide expanse of snow and ice. Smoke came from the pipe protruding through the wall, drifting in the almost still air, and light gleamed through the frost covered window. Carl had agreed to see to these things this morning and as Brock pulled open the door, the lingering scent of fried bacon and eggs and freshly perked coffee let him know he had more than kept his word.

Only Oscar was there now, sitting on one of the chairs with his injured leg propped on the end rail of the bunk he had been lying in for the past few days.

"Hey, look at you." Brock grinned at him, putting the packages he had brought with him on the table. "Love will never know.. A few more days of growth for that beard and…"

"Oh, yes she will. All I'll need to do is look at her…"

"Yes, I know. Not even that. She will only have to be in the same room."

Sensing the depth of the other man's emotions Brock turned from him, removed his mackinaw, put his gloves and ski mask into the pockets and hung it on the nail by the door. Then he went to warm his hands near the grate.

"I told her some of what happened. She would need to know that you had gotten a bit banged up. We've moved what she'll need for the next week from the house to the cottage. Grandfather, Rosella, and I will stay at the house until the movers come on Monday."

Oscar was almost afraid to ask, but…"Have you made arrangements for after Monday?"

"No, not yet. Things are a little up tight right now with Linda. I got a little ahead of myself Tuesday night – off on the wrong foot so to speak. So it will have to come to her as a settled fact, something already happening."

Brock turned back to the packages he had put on the table. "Doc said you could be up and move around a bit today, so I did some shopping." He tossed two of the packages into Oscar's lap noting a slight tightening of his jaw as they landed. "There's still some pain, huh?"

"Only when my leg is bumped, or someone clobbers it with…"

"Sorry about that." Brock grinned. "You won't notice a bit of pain by Saturday."

Then referring to the packages, he continued. "After Doc changes the bandages this afternoon you can try these on. They may be a bit too big right now, but after a few days of a certain loving woman and her cooking you'll begin to fill them out. The ice cut through your dungarees and tore up your jacket and we had to cut your one boot off. You can't travel, even from here to the cottage in over-sized pajamas and flannel robe."

As Oscar opened the packages, Brock poured coffee into two mugs, added two spoonfuls of sugar to one and placed it on the up-ended crate near his chair then relaxed on the edge of the bunk.

"There is everything you will need for a few days either in these packages or at the cottage, except Love. She'll be there when you arrive."

"Man. What can I say?"

"You don't need to say a thing, Oscar. You know what your returning means to all of us. All you need to do is..."

"I know. Get well."

"And get on with your life from where you left it over three years ago. Now," he got up from the bunk and rinsed the coffee mugs at the counter, "this is Christmas Eve. I need to be at the airport at five o'clock. Harold and Steve will be in and out today to see that you behave yourself. So don't try to do too much the first day up."

After a quick lunch at the corner cafe, Brock hurried to the lot where the local YMCA was selling Christmas trees. He loaded the six-foot silver spruce he had selected a few days earlier into the back of the wagon. His next stop was the department store for the many packages they were holding for him; then to the little house.

Love clasped her hands in front of her after she opened the door for him and stepped back for him to take the tree into the house.

"Oh, Whit, a tree!"

"Of course, my darling sister. Who would expect a small child to come to her Mummy's house on Christmas Eve and not find a tree there?"

The stand had been put on the tree at the lot so in a very few minutes that symbol of the Christmas season was filling the small house with its aroma. They worked together as they had done years ago in their family home on the Hudson. Brock strung the lights through the soft branches, placed the star at the very top and hung the ornaments on the higher branches, arguing cheerfully with Love as to where they should be put.

As the last ornament was in place they noticed the time. "Oh, Whit, it's after four, you need to go to the airport."

"I see." Quickly, he began closing boxes. "When Brombke calls, you can take the message."

"Of course. Now leave that." She referred to the bits of paper and tinsel around on the floor. "I will get that."

"I have some more things to bring in from the wagon." He shrugged into his Mackinaw. "I'll bring them to the door and you can put them around the tree." He talked over his shoulder going to the garage. Don't bother too much with dinner."

"Dinner is nearly ready." She put the brightly wrapped packages on the kitchen table as he handed them to her. "Now, go, and drive carefully. They will wait for you inside the airport waiting room if you are a bit late."

Later, driving away from the small commercial airport located a few miles out of town, he again needed to offer assurance. This time to his grandfather, that the wait was over. Oscar was well and recovering rapidly from his injuries and that everything was going smoothly.

"It has been a long time coming, Whitaker, and you have earned a long vacation. Take some time for yourself."

"Yes, Sir." Brock assured him. "I am thinking seriously along those lines and I wonder – how many can you spare from 'Brockridge' for a while?"

"It depends on what..." "I would want someone for general cleaning, airing, checking the linen supply, that kind of thing."

"I think we could manage a reliable company."

"By the end of January?"

"That soon?"

"Well, I should think that I would want it finished by the end of March. It has been closed for three years so I want everything double checked the heating and air conditioning, the grounds, the pool, the drives. After just doing the smaller house over for Lovellyn and Oscar you should have a very good idea of what will need to be done. And you know you'll enjoy doing this one also."

"You seem so sure, my boy."

Brock allowed his eyes to meet the questioning ones of the older man seated beside him for a moment. "I'm sure it's time for me to go home, Grandfather. If I can just crack an iceberg, I don't think I'll be going there alone." He watched as understanding flowed into the expression of his grandfather's face, then turned his attention back to the almost deserted highway stretching ahead of him.

But could he be sure? Even if the ice did melt, if she should become a warm happy person again, it would not necessarily mean...Yes, it would. He would make it so.

There had been some response. Necessarily his thoughts returned to his driving as the Christmas Eve traffic intensified with last minute shoppers and shop owners going to their homes; revelers and celebrators leaving the small town for family gatherings and others coming into town. It was still a bit early for the party goers, but the volume of traffic had increased in both directions and at the small house an anxious mother waited. Rosella, cuddled on her grandfather's lap, slept peacefully, awaiting the excitement of the anticipated day. She had not been told of the meeting planned for Sunday. How would she react? Could she accept? Would she know Oscar from the pictures? Surely he would know how to handle it. The small house was ablaze with festive welcome. The tree lights blinked on and off through the living room windows. The amber lights of electric candles shone from the kitchen and den. It would be hard, not having Oscar here, but there was still that slight chance of discovery of his arrival. There would be many more Christmases.

He pressed the button on the garage door opener which he had borrowed from Love and drove into the garage as the door opened for him. Immediately he was out of the car and around to the passenger door. "I'll take her, Granddad. You get the doors, if you will. We'll get the luggage later."

By Friday afternoon the excitement of Christmas gifts and pleasures had dimmed a little and being with her mother seemed again to be the normal thing.

Brock was now again in the small bedroom. This time the sleepy eyes met his from the depths of a billowy ruffle-trimmed pillow and matching coverlet. He sat on the edge of the bed after just kissing the rosy cheek that had been sleepily offered to him.

"You must sleep for a while now, Sweetie, and when you wake up Grandfather will be here with you and perhaps Francis will be here, also." Rosella smiled excitedly at this last suggestion. Mr. Brockman's private secretary and chauffeur was a favorite guy to her. Brock continued. "Your Mummy has to go away for a few days, but I'll be back tonight and then on Sunday you can go with me and then be 'with her – for always."

"Will Grandfather be there?" "No, not this time – now, say your prayers, and go to sleep. Have sweet dreams." He tucked the ruffled softness around her and touched her lips gently with a tender fingertip caress, then quietly shut the door behind him. Still desiring to keep the events of the week secret, he had made arrangements with Harold. As he turned the wagon from the road into the drive up to the farmhouse he noted that all of the draperies to the front had been drawn shut. If his timing was right, the family was at dinner. He turned off the headlights and continued up the drive. The woman in the front passenger seat had not spoken since they left town. She sat relaxed, her eyes closed and her hands folded around a small package resting in her lap.

"Love." He spoke to her as he parked as near to the cottage door as possible.

"I'm awake, Whit. Just relaxing, thankful that he is home."

"But not apprehensive?"

"Of course not. Why should I be?"

He did not answer the question, but slipped out of the car and around to open the door for her. Inside the cottage he pulled the drapes closed and switched on the lights to the small Christmas tree on the desk that had been cleared and draped with a brightly sparkling cloth. "You have described it to me so well that I'll not have any problems finding what I need."

"Good." He smiled at her. He held her coat for her as she slipped her arms from the sleeves. "I'll hang this on the rack for you. You make coffee, fix whatever you want. I'll be back here in about an hour."

Later, on the return trip, the moon's soft glow seemed to bathe only the cottage and its surroundings, isolating it from all else. He again stopped the wagon as close to the door as possible, having come out of the wooded area with headlights off and the motor slowing to a stop of its own accord. They opened and shut the car doors quietly.

The two men moved as silently as possible from the side of the station wagon into the cottage.

Tired and alone, guiding the empty station wagon through the brittle cold of the moon-bright whiteness of the now so familiar country road, Brock recalled the scene that had unfolded as he closed that cottage door behind himself. Love's softly murmured words as she hurried from the kitchen. Oscar, heedless of his injured leg and other injuries grasped her into his arms, burying his face in her hair where it caressed and wrapped around her neck and chin. They clung to each other out of Brock's view now.

Their need being satisfied to gaze into loved and longed for eyes, hungry lips, beloved features, only to reach again to wrap each other around in deep rapturous emotions.

"Thank you God. It's over. He's home. We can go on with our lives." He parked the station wagon in the driveway of the small house in town. The other half of the drive was filled with the dark gray Rolls

Royce that Francis drove for his grandfather. Things were going well in this house tonight. *Thank you, God.*

Chapter Sixteen

The roads and driveways were reasonably clear as Linda and her mother visited the many friends and neighbors, leaving packages of fancy breads, cookies, and candy. At the home farthest away they were invited to pause for a quick lunch before continuing to complete their calls. Many had gifts to exchange, others extended invitations to informal gatherings between Christmas and New Year's Day.

When they returned late in the afternoon the baskets they had carried were nearly as full with other women's gifts as when they had left home. The lights shining their Christmas greetings through the windows completed the Christmas card setting of the snow covered lawn and shrubbery surrounding the house.

Linda was pleased to see that someone had decorated the door of the cottage, candles glowed in the den window, a faint glimmer of tree lights showed beyond the drawn-back drapes in the small living room. *Evidently Steve's handiwork*, she surmised, recalling his frequent visits to the cottage the day before. *The station wagon is gone. What do you expect?* she asked herself. *Why would he spend Christmas here, when the one person most important to him is so near in the small house in town?*

She helped her mother carry the baskets into the house, depositing them on the counter just inside the door from the garage. Agnes and Marci were busy in the dining room. The festive Christmas Eve buffet was nearly ready. Her mother's breathless, "we're home," and her exclamation, "Oh, you have everything nearly ready," followed Linda through the hall, on her way to her room.

The joyous words of "Joy to the World" caused her to stop for a moment at the door to Richie's room. He was happy. There was one feeling of peace for her to cling to this holiday season.

Linda deliberately hung the white dinner dress in the back of the closet where it would probably stay in its department store plastic covering until... He was not here. It would not matter if he were. She would not wear it. Her green velvet dress was warm and comfortable.

Today she could hold it close to her, feel the rich softness of it in her hands. The painful memories of the first Christmas after her wedding were faint shadows; this would be the time to wear it.

The dress had been a gift from her mother and she would be pleased to see her finally wear it. She gathered it into soft folds and held it over her head to let the weight of the fabric pull the sleeves over her arms as it fell around her. It fit the same as it did five years ago, but then she had been ill and there was a reason for her being so thin. The sleeves were long and tapered at the wrists. The neck, although high in front scooped low in the back to between the shoulder blades with a ribbon embroidered with silver threads dropped to the waist, gathering an extra fullness in the skirt to sweep to the floor.

She slipped her feet into black velvet shoes with high crystalline heels and paused a moment before the full length mirror. Her hair was drawn into the familiar soft bun at her nape and she thought of herself as she was at eighteen, trying to dress up as a twenty-five-year old sophisticate. In her hand she held a perfect circle of twisted gold braid with tiny holly-leaf forms imbedded with minute chips of rubies and emeralds. It was beautifully delicate, not more than an inch and a half in diameter. This she pinned high on her left shoulder. It was the last Christmas gift she had received from Philip, and this was the first time she would wear it since his death.

Well, it's time.

Her thoughts were interrupted as Richie knocked on her door and called, "Aunt Linda, Grandee says we are waiting for you." There was a slight pause, then an anxious,

"are you all right?"

"Yes, of course, Dear." She assured him, tucking her hand under his arm after closing the door behind her. "Shall we go in to dinner?"

The house glowed with many candles and the brightness of Christmas. Harold and Steve were prolific with praises on the "dressing up" as Angela called it, of the house, the dinner and all of the extra goodies that accompanied it, and especially the simple elegance of the five, Angela included, ladies who were responsible.

Happiness seemed to fill the house again as the hours passed. The sound of their voices, their laughter mingled with their words were all wrapped together and tied with the softness of muted seasonal music from the stereo. A few of the neighbors whom they had not seen dropped in for short visits, exchanged greetings and exclaimed over Richie's recovery.

Linda was in the kitchen refilling the coffee server and had just handed it to Harold to take it to the dining room when her body tensed. Her heart seemed to go at double time and for a moment she wished for the white dress to replace the green as she noticed the automobile lights near the cottage. She put the cup down and hurried to the fireplace area thinking to sink down onto one of the chairs. *Brock would come in the back door, unless he brings her. Surely he wouldn't, not without letting Mother know.*

Well, they won't find me hiding.

A familiar voice sounded, although not the one she had feared, after the back door was pushed open. "Merry Christmas! It's just us." Carl called as he knocked loudly on the already open door. "We thought we'd come through the back because we feel like family, and not special once-a-year guests." He laughed as he ushered a giggling little girl into the house, along with his happy expectant wife. With a relieved sigh and a little harsh reprimand at her inner disappointment, Linda hurried over to greet Carl and his happy family and show them into the living room. She was pleased and happy for her friend as she noted the change in Carl. Surely now he had developed his mature, adult personality evident in his manner of greeting everyone and his sincere expression of pleasure in Richie's recovery. She recalled the visit Maria had made a few weeks ago; had that been the cause? Whatever had brought it about – she knew now that she could smile as she greeted. Smile? Yes, there had been a few flit across her face that evening.

Richie had noticed and on one occasion had gripped her hand tightly in his. "You're doing it again, Aunt Linda." She understood what he was referring to and smiled. "Can you be happy now?" he had questioned.

Happy for him? Oh, yes! For Maria and her family; Harold and his family, yes, she knew that she could smile for their happiness. But what of Brock and Mrs. Johnson, his 'Love.' Would she ever be able to smile and wish them every happiness?

It was simply ridiculous to allow it to bother her. Especially to the extent of spoiling an otherwise perfect day. So, Brock had not chosen to spend any time at all with them. At least he could have called Richie.

Christmas Day had seemed to hurry by, the gift exchange had gone much too quickly. Why could he not have arrived in the middle of it while everyone was laughing and enjoying... She couldn't hold back her silent prayer. *Dear Lord, wouldn't it have been better if we had managed within the family to care for Richie? Why had we brought this man into the picture?* Her thoughts would not leave the subject. She did not need this feeling of wanting, yearning, for what?

She turned away from the windows, closed the drapes, there was nothing there.

Her eyes were dulled to the glitter, the snow on the ground and the nodding and bowing of the tall, snow-draped pines. Now, instead of the impression of a day passing too quickly, the early morning hour which had been the happy beginning, seemed four or five times as far away. The gifts had all been exclaimed over, enjoyed. Brock's gifts of gloves or scarves for everyone had shown no special thought for any of them. No special thought, of course that would be the way he would want it. What had she expected, a token of his love, his deep affection? Dear Lord, was that what she really wanted from him? How could she? All of that belonged to Mrs. Johnson.

Now it was midnight, the day was over. Her need to pretend, to force a smile for his benefit had not arisen. Richie would not need to ask again if she were happy.

Dejected, she clipped the hanger to the waistband of the long, rose velvet skirt, put the pale pink floral blouse on the padded hanger and placed them on the rod in the closet in front of the green velvet that hung so obviously blocking from her sight the soft, white dinner dress still in the store wrappings. The soft illusive scent of her favorite perfume drifted from the closet as she slid the doors closed.

How she wished it was over. Almost another full week of visiting and receiving visitors, exchanging greetings and small remembrances. It would continue through New Year's Day. After that Richie would be back in school, it would be time to close out the business year, Brock would be gone, indeed he was gone already, it seemed. They would agree to Steve moving into the cottage if he wished. He would have more room and privacy there. There would be time after New Year's Day to decide that, however.

Right now she needed to sleep. She would be glad when the doctor took her off this sleep medicine. *Thank you for Christmas, Heavenly Father.* That was the extent of her evening prayers. Her hands slowly relaxed to clasp each other and form a rest for her cheek. Soft pink lips quivered slightly to emit an unheard sigh and sob, and then she slept.

Marci and Agnes greeted her from the midst of crumpled wrapping paper, name tags, and discarded ribbon they were sorting and folding on the living room carpet in front of the tree. She paused as the housekeeper related, "your mother is making fresh coffee in the kitchen."

"Thank you, Agnes." Linda glanced at the clock on the mantle. "I didn't intend to sleep so long."

"Nonsense, there wasn't any reason for you to be up early this morning."

Marci smiled up at her from her sitting position on the floor. "Richie and Angie have gone into town with Harold, and Steve has gone out to replenish the supply of firewood for the cottage..."

"Oh, has Brock..."

"No, he isn't there. He will be here later. Harold talked with him earlier this morning on the telephone."

So, how soon would later be, Linda wondered as she finished the omelet and orange juice her mother had so insistantly and lovingly prepared for her. What did she have to do that would keep her thoroughly occupied at the time of his arrival?

She helped in the house; put fresh candles in some of the holders, gave the centerpieces fresh water. Then completed a few little chores in preparation for the small open house planned for early afternoon the next day. These small tasks were quickly completed. They had lunch and the clearing away took no time at all.

Harold and the children had returned after having lunch in town and now they were skating on the frozen creek that ran through the orchard. Harold had collected the mail from the box at the corner where the drive joined the road. It now awaited her Linda's attention on the desk in the study. That would be a good place for her to be when Brock returned. She would see the wagon when it turned into the drive. Marci and Agnes were putting things in order upstairs and Mum was sleeping. Most of the pieces of mail were New Year's greetings from business places and announcements of special events in the community and from their church for the coming year. Three belated Christmas greeting cards and one rather bulky envelope addressed to Linda in a feminine handwriting marked "personal." She turned it over slowly in her hand, wondering. She stood up from the chair at the desk and, concentrating on the envelope turned her back to the window.

"Who?" she wondered out loud. There was no return address and the postmark was blurred. Could it be another insult from Miss Tucker? Hesitantly she slit the envelope across the top and withdrew another envelope. The second one was of pale yellow paper, perhaps from age for it seemed to be crackly and old. Across the front was written in a spidery penmanship...

MRS. PHILLIP WILSON

It had a strange mustiness clinging to it as though it had been shut away in a desk or dresser drawer for a long period of time. Realizing now that it had not come from Miss Tucker, she wondered again, "WHO!" Opening the second envelope she removed two folded sheets of matching stationary. As she unfolded it she noticed again the spidery penmanship, then began to read.

Late that same morning Brombke radioed to the small house in town. Everything in Chicago had gone as smooth as clockwork. Oscar's "replacement" had passed customs.

That man would now fade into oblivion. Oscar is now free.

"Yes," Brombke assured Brock, "we notified them earlier. I see no reason why they should not feel safe. I think it's time all of you get back to that part of the Hudson Valley and go on with your personal lives."

Leaving his grandfather and Francis to dismantle the radio, undo the Christmas tree and otherwise put the small house in order for the rental agency, he picked up a specially wrapped package, placed it on the front seat of the station wagon and once more started for the farm. The sun was nearly finished with its downward journey seemingly in a hurry to hide itself behind the dark pillows of clouds coming to meet it. More snow was on the way, he noted as he again parked the wagon in the space near the cottage. There was no evidence of anyone present.

All of the curtains were drawn in the cottage and the back part of the house. He left the package in the wagon and hurried against the rising wind, into the house through the patio and kitchen. The house seemed strangely empty and quiet, and then... Suddenly it was filled with terrifying sound. Wild hysterical laughter sharply accented with the shudder of harsh sobbing rushed at him as he hung his mackinaw over the back of a chair. "MY GOD! LINDA!"

He rushed to the study. The laughter ended on a shuddering sigh as he caught her limp body in his arms before it sank to the floor. All of the evidence of the heartache, the ice wall it had erected, the pushed down unshed tears was revealed now in the paleness that flooded the lovely face of the woman he held so close to him.

"Linda!" Gently he slapped the side of her face. "My dear." He hurried to put her on the sofa near the window, put the pillows from the back and end beneath her feet.

"Brock!" Marci hurried from the stairway. "What has happened?"

"She fainted!" Of course that would be obvious to the other woman. "She has had some kind of shock, Marci, call Doctor Browne, please."

Her breathing was shallow and he saw just a faint quiver of a pulse in the deep hollow near the base of her throat. He knelt beside her rubbing her wrist. He recalled faintly that all tight clothing should be immediately released, but she was so thin there was nothing she ever wore that fit tightly. *Dear God! She's so pale. What next?* His mind raced on. *What could have caused this?* The telephone was still on the desk so it could not have been a call. She had been standing near the desk and the window.

"There, that must be it.," he answered himself aloud as he carefully gathered the folded sheets of writing and envelopes from the carpet and put them into his inner coat pocket; it was Linda's business what they contained, but he needed to know. He was back kneeling beside her when Marci returned.

"He's on his way, Brock. We are to get her to bed and keep her warm. Try to rouse her gently, but not to shock her awake."

"You prepare her bed, I'll bring her." As he carried her, he brushed his lips against her hair, her cheek, softly whispering her name near her ear and on her pale lips, yet she did not respond. Her shoes dropped to the floor in the hallway. Marci had turned back the spread, top sheet and blanket on the bed. She was filling water bottles from the tap in the bathroom as he entered. He put Linda in the middle of the bed, unbuttoned the cuffs of her sleeves and the top two buttons of her shirt while Marci placed the warm bottles, now wrapped in thin toweling, on top of the blanket.

"Her mother?" Brock's voice was barely audible as he asked, pulling, tucking the covers around the still unconscious woman, and placing the warm towels on either side of her.

"I'm right here, Brock." Mrs. Farnsworth answered him as she entered the room, the shoes from the hallway in her hands. "I heard her cry out, but it seemed as a dream.

Then I heard you come in here. What has happened to my girl now?"

"Marci called Doctor Browne. She fainted." He quietly explained as he helped her to the chair near the bed, but he omitted everything concerning the letter.

Later, in the kitchen. "Is there enough there for another cup?"

Brock did not bother to answer but reached another mug from the rack, filled it with some of the freshly brewed coffee and placed it on the table across from where he had been sitting and returned to his seat.

"I'm glad you asked, Doc." He motioned for the doctor to sit across from him. "I need some answers, I think from you, Doctor Browne."

"You found some letters?" Doctor Browne asked, pulling out the other chair and sitting down. He spooned some sugar into the waiting mug of steaming coffee.

"Yes. But first..."

"She woke up almost as soon as I spoke to her, after a lot of tears, near hysteria. I heard about the letters, promised to find them, and had Marci help her get into bed properly where she is to stay until noon tomorrow." He sipped the hot coffee, glanced at his watch. "It seems they have guests coming tomorrow?"

"The open house brunch." Brock had heard that mentioned somehow.

"I will call the pastor of the church. It is usually that group. Neither one of them should have to..."

"Neither one...?"

"I have ordered Mrs. Farnsworth to bed also, and she is not to do anything but sit in her easy chair or lounge in her bed until further notice. He drank half of the coffee in the mug while Brock continued to stare into his.

"Marci is the night nurse. You will have Agnes to help tomorrow."

Brock lifted his glance from the coffee and fixed them steadily on the other man's face as he reached into his inner coat pocket. "I have read these." He put the letters on the table in front of the doctor. "Now you explain." He watched as the other man read the faded letter then heard...

"SO! This does explain it!"

"IT EXPLAINS WHAT?"

"Five years of a wasted, sorrow-filled life, self-incrimination."

He folded the letter and put it into his own coat pocket, looked at his watch again. "I do have a few minutes. Come." He left the coffee mug on the table and went to a chair near the fireplace, motioning for Brock to join him.

"These letters set her free, Brock!"

"FREE! Do you mean she was still married?"

"The story is complicated, but I'll make it as brief as possible. "It was their wedding day, and in his excitement Phillip had forgotten to bring her wedding gift with him. They had already changed to leave on the honeymoon and she was packing gifts to be moved to their apartment. He took her brother's motorcycle to the lodge, where he had been living, to get her gift. On the way back the cycle hit a tree root and threw him over the front and then ran over him. He lay there for too long before he was found. She was in shock for three days after. He was in intensive care on life support for three weeks after the accident. How he lived that long I never understood. We didn't tell her the extent of his injuries.

"One morning early, the nurse noticed that the warning light was flashing, the connections had been pulled and her explanation was that the cords were in his hand.

And that is the way the doctor found them."

"But if he could not live, where did he get the strength to pull?"

"That was the mystery. Linda blamed herself, thinking he had done it deliberately because he did not want to live in that condition." The doctor removed his glasses, rubbed his eyes and ran his hand down his cheek and behind his neck. "The insurance company and the doctors also were sure of this."

"What a thing to live with all of these years. What about this nurse?"

"She was a specialist, but as I remember, and as the letter states, she had been out on sick leave, and had just returned to duty. According to this letter she had been to the bathroom on a personal emergency."

"There had been no hope of his recovery?"

"No, and he would not have wanted to live in his condition. That cycle turned on him with a vengeance, gouged, mutilated. He never awoke."

"Did Linda know?"

"No. Not then, but that is one of the things we discussed a few minutes ago."

"But five years of torment."

"It would not have helped, not until now." Doctor Browne was insistent. "They were the happiest, most suitable young couple I had ever known." The eyes of the older man searched Brock's face.

"You know why I had to know this, Doc? I knew there was something that had to be cleared away, and I could not put her through the telling of it, whatever it was."

"After his death she was like a zombie for six months or so, then she gradually changed into the cool remote person she is now." He removed the letter from his pocket, held it out to Brock. Perhaps, if you just give her this, let her know that you know the full story..." he prepared to leave, "but not until tomorrow; she needs to sleep." He hurried to the door to the patio and outside. "You can have Marci tell her that I have seen the note. That should suffice for now."

The slight click of the latch on the door brought her to full awareness of something different. She lifted her head from the hollow place in the pillow, and her eyes to the young boy standing near her bed.

"You did it, Aunt Linda. Doc said you would need to, and you did."

"Did what, Richie?"

"You slept until noon. Grandee is still sleeping."

"But, Richie, there are people coming to brunch."

"No, Doc told Harold to call them, and Doc called the pastor."

"But all the preparations. The food."

"Oh, Brock said there would be people here to take care of that. Carl and Maria are coming later, and Brock's grandfather and his associate, the man who travels with him, Francis Huffard, are coming later this afternoon."

"Oh, then I must get up."

"No, no." He said smiling. "Agnes and Marci are going to do it. The guests are not supposed to be here until after four o'clock."

"Richie, sit down here beside me for a minute." The need to pause, to think, suddenly seemed very strong. Here beside her now, held close in her arms was her sanity for the last five years. She had watched him grow, assisted in his training, education, discipline, always believing she would never have a child of her own. She recalled his teasing, his laughter and childhood pranks – and his own tragic loss and injuries. She held him close to the softness of her fleecy pajama top, pressing his head into the hollow place of her shoulder. Nestling her cheek into the softness of the auburn curls she closed her eyes and felt the warm moistness of her own tears as they sparkled there.

"Aunt Linda?"

"Hmmm?"

"Can you be happy, now? Marci said you could be"

How can I answer that yet, she wondered. *What is there to be happy about? Is the absence of guilt the assurance of happiness?* It was too soon to say. There was a different feeling, a release of something, but the ache was still there, the lump in the throat.

Richie pulled away from her embrace and looked sternly into her face. "You scared Brock something awful when you fainted yesterday. He was as white as a sheet and walked the floor all the time Doc was in here." Richie picked up the corner of the sheet and gently wiped away the tears still glistening on her cheek as he continued. "He came into the house just before you cried out and he caught you in his arms before you fell."

So he had been there. Did he have the letter? Should she have Richie ask him? How could she. "Richie, is Marci down stairs? I would like to see her."

"She's in the kitchen."

"No, I'm here." The soft voice interrupted from the doorway. "I missed you, Richie, and rather thought I would find you here." She brought the tray she was carrying into the room and Richie took it from her and placed it in front of Linda, across her legs where she could look down on it.

"Lunch in bed, by order of the men in the house." Marci smiled at her. "Your mother is being served by Steve in the same manner."

At Linda's quick questioning glance and gasp, Marci continued. "She was a little upset, as we all were, and Doctor Browne ordered her to bed until after lunch."

"You are not hiding anything?"

"No, it is only a precaution." Marci thanked Richie for his help and informed him: "The men are having lunch in the kitchen, sir."

He laughed and with an "I'll see you ladies later," he went to join the men.

"Marci?"

"Hmmm?"

"Was I so terrible yesterday?"

"You frightened a few people, and we do not know why yet." She went to the window and pulled the drapery cord to lighten the room a bit.

"I received a letter. Did you find it? Has anyone?"

"The doctor knows about it. He said for you not to fret over it." She came away from the window and sat in the chair by the bed. "My dear, we haven't known each other for very long but you are my dearest friend. Can I just say this. Something has come to you to release some of that pent up sorrow, something has happened now don't permit anything to rebuild that wall that is beginning to crumble. When things hurt, for your own sake scream or cry about it, or slam doors, or kick cans, that's what Steve and I used to do. Now we pray more often than we used to."

"No. I must not. I just won't let myself be hurt any more. I'll pray more, too."

"If I can be of help let me know."

"We'll not talk about it now." Linda was still not certain how much to share and with whom. "Thank you for being here, Marci, and for this lovely lunch." She needed to change the tension in the room or the tears would flow again and she was not sure they would stop so easily if that happened. She lifted the silver cover from the plate.

"Ummm, scrambled eggs as only Agnes can do them" She was surprised at her hunger and finished the eggs and raisin muffins then sipped from the frosty glass of fresh orange juice.

"Richie informed me that the open house has been cancelled."

"Yes. Your mother agreed because of you and the doctor insisted because of both of you."

"Carl and Maria are still coming?" She placed the empty juice glass on the tray and set it to one side. "I'll need to be up and dressed before they arrive." She pushed the covers aside and swung her legs around to place her feet firmly on the floor. "I think I'll...Oh!" The window tilted with the floor, up, then down and up again.

Strong hands grasped her by the shoulders. "Here bend over a little," she heard as those same hands directed her head down between her knees. "I think that you will just take things easy for another few minutes."

She had not heard him come into the room, but his presence there sent excitement racing through her. The touch of his hand, the sound of his voice. She needed to keep her head lowered for a moment longer before she met his glance.

"Better now?" The questions came from his voice, his eyes, the tenderness in the strength of his hands as they steadied her.

"Yes, thank you." She noticed the smile in his eyes as she rebuttoned the two top buttons that had come undone.

"Here," he handed her the velour robe that was across the foot of the bed. "Put this on over your frazzled head and zip up."

She gasped at his grinning face. Her hands flew to her hair, realizing that it was loose from the snug roll and was hanging in soft waves below her shoulders. The short bangs were in disarrayed curls.

Suddenly Brock clasped his hands over hers. "Leave it. It's beautiful that way, and you do need to put on your robe. He still held her hands. She felt the color rise up to her cheeks. "And don't forget your slippers." He smiled again.

He released her hands and turned to Marci, who was just leaving with the lunch tray. "When you have finished with your own lunch and seen to little Angie's needs, could you come back and... "

"I'm perfectly able to take care..." Linda declared as she stood beside the bed, pushing the robe down so it would fall free around her feet, and pulling up the zipper tab.

The sudden lifting of her head seemed to cause her eyes to swirl. *What is the matter with me?* She blinked her eyes rapidly and then met Brock's steady glance.

"Are you all right now?"

Marci's quick, "I'll be back in about half an hour," reached them as she closed the door.

"I'll be all right in a few seconds." She blazed back to meet the fiery light in his blue eyes. What was happening to her now. She did not want to do battle with this man.

She wanted to feel his arms around her, wanted to be near. *Am I going to have to put up another barrier because this will never happen?*

He turned her favorite lounge chair around so the back of it was toward the window and motioned her to it. "All right. Spend the next thirty minutes in this." He pulled the satin covered chair from the other side of the window nearer to hers and sat down on it.

He looked so strongly masculine and yet so right, sitting there. His strong, vigorously healthy frame stretched full length as he leaned back as far as he could in the high back chair, his legs out in front of him. Dark green, brushed corduroy jeans, ribbed knit V-neck matching sweater over brown plaid shirt emphasized his lean strength.

She could not, indeed did not, keep her eyes from following that line from brown loafers to the lingering, knowing half smile. No farther. She could not meet his eyes.

What would they ask of her? What would they discover in her own?

Suddenly, as though he found his position on the chair uncomfortable he pushed his hips back into the curve of the seat, drew his feet back and put both elbows on his knees. Now she could not control where her eyes turned. The magnet in his blazing blues drew hers relentlessly.

"Your little episodes can be very frightening, you know." He charged.

"I know. I'm sorry." What more could she say. She could not tell him about the letter. She turned her chair slightly so that she could see the snow-burdened pines. There seemed to be a thicker layer of white.

"Did it snow again last night?"

Accepting the fact that she needed a change in topics he went to the window.

"Yes, it was quite a storm. People were stranded."

"Is that why you stayed all night?"

"You are why I stayed here last night, Linda. You fainted from shock and no one knew why. Your mother had a slight attack." His voice was forceful.

She trembled at the power in his stride as he came to sit on the ottoman near her chair.

He calmed his voice. "I didn't even know there was a storm outside as well as inside."

The soft change in his voice came through to her. She watched his hands, fascinated with their strength as he worked them into fists, gripped his knees, ran them through his hair and around the back of his head. *What does he really want to do with those hands?* She wondered. Would he pull her close to him and hold her there? Push her back into her chair? He loves Mrs. Johnson, how can I listen to my heart?

Actually, she noticed his hand had taken a piece of paper out of his shirt pocket.

It looked old as he held it out to her. *The letter. How did he get it?* Her eyes shot to his.

Her mouth trembled. Refused to open because her teeth were holding her lower lip.

"I know, Linda. I found the letter."

"But Marci said Doctor Browne had it."

"I let him read it."

"You had no right to read it." The words slipped through her lips in a whisper.

"The effect it had on you caused me not to consider that at all." He still held the letter. "But, I know more than what the letter tells. After I showed it to Doctor Browne and made a few facts clear to him, he told me what happened five years ago. And he told me all the facts, not just the simple ones that you were told." Still he held the letter, but she turned her chair completely around with her back to him. She heard him get out of the chair and move it back to its original place. Now her hands were gripping the arms of the chair she was in. She did not want to look at him. What could she say.

"You were the judge, the prosecutor, the jury at the 'trial.' The verdict was guilty. The sentence was life imprisonment in an icy walled barrier." His voice caught in his throat even as it cut through her. She heard him move away toward the door. She swung the chair around to face the strange fierce fire glowing in his eyes. His jaw was set hard and there was no tenderness apparent in his face. "The case has been re-opened, Linda. The same prosecutor, the same judge and jury, and the same plaintiff. The evidence this time is truth. Can you now release the prisoner?"

Quietly he closed the door as he left her. Silently she let the tears flow.

Her afternoon visit with her mother and Richie in the older lady's room had been a tearful but relieving one. Why had she never told her mother about her guilt feelings before this? Perhaps the last five years would have been different. Richie had seemed bewildered at first, but he finally understood most of what was discussed. How could she have thought that Phil would have been so weak as to take his own life? But surely he would have known the extent of his injuries, but if he had, then he might have. Oh no. I'm not going over all of that again. Linda chided herself. How foolish she had been.

All of that heartache. Yes, there would have been sorrow, for Phil would have died very soon anyway, she realized that now. What had the letter said. That poor woman. Her guilty feelings must have been as overpowering as Linda's.

The daughter who sent the letter had not read her mother's note, but had explained in a brief statement. Her mother had died recently and she found the sealed and addressed envelope in her mother's writing desk. She had mailed it, unopened, with her own note. The letter was two pages of spidery handwriting filled with self-incriminating words concerning Phillip's death and finally the explanation:

'The arm restraint on the patient's bed was left unfastened.

In his delirium, he had flung his arm up and over, pulling loose all life support lines. I had been away from my station because of personal discomfort and when I returned the warning signal was flashing, but

I was too late. In a panic I arranged the patient so That it seemed as though he had pulled them.'

Now, it was five-thirty. The open house that had been cancelled was now on again. The buffet had been set up in the dining room. Guests were arriving slowly as having been delayed because of the storm of this day.

She had needed this time alone for the 'whys' that kept racing through her mind.

Why had the doctors accepted this? Why had there not been an investigation? Why?

Why? Then the answers were 'accidental cause of death.' Now the nurse was dead.

Mum and Richie now know the truth. Doctor Browne and Brock know the truth now.

The truth. Oh Lord, thank you. Now I also know the truth. The guilt is gone. The prisoner is free.

The sun flashing on the windshield of a dark gray Rolls Royce just turning into the drive drew her eyes into focus.

This is not a familiar car. It must be Grandfather Brockman. She brought her thoughts back to the present, turned from the study window and hurried to the powder room. In the mirror there she saw her features arranged perfectly. Her hair was neatly tucked in, a light touch of makeup hid the pale effects of her recent emotional battle. The soft white dinner dress clung and flowed at the proper places, as she had known it would.

She entered the small entryway just as the door bells chimed once. She paused just a moment and then opened to them.

"Good evening." She greeted the two men standing there. "You, of course are Mr. Brockman." She offered her hand to the older man as she welcomed them, stepping back for them to enter. The other man was of light brown skin, his eyes were hidden by sunshade driving glasses, but she was sure they would be nearly black to accompany the black brows and neatly trimmed mustache. In one hand he carried a tan briefcase, and in the other a small child cradled against his shoulder.

As she closed the door against the cold, the older man smiled at her. Although she had not met him until now, the smile was vaguely familiar.

"You are Mrs. Wilson, I'm sure." He turned to the man who had accompanied him. "Francis, I would like to present you to our hostess. Mrs. Wilson, this is my very good friend and associate, Francis

Hubbard, and the pretty little package he is carrying," he paused as the small child raised her head from Francis's shoulder, "is my great-granddaughter, Rosella." He took the child from the arms of the other man, hugging her close to him.

"How do you do, Rosella. It is nice to have you here."

"I am fine, Mrs. Wilson, thank you."

There was no other explanation. *Who is her parent? Is this beautiful little girl Brock's child?*

Chapter Seventeen

Her voice was somewhere behind the lump in her throat. Questions would be inappropriate. She had to say something.

"Francis will see to your things, Rosella dear, and you may join us later." Mr. Brockman returned the child to his associate and removed his overcoat.

Linda rallied.

"It's the first room on the right at the top of the stairs, Francis."

She smiled into the very dark brown eyes, thankful that the older man had taken the initiative and broken the silence. Francis nodded slightly, put the child on the stairs ahead of him, and took Mr. Brockman's coat and accessories with him up the stairs.

Warm greetings awaited the visitor as he and Linda joined the friendly gathering already in the living room. Carl and Maria had arrived earlier. They were enjoying some pictures that Harold had received from Australia as gifts from friends there. Mrs. Farnsworth was obeying the doctor's orders by remaining in her easy chair by the living room fireplace. A light dusting of simple makeup and her joking remark of being 'Queen for a day' helped to conceal the effects of her distressing upset of the previous day.

Three little girls were now gathered around Richie on the area rug in front of the fireplace in the family room. Light chatter and sweet laughter joined with his voice as he read to them from a favorite children's Christmas book. The dark, curly hair of Rosella, the youngest one, fascinated Linda. Whose child is she? The question troubled her.

Linda had come to the kitchen for a glass of water, but had paused at the sink as Richie read something not especially witty, but it referred to 'Mother and Father,' and a small voice, very excited, exclaimed:

"My Mummy and Daddy are going to be here soon and we are all going home together!"

The small Dixie cup crunched in her hand spilling water on the counter. The pill she was scheduled to take rolled on the floor when she dropped it. She must have made some sound for Richie was now at her side.

"Aunt Linda. Are you all right?" His young voice quivered in apprehension.

"You are pale, and trembling."

"I dropped my medicine, Richie. It must have rolled out of my hand." She gripped the edge of the counter as she looked at the floor, searching for the pill. "I'll need to find it."

"Wait, I see it." He picked up the pill from the floor and deposited it in the sink drain. "I'll get another one." He hurried through the house.

So, her parents are coming. But if Brock is her father, who is Mrs. Johnson?

And, if she isn't the mother, who is? Why? Again the simple question whirled through her thoughts. *Where is Brock?* Did what the child say really mean him? Would he be taking this lovely little minx of a girl and her mother home with him. *Dear Lord, help me.* Again the tears needed to be pushed down. There was no relief in letting them flow. Only more pain. Push them down. Push them down. The ice barrier needed to be rebuilt. How foolish she had been to think she could manage without it.

She reached for another Dixie cup and filled it with water as Richie offered her the small plastic medicine vial.

"Agnes said that everything is ready in the dining room except putting the hot dishes out."

"Fine, Richie." She swallowed the pill, needing an extra cup of water. "It seems that Rosella's parents are coming and Brock is not here yet." Now why did she mention that. The doorbells chimed as she crumpled and discarded the Dixie cup.

"It must be..." She turned away from the boy standing so near. "Someone else will need to answer that. Richie, will you?"

But voices were even now coming from the hallway. Harold, saying "Come in," and Brock saying "Thank you," and a softer, sweeter tone – Mrs. Johnson! There was no avoiding it any longer, Linda knew. She must go, make them welcome.

All of a sudden there seemed to be no time left. Why would she want more time?

She felt the presence of the small, curly-haired girl near her as she forced her feet to take her to the newly arrived guests. It was Brock and his wife, but her name was not the same as his, it was...

"Oh, Mummy, Mummy!" The small sound came around Linda as the little girl rushed to meet Mrs. Johnson.

But who was the tall, thin man beside her?

Harold was greeting them now – but how did he know...

She waited there near the entryway as Harold put their hats and coats, gloves, and scarves into the hall closet, and then – she could no longer avoid them. Her eyes flashed to meet the deep blue fire-lit ones as though they had commanded hers. What was it now that she saw there? Not shadows, not anger, just clear blue fire – but she could not let him see the hurt that must be clear in hers. She turned away. This was his family.

"Linda." It was not a command nor a question, just his voice – and her name. Then he continued as she turned to face him, keeping her eyes on the level of the perfectly knotted tie at the base of his throat. "You have met Mrs. Johnson..." "Yes." *Dear Lord, help me now.* "It's nice to have you here." Her eyes met briefly the soft glow in the other woman's eyes. Brock continued with the introductions. "But you have not met her husband, Oscar Johnson."

The words thudded through her mind. *Her husband. Her husband.* The rest of the information Brock was offering became a blur as she automatically offered her hand in welcome to the tall, thin stranger.

In the mingle of voices the little girl voice whispered the question. "Daddy?" And then happily exclaimed, "Yes it IS my DADDY!"

The soft woman's voice offered assurance, "Yes, Darling." Rosella grasped the man around the legs and hugged them.

Through the blur of her confusion Linda fixed her eyes on the face of the woman still standing in front of her. She did not try to hide the hurt, the utter contempt that flowed through her for the association of this woman and her 'Whit' as she had called him.

"It's over now, Linda. I hope you'll allow my brother-in-law a chance to explain."

"Your brother-in-law?" She flung a glance at Brock. Of course, he had said that his sister called him Whit. She caught his slight nod and his comment, "It was best for no one to know," just as Agnes came from the dining room.

"Linda, everything is ready. Please bring our guests to dinner."

"Of course, Agnes, I'm sorry. Give us just a minute or two more."

Still determined not to reveal the tumult inside her; she only glanced at the necktie again and then a quick glance upward to catch a glimpse of the gentle smile lingering above the strong determined chin.

"Will you introduce your family to Mother, Brock."

The meal was delicious. The laughter of children, the soft background of familiar Christmas music, and the muted conversations of the people filled the house. It had been a long time returning, but it was almost the same. Some faces were new; others were lovingly missed, but the heartache had gone.

Now the laughter of small children had silenced in sleep, the music had ended and only voices filled the living room. Carl, Maria and their daughter had said goodnight soon after dinner. Mrs. Farnsworth had changed to a lounging robe and was again in her chair by the fire enjoying the firelight and warmth that filled her home.

Linda helped Marci as she wheeled the tea cart laden with freshly brewed coffee, cups, and an assortment of snacks. Brock stood leaning against the brick wall of the fireplace, in the reflections of the Christmas tree lights, one foot elevated to rest on the hearth. Linda could feel his gaze surrounding her; had sensed it during the meal and after. Their hands had met briefly in the serving of the food, but only a few words had passed between them.

Linda had talked briefly with Mrs. Johnson – Lovellen. Of course a brother would shorten it to something – it could have been Ellie or Lynn, but Brock had chosen 'Love,' his sister had informed her, and the feeling between them merited the name. But oh, how it had hurt; and what now? There was still that doubt, that lingering hurt.

"Love," Brock interrupted her thoughts as he addressed his sister, "if you and Oscar will permit me," his voice had an urgency and a requesting tone, "I think I should tell your story."

"Oscar?" She looked at her husband.

"Better you than me." Oscar granted permission as he knew what Brock had in mind.

Everyone in the room had by now helped themselves or been served refreshments from the cart. Oscar and Love were comfortable in the small sofa, their feet sharing the top of the matching ottoman; Mrs. Farnsworth in her chair by the fire; Richie, zipped and snug in his wrap-comforter on the floor near the lounge chair where Linda sat. Harold and Marci were on floor pillows near the other end of the fireplace, and Steven sat cross-legged on the floor in front of the tree. Mr. Brockman and Francis sat at either ends of the sofa, a temporarily forgotten chess game on the sofa between them.

"It's a long story," Brock began, "Oh, not so long in the telling, but it began three, almost four years ago."

"Just the high spots, please, Whit." his sister pleaded. "The details can be gone over some other time if necessary."

"Of course, Love." He scanned the up-turned faces of his interested audience.

"Oscar was a member of a photography team in Southern Europe. It was a small group working for an independent agency. Everything and everybody was legal, except in a storm their plane was blown off course and crashed. Two were killed. Oscar and another man were badly injured. They prevailed upon the other three to leave them and seek help from somewhere. The local authorities found the two injured men; they were arrested and taken into custody. A year later they were officially tried and put in prison where the other man died. We, and I cannot reveal who the 'we' is, but we finally discovered where Oscar was being held and managed to unofficially release him. It was a long, hard, dangerous, and secret trail from where he was held to Norway. It took time to find the right job on the right Norwegian freighter coming through the St. Lawrence Seaway to arrive here at the right time." "You mean you were a prisoner behind the Iron Curtain, Mr. Johnson?" Richie gasped. "You escaped." He exlaimed, wide eyed. His glance flew to meet Brock's. "And you helped. GEE!!"

"Well, Richie, I only helped with the planning and communication. But many brave men were responsible for Oscar's escape, as well as many before and after him.

"The plan originally was for him to go directly to Chicago and leave the ship there, but problems developed and we had to plan it for here."

Linda watched intently. His smile broadened as he looked at Richie and continued.

"You were an answer to a prayer about this great problem, young man. I was at the end of my thinking when I saw your Aunt Linda's ad in the Detroit News. I had picked it up at a New York City news stand. It worked out, and we all have benefitted."

"So that was why you did all that fishing?"

"Yes!" Brock smiled as Richie put the pieces together.

Linda realized there was much more to the story, but what of the man telling it? Who was this man if he was not what he had said? But then she recalled the story of the events in New York City and was assured he was worthy. Worthy of what? Her love, her devotion, her life? But surely he did not want that, not from her. But she could respect him. *That is not what I want.*

"The fishing huts were needed," Brock continued, "because we thought that he could swim beneath the ice from the ship and come up through the hole in the middle of the floor. But that was not feasible because of many dangers and the distance, so."

Linda noticed the expression of worship on his sister's face as he told the story.

First with awe as she listened intently. Hadn't she known what had been happening?

Hadn't Brock told her? As Love's face paled at the thought of the danger, Linda realized she had not known, and she was happy for these two as she watched their hands tighten around each other's as the story continued.

"The cable reached from the truck to the winch on the ship with a little to spare, but just as Oscar cleared the channel and was above the jagged ice chunks, the cable hook that was fastened to the winch broke and Oscar took a nasty fall. But, at least he was on land. Doctor Browne took care of the gash on his leg and bound up his ribs. We hid him in the hut for a few days." "That's enough of the story for tonight, Brock." Oscar interrupted. "We have an early plane to catch tomorrow, and Grandfather Brockman and Francis will be driving us to the airport." "Surely not before breakfast;" Mrs. Farnsworth wondered. "Agnes will have it ready."

"Mother..." Linda began to object.

"We will not disappoint Agnes," Brock assured her, with a smile, remembering the culinary skills of Agnes.

As Brock went to the hall closet to collect coats for his sister and brother-in-law, Linda was suddenly confronted with the two people who were even now offering their hands in thanks. What could she say to them, how did she make amends for the misguided thoughts that had gone through her mind, the way she had felt.

"Mr. and Mrs. Johnson, it was so good to have you here this evening. What can I say..." "Please, just say that you will let me call you Linda, and be friends. Whit is very dear to us and we are indebted to you..."

"Oh, no. There is no debt on your part. Brock was just what Richie needed."

She accepted their hands in friendship, wondering if it really would have the depth to develop into first name associations.

"Please, call me Linda, and I will..."

"Love is Whit's and Oscar's special name for me, but Grandfather calls me Ellen, and I would like for you to, also."

"Of course, Ellen. And Oscar, I'm glad the ordeal has ended for you and you are able to reestablish a happy home with your lovely little girl." Her almost rambling farewell (as she thought of it) was interrupted as Brock returned with their coats.

"Brock, Rosella is up in Angela's room." "Yes, I know, Linda, and her parents are my guests in the cottage. We will collect her in the morning. If there is any problem during the night, Francis will be delighted to take care of it. She adores him."

"Then why not take them through the family room and out that way, Brock. There is not so much snow."

Still unable to comprehend all of this new information, Linda helped Marci clear away the tea dishes, said goodnight to Richie, and made certain her mother was settled comfortably for the night.

The fire was still burning in the living room fireplace and the house was quiet. Quickly she changed from the white dress into her favorite, simple gown and snug robe and slippers, then went through the rooms turning out lights, straightening doilies here and rug edges there. The tree lights were still glowing. Feeling the need for a relaxing moment, she curled her legs beneath her on the end of the sofa facing the fireplace. Her back rested against the arm of the sofa and toward the kitchen. The fire had now burned low. Its crackling and snapping had ceased, but there was a sound from behind her. The kitchen door to the patio, and a voice.

"It's Brock, Linda." And he was there, coming toward her as she stood up in front of the sofa. A large, beautifully wrapped package was in his hands. His hair was rumpled from the wind, and he was without his mackinaw. "I have your Christmas present." He put the package on the sofa. "There is no mistletoe here, but a Christmas wish and a mistletoe kiss comes with it." His firm lips caressed gently first her forehead and then closer, her cheek and then both arms were around her drawing her snugly nearer. His mouth captured hers and her lips trembled beneath his. He did not resist as she pushed away.

"Brock."

"Shhh." He covered her protest with two fingers against her still trembling lips.

"Before you open it I want your assurance that you will accept it. It is a lovely gift for a lovely lady. I bought it because it is perfect for you, and because I know that on you it looks lovely. He frowned at her. "I never have had to apologize for a gift before." "Brock! What." She sat down on the sofa and with trembling fingers slipped the ribbon over the corners of the box and tore away the papers. Her heart raced unheeded as she lifted the lid. "Oh, the coat from the store."

"Yes! You like it. You said you did. Remember? And it is you." He knew that she recalled that day in town.

Slowly she stood again, her knees unsteady as she lifted the coat from the tissue- lined box. "But I cannot..."

"You can, and you will." He took the coat from her hands and wrapped it around her, capturing her arms in its folds as he pulled the hood up over her head and around her face with one hand and pulled her close again to him. "It is yours. I have thought of you as you looked that day. It is something soft to wrap you in and to keep you warm." His hand brushed from the fabric surrounding her face to the soft warmness of her cheek.

"The warmth is returning – isn't it? The ice barrier is melting further away." His voice was also soft and warm.

Oh, yes. The ice is gone. It had washed away in the flood of tears, and in the pleasures and disclosures of this day, but still there was the lump and the uneasy, unfamiliar pressure inside and he was adding to it. Now both of his hands were wrapping his wonderful gift tightly around her. She could not move; could only watch as his eyes held her gaze. What could he read there, she wondered briefly as his mouth again descended to capture hers. This time it pushed, pressed and moved against her slowly yielding, quivering answer. Almost as quickly and forcefully he released her mouth, staring into her startled, up-turned eyes.

"It still gets very cold along the Hudson River in March. You will need this then, and for the immediate next few weeks."

She continued to watch his eyes as their expression changed from desire to wonder to a bit of teasing. Finally he released his hold on the coat letting her arms relax beneath it.

"Brock, I..."

"No more tonight...Linda."

She noticed the pause before he said her name as though he had been about to say...say what, she mused but did not dare to dwell on it.

"Get a good night's sleep. I'll see you at breakfast."

She felt his lips brush the curls of wispy hair and her cheek near her ear as he moved away, her own hands now holding the beautiful gift snugly around her. She watched as he went out the door as quietly as he had entered.

Breakfast had been hurried through. Scrambled eggs, sausages, English muffins and toast with butter and jam, coffee or tea and juice. The conversation was lightly mixed with a few giggles from the little girls and Richie's gentle teasing to make them squeal. Linda kept busy with the preparing and serving and there was time for only casual greetings and small talk between the adults. Harold and Steve had helped with all of the different luggage, seeing it was put into the proper cars. Then he helped Brock clear the cottage. Linda had not even known of the radio equipment. The time of Brock's arrival seemed so long ago, so much activity, so many changes.

Now everyone was gone. Harold, Marci, and Angela were on their way in the yellow VW for a week in Saulte St. Marie with Marci's parents. Mr. Brockman, Love – no, she must remember to think of her as Ellen, just in case they should ever meet again – and the little girl were with Francis in the Rolls Royce. Brock and Oscar were in the loaded station wagon. They had hurried away to the airport for the ten o'clock flight. Five p.m. came slowly. Steve and Linda's mother had gone to take Agnes to a friend's house for a few days vacation, and Richie to exchange the shirts he had received as gifts for larger sizes. The house was strangely empty. She walked through to the cottage. Even it seemed different. Why? It was just the same as she had seen it in August. Had she been in here since. No. Agnes had remade the bed, the fireplace had been thoroughly cleaned, and new logs laid for a fire; but there was still a lingering fragrance, a certain aroma tangy and slightly sweet. She turned away from the small kitchen window where she had been heedlessly watching the snow-carpeted orchard, where the light from the window now lit a path over it. She turned to the small living room.

The mantle! There it was – his sweater. It was the source of the haunting aroma!

Slowly she wrapped it around her fingers, He had forgotten it. *Was this the only thing he left behind?* The light from the kitchen spread another path which she followed into the den and to the lounge chair there.

His sweater, her coat, was that all she was to have, no more? What of the house on the Hudson? *Did he really mean what he said? Had he really gone? Yes, with his family, and with not a word about anything.* Was this all she would have besides a few memories? Must she rebuild the ice wall? NO! She would not allow it. His answer to Harold's inquiry of what he would do had been definite. There was a family business in finance and accounting that he was responsible for; a house and estate on the Hudson that needed him. She folded the sweater in her hands, held it close to her cheek as she curled up in the large chair as though she would receive some assurance from the fragrance. She watched through the open drapes, lost again in the swaying movement of the snow-blanketed pines. *Why did he go? Is he even now with them in that house on that far away frozen Hudson River?* The desired comfort of the sweater, the lingering scent of after shave, burning logs of applewood, and the motion of the trees filled her senses and she...

"Thank God, Linda." You scared me senseless." He seemed to burst into the cottage through the open door. His strong hands pulled her out of the chair, slightly shook her awake as the sweater fell out of her hands to land on the chair.

"Why are you here? Don't you know they're looking for you?" He pulled her hard against him as she trembled awake. "Why are you here?" He demanded this time.

"It's getting cold. There is no fire..." "Your sweater..." was all she could manage as she stared into his angry eyes. "Why are you so angry with me?" She pushed herself away from him and picked the up the sweater from the chair.

"You forgot this..." The tears she could no longer control began to flow, welling up and running over. "I thought you would not be back and I wanted..."

He stared at the sweater she held out to him. "You wanted what, Linda?" He took the sweater from her hands and put it on the table near the chair. His eyes never left her face as he continued. "Don't ever push away from me again." He wrapped her again into his closeness, buried his face in the sweet scent of her hair at the nape of her neck. She felt his lips touch her ear as he murmured. "Is this what you want, my darling? Can I give you warmth enough to melt the ice?" He brushed away the streams of tears with gentle fingers and then caught the few that remained on her lashes with the tip of his tongue as he continued the warming up session.

"Oh, Brock." She was breathless. "I thought that you had gone – you didn't say..."

"No, I didn't say, because I knew that once I began it would take a while to finish."

"But why were you so angry when you came in? You..."

"It's eight o'clock! Do you realize that? Your mother and nephew have been worried to distraction since six-thirty..."

"But it can't be! It was only a little after five when I came here."

"You've been sleeping since."

"Not all the time. I've been watching the trees, and wondering..."

"If I would be back? Oh, Linda."

"More than that, it was more if I was going to have to begin again building the wall..." The sob that slipped through was quickly caught as his lips gathered her trembling ones again into the gentleness of his, holding them firmly for a moment and then softening to allow her to catch up with him. Her responsiveness ignited his desire for more. As her arms reached to pull him still closer, the heat of his breath melted the ice forever.

Linda hadn't been kissed for so long and so well in what seemed a life time.

"Do you know what you are doing to me, Woman?" His husky question filled her ear as he released her mouth to brush his searching lips along her cheek. "How could I have started this at breakfast time?" The light in his eyes now smoldered with desire; her eyes sparkled with the moisture of unshed tears and an answering flame like fire through a rainstorm. He pulled back from her, holding her lightly in the bend of his arms. "How could I not have come back?" he teased. "when I was so sure of what was here, my love. I have battled too hard and long to get this flame started. I intend to warm myself at it for the rest of my life."

He turned quickly as a knock sounded at the cottage door.

"Oh, yes, I promised I'd be right back." He hurried to the door and opened it to

Steve's question. "Brock?"

"She's here, Steve. She had fallen asleep in the chair. Everything is fine. We'll be in shortly."

Linda was hastily gathering her thoughts. He still had not said – but what more did she need? Hadn't his actions, his kisses told her what she wanted to know? She walked toward the window as he shut the door to come and stand behind her.

"Darling." He slipped his hands around her waist, drawing her back against him, his warm desire heated her body. "How long has it been since you heard those words?"

"It's been so long – but never from you. Oh, Darling." She could wait no longer.

Turning in his arms she faced him. "Do you? Oh, say it, for I love you so much, and if you don't..."

"Do I ever love you. How could you not know?" As if there still could be some doubt in her mind, he continued to kiss her and murmur his love to her. "I love you my darling."

"We should sit. I have something here." He looked around the chair. "Here in my jacket. There's a small box in the right hand pocket."

She questioned him with a look.

He wrapped his arms around her drawing her closer to him as he opened the package and flipped up the lid of the velvet-covered ring case.

Her heart raced and pounded. She clenched her trembling hands together as the exquisite green of the emerald sparkled on the band of platinum caught in the slot of the satin lining.

"This is why I needed to go into town this morning, and why I had to stay so long. I had to wait for the jeweler's representative to arrive with it. Will you wear it, my darling, along with the circle of emeralds that is its mate? Will you warm my heart, fire me with your fire in exchange for mine? I have a house on the Hudson. Everything is there that I need, except you."

She boldly answered with her lips eagerly seeking his. He was the source of her life's fire. *At last.*